International award-winning author Bronwyn Parry has previously written six romantic thrillers set in outback Australia, published by Hachette Australia. Her first novel won the Romance Writers of America's prestigious Golden Heart Award, and two of her books were finalists in RWA's RITA™ and Daphne du Maurier awards. She has also won the Australian Romance Readers award for Favourite Romantic Suspense three times.

With *The Clothier's Daughter*, Bronwyn turns her pen to another genre she loves, historical romance, and draws on her long interest in history and particularly textile and costume history to weave a story of intrigue, drama and passion. When she's not working at her keyboard, she enjoys researching and making historical clothing, and she's a skilled spinner, weaver, seamstress and knitter. *The Clothier's Daughter* is in part inspired by her Honors thesis research on British worsted textiles.

Bronwyn lives with her husband and two border collies on 100 acres of beautiful bushland in the New England tablelands of northern New South Wales, Australia. and loves to travel.

ALSO BY BRONWYN PARRY

Bronwyn has also written six romantic thrillers, set in outback Australia (published by Hachette Australia), and a novella. Although the books are in two loosely-linked series, each book stands alone.

Dungirri series:
As Darkness Falls
Dark Country
Darkening Skies
The North Wind (A Christmas novella)

Goodabri series:
Dead Heat
Storm Clouds
Sunset Shadows

THE Clothier's Daughter

The Hartdale Brides
Book 1

Bronwyn Parry

Firetail Press
Armidale NSW Australia

Copyright © Bronwyn Parry 2019

Published by Firetail Press, Armidale Australia

Cover Design by Lauren Sadow

Cover photography by Andrew Sadow

ISBN: 978-0-9941970-5-4 (Ebook)
ISBN: 978-0-9941970-4-7 (Trade Paperback)
ISBN: 978-0-9941970-6-1 (Large Print)
ISBN: 978-0-9941970-8-5 (Hard Cover)

This is a work of fiction. Names, characters, places, and incidents are either the product of the author's imagination or are used fictitiously, and any resemblance to actual persons, living or dead, business establishments, events, or locales is entirely coincidental.

DEDICATION

For all the teachers of literature and history at school and
university who inspired and nurtured my love for both, and
encouraged me to find the people of the past, especially:
Kerrie Crimmins
Helen Pilkinton
Bethwyn Wilkins
David Kent

CHAPTER 1

Friday August 9th, 1816, West Riding of Yorkshire

If the rain kept falling, her business might not survive. Stretching the crick from her neck, Emma Braithwaite stared out of the warehouse window. Spattering against the glass, the rivulets of water dissected the view out over the lower buildings across the road to the waterlogged field behind them. Across the field, row upon row of tenter frames usually had long lengths of cloth stretched to dry on them, but in this unending wet they all remained empty. On the hillside beyond the tenter fields, beyond the stream that gushed down from the fells, the new steam-powered cotton manufactory belched out smoke, darker than the grey of the clouds.

She closed her eyes against the depressing sight and concentrated on listening instead to the rhythmic sounds of the drawloom at work in the room behind her. The thunk of the treadles alternating, the wooden clatter of the shafts, the brushing of the hundreds of threads as they passed each other, and the murmured counting of Tom the drawboy, sitting on top of the loom pulling the batches of pattern threads as Jacob the weaver threw the shuttle and beat each weft thread into place.

Familiar sounds, sounds she'd known since childhood. As a small girl, she'd watched the drawloom weavers at work, awed by the delicate patterns that slowly emerged, thread by fine thread. In her innocence, she'd envied the drawboys, perched up high, pulling the cords that manipulated the pattern threads. She hadn't understood then that few children lived in large houses, that many had to work full days to earn a wage for their families instead of playing with dolls and dressing in pretty clothes as she did.

But in her childhood there'd been six drawlooms working full-time in this uppermost floor of Braithwaite and Co's warehouse, each loom producing fine figured worsted textiles for clothing and furnishings. Now five stood idle, the hand-made worsted fabrics no longer able to compete with the much cheaper, factory-produced cotton textiles. Dozens of other weavers still worked for Braithwaite and Co, on simpler looms out in farmhouses and cottages across the valleys, but fewer than there used to be.

And now it was her responsibility to continue the company founded by her great-grandfather, to oversee production and manage the business to protect the livelihoods of the weavers, spinners, dyers and finishers who had relied on Braithwaite and Co for decades. Her responsibility, alone. Until her brother returned from Canada. If he returned from Canada.

Emma turned away from the window and from that unproductive chain of thought and returned to the table where she'd spread the pattern book alongside the warehouse ledger. With its large windows facing south, the weaving loft had better light than her father's office on the floor below, and she sometimes brought her work up here.

She gently touched the small samples of fabrics in the open pattern book. Jacob, about to complete a thirty-yard length of figured cloth, needed to know what design to weave next. With its record of the firm's designs, the pattern book offered a multitude of possibilities, but the ledger contained Emma's lists of the bales of wool fabric stacked in the warehouse rooms on the ground floor. Potentially hundreds, maybe a thousand, pounds worth of woven goods, if only the weather would allow for the dyeing and finishing processes so that they could be sold. If they could be sold.

But until that happened, they only represented hundreds of pounds of debt. The combers and spinners and dyers must be paid. Jacob and all the weavers must be paid for their completed pieces.

Mr. Hargraves, the factor, and the warehouse lads must be paid their wages. So did the two clerks and the copy boy in the main office on the middle floor of the warehouse. She had little spare money to pay any of them.

If the fabrics Mr. Hargraves had taken to Halifax today for tomorrow's market in the Piece Hall sold for a good price, she could pay the wages for this week. She should not ask Jacob to begin another piece until she could pay him for this one. But if he had no work, his family would go hungry.

Her head ached from constant calculations, constant decision making, constant worry.

She pulled her shawl closer around her shoulders. The persistent damp weather chilled the air despite the fire in the fireplace at the end of the loft.

The fire that seemed to be smoking. The smell tickled her nose and the drawboy coughed. Glancing across to the closed door of the stairwell, she saw a very faint haze of smoke drifting in the air.

At the other end of the room from the fireplace.

Her chair scraped loudly on the wooden floor but Jacob the weaver was already alerted and on his feet.

"There's a fire," she said. "But where?" She checked the fireplace but the wisps of smoke were too elusive and she couldn't tell exactly which way they came from.

Emma stood in the middle of the room, slowly turning, listening, searching for the entry point of the smoke. Where was the fire? *Where?* Was it merely the fireplace in the office below them smoking badly? Or was there a fire in the warehouse on the ground floor, packed with bales of fabric? In the stables adjoining the building, on the other side of the stone wall?

"I'll check downstairs, Miss Braithwaite," Jacob said, opening the door to the landing.

A roar of sound, air, heat and flame shook the building, throwing Jacob backwards, making the shafts of the loom clatter. The floor seemed to move and Emma staggered back against the table, sending her inkwell crashing to the floor. And all around her, a shower of ash

3

and burning embers fell, on to the looms, on to her accounts, on to the wooden floor, and on to her and Jacob and Tom.

She could not think of how or why. No time to make sense of it. Because Jacob lay still, flames leapt through a hole in the wall between the hay loft of the stable and the stairwell, and the old timbers of the stairs were catching alight.

Young Tom helped her drag Jacob away from the doorway, and using the door as a shield she slammed it shut against the heat and flames. And against their only exit from the top floor of the warehouse.

Tom stamped out embers and smoldering clumps of hay with his feet, and she dragged her shawl off her shoulders to beat out sparks.

They might have little time before the fire spread, through floorboards, walls, roof beams, into this room. She had to think of some way they could get out of the danger. The lads in the office below, one floor up from the ground, could probably jump out the window without major hurt, assuming they were uninjured, or rescuers could bring a ladder, but the windows here, ten feet higher, could not be reached by a ladder.

Tom stared at her, just nine years old, his eyes wide with terror. "Are we going to burn, Miss Braithwaite?"

"No." She wouldn't let him die. "Open the window. The far one. I'll get you out of here."

Somehow. There had to be something up here long enough to tie around Tom so she could lower him to the ground.

But there'd be no way to get the unconscious Jacob out through the window and she wouldn't be able to bear his weight, to lower him safely. And no way could she leave him to die.

~

After more than a day travelling in the jolting mail coach from London, Adam took pleasure in riding the last eight miles from Halifax on a hired horse, despite the steady, soaking rain. His greatcoat and beaver hat protected him from the worst of the damp, and the fresh air and solitude after the close confines of the coach made up for the minimal discomfort of the weather. Rain no longer rated as an annoyance after his years away at war.

The hired mare trotted along with an easy gait. Easier than Adam's mind. The mix of familiar landmarks and signs of major change made his thoughts see-saw between a sense of *home* and the unsettling sensation of strangeness, of being a stranger. Less than three miles from his family home at Rengarth, and he no longer belonged, no longer recognized some places.

Here, in the small town of Hartdale, a new bridge crossed the now-finished canal that flowed south from the fells into the river. Two new factories and several new warehouses lined its banks.

Smoke billowed out from the factory chimneys, dark against the grey of the clouds, and the noise of the steam-powered machinery vibrated in the air.

Only those with urgent purpose ventured out into the rain, and Adam saw few people about, even in the market square. They dashed from the shelter of one building to another, under an umbrella, or with coat collars pulled high and heads bowed under hats. No-one recognized him. No-one even looked twice at him, more concerned with keeping dry than acknowledging passers-by.

But as he passed the Hartdale Arms, a shout caught more than one person's attention.

Adam didn't hear the words the first time over his horse's hoof beats, but he heard the urgency, and he heard them the second time as a young man raced down the road.

"Fire! Get the fire cart!"

Adam kicked the mare forward, around the crook in the street. The grey smoke he'd assumed rose from a chimney came instead from a warehouse, and flames leapt up from behind it.

Josiah Braithwaite's warehouse. And a neatly-dressed lad leaned out from an upstairs window, calling for help, for a ladder, for water.

A boy—a child—struggled to lift a full bucket of water from a water butt almost his height.

Adam swung off his horse, lifted the bucket, and tossed the reins to boy. "Take her to the Arms," he ordered, as if the boy was one of his soldiers. "Tell them Major Caldwell says to bring every ladder and bucket they can find. And stout ropes."

Still puffing from exertion, the boy's grimy face was wide-eyed with excitement and trepidation. Just a child, not a soldier. "Johnno's gone for the fire cart."

Adam softened his voice. "Good. We'll need them and more. Hurry now."

Underneath the window, Adam called up to the desperate lad above, "How many of you up there?"

"Three here, sir. But-"

Someone near Adam took up the shout of *"Fire! Get the fire cart!"* and he barely made out the trapped lad's panicked words, "-Braithwaite is in the loft."

Josiah Braithwaite? Or his son, Matthew? It didn't matter. Adam sized up the height of the building and swore. Too tall for a ladder to reach the weaving loft.

He remembered the basic layout of the warehouse from the one time he'd been inside it and rapidly assessed the situation. The entrance at one end, off the street, leading into the showroom and the warehouse rooms with all the bales of finished and unfinished fabrics. The stairs to the middle floor led to the large counting room where the clerks worked, with Josiah Braithwaite's office at the opposite end of the building from the stairs. Above the counting room, the weavers' loft, with large south-facing windows for light. At the rear of the building, the double warehouse doors opened on to the courtyard, with the stables to the side, abutting the warehouse.

The main roar of the fire seemed to be coming from the back, from the stables, but thick smoke swirled in front of the window glass near the main entrance door, pierced by the orange-red flicker of flames.

No way out through there. A decade of war and too many burning buildings had taught the harsh lesson that to even open that door would send a rush of air to feed the flames into an inferno.

He pushed aside memories of a burning farmhouse and the

screams of trapped soldiers. Not here. Not today. The continued rain and damp must reduce the heat and power of the fire. He would get these people out of the building, alive.

He slipped into battle readiness—focused only on the job to do, allowing no time for feelings or fear—and gave orders because there was no-one else to take charge.

"Get into Mr. Braithwaite's office," he called up to the young clerk. "Close the door and open the window."

The clerk coughed and disappeared from view. On the top floor, someone shattered some of the panes of the end window. He couldn't see who.

Several men with buckets rushed up the street. "Don't open the front door!" Adam ordered. "Go round the back. Do what you can there to douse the flames." There'd be water butts and troughs for horses around the stable yard. Not much hope for any horses in the stables, but he could hear none, and hoped there were none.

A woman hurried from a house across the street awkwardly carrying a ladder, tears running down her cheeks. "Please sir," she gasped, "My boy...my boy's in there."

With a brief word of reassurance, Adam set the ladder against the wall of the warehouse. It barely reached the window of Braithwaite's office on the middle floor. But it was close enough. Close enough for the clerks in the counting room. Nowhere near close enough for Braithwaite and anyone else on the top level.

The woman—sensible despite her anxiety—held the base of the ladder steady while he quickly ascended and hauled himself in through the window. The three clerks—two youths, and one boy around twelve years old—gathered close to give him little-needed help. They'd had the sense to close the door between Braithwaite's office and the larger room and although smoke scratched his eyes, the flames had not yet reached here. They had several ledger books and the cash box stacked by the window.

The tallest of the clerks pushed the boy forward. "William must go first, sir."

Adam nodded agreement and lifted the lad to the window sill, holding his arms while William felt with his feet for the top rung of the ladder. The boy's mother called encouragement and William made his way down to be hauled into a close embrace. As Adam assisted one of the clerks over the window ledge, a man took the goodwife's place, holding the ladder steady.

The younger clerk was half-way down when the man at the base shouted, looking up, and Adam twisted to see above the window. Two small legs dangled, one shoe hanging loose, as someone in the loft lowered a child, inch by inch. As the legs came level, Adam grabbed them, guiding the swaying child towards the ladder. A wide strip of fabric wrapped around his chest, tied in a knot almost thicker than the skinny body, long ends of threads hanging. Braithwaite must have cut a web from a loom. Good thinking. Up to thirty yards on a piece of cloth, long enough to reach the ground.

While the boy—young, maybe eight or nine years old—clung to the ladder, Adam tugged the knot loose so the cloth could be used for another person.

"Down you go, lad. You're safe now."

The boy's lip trembled. "Miss Braithwaite and Uncle Jacob—you'll save them, won't you?"

His words shattered Adam's detached focus. "*Miss* Braithwaite? Miss Braithwaite is up there?"

He must have said it forcefully, because the boy barely nodded before he scampered down the ladder.

"Yes, sir," the clerk behind Adam said. "Miss Emma Braithwaite. She's the senior partner now, sir."

Barely hearing anything past the confirmation, Adam leaned half his body out the window, straining to see upwards.

"Emma!" The length of fabric obscured his view and he pulled it out of his way. There was no-one at the window. She was somewhere inside there, in the smoke and the fire. "*Emma!*"

He saw movement, and then her face, almost as pale as the white lace of her collar. She saw him but with the smoke all around she didn't recognize him, didn't know him.

"I can't lift Jacob," she called down to him, to those below, panic sharpening her voice. "I can't lift him and I won't be able to hold his weight."

He closed his fist around the fabric, griping it tight. "Fasten the cloth to a beam or something heavy. I'm coming up."

She properly saw him then, visibly startled. "*Adam?*" She shook her head, urgency overpowering her astonishment. "I can't. There's only the loom, and it's not heavy enough. It just moves."

Adam swore. He strode across and opened the office door so that he could check the door to the stairs, twenty feet away, near the front wall of the building. The smoke flowed under it, but he could see no flames licking the edge of the door itself. At the other end of the wall, where it met the back wall, the paper curled and smoked, but not near the door.

He returned to the open window and called up again, "Stay near the window, Emma. I'm coming to get you."

He still wore his great coat, thick wool wet through after hours in the rain. Woolen breeches, leather boots, leather riding gloves. His beaver hat had fallen to the floor when he'd clambered through the window, and he swept it up, jamming it on his head as he pulled his damp cravat up over his face.

The clerk began to follow as he crossed the room. "Sir, you're not going to…"

"Yes. Get down that ladder, man. Now."

The metal of the door handle was warm through his gloves, but not searing hot. Not yet. With his ear to the door he held his breath and listened. Over the sound of his heart beats, the harsh crackling of fire eating wood, but not right outside the door. He opened it cautiously, keeping behind it. Smoke rushed in, and noise and heat, but not flames.

Immediately to his left, the stairs rose from the small landing to the upper floor. But there was a hole in the back wall, near the top landing, and the stairs leading to the lower floors were well alight, flames leaping upwards, and thick, choking smoke filling his nose and throat despite the small protection of his loosened cravat.

Flames worked on the bannisters, and some of the steps smoked, small pockets of flames breaking through.

He could make it. He had to make it.

He sucked in a breath and took two paces backwards, then ran into the hell of flames and smoke. Up the stairs, two by two, heat singeing the cotton around his face, throwing himself forward as the wooden treads shifted under his boots, reaching the top landing and grasping the door handle as the supports below the flight of stairs gave way.

With his weight yanking the door handle down, he swung himself inside the loft, slamming the door shut against the roar of the flames as the stairs collapsed to the floors below.

The floor directly beneath him shook but held. His lungs screamed for air and he coughed violently, staggering a few feet.

"Adam!" From the far end of the room, Emma rushed towards him but he drew enough breath to meet her part-way, taking her arm to guide her back to the fresh air coming through the open window. If the flames burst through—*when* the flames burst through—he wanted her already gone, already safe.

The weaver lay unconscious, near the window. A good-sized man, thick with muscle. She had done well to drag him this far.

But her attention now was on him, checking him for injury, smothering a smoldering shirt cuff with her shawl. "You shouldn't have risked yourself, Adam. They'll be here with the fire cart soon." Her breath caught. "You could have died."

"Wet wool is armor," he said. "But we must hurry. I'll lower you down, then him."

"No. Jacob goes first. He has a family to support. And it will need both of us to lift him."

Adam knew her well enough not to argue. He knelt beside the weaver, checking for signs of life. Blood seeped from the man's head, but a pulse tapped evenly against his fingers.

Emma had already hauled back the length of worsted fabric, and had one end tied to the loom, the other near the man. As Adam lifted him by the shoulders, she wrapped it around his chest, the knot she tied thick enough to give a little support to his drooping head.

Flames broke through the wall at the far end of the room, and something else collapsed with a resounding crash. Choking smoke billowed into the room.

She gasped but didn't scream, focused on helping him to lift the dead weight of the weaver up onto the window sill, his legs over the edge. She guided the weaver's body as Adam stripped off his gloves and gripped the makeshift rope, the taut, bunched fabric harsh against his hands.

He battled against the desire to let the man drop quickly so that Emma could go. But to drop him too fast might kill him, if his injuries weren't already deadly. Inch by inch, foot by foot, it seemed to take forever. In reality, it might have been a minute. The flames had hold of the far wall.

"They've got him," Emma said, and the dead weight suddenly lessened as the man reached waiting arms below.

"Untie him," Adam bellowed through the window. While he hauled the makeshift rope hand over hand back up, Emma wrapped two thick ledger books in her shawl.

"Leave those," he said, as he readied to tie the cloth around her.

She held the bundle tight to her chest. "No. I need the records of debtors and creditors. And the pattern book has our history."

Logical, and it took no more time to save them than it did to save her. He passed the cloth around her to tie it over the books, the cloth helping to hold them in place. Her skirts hampered her as he helped her climb to the window.

He put a hand on her shoulder to guide her. "Back out. Use your feet against the wall. Don't look down." He gripped the makeshift rope with both hands and braced himself as she maneuvered out the window.

Another few seconds, another minute, and she would be safe.

He wasn't sure if he had much longer than that to get out alive himself.

~

Hands steadied her as she came close to the ground and she reached with her feet for solidity. Above her, Adam's face strained to lower her steadily, his gaze never leaving her.

Adam. Adam Caldwell. That he should be here, now, after eight years...

Her feet found the cobblestones and she steadied herself with a hand against the warehouse wall.

Voices shouted all around, people crowding her, and someone took the ledgers from her but she could only think of Adam, still up there in the burning loft, and she tugged at the thick knot around her chest, coughing in the wet, cold air, sobbing as she struggled to undo the now damp cloth.

Work-worn hands came into her vision, gently pushing hers away to take over the task. Goodwife Harris, the mother of young William, the new copy boy.

"It's all right, Miss Braithwaite. I'll get you out of this." Her fingers worked nimbly as she soothed with chatter. "Someone said that it's Captain Caldwell up there. The old Earl's son, isn't he?"

"Major Caldwell." She'd read the notice in the Gazette, after Waterloo. His promotion, and his appointment to the Duke of Wellington's staff in the Paris embassy.

Freed from the twisted cloth, Emma allowed herself to be drawn back, away from the warehouse, away from the heat and danger. The warehouse door hung open, half off its hinges, flames flicking out above it. A chain of men with buckets kept a constant pace, throwing water at it, held back by the heat, the liquid only sometimes hitting the flames in a hiss of steam.

Horses hooves clattered up the street, sending bystanders scattering. The fire cart, at last. Only one, in this small town. Owned by the insurance company in Halifax, to whom Emma paid the premium sum to guarantee the services of the fire cart. Guaranteed, if not prompt. It seemed like hours since the fire had burst through from the stables. But the men on the cart began pumping before the horses had fully halted.

At the high window, Adam straddled the window sill, maneuvering to get a good hold of the cloth rope. She could just see the shape of the loom, drawn hard up against the wall. Good, it should hold there for him. He swung his body over the sill and began a slow descent, hand over hand, his feet walking down the wall.

Emma breathed out and looked away. He had to make it down safely, without falling, without fire billowing out through the window or walls. She couldn't bear to see it if anything went wrong.

"Miss Braithwaite!" Ned, the senior of the two young clerks, pushed his way through to her.

"You're all unhurt?" she asked. "You and Theo and Will are all safe?"

"Yes, Miss. We all got out fine. And Jacob woke up just now. He's spoken quite clearly, Miss, and he can move all right. They've taken him to his sister's."

Relief made her head spin. They were all safe, all her employees. No-one left in that inferno. She made herself think straight. She still had responsibilities to see to. "I'll go there. Ned, find the constable and tell him where I am. He will want a report."

"Out of my way!" The commanding voice parted the crowd as a tall, well-dressed man shouldered his way through. Emma smothered a groan. Not Robert. Not here. Not now. With an effort, she straightened her shoulders to face him.

"Cousin Emma! I heard... Good Lord, you *were* in there!" He jabbed a finger at Ned. "Don't just stand around, man, go and fetch a doctor this instant!"

She took a breath to protest but the sudden air scratched her raw throat and she coughed, again and again, unable to stop. Made giddy by the wracking convulsions, her head became heavy and the street beneath her feet tilted this way and that.

She would not faint in front of Robert. She would *not*. But she could scarcely draw breath, her lungs screamed for air, and black spots danced in front of her eyes.

"Smelling salts!" she heard Robert call. "Someone fetch some smelling salts!"

The mere thought of the biting aroma of the salts made her throat close further. She tried to shake her head, but the spots in her vision swelled into darkness. Her head hit Robert's arm as she collapsed.

CHAPTER 2

Adam let himself drop the last few feet to the ground as another crash inside blew a cloud of smoke and cinders out of the door, sending those in the bucket line staggering backwards, out of the way. The men on the back of the fire cart ducked but hardly missed a beat in their pumping, pushing the handles alternately up, down, up, down as others aimed the hose through the doorway.

On his way down, past the counting room window, he'd seen few flames encroaching from the stair well. In this damp weather, there might still be a chance of saving some of the building, now that the fire cart had arrived.

But while he looked around for Emma, Adam used his officer's voice and stance to direct the gathering crowd further back, away from the building. A huddle of people across the road ignored his directions. On the edge of the group he recognized the older of the two young clerks, the thick ledger books and cash box still clutched to his chest, and crossed to him.

"Miss Braithwaite swooned, sir," the clerk told him, nodding towards a wooden bench outside the shop, where Emma sat, a handkerchief to her mouth, strands of loose hair falling across her pale face. The goodwife sat beside her, and a gentlemen stood in front of her in a proprietary manner, as if to shield her from view. "Mr. Braithwaite has sent for his carriage to carry her home."

"Matthew Braithwaite?" Adam guessed. The man stood too tall

to be Josiah, Emma's father. But Matthew would be twenty-six now, a man, not a youth.

"No, sir. Mr. Matthew is in the Canadian colonies. Mr. Robert Braithwaite, of the Braithwaites of Sowerby."

Robert Braithwaite. Adam vaguely recalled a stiff, reserved boy at school in York. A cousin—second cousin?—of the local family.

"You are familiar with the family, sir?" the clerk enquired, politely curious.

Of course he was curious. Adam had called her Emma, shouting it out the window for all to hear. Emma, not the 'Miss Braithwaite' he should have used. He'd barely arrived back and already he'd possibly put her in a difficult position. Again. And there was Robert Braithwaite, attending to her as if he had the right to do so. For all Adam knew, he might have. Her employees still referred to her as 'Miss Braithwaite' but she could easily be betrothed. What man in his right mind wouldn't want a woman like Emma? Her beauty and common sense at seventeen had become more so, now. She hadn't panicked in the fire. She didn't fall apart now. Her composure and practical actions had saved the lives of her employees.

"Our families are neighbors," he explained to the clerk, as if that might douse any gossip. "I am Adam Caldwell."

Hampered by the burdens he carried protectively, the young man bowed. "I am honored, sir. I am Ned- Edward Langton, at your service, sir."

On the bench, Emma made an attempt to tidy her hair as she rose to her feet. Braithwaite hastened a step closer and said something Adam didn't hear, but Emma replied clearly despite some huskiness in her voice, "Thank you, Cousin Robert, but I am quite recovered."

A postilion, holding the harnesses of a well-matched pair, led horses and coach along the street, stopping some distance from the fire, the horses already skittish.

"There's my coach," Braithwaite said. "Cousin, please allow me to escort you home. Perhaps this good woman would accompany you? To attend to your needs. Unless you have a maidservant here?"

At least Braithwaite had some sense of propriety. Either that or he feared being alone with a lady who might be taken faint again.

Not that Emma appeared to be unsteady now. "No, I have no maid here. I must ensure that a doctor is sent to Jacob." She searched the crowd, and Adam stepped back in to the shadows. Langton excused himself, and went to assist his employer.

A polite cough behind him made Adam spin around. "Begging your pardon, Major Caldwell. Could I have a word, sir?"

The man supported himself on crutches too short for his height, his left leg missing below the knee. He wore the remnants of a soldier's uniform, a tattered and worn coat, the facings signifying Adam's own regiment. It took Adam several moments to place the face.

"It's Garrett, isn't it?"

"Yes, sir. Nathaniel Garrett. I were a sergeant."

The rain had begun falling again and Adam waved the man towards an old shop from Tudor times, with an overhanging upper floor.

Suspecting he was about to receive a supplication for money, Adam asked brusquely, "What is it, Garrett?"

"The fire, sir. I haven't heard anyone saying it yet, but the constable needs to know, and better that this comes from you, rather than the likes of me. There was an explosion, sir, not long after the fire started. I were just in the lane there. First I sniffed the smoke, but everyone that can has a fire burning today. But then there was the explosion. Not mighty loud, but loud enough. And the smell of black powder, in among the smoke."

"You're sure? It wasn't just some part of the warehouse collapsing? Or the stables behind it?"

The man eyed him steadily. "No, sir. I know the sound and smell of black powder exploding."

An explosion. Adam surveyed the warehouse, where the bucket brigade and fire cart seemed to be winning against the flames. What on earth was there to explode, in a warehouse full of worsted goods? In the *Braithwaite's* warehouse of worsted goods? He could hardly imagine Josiah—or Emma—running smuggled goods, let alone gunpowder. Enough gunpowder to do damage. Josiah leaned towards Quakerism, had never even taken part in shooting sports, to Adam's knowledge.

"Do you live here in town, Garrett?"

He shrugged. "Here and about. Not much work for an old cripple."

Old? The man was scarcely older than him. But there was a weariness in the harsh lines of his face, and he was only one of many former soldiers, out on the roads of England, searching for work. Little enough work around, and even less for a one-legged man. He doubted a military pension was enough to live on.

He remembered Garrett as a quiet, taciturn man, and a good sergeant, tough but fair with his men, and with a better understanding of soldiering than many of the young officers. Wise enough not to openly refuse or disobey orders, but to circumvent them when necessary. A man with more intelligence and sense than many. The kind of soldier that called officers 'sir' to avoid accusations of insolence, not out of any degree of respect.

"If you're willing to do some work for me, Garrett, I want to know more about that fire."

Garrett hesitated but eventually nodded, and Adam gave him some coins. "I want you to keep your eyes open and listen to the talk. Get yourself a good meal at the Arms. And meet me there tomorrow at ten."

Garrett studied the coins for a moment, wary, before he pocketed them. Adam figured they'd earn him at least twenty-four hours of conscientious listening and observation.

After Garrett limped away, Adam went in search of the town constable. He found him watching the fire from the dry shelter of the stationer's shop.

Not a man Adam remembered. Stout and ruddy-faced and years younger than the old constable, who often had good reason, long ago in the past, to issue stern warnings to a reckless lad from the castle.

The man pushed himself to his feet. "Major Caldwell, I believe?"

Adam nodded assent. "And you are?"

"Bert Williams, sir. Would your brother, His Lordship, be returned to the Castle, perchance?"

"No. He and Lady Rengarth remain in London for now."

"Ahh. I see. Then perhaps if you would be so kind as to inform her ladyship, the Dowager Countess, of this incident? Blasted Luddites are causing trouble everywhere. But who'd have thought they would strike here, in the heart of our town, in day light?"

"You believe this is the work of Luddites? Of machine breakers?"

"Started in the stables, it did. The horses and the stable boy went off to Halifax this mornin' with Hargraves, the factor. No-one there, see. Lucky for the horses."

"Indeed. But if the fire started in the stables, how do you believe it broke through into the warehouse?"

Williams shrugged. "It's an old building. Nigh on a hundred years. Roof rafters could have lit up."

"It's an old stone building," Adam corrected. "And the fire has yet to take hold in the roof." He didn't say anything about the hole he'd seen in the wall, or Garrett's report of an explosion. Not yet. Not until he had more of the constable's measure. A good constable would be asking these questions himself.

He had plenty more questions, and a number of possibilities, but he did not wish to put anyone on guard, until he had a better idea of the context. The last year on the Duke of Wellington's staff had certainly honed his instinct for holding his cards close.

He took his watch from his pocket to check the time. A plain watch, the case marked by years of hard use. But he did not miss the constable's quick, assessing glance at it. An avaricious man, the constable. Interesting.

"I must be on my way. My mother is hosting a ball this evening."

"Yes, yes, Her Ladyship's ball. Many fine people attending, I understand."

Anyone of any social standing in the West Riding. His mother's annual ball was the highlight of the summer, and an opportunity for the introduction of the season's crop of young ladies to society. For which reason Adam, a single man, would have preferred to face a hundred diplomatic conferences in Europe than to attend the ball. But duty called. He owed his family, and Rengarth, much more than that.

He nodded across to the warehouse. "They will have that under control shortly. Make sure that they keep watch overnight to prevent any flare-ups. And set a guard so that there is no looting. Meet me here in the morning, at nine o'clock. We will investigate further, then."

The constable started to protest. "But sir, the insurance agent-"

Adam raised an eyebrow. It sufficed to remind Williams who he was. "The agent will not be out from Halifax before nine. We will meet here then."

As he strode down to the Arms to retrieve his horse, he went over and over what little he knew so far. Matthew Braithwaite was in the Canadian colonies. There'd been no sign of Josiah and no-one had mentioned him. Perhaps he was dead, or infirm. But if he was, that left only Emma and her younger sisters. And Emma had been there, working in the warehouse, an ink stain on her fingers, the staff speaking respectfully to, and of, her.

Even at seventeen she'd had a strong head for business. Perhaps better than her father's. It made sense that with her brother away, she would have charge of things.

But she'd been in that warehouse when someone had likely set it alight, and she could easily have died.

CHAPTER 3

In her room, Emma sent her maid for washing water, and stripped off her sooty and cinder-singed gown, and then her petticoat, her stays and her stockings. The thick odor of smoke clung to it all, clung to her, her skin and hair, and she had to repress, yet again, the urge to cough. She took a fresh cambric handkerchief and dabbed it with lavender oil, breathing in the soothing scent.

Her maid returned with the water, and Emma washed quickly, her thoughts racing through all she needed to arrange and to do.

"The blue gown for now, thank you, Kate. And the lilac ball gown for this evening."

"This evening? Pardon me, miss, but wouldn't you prefer to rest?"

Yes. "My cousin is waiting for me now. And I must attend this evening's ball. It's more important now than ever."

Kate helped her to dress in the plain day dress and tidied her hair, spraying it with a misted scent that didn't quite succeed in masking the clinging odor of smoke. Emma dabbed some lavender on her throat before she tied her chemisette closed. Perhaps it would keep her mind from straying back to the fearful minutes when she'd thought she would not escape the fire. Until Adam had walked through the flames.

Adam Caldwell. After eight years away, he'd appeared without warning, without any time to prepare for seeing him again. Without any time to think about how she felt.

No, she'd had *eight years* to think about how she felt. Eight years in which she'd relived his kisses and caresses, regretted her words, wasted thoughts and imagination on what could never have been.

Breathe. Think. Be sensible.

She'd left her seventeen-year-old self far behind. Adam would have changed, too. Perhaps he hardly remembered her. There'd have been other women in his life. She'd not heard of a marriage, but she had not seen the Dowager Countess or others in the family for many months, and the marriage of a second son might not make the newspapers. Especially when he'd been overseas for so long.

And his marital status was none of her business.

Her business involved a struggling worsted manufactory, a fire in her warehouse, a missing brother, and her second cousin Robert waiting downstairs in the library, doubtless with unsolicited advice on any or all of those matters.

Robert stood at the window, gazing out over the rain-soaked lawns. He dressed as impeccably as always in the finest cloth, beautifully tailored. They'd known each other since babyhood, their families maintaining cordial relations despite the disagreements between their respective grandfathers that had split the old family company into two. Yet although they continued to use first names, their differences in opinion and character often strained their relationship.

He had been unremitting in his concern for her in the carriage on the two-mile drive, and painstakingly polite to both her and Mrs. Harris. To steer him from constant questions about her well-being, Emma engaged him in small talk on the drive. He'd come from Sowerby for the Dowager Countess's ball tonight. He'd just arrived at the inn when he heard about the fire. He was well. Business was as good as could be expected, in these difficult times. When a small silence fell in the conversation, he filled it with more questions about her comfort, whether she was in pain, whether she felt faint. She'd been glad to arrive at Larkfell, and escape his persistent worry for a few minutes while she changed.

He'd carried in the ledgers and letter books saved from the fire and placed them on the corner of the large mahogany desk. She did not doubt he had resisted any desire to examine them. Honor mattered to Robert.

Mrs. Barnden, the housekeeper, followed her in to the library, carrying a tea tray.

"On the desk, thank you, Mrs. Barnden," Emma said. Robert had said he had important matters to discuss. She would make this business-like and, preferably, brief.

She took her seat behind the desk so that he would have to sit, too, and directed Mrs. Barnden to leave the door open as she left. She never felt unsafe with Robert—he was far too proper a gentleman to commit any indiscretion—but he did need reminding, not infrequently, that a grown woman with intelligence did not require his counsel on every small matter. With the portrait of their great-grandfather, Sir Francis Braithwaite, high on the wall behind her, and Robert seated in the chair opposite her, she held the marginally more powerful position. Not that Robert would acknowledge that.

She poured tea into two cups. She needed it, even if he didn't. "What is it that concerns you, Robert?"

"You know how important it is that we find out what has happened to Matthew," he began. "Have you heard any news of him?"

She raised an eyebrow at his use of 'we'. Important to her, yes, to locate her brother and bring him home to take on his responsibilities since their father's death. Important to Robert? Braithwaite and Co, her family's company, had had no business connection with Robert's branch of the extended family for more than thirty years. The woolen manufacturing company in Sowerby owned by Robert and his brother Francis was entirely separate, the business split a legacy of their grandfathers' disagreements.

Emma kept her voice calm. "I have not heard from Matthew. Yet." Robert must have some reason for broaching the topic, so she confronted him outright, "Why do you ask?"

He hesitated, stirring sugar into his tea with precise, elegant movements. "You may know that my brother, Francis, has recently returned from the colonies. I hesitate to tell you this, after the distress you have endured this afternoon, but I feel it is my duty…"

"I will not faint again, Cousin Robert. Please tell me what you know."

"Matthew spent the first winter in Montreal. He travelled to Kingston in March last year."

Emma tried to conceal her impatience. "I am aware of that. We have received orders from some of the merchants he visited. Our last letter from him is dated June fifteenth of last year, in which he mentions interest in an expedition to explore the waterways to the north of Kingston. Has Francis heard anything since then?"

Robert's long hesitation set Emma on edge. "He was in Kingston earlier this year, and heard that Matthew had joined the expedition." He watched her closely, all solicitous concern, as he added, "But he also heard rumors that the expedition was attacked, and that all are lost."

Emma carefully, very carefully, loosened her tight grip on her tea cup and placed the delicate china back on its saucer. She sat back in her chair, and clasped her shaking hands in her lap.

Pretending calmness, she queried, "You say 'rumors'. Is there any confirmation of this? Or an official investigation?"

"Not that he is aware of. But perhaps, cousin, with your permission I could request the authorities to enquire officially in to the reports?"

"There is no need, thank you, Robert. As it happens, I have employed two men to search for news of Matthew."

He raised an eyebrow. "You have? But are they good, trustworthy men?"

"They were recommended by Lord Castlereagh's office. I think I can rely on the judgement and experience of the Foreign Secretary's staff."

"Yes. Quite. Of course." The admission came reluctantly, and he found a way to qualify it. "Strange sorts, those spies the foreign office uses. Not proper gentlemen at all. Not the kind a lady should have dealings with." His curiosity got the better of his censure. "Have they reported any news yet?"

"The weather has delayed shipping and mail and few ships have arrived yet from Quebec," she informed her cousin in case he was not studying the shipping intelligence as assiduously as she was. "I did receive a letter three weeks ago, from the agent in Quebec. He is aware of the expedition and believes they may have planned to over-winter in one of the fur-trading posts north-west of Ottawa. He believes the other agent may have more news soon." Having pored over maps and books, she now knew a hundred times more about the wild country beyond the main settlements than she'd known twelve months ago.

Robert made a slight sniff of disdain. "Going into the wilderness was irresponsible in the extreme."

Emma allowed the criticism of her brother to pass, coming as it did from a man who considered having to change tailors more than enough adventure for any gentleman's lifetime.

"Matthew is still young and has no dependents. He went to Canada for business. Father's death was quite unforeseeable."

"As an only son his duty lay with his father."

"Who encouraged the possibility of expanding markets," Emma said more mildly than his presumption deserved. "I hope to hear good news shortly, that they have made the journey back to one of the towns once the waterways were navigable again."

"The weather has been bad there as well as here. No summer at all, yet. Francis travelled down to New York and said it was bitter there when he left in late May. And they were still getting frosts in New York in June."

She read the newspapers thoroughly and was familiar with the reports of unseasonal cold weather from all over Europe and the Americas. They did not bode well for an expedition into the vast wilderness of Upper Canada. But she would not give Robert the satisfaction of seeing her anxiety, or the excuse to meddle in her family's business.

"So since there is no other intelligence to the contrary, we will assume that my brother is alive and well and spent the winter at one of the settlements in the interior. I expect we will hear confirmation of this very soon." She prayed there would be a letter soon. Even today, first thing on arriving home she'd gone straight to the silver tray in the hall to check the day's post for a letter with Matthew's handwriting. Nothing. Like all the days in the past year, nothing from Matthew.

She could not allow emotion to overwhelm her in front of Robert. She took a sip of her strong, sweet tea, and asked, "Was there any other matter that you wished to discuss with me?"

"There is. It is somewhat delicate, however. I hope you will not take it amiss, Cousin, but I believe it is my duty to ensure that you are aware, that there are...some concerns. While I generally dismiss rumors, two of your creditors have directly approached me to enquire about the solvency of Braithwaite and Co. And now with this fire, I expect there will be rather more concern."

They'd approached *him*, not her. The masculine trade and social circles excluded women, as if none of them—wives, widows, daughters, sisters—were capable of thinking beyond what to order for dinner. Yet she had far better business sense than her father, who would have driven the company to bankruptcy in his efforts to please everyone, and his reluctance to acknowledge the changing world.

Emma held her cousin's gaze. "The company is solvent. The warehouse and its contents are insured. The creditors need not be concerned. They will be paid within normal terms of trade. Should anyone else enquire, please direct them to me or to Mr. Winslow." Not that Ralph Winslow, her father's old friend and the 'and Co.' in the company, had contributed significantly to keeping the business running in the past ten years. More of a silent partner than an active one, although he had no qualms about her continued role and whenever she consulted him, seeking his advice, he listened carefully, discussed the issues, and generally agreed with her decisions.

She placed her tea cup on the table and rose to her feet. "If you will excuse me, Robert, I do have to write letters before this evening's ball. I will send you word when I hear any news of Matthew."

He stood reluctantly. "I am surprised that you are going to the ball. Surely you should be resting after your ordeal. And it is so soon after your father's death."

The critical glance he cast at her dark blue calamanco gown made her almost wish she'd asked Kate to put out her crimson gown.

"It has been more than six months. My father did not agree with extensive mourning periods, and neither do I. They isolate women from the support of society and from practical activity. Not to mention," she gave a slight smile, "they are bad for our trade. As a partner in this company, it is my duty to encourage moderation in such practices. And it's also my duty to participate in major society events to encourage confidence in the company."

"And what if Matthew doesn't return?" he asked, but he said it with a paternal gentleness. "You can't seriously expect to continue running the business. We both know Winslow isn't doing it."

She paused with her hand on the door knob and took two slow breaths to remind herself that Robert spoke out of concern, more than criticism. As the eldest Braithwaite male remaining, Robert saw himself as responsible for the extended family, and his sense of duty was strong. Too strong.

"I keep Mr. Winslow informed and as a fellow partner he has supported my decisions. *If* my brother has met with tragedy…" She kept her voice even with difficulty, "I will deal with the consequences in accordance with his wishes and in consultation with my sisters and our family lawyer."

For once he nodded and didn't argue, or lecture her any further. She saw him out through the hall, and he paused as he took his hat from Jarvis, the butler. "As I will also be attending the ball this evening, perhaps you will grant me the honor of saving me a dance?"

"Of course," Emma consented, out of courtesy rather than pleasure.

He carefully straightened his hat on his head, just so, and as he pulled on his gloves he commented, "I was surprised to see Caldwell. I had no idea he had returned."

He mentioned it as a curiosity, a piece of local news. Perhaps he did not realize the part Adam had played in saving Jacob and herself. He certainly could not know what Adam had once meant to her.

She murmured a polite response, but the drama and emotion of the day threatened to overwhelm her, and she barely kept her composure in front of him as he left, and in front of Jarvis as she hastened back to the library. She closed the door behind her and let it take the weight her shaking limbs almost refused.

Alone, with no need to be strong for others, she allowed a few tears to fall. But not for long. She drew on her self-discipline to lecture herself out of the weak moment.

Breathe. Pull yourself together. You will manage this. All of this.

She pushed away from the door, walked almost steadily to her desk.

This was her life. This desk, these ledgers, the bales of fabric in the burning warehouse. This responsibility for the livelihoods of the warehouse staff, and dozens of skilled weavers, wool combers and spinners. This responsibility for keeping Matthew' inheritance intact—the business and this family home, Larkfell House.

All of them responsibilities that she carried alone.

The younger sisters she'd raised after their mother's death no longer filled Larkfell's rooms with their laughter and activity. Both her sisters, married to army officers, were in the East with their husbands. And Matthew stranded somewhere in Canada. All thousands of miles, months of travel away.

But now Adam Caldwell was home after eight years away, to remind her of all that she'd given up to do her duty by her family.

CHAPTER 4

Adam reined in his horse to a halt when he reached the top of the ridge overlooking Rengarth Castle. The entire estate lay before him, the rain muting the soft greens of the fields, the darker green of the woods, and the greys of the stone buildings, from the smallest cottage in the village to the vast façade of Rengarth Castle. Not a castle proper—the ruins of the old medieval fortified castle towered over the trees in the north wood—but a grand house, built in stages over fifty years by his ancestors and added to by every generation. The conservatory his father had planned now graced the east side of the house. His brother's new carriage house was just visible behind the stables.

The mare fidgeted and rain dripped from the drooping brim of his beaver hat on to his cheek, but he did not move on. The once familiar ache in his chest pulled tighter, almost physically painful. How many times in his life had he stopped here, on this rise, to look out over Rengarth? Hundreds. Maybe thousands. He'd never tired of the view. Could never tire of the view. In all the years away he'd dreamed, often, of being here, and in dark times in the hell holes of war he'd doubted he would ever make it back.

But the war that had swept its bloody scythe across Europe, from Portugal to Russia, from Italy to Calais, had not invaded this quiet corner of England. Rengarth stood untouched in its peaceful valley, the same as it had always been. Only he had changed.

Less than two miles to the east, beyond the woods, the white walls and dark slate roof of Larkfell House were just visible among the treed slopes of its gardens. Emma would be home by now. Robert Braithwaite had stepped in quickly to ensure her well-being and her transport home and would surely have called a doctor if there was need. As an affianced gentleman should.

Adam turned his gaze away from Larkfell. Nothing for him there. Only memories, and the bitter knowledge of his own stupidity.

A cart with a covered load made its way up the lane from the village towards the castle. Perhaps the carter from Halifax bringing his luggage. More probably supplies for his mother's ball tonight. If he'd stayed in London another day or two he could have avoided the ball and all the polite socializing it demanded. But his brother George had asked him to attend in his place, his mother would appreciate his presence, and it was an important event for at least two of his sisters—one just married, one coming out. And another, making her first major social appearance since her husband's death at Waterloo, over a year ago. A rare occurrence to have almost all of the family at home at once.

Family. He'd swapped military responsibility for family duties. And no-one in his family had ever been inclined to follow orders. Including himself.

A gust of wind whipped rain into his face and drops of water seeped in under his cravat, cool against his throat. He flicked the reins and the mare took off down the bridle path at a trot, as if keen to get out of the weather herself.

He rode around to the stables, and one of the stable boys ran forward to take his horse; a lad who must hardly have been in breeches when Adam was last at Rengarth. With perfect courtesy, he held the mare while Adam dismounted and offered to carry his saddlebags inside. A good stable boy. Except the curious glance from under the brim of his cap, the unruly brown hair, and his mostly clean hands gave him away.

Concealing a confusion of amusement and regrets, Adam unbuckled his saddle bags and let the boy lead the horse away.

But he took the risk and called out when they were half-way to the stables, "Don't forget to clean your fingernails before you come back to the house, Benjamin."

The boy shot him a grin, echoing the one Adam saw on the rare occasion he had reason to grin at a mirror. Definitely his youngest brother. The youngest of ten children, only three years old when Adam was last at Rengarth.

Adam strode along the gravel paths through the garden to the terrace, regrets and guilt gnawing away at his pleasure at being home. He barely knew his youngest brother, had barely recognized him. Only the recollection of his own childhood escapades masquerading as a stable boy had led him to suspect that the curious, well-spoken boy might be Benjamin. Would he recognize Cecilia, who must be fourteen now? Or Jeremy, assuming he was home from school? Or Susanna, properly out in society this season? At least he'd seen them in London, five years ago, on a leave too-brief to make the journey to Yorkshire. And Phoebe and Lilian and Louisa and Oliver three years ago, on another brief leave. And George, of course, this past two weeks. But with Lilian now married there was a husband to acquaint himself with, and Phoebe's baby son, his father killed at Waterloo before his birth, and...and maybe he'd been neglectful of his family for too long and he was a fool to think he had any right to regard Rengarth as *home*. Perhaps Rengarth had changed as much as he had.

He paused at the steps up to the terrace. Voices and laughter came from the drawing room. Too many voices. He had no desire to walk in, dripping wet, on the whole family and guests at once. Instead, he headed to the end of the terrace, where the study doors opened out in to the garden.

The unexpected presence of his mother at the door, watching his approach, waylaid his plan to attend to his scorched, smoke-reeking attire before he encountered any of the family.

Caroline, the Dowager Lady Rengarth, who had taken all his boyhood adventures without panic, smiled warmly but did not embrace him until he'd shed his wet greatcoat into the care of a hastily summoned footman.

As she kissed Adam on the cheek, he inhaled the sweet scent of her favorite rosewater, as much a part of his memories as the view of Rengarth from the ridge.

"Welcome home, Adam." She held him at arms' length while she inspected him for wounds as if he was still ten years old. Or perhaps to see for herself that he was still whole, after Quatre Bras and Waterloo and the other battles in the years since his last visit to London. He *had* changed, but he doubted she could see those changes. So had she, but only in small ways. The wisps of hair escaping from under her cap, fine and soft as always, but silver in among the brown. The fine lines around her eyes, the indentations deeper, most of them smile lines, but not all of them. Curiosity chased concern in her eyes.

"I trust your disheveled state is not the sign of a terrible journey? Were all your fellow travelers smoking dreadful pipes?"

"The journey was fine." Crowded in with three portly gentlemen for much of the way from London, but he'd been dry and able to get some sleep. "I had some business to see to in Halifax, so I hired a horse from there. But there was a fire at Hartdale, hence my delay."

"A fire?" She indicated the chairs near the fireplace and folded her hands in her lap when she sat down. "Where? Was anyone injured?"

Instead of the brocaded arm chair, he carried across from the desk a straight-backed, wooden chair that would not be damaged by his damp clothing. "It was at Josiah Braithwaite's warehouse. The clerks escaped without difficulty. Miss Braithwaite was in the loft with an injured weaver and required some assistance to escape."

"So you rescued Miss Braithwaite?"

"She rescued herself, and the draw boy. I merely helped with the weaver. He was knocked senseless for a time, but has since recovered."

His mother considered him as if she knew he'd only skimmed the truth. "I hope Miss Braithwaite was not scorched assisting him as you were."

He didn't think she'd noticed the burn marks on his coat or

his cuff. He should have learned that lesson years ago—an astute mother of five sons and five daughters noticed every detail. "Miss Braithwaite was not near the flames," he assured her. "She suffered a little from the smoke but is unharmed."

He considered mentioning his suspicions about the fire, but decided against it for now. No sense in concerning his mother until he had further information. Not when he had other, graver news to impart.

He shifted in his chair, wishing he could stand and pace, his usual ease in her presence tempered by the knowledge of the conversation that must come. "George sends his love and respects to you."

"Has he seen the new physician yet? The one from Paris?"

"Yes."

"Does he offer more hope?"

There was the question he dreaded, and despite all the long hours on the journey to prepare for it, he had no soft words but the truth. "He offers some hope. He claims several successes with his treatments, but admits they are few."

Silence. Not even the rain outside. Sometime in the past few minutes, it had stopped raining. His mother sat breathlessly still, the whiteness of her tightly clasped hands in her lap the only sign of the distress she must be feeling.

It took some moments before she asked, almost calmly, "Will George live to see the birth of the child?"

"Probably. He may have some months yet. And perhaps the physician is right, and there is a chance." A chance for a man, only thirty, who struggled to breathe? Who could barely rise from his bed, let alone sit at a table for a meal?

Adam hoped the French physician had more answers than the previous one had. His brother was battling consumption, coughing frequently to clear what little remained functioning in his lungs.

His mother's blue eyes shone with unshed tears she would not, yet, give in to. "You're not truly optimistic, are you?"

"No," he conceded. "He is not, either, and he seemed to decline even while I was there. And he insisted that-" He swallowed against

33

the difficult words, "That we make arrangements for the future."

She dabbed at her eyes with a lace-edged handkerchief, but dealt with her concern in practical decisions and actions. "I will return to London in a few days, after Lilian and her husband leave. Hannah will need support. And I want to be there."

To be there if her son died. Adam could barely even consider the eventuality; his brain kept skittering away from the thought. But after several years of illness, the outcome was a distinct possibility, and perhaps sooner rather than later.

He'd always imagined he would be the first one, brought home in a box or buried in some foreign field, long before George said his last farewell to the world. A world without steady, reliable George seemed impossible, and immensely unfair. Why should he, Adam, who had lived a far from faultless life, outlive George, who had only ever strived to do good?

But then, the world was far from fair or just. In all the years of war he'd learned that lesson again, and again, and again. No fairness or justice in where a cannon ball fell, or where a bayonet struck in the madness of a charge. And if there was any divine will, it was from a Divinity who practiced no earthly logic of compassion.

His mother wasted no time in philosophy, finding her way through practicality. "Oliver and Louisa will wish to come with me, I am sure. They are close to him. And Phoebe has business she must attend to in London. Will you—can you—stay here at Rengarth while we are in London?"

"I can stay." He'd discussed the matters his brother wished discussed, made his promises. And his goodbyes. Although a large part of him refused to accept that he might not see his brother again.

"Good. Jeremy needs something of a firm hand at times. And so does Benjamin. Your sisters will be no trouble."

As easily as that, the immediate future was arranged. He would stay at Rengarth for now, and oversee the younger brothers and sisters he scarcely knew.

Neither he nor his mother spoke aloud the reasons why it should be him, rather than one of his sisters. Because George might be dying, and unless the soon-to-be-born child was a son, Adam would become the next Earl of Rengarth. Even if the child was a boy, if George did not recover, the estate would need a guardian until he came of age. And Adam had promised his brother that he would be that guardian.

Hannah and her mother were both convinced that all the signs indicated that the child was a boy. He could only hope that they were right. He had little faith now in the wisdom of kings and emperors and princes, in the ability of the aristocracy to guide the realm—any realm—and maintain a just peace, and he had no desire to be an earl.

But this evening he had a more pressing concern. The fire in the warehouse could easily have killed Emma and her employees. Yet fires rarely started by accident in stables unless a lamp was overturned—and from all accounts, there'd been no-one, and no livestock, there. And fires in stables even more rarely blasted through a stone wall.

He'd checked, and the warehouse roof remained intact. No burning rafters to spread the fire from one building to the next. Only the hole in the wall between the stables and the stairwell.

Garrett's report of hearing an explosion and smelling powder made a logical explanation for that hole. Unless the Braithwaites stored powder in the stable—and why on earth would they?—it was far more likely that someone had intentionally set the fire and the powder to harm the Braithwaite's business. He intended to find out who and why.

CHAPTER 5

The lantern lights of the long row of carriages formed an arc leading to the sweeping entrance steps of Rengarth Castle. The magnificent portico framed the windows of the hall and the ballroom, lit to brilliance with chandeliers.

Her coach rolled forwards a few yards. One place closer. Emma made herself breathe slowly and deeply. The fire was sufficient reason to excuse herself from the Dowager Countess's ball. No-one would have considered it amiss of her. Any lady would be forgiven for preferring to rest and recuperate. But she was not any lady. She bore the responsibility for Braithwaite and Co, and for presenting confidence and calm in the wake of the afternoon's disaster.

The coach moved again, stopped after a few moments, and a footman opened the door, standing ready with an umbrella and holding it over her while she crossed to the steps up to the portico, although the rain had almost ceased for now.

In the drawing room off the grand foyer, guests greeted each other and discussed the unseasonable weather as they discarded cloaks and changed shoes. Gossip swirled in whispers. The Earl had not come. The Earl and his lady remained in London, for their health. The Countess was said to be expecting. Surely it would be a son, this time. Three daughters already, but no heir to the title.

Emma nodded at several acquaintances but did not see, in the immediate vicinity, any of her small circle of friends. The awkwardness of arriving alone at such an event added to her unwelcome nerves. Not that she particularly needed a chaperone; at twenty-five she was hardly a sheltered girl, and the Countess's invitation list could be relied on to be respectable. Yet her arrival this time was so different to the last ball she'd attended at the castle, two years ago, with her father and her sisters and her brother. So much had changed, since then.

A few acquaintances had heard of the fire and enquired after her well-being, although it seemed the details had not yet made it to the drawing rooms of the well-to-do. No-one mentioned Adam. It must not be generally known that he had returned.

She returned to the foyer to join the reception line, winding up the staircase to the ballroom, at the same time as Robert and his brother arrived.

"Cousin Emma." Robert bowed courteously. "I trust you are recovered well from your frightening ordeal."

Francis, as finely dressed as his older brother, bowed with rather less formality and a sly grin she wasn't sure how to interpret. It seemed his sojourn in the colonies had done little to polish his manners. But then Francis, named after their great-grandfather knighted for his success in the industry, had always deemed himself superior to her side of the family.

"Blasted Luddites," Francis drawled. "They should all be rounded up and hung for their insolence and violence. Thieves and murderers, the lot of them."

Emma could see no reason why machine-breakers would target a business using primarily traditional methods, but she did not voice her disagreement. She'd written to the constable this afternoon, formally engaging his services to investigate. Tomorrow she would see him and find out what he'd learned.

"I read of the attack on your cotton factory last week. Have you resumed production yet?" Emma enquired.

"Of course we have. We're making more than enough profit that repairs were done quickly. We won't be stopped by thugs."

He'd spoken loudly enough to draw attention to his proclamation.

An intentional play to differentiate his arm of the family from hers. The intense rivalry that had seen their respective grandfathers split the original Braithwaite and Sons company into two still ran strongly in her cousin's veins. Although the two companies didn't directly compete—the Sowerby company producing woolen cloth, while Emma's family produced worsteds—Francis rarely let an opportunity pass without expressing pride in their company's financial successes. More specifically, *his* financial success. His drive to mechanize production for Braithwaites of Sowerby with scribbling and spinning mills had been so successful he'd formed a partnership with other men to establish cotton factories.

Mechanization was not an option for Emma. Most of the fine worsted textiles that Braithwaite and Co specialized in required skilled hand spinning and weaving that could not be replicated by machine. A fact that might lead to their extinction within a few years if the pace of change continued with the rapidity of the past decade. And that worry underpinned all of her other concerns; move to coarser, cheaper worsteds, or watch her business shrink and eventually die.

The receiving line moved forward, Emma and her cousins with it. She almost wished she could attach herself to another party, but those around her were mere acquaintances, not friends she could desert family for, however distant the relationship. Not that the presence of family stopped Francis from greeting a friend and drifting away. So it was that when they reached the entrance to the ballroom, the butler announced "Mr. Braithwaite of Sowerby, and Miss Braithwaite," and Robert waved her in ahead of him, as if their relationship was closer than it was. And wouldn't that just feed the speculation over the years that a marriage between them would bring the two companies into one again.

Her face heated, Emma curtsied to Lady Rengarth, the Dowager Countess.

"My dear Miss Braithwaite, it is a relief to see you unharmed. My son told me of the trouble this afternoon."

Of course Adam would have told her, given his presumably

38

disheveled state after walking through flames and scrambling up and down ladders.

"Thank you, my Lady. Only one person was injured, and thanks to Major Caldwell, he is safe and recovering."

To Emma's relief, Robert occupied himself with bemoaning the weather with the Countess. Emma moved on to exchange greetings with the Lady Lilian and her new husband, a baron's eldest son.

And then Adam was the next in the line, tall and solemn in his evening clothes, the crisp white collar and cravat stark against the tanned skin of his jaw. He answered her curtsey with a deep bow. "Miss Braithwaite. I am thankful that you have taken no lasting harm."

In the crisis of the fire she had barely had the chance to look at him, save for the few moments when he'd tied the cloth around her, his face close to hers. Her brief impression then was confirmed now. No more the laughing, light-hearted young man of her memories, quick to smile, brimming with energy. His face had firmed, his cheek bones become more prominent, echoing some distant Viking ancestor. Dark brown eyes that had once sparkled regarded her gravely, shadows clouding them. After years in an army regiment that had seen hard action, again and again, of course he had changed. He might have escaped physical injury, but there were other hurts there, hurts that must have cut him deeply.

Would he see as many changes in her? No, impossible that there could be. Her concerns had been domestic, emotional; nothing on the scale of war and hard-fought battles over months and years.

The sweet summer of their romance seemed impossibly long ago, a story involving different people, and this man was almost a stranger to her.

She took her cue from his formality. "I am grateful that you have returned safely from the wars, Major."

He inclined his head, acknowledging the courtesy. "I understand that Matthew is in the Canadian colonies?"

Uncertain what he had heard, she lifted her chin with a show of confidence. "Yes. Although I expect to hear news of his return very soon."

"Good. And your sisters? They are not here this evening?"

"They are both married to officers, and gone to the East Indies, more than a year ago." Uncertain if his questions were mere politeness or genuine interest in the family, she added, "Sophia has a daughter. And Lucy's first child will have been born by now, too."

Babies that she might not see for years. Might never see, if the children succumbed to the heat and the many diseases of the tropics.

For an instant, there was an echo of long-ago laughter in his eyes. "I do hope, for Lucy's sake, that her child is not quite as much of an imp as her mother was."

The shared memory of a picnic and twelve-year-old Lucy's insistence she could climb a tree as well as Matthew, requiring Adam to rescue her from a high branch, made Emma smile. He remembered, too. Not quite such a stranger.

But Robert had finished his greetings with the baron and she must not hold up the line.

Light filled the ballroom, the candles of the vast chandeliers reflecting off the ladies' silk and lace dresses. The young girls, in their first or second season, wore the ever-fashionable white, although this year heavily trimmed with flounces and flowers, and overlays of embroidered net. Some of the married women and older single women, like Emma, wore soft colors, or even—for some of the mature ladies—rich, bold, crimsons, blues and purples. Elaborate head-dresses adorned hair piled high, crowned with flowers and profusions of jewels and ostrich feathers.

For the ladies of this corner of Yorkshire, far from London and the society of the southern counties, the Rengarth ball offered the best chance for a display of wealth and fashionable taste.

Emma had not gone to the expense of a new gown for the event, and there had been little time to add anything more than some simple rouleau trim to the bodice and front of her skirt to update it. But at twenty-five, she preferred simplicity, and the cost of new dresses and fancy trims could not be justified.

The crush inside the door slowly moved forward, Emma with

it. Although the very center of the ball room remained mostly clear, people were standing a dozen deep around every wall, waiting for the grand entrance of the Countess and her family. Even those who didn't dance, who would eventually wander off to the whist tables or the billiards room, lingered to witness the opening of the ball.

"Can't be an ostrich left in Africa with any feathers," Robert remarked drily behind her. Of course he had followed her, a self-imposed duty to ensure her well-being. More paternally protective than her father, who had trusted her good sense even at seventeen.

Her generally good sense. Maybe she hadn't been entirely sensible with Adam on their trysts in the woods that summer...but ultimately she had, hadn't she? Made the sensible choice, done the right thing.

The crowd at the door parted as the musicians struck a chord and began to play, and the Dowager Countess led Lilian and her husband in, followed by Adam leading a lady resplendent in rich blue satin, and they processed up the ball room to begin the ball.

Eight years ago, it was her beside Adam, blushing and honored and overwhelmed that he'd invited *her*, out of all the more beautiful young ladies present, for the first dance of the evening.

When the family party reached the top of the room under the musician's balcony, and the Countess made her brief speech of welcome, other couples fell in behind the beaming newly-weds and Adam and his beautiful, laughing partner, to form the long lines of the country dance sets.

Robert held out his hand to her and she could not refuse his invitation to dance.

The past and her youthful dreams were gone, years ago. She held her head high and walked out on to the dance floor beside him. They were half-way down the long set of more than twenty couples, so there was standing time through several repetitions of the dance while the lead couple gradually progressed down the set.

While she responded to the friendly chatter of the ladies on either side of her, she overheard Robert saying to the gentleman next to him, "Oh, yes, quite sound. I keep a close eye on things, but Winslow and Miss Braithwaite are managing very competently."

He caught her look, his gaze candid as he gave her an almost imperceptible nod. Her moment of irritation faded. Robert prided himself on practicality, on well-considered decisions and actions. He was a single, well-respected, wealthy gentleman. He could have invited any woman in the room for the first dance.

Whether he had thoughts of a marital partnership or not—and why would he, when her inheritance from her father was no great sum, and there was no passion between them?—his actions in dancing with her, and speaking up for her and her family business, were a purposeful and deliberate demonstration of support.

Her grateful smile may have been the first natural one she'd given him for a long time.

~

Regimental duty and friendship required that Adam dance with the lady of his former Colonel, for she loved to dance but her much-older husband could barely walk. Not an unpleasant duty, by any means, for he and Julia had been friends since she followed her husband to the Peninsular. She danced lightly and well, her merry chatter requiring little effort from him. Later this evening, he planned to quiz the Colonel about black powder. Hampton's family had a long involvement in mining in the district, knowledge that he'd effectively used against fortifications during the war.

As each repeat of the dance progressed Adam and his partner one place down the long set, he greeted old friends and acquaintances, but found more faces he did not know. New people had flooded in to the West Riding with the rise of investment in the factories and the businesses that supported them. He was the stranger here, now.

Each turn through the dance brought him closer to Emma and her partner. Robert Braithwaite treated her with perfect courtesy, although his serious demeanor seemed polite rather than demonstrative. She appeared happy enough. Not with that soft glow of affection and joy as he'd remembered her all this time, but she was twenty-five now, the demure seventeen year-old transformed into a woman with a quiet dignity and composure. He'd just have to become accustomed to seeing her with Braithwaite.

But when he took both her hands for a wide turn, her fingers in her kid gloves curving naturally around his, the gray-blue of her eyes shining into his, he was back in time again, dancing with her, meeting her in the woods, courting her, kissing her, loving her.

The memories flooded his thoughts so completely he lost count of the music, almost forgot the next figure. His heart beat thudded in his ears, but the phrases of the music swept on, and the dance, and within moments he and Mrs. Hampton danced with a new couple, and Emma and Braithwaite moved up the set behind him.

He didn't see them in the mingling crowd when the dance finally finished. He escorted his partner back to her husband, and found his young brother Jeremy, not yet seventeen, engaged in a lively discussion with the Colonel about an army career. Not a plan Adam would ever support. Not for this bright lad he was only just getting to know. But he'd acquired some skills in diplomacy accompanying Wellington around the courts of Europe this past year and he extricated Jeremy from the conversation by reminding him of his duty to ensure no young ladies who wished to dance sat out for lack of a partner. Tomorrow he'd enlighten his idealistic young brother about the brutal realities of army life and war.

The Colonel's request to assist him to the card room—slow progress, given his lameness—waylaid Adam's intention to seek out Emma and invite her for the next dance. It was already underway when he returned to the ballroom, and she danced with another man.

He ran a quick check around for his younger family members. They'd be his responsibility within a few days, so he had better get in to the practice of keeping an eye on them. Phoebe and Oliver, not surprisingly, remained in a quieter salon, away from the crowds. Jeremy, not particularly enamored of young ladies just yet, had fulfilled his duty by inviting the vicar's eldest daughter, a spinster nearing thirty. But he paid her kind attention, and she seemed to be enjoying herself. Susanna, only eighteen and just out in society, danced with a young man he didn't know. His mother would be keeping a close watch on her, though, so the partner must have her approval. Lily had her husband now and no eyes for anyone else. And Louisa... he'd never had to worry about Louisa. Except that her partner had no sense of rhythm and he could only imagine the effort it took her to keep smiling while her teeth must be grating. At twenty-five, she was not yet married. As far as he knew, no man had caught her affections yet. She danced in the same set as Emma, who gave her a sympathetic smile as they both guided Louisa's clumsy partner into the correct place.

They were the same age, Louisa and Emma, and friends that long ago summer. Louisa spent much of her time in London now, but perhaps she would know if Emma and Braithwaite... He cut that line of thinking short. He'd only just come home. *Eight years* had passed. She'd probably barely given him a thought in all that time. And she'd drifted from his constant thoughts, too, as he'd been thrown into the hell of war, and he'd almost convinced himself that she'd fallen for a better man, was raising a family, leading her life in this peaceful corner of England.

Adam dragged his gaze from the graceful figure in the lilac dress and spied his youngest brother and sister watching proceedings from the gallery. There was his new reality. He could make polite conversation down here with guests and go over the same courtesies and curious questions again and again...or he could go upstairs and watch with them for a few minutes. He chose the latter option. Cecilia and Benjamin were old enough to join the family for dinner— his mother had liberal views about that—but not quite old enough, at fourteen and eleven, to attend the ball, despite all their desperate promises of good behavior.

At least Benjamin hadn't disappeared off to the stables again. And Cecilia showed more interest in the ladies' gowns than in the opposite sex.

"Can you persuade Mama to let me go next year?" she begged him. "I'll be almost sixteen."

The girls will be no trouble, his mother had said. He suspected

Cissy's angelic face, blonde curls, and soft pleading could lead to a whole lot of trouble, for her and for any boy who saw her.

"You'll be barely fifteen," he corrected. "And you forget that I know what young men are like. If I have anything to do with it, you won't be out until you're at least twenty-three."

Those innocent blue eyes filled with tears. She didn't know him well enough to know if he was teasing or not. With his own memories of what he'd got up to with Emma, he wasn't entirely sure himself.

He could command a regiment of men. A household with four brothers and sisters eighteen and under? It might be a long, long few weeks—especially if the foul weather continued.

Fortunately, his mother appeared and they obeyed her firm instructions to go to bed without argument.

She paused to spend a few minutes watching over the throng below, resting her hands on the balustrade beside him.

"I am glad that you arrived in time for tonight," she said. "I know that's a kindness on your part, not a pleasure."

"George asked me to." And despite the sense of strangeness, he was glad he'd come. Not only because of his fortuitous arrival in town to help Emma at the fire.

"Is there anyone you'd like me to introduce you to?" his mother asked. Their discussion this afternoon of George's illness and current lack of a direct heir had touched lightly on the topic of Adam's marital status, but with her usual tact she'd merely enquired if he had intentions towards any particular lady yet.

"No. Thank you." Looking down over the dancers weaving the figures of the cotillion he easily found Emma again. The words were on his tongue to ask about Braithwaite, but he held them back. Mothers—particularly his—had a way of reading more into words than he wanted to say. Especially now, with this barrage of unaccustomed emotions and memories throwing him right off-balance.

He hadn't counted on his mother noting the direction of his attention.

"Miss Braithwaite appears none the worse for her close call this afternoon," she commented. When he didn't respond, she continued, "Mr. Braithwaite fears the warehouse loss may be total. That the business may fail."

"Robert Braithwaite said that?" His irrational dislike of the man burned even hotter. Spreading rumors of impending business failure could ruin Emma's chance to recover from the disaster.

"Francis Braithwaite. I overheard him in the card room. Not quite so much of a gentleman as his brother."

"The men on the fire cart kept the fire mostly out of the main storeroom," Adam argued, as much to convince himself as his mother. "The warehouse is insured and she saved the account books."

"She's a very sensible woman, and has managed exceptionally well in difficult circumstances," his mother observed. Just when he thought he might casually ask about Robert Brathwaite, she added, "You had a fondness for her, I recall."

"It was a long time ago. And I was a fool."

The Countess's delicately-shaped eyebrows rose high. "A fool to be fond of her?"

"No. A fool the way I... An idiot to..." His tongue tied itself in knots worthy of a cravat. Might as well just confess straight out, although he didn't dare look at his mother as he did. "A fool to propose a rush elopement to Gretna Green so she could come with me when the regiment shipped out."

"Oh." Silence, after that one word.

He'd just shocked his unshockable mother. "I was so sure, then, that we were going to the West Indies and I'd make my fortune within a couple of years and give her a comfortable life. She refused me, of course."

Even when he was a wayward boy, his mother had never responded with anger or harsh criticism. But now, as then, her thoughtful silence before she spoke gave plenty of time for his conscience to whip him harder than her words ever could. "I'm sure that her refusal hurt," she said eventually. "But I think I'm glad she did. These past years would have been very hard for her, otherwise."

Hard for his mother, too, but for a wife? Yes, perhaps even more so. He thought of his sister Phoebe, her vibrancy shattered, and the lies he told her in his letter after Waterloo of the gallant and swift death of her husband. If Emma had been his wife, she'd have waited and fretted and read every newspaper report of every battle, and watched for the post every day, dreading a letter like the one he'd sent Phoebe. For years. With little time together because he'd fought all over Europe.

"I was sixteen when I fell in love with your father," the Countess said after some moments. "He was barely twenty."

Sixteen and twenty. Seventeen and twenty-one. Not much difference between his parents and him and Emma. "But you didn't marry Father then."

"No. We waited until after he finished at university. And married with our parents' blessings."

He accepted the mild, well-deserved criticism. "Would you have given it? Your blessing? If I'd asked for it?"

"Her parents were well-respected. But you were both very young. Your father and I would have counselled waiting, I am sure."

Exactly as Josiah Braithwaite had counselled, in the uncomfortable interview when Adam had sought permission to address Emma. Before his arrogant, self-righteous decision to ignore the advice and propose the elopement.

"I trust-" His mother's gaze pinned him like a bug on paper, "that you treated her as a gentleman should."

At least his conscience was clear—mostly—on that point.

His mother may have read straight through him but, as the musicians played the last figure of the dance, someone upset a large vase of flowers at the end of the room, and she hurried off to placate water-splashed ladies and supervise the removal of broken porcelain.

Adam assisted a footman to discretely escort outside the thoroughly drunk baronet who had knocked over the vase while attempting a Highland jig and waited with him while the carriage was brought around and the gent persuaded to go home.

By the time he returned people were taking the floor for one of the new waltz country dances, one couple facing another in a large circle around the room. Emma already had a partner. A man with the Braithwaite jaw but not the same level of courteous attention that Robert Braithwaite had given her. Francis Braithwaite, presumably. *Not as much of a gentleman as his brother.* But his mother had still invited him, so his reputation must be reasonably decent.

Emma was wise enough to know her own mind and it was none of his business who she danced with. He had no claim on her at all, no indication any of her feelings of the past remained. And no reason he could fathom for this inability to shake her from his mind since this afternoon, when he believed he'd come to terms with her refusal, years ago.

But the circumstances of the fire still worried him, so he went in search of the Colonel.

CHAPTER 6

If she'd known it was going to be a waltz, Emma would have found some way to politely refuse Francis. Although half of the dance involved a sequence of figures with another couple, the sixteen bars of waltzing on to meet the next couple required a closer hold of one's partner than she was entirely comfortable with. Especially with Francis. Her hands on his shoulders. His hands at her waist, his palms at the side seams of her dress. A good foot of space between them, yet more intimate than the open turns of the older country dance styles.

She had no wish for any form of intimacy with Francis. Not that she actively disliked him, but at least with Robert she could respect his sense of responsibility, and his earnest courtesy. Francis had less esteem for others, and a high opinion of his own abilities—not unwarranted, given the financial success of his steam-powered cotton factory. Assuming one was not disturbed by the conditions for the workers. Not conditions that Emma could justify, despite Francis's factory being no worse than any other in the district.

But this was only a dance, and she merely had to remain polite and soon enough it would be over and she could escape the heat of the ball room to the retiring room. She smiled at the next couple as they danced the foursome part of the figures but her smile strained as she joined Francis again to waltz on to the next pair.

Her smile faded completely when he pulled her a little closer than necessary and said quietly under the music, "I'm surprised that you came tonight, given the fire this afternoon and the news about Matthew that Robert conveyed to you."

Tact had never been one of his strengths, but to broach such a topic in the circumstances had to be deliberate, no mere lack of sensitivity. "I was not injured," she retorted under her breath, "and hearsay is not news. My own sources have mentioned no such rumors."

She found it hard to smile for the next couple and pretend there was nothing wrong as they danced together.

But he ignored her censure and continued the moment they resumed the waltz hold. "You have to face the truth, cuz. Matthew is not coming back. Robert thinks it is his duty to marry you, now that you're alone in the world and facing bankruptcy."

To say such a thing, in the middle of the ball room.... She pushed back against unyielding shoulders and whispered, "Matthew is alive and I am neither alone nor bankrupt. Please dissuade Robert from the notion and save us both the embarrassment of my refusal."

She turned under his arm as the phrase of music finished and faced the next couple with relief. But the short interval of dancing with them was soon over, and he started murmuring again the moment it was just the two of them again.

"You need a stronger man than Robert, Emma. You have so much more fire, sweet cuz, than he knows what to do with." His gaze dropped to her breasts, and his hands on her waist tightened, drawing her almost close enough to touch her body against his. "You need a powerful man to tame you," he whispered near her ear. "Marry me and you won't go to debtor's prison."

Emma's cheeks flamed hot. "I will do neither," she retorted, but he just laughed lightly as he spun her under his arm and they began the dance again, this time with Mr. Stratham, a partner from her bank, and his wife. She could not make any sort of scene in front of the banker. Could not give him any cause to doubt her reason or her health. Her forced smile made her jaw ache. She dared not look at Francis but the way Mr. Stratham seemed to share a knowing grin with him made her spine crawl. As if he thought Francis was making sweet talk to her.

After the short sequences of turns and figures, the Strathams moved on, and Francis began his whispers again.

"Matthew's estate will take years to settle, if they don't find his remains. So will your father's estate. You can't hope to keep the company solvent with just your annuity."

She lifted her hand from his shoulder to grip the fan hanging from a ribbon at her wrist. "Francis, if you say one more word, I will strike you on the face."

He merely grinned, daring her. "Your reputation will suffer, dear cuz, not mine."

She hated him for being right. She couldn't do it. Over-emotional lady hits respected manufacturer—that's how it would be seen and talked about. And she could hardly swoon, because he'd do the 'gallant' thing and carry her off, and she could not bear his touch any further.

While her thoughts raced to find ways to escape, the next couple glided towards them. But the lady saw her and stopped abruptly, holding her partner back. Her head haughtily high, she glared at Emma and announced loudly, "I will not dance with *that woman.*"

Shock jammed Emma's breath painfully in her throat, stole her ability to form words.

"Why ever not, madam?" Francis drawled beside Emma. He sounded more amused than outraged. The couples around them ceased dancing. Others craned their necks to watch as they danced.

Emma tried frantically to place the lady's face. Only slightly familiar, the man even less so. She'd perhaps only met her once or twice. The name fell in to her memory. Lady Beatrice Farringdon. An earl's daughter married to a baronet. A baronet who stood by his wife, silent.

Lady Beatrice's ostrich feathers wavered as she tossed her head indignantly. "Meddling in men's affairs. Running her father's business into bankruptcy. She's no *lady.* I can scarcely believe that the Countess invited her."

"It's unnatural," a man muttered behind Emma. "No wonder the Good Lord sent the lightning bolt today, to punish her. "

Frozen by their vehemence, unable to think of any response, let alone anything polite, Emma stared at the floor, biting her lip as a wave of panic threatened to overwhelm her. A lightning bolt? Is that what people thought? Could it have been one? If the insurance company declared the fire an act of God, they wouldn't pay. Everything might be lost.

Francis had moved a step away from her. She could no longer see his shoes in her small circle of vision.

The music drew to an untidy close, mid-dance. In the sudden silence that fell, there sounded only a rustle of silk and soft footsteps on the polished floor. Emma lifted her head to see people stepping back to make way for someone. Lady Beatrice's mouth fell open in an indelicate gape and an ostrich feather drooped over her face as she curtsied low to Lady Caroline, the Dowager Countess of Rengarth. Adam's mother.

Every inch the Countess in her satin and lace, Lady Rengarth turned a glittering, ice-laden smile at Emma's accuser. "My dear Lady Beatrice, I fear you have been misinformed." Every word enunciated crisply, her voice carried clearly across the room. "Braithwaite and Co is such an excellent, respected business that I'm considering investing in shares myself. Of course, it's not quite on the same grand scale as the estate business here that I oversee for my son, but it *is* a lady's sacred duty to support her family, is it not?"

Emma had to close her eyes briefly against the wave of giddy relief. Her breath came unevenly, and she might have swayed on her feet but for a soft arm linking through hers. Not Francis. Louisa Caldwell, her smile warm and encouraging. Louisa had lived more in London than Yorkshire but they'd renewed their friendship of the long-ago summer in the last dance, as if hardly any time had passed at all.

"It is so stifling hot, isn't it, my dear Emma? I fear I am ready to faint." Keeping her arm linked with Emma's, she bobbed a curtsey to Francis. "Mr. Braithwaite, I beg your forgiveness for stealing your partner. But I must have some fresh air. Emma, will you be so kind as to come with me?"

Emma straightened her spine. Dignity and calm. The kindness of Louisa and Lady Rengarth gave her strength to face the crowd. Lady Beatrice's shoulders drooped even more than her feathers, her face red. Her husband stood helplessly by her side. Gentlemen and ladies shifted uncomfortably on their feet, uncertain where to look, what to do.

Lady Rengarth clapped her hands and called to the orchestra for "One more country dance before supper." And then she touched her hand to Lady Beatrice's shoulder in a friendly gesture. "My dear, do come and have some refreshment with me. I can tell you a little about some of the good works the Braithwaites have engaged in for our district." She smiled across at her daughter and Emma. "Louisa, Miss Braithwaite, I will join you shortly."

As simply as that, the Countess and her daughter managed the situation. A public pronouncement of the family's favor and friendship for Emma, while the Countess enabled Lady Beatrice to retain her dignity with her insistence that it was all just a misunderstanding as she led her to a small salon off the ball room. And Louisa gave Emma the perfect reason to walk away from Francis.

The musicians struck up a chord, and couples hastily formed long ways sets.

Despite her claims of faintness, Louisa held her arm firmly and steered her out of the ballroom. Emma stammered her thanks, but people milled around them in the gallery and she could not explain.

"We'll go downstairs to the conservatory. We can talk in private there if you wish," Louisa said. "Unless you need to lie down?"

"No, I'm not faint. Just... unsettled still, I think. By more than Lady Beatrice's remarks."

"I thought so. I saw that you were already distressed before that odious woman started with her nonsense. Was Mr. Braithwaite dreadfully ill-behaved? Should I have Adam ask him to leave?"

"No, that's not necessary." And she could not risk another scene, or earning her cousin's resentment. She glanced back over her shoulder as they descended the grand staircase. No sign of Francis. She breathed a little more easily but when they reached the magnificent hall she checked again and he was there, watching her from the top of the stairs.

The instinct to flee almost won. *Don't let them see that you're afraid,* Adam once told Matthew long ago, when he'd been threatened by bullies. She should have remembered that, facing Lady Beatrice. If she hadn't been so stunned by Francis's callousness, she might have remembered it. She'd followed the advice herself when she'd had to take on more of the management of the company and meet with men to negotiate contracts and arrange business.

So she stood her ground, looked directly up at Francis, and gave a slow, emphatic shake of her head. Then she turned her back on him, linked her arm through Louisa's again, and walked out of the hall with her.

~

In comfortable arm chairs in a corner of the spacious cards room, Adam poured Colonel Hampton a second glass from the bottle of fine claret he'd had the butler fetch from the cellar. He respected Hampton; respect earned in the long months and years of the Peninsular campaign, before the colonel's injuries in action forced his retirement from the field. The conversation so far had covered the fates of mutual friends and fellow officers, only some of them returned safely from the wars. They'd drained their first glasses in toasts to those who had not.

The Colonel swirled his wine in the glass and studied the color against the candlelight. "I hear you saw some more action today, Caldwell. Damned Luddites, burning and wrecking."

"I only did what any man would do."

Hampton snorted. "Yes, walked through fire, as I heard it. You'd never have ordered one of your men to do that."

Adam dismissed the comment with a shrug. "Has there been a resurgence in Luddite activity recently? I thought most of the ringleaders were hung or transported several years ago." A fact about which he had mixed feelings. The rapid pace of change in the last decade astounded him, but machines, for all their wonders, took the jobs and livelihoods of too many working men. Progress brought wealth to some, and misery to more.

"The leaders were made examples of," Hampton said. "But there's been a few attacks recently. Bad one down Nottingham way last month. Twenty stocking frames broken, the papers said. And a cotton factory near here attacked by a mob not long ago, too, with looms destroyed."

"I'm not so sure," Adam said slowly, "that this fire was the work of Luddites. There was no machinery to break. It's a warehouse of hand-spun and woven goods. And draw looms that have probably been operating in that loft for fifty or more years."

"An accident, then?"

"Perhaps." Adam leaned forward to speak more quietly. "Tell me, with your experience, if you—hypothetically—wanted to blast through the wall of a stone building, how much powder would you use?"

The Colonel's eyes lit with interest. "Hypothetically or not, it would depend on the type of stone, how thick, how you set the blast. But an old warehouse—you wouldn't need much. A small cask, packed to blast in the right direction, would blow a hole, right enough. Probably even bring down the wall."

Exactly as Adam had figured. Easy enough for someone to smuggle a small cask of powder, or even less, in to an empty stable. It hadn't been a huge hole. A few feet, maybe a yard and a half wide. The wooden framework of the stairs might have helped brace the walls, but there'd been a large enough hole to blast burning hay and heat through on to the timbers and set them alight.

But there might be no evidence left in the ruins to prove it, and even if he found something, it would not answer the question of who had deliberately placed Emma and her employees in danger, and why.

A footman coughed discreetly at his side. "Pardon me, sir. Her

Ladyship requests your attendance in the conservatory, on a matter of importance."

He excused himself to Colonel Hampton immediately. A summons from his mother to the conservatory, when she had a ball in progress, had to mean an emergency of some kind.

As he strode through the throng in the gallery, several groups of gossips whispered behind fans, and a small gathering of gentlemen guffawed loudly but broke off the moment they saw him.

Whatever had occurred must be a matter of honor, rather than physical injury.

A matter of honor involving Emma, he discovered, when he reached the conservatory. She sat on the chaise, flanked on either side by his mother and his sister. Despite her shield of composure, her white face matched the pearls around her throat, and her gloved fingers curled tightly around each other in her lap.

He drew a chair up to face them. Emma remained silent while his mother succinctly summarized the events for him. "Just moments after Francis Braithwaite made a threat to Miss Braithwaite, a woman who cannot even balance her own pin money publicly insulted her to her face and called into question her financial management."

Damn. That meant that rumors were circulating—and they would spread even more rapidly after a public confrontation. The whispers and guffaws assumed new significance. Many in the landed aristocracy still nurtured the old prejudices against the merchant-manufacturing class. But neither wealth nor breeding made a man a gentlemen, in Adam's experience.

That Emma had been insulted and threatened, by guests at Rengarth, sent anger running hot through his veins. He endeavored to keep his voice even so as not to distress her further, but it still came out as gravelly as if he'd thirsted for days. "What did Braithwaite threaten?"

Her composure wavered and she swallowed before she met his gaze. "He threatened..." She paused, and corrected herself. "He *implied* that if I did not marry him, I would go to debtor's prison."

Adam muttered a phrase under his breath that he'd picked up in

Spain. A phrase that came in handy when 'bastard' wasn't a strong enough condemnation. He no longer wondered why a man would try to coerce a woman he didn't love into marriage. Money. Possessions. Power. Revenge. From the heights of royalty to the poorest peasants, men existed in every country and every class who used women for their own ends. Francis Braithwaite should be consigned to the pits of hell alongside them.

The warrior within him clamored to call Braithwaite out to meet him at dawn. Shooting him would not, however, meet with Emma's approval. Or that of his own war-weary conscience. There must be a solution that did not involve violence.

"Are you in debt to him?" he asked. "Has the fire ruined your company?"

She did not object to the question, in word or manner. "No, I'm not in debt to him. The company has sufficient assets. Our stock wasn't all in the warehouse. Much of it is still put out to hand-spinners and weavers. And there is a wagon-load at the Piece Hall for tomorrow's market. The fire will not ruin us. Unless-" She took in a deep breath. "Unless the insurance company determines that the fire was an act of God, or otherwise decides not to pay. Or our creditors all demand immediate payment. If Francis persuaded them to do that...I am not sure if I could."

Adam had little experience of trade beyond his own investments, but he assumed that, as in politics, army operations, and diplomacy, only a fraction of what went on was enshrined in writing and contracts. Power brokers easily influenced negotiations, decisions, and confidence in a company and its reputation, with a word here, a word there. If enough creditors became concerned, they could press for payment or threaten bankruptcy.

His suspicions about the fire hardened, although with little to go on he did not wish to alarm Emma. Not until he could assure her of safety.

In order to uncover who might have targeted her, he needed to understand more about the business situation. About who might want her to fail. "If that happened—do you have assets you can sell?"

"With Matthew still away and..." Her voice trembled and pain darkened her eyes. "And his fate uncertain, my father's estate cannot be finalized. I have only my annuity to draw on. Francis knows that." In spite of everything, of the threat to her world, her security, even her freedom, she raised her chin, quietly courageous, her earnest gaze alternating between him and his mother. "I am grateful for your kind support this evening, my lady. I sent word to Mr. Winslow this afternoon, and I will see him tomorrow, and my solicitor. We will explore the possibilities for action."

Just like the Emma he remembered, that practical determination to find solutions to challenges without surrendering to them.

Before Adam had the chance to offer to accompany her, his mother spoke, as decisive as a general on the social battlefield. "A continued show of our family's support is in order, I think. Miss Braithwaite, will you do us the honor of having supper with us at the high table? And Adam, if you do not already have a partner for supper...?"

His mother's suggestion accorded exactly with his own thoughts. And when it was seen—he'd make sure it was seen—that Emma was an honored guest of the family, anyone who spoke against her reputation would be unwise.

He rose to his feet and bowed before Emma. "I would be privileged to escort you to supper, Miss Braithwaite. If you are not already engaged." Too late, he remembered Robert Braithwaite's proprietary behavior and caught the unintended double meaning of his question.

Her hesitation lasted only as long as it took her to search his face before she answered both the asked, and unasked questions.

"I am not engaged." A slight smile softened some of the anxiety in her eyes. "If you are certain it is no inconvenience to you, sir."

How carefully they tip-toed around each other. The past was there, rippling under the surface of the formality that his long absence created between them.

"Nothing would please me more." He hoped she heard his

honesty despite his reliance on the polite phrase.

It truly would be a pleasure to have this beautiful, graceful woman by his side. In the few hours since his return he'd learned that all that he'd loved in her as a girl had been but a promise of the woman she had become. The classic simplicity of her gown suited her nature. She had no need of an abundance of frills and flowers. The pale lilac of the silk bordered the smooth skin of her throat and her face, framed by the rich waves of tawny brown hair drawn back softly and wrapped with pearls.

He'd overheard someone tonight describe her as plain and cool but they didn't see beyond her reserve to the warmth of compassion in her eyes, to the way she paid attention to people, no matter their station, responding to them as individuals. Her quiet dignity and pride masked a genuine care for others, even above her own needs and desires. A woman who'd single-handedly saved the draw boy, and risked her own life to ensure the safety of the injured weaver—a courage equal to anything he'd witnessed on the battlefield.

In her silver-grey eyes he saw an echo of her youthful fondness for a restless young man. Once he'd delighted in making her laugh, in seeing the shadows of responsibility and care slip away in moments of pure enjoyment. He'd kissed her and caressed her and been inanely proud of his restraint and gentleness and respect for her, despite the desire raging in him for more. In his youth and naivety he'd imagined himself capable of providing a happy life for them.

Before his first battle. Before he rammed his bayonet into a man. Before he understood the hell of fear, the stench of the dead and dying, the horror of the human cost of war.

He hadn't laughed in a carefree way in a long, long time, and doubted he could make anyone laugh anymore, least of all Emma.

But since his birth had decreed that he held a position of influence, he was determined to use it to support her, and to shield her from the lies and prejudices arrayed against her. And from Francis Braithwaite. He would not have the satisfaction of calling him out, but he would ensure, before the night was over, that Braithwaite was left in no doubt that Emma was under his protection.

He offered his arm, and she rose gracefully and took it, her gloved hand light on his jacket. "Are you ready for this, Miss Braithwaite? I can have your carriage brought around if you prefer to go home."

She raised her face to look up at him, trepidation in the fine creases on her forehead, yet resolution in her words. "I must return to the ball. It will not help if I am seen to be weak, or afraid."

She had every right to be afraid, with the threat of financial ruin hanging over her head. And to be facing it alone, without her family...yet she refused to panic, to give in, or even to plead for help.

"You are one of the most courageous women I've ever known, Emma," he said quietly. He didn't realize he'd used her given name until he caught the quick exchange of smiles between his mother and Louisa. So much for being proper and formal. She'd been 'Emma' in his mind for so long that he would have to watch his words in public, lest that familiarity be interpreted the wrong way and make her uncomfortable.

Whatever affection she once had for him was for another person, not the man he was now. The difference between the youth he'd been and the man he'd become was the difference between a warm summer's day and a dark winter's night.

CHAPTER 7

There were gapes, whispers, stares, as Emma and Adam made their way through the gallery. Not many smiles, although here and there some of the older ladies seemed delighted to read more into his presence by her side than it meant.

The Countess and Louisa had hurried ahead to ensure supper arrangements were well in hand, and people milled, waiting for the country dance to finish and the meal to be announced.

Her heartbeat sounding so loud in her ears she feared everyone might hear it, Emma made her mouth form a smile. Perhaps the smoke from the fire this afternoon had affected her, because she found it hard to draw a deep breath. *Not afraid. Not afraid.* Her heart and her nerves ignored her head. She dreaded meeting Lady Beatrice. She dreaded meeting Francis. She dreaded facing all the guests who had witnessed the scene in the ball room and who likely had spent the past half hour talking about it. About her.

She could make no sense of Francis's behavior. He'd been away for almost a year, and in all truth even before that she saw him less frequently than Robert, who had at least visited her father occasionally.

That Francis had suggested marriage—attempted to coerce her—disturbed her well beyond the initial shock and anger, and her thoughts kept returning to gnaw at the question of *why*. He hardly knew her, did not like her or even respect her, and she knew full well she was no beauty. Nor would she bring a title or wealth to a marriage. The social stigma of her unconventional participation in business also reduced her marriage prospects, a fact she was well aware of, long before yesterday's events.

A fact she must keep firmly in mind. Adam's kindness and concern were just that, a courtesy from an old friend. No matter the disconcerting fluttering of her heart when he stood near, or whenever his thoughtful gaze settled on her. What had been between them was long ago, and as the son of an earl, respected for his war service, he deserved to find a partner from his own station in life. The wealth that had seen her family rise to gentry status in her great-grandfather's time might not hold in the new world of factories and steam power.

Part-way down the gallery, Adam paused and introduced her to his former commanding officer, Colonel Hampton, and Mrs. Hampton, a charming couple newly arrived in the district, who obviously held Adam in high esteem. Perhaps ten years older than Emma, dressed in a stylish blue satin gown, Mrs. Hampton greeted her with genuine warmth, and a self-confidence that Emma envied. Much like Lady Rengarth's poise, and even Louisa's. Women who seemed to thrive in social situations, whereas she—even before tonight's unpleasantness—preferred much smaller social occasions. And until last year, she'd always had her sisters, for company and to chaperone.

While the Colonel took the opportunity to quiz Adam about a local horse breeder, Mrs. Hampton drew Emma aside, ostensibly to admire a portrait. Her knowing eyes regarded Emma gently as she murmured behind her fan, "Do not distress yourself about the incident earlier, Miss Braithwaite. I believe the lady in question has now gone home. Her views were not widely shared, and her behavior is generally regarded as intolerable. Such people are dreadfully old-fashioned."

Mrs. Hampton's words eased some of Emma's disquiet, although they did confirm that the incident had been the topic of much conversation. And she did notice the qualifiers—'Not *widely shared*',

'Generally regarded'. Going by the glances directed at her, not all of them friendly, Mrs. Hampton's circle of acquaintances might not encompass many of Lady Beatrice's friends.

Nevertheless, her new friend's confidence gave Emma a much-needed boost to her courage and her smile came more easily as she thanked her for her reassurances. She'd have taken pleasure in prolonging the conversation, but the music in the ballroom drew to a close. The chatter around them quietened as the guests watched for the announcement of supper.

Adam offered her his arm again, this time a very public gesture. "Miss Braithwaite, will you honor me with your company for supper?"

She did not make the mistake, either now or in the conservatory earlier, of assuming anything in his invitation but respect for a youthful friendship and a chivalric desire to defend her reputation. And she accepted his invitation for the same reasons, with gratitude.

In the past, Adam had always smiled quickly and often. But the slow, wistful smile he gave her now in response to her acceptance warmed her more than a hundred easy grins.

People stepped back and gave way to them as he led her along the rest of the gallery towards the supper room. In a small knot of gentlemen at the wide doorway into the ballroom, she caught sight of Francis. The man had the gall to smile at her. A sly, insolent grin that made her skin crawl. Adam's arm stiffened under her hand and she heard his sharp intake of breath. She pointedly looked away from Francis and smiled brightly at the next people they passed, as if seeing him hadn't affected her at all. He would not have the temerity to approach her while she was with Adam. Surely.

Adam's jaw was tight with anger. "I will have him removed from the house," he said, through his clenched teeth. "If you wish it."

Yes. "No," she murmured, Francis's contempt fresh in her mind. "He would likely cause a scene. He may leave after supper, anyway."

Despite her determination not to allow Francis to disturb her composure, her legs were shaky under her skirts and she was glad when they entered the supper room, and Adam drew out a chair for her at the high table.

She did not see Francis enter the supper room. Perhaps he left early, because she did not see him at all during the meal. She gradually relaxed to enjoy the conversation and the congenial company of her friends, the vicar, Mr. Timms, and his daughter Letitia, and Adam's friends, the Colonel and Mrs. Hampton. The Hamptons, they quickly learned, shared Emma's and the Timms' commitment to the education of girls, and their concerns about conditions for workers, particularly women and children, in the cotton factories.

Adam was attentive to her, passing her the tastiest dishes, but he mostly listened to the discussion rather than contributing to it. It wasn't that he disagreed with them—when asked for his opinion, he agreed whole-heartedly with their concerns—but he seemed distracted by his own thoughts.

She could no longer read him. If, indeed, she ever had been able to. Perhaps that had just been a young girl's foolish dream, thinking that she understood him. He was perfectly polite and gentlemanly, but his formal courtesy emphasized the distance between them that those years had created.

Perhaps there was, in London or Europe or somewhere, a woman who held his heart. But when he presented her with a crystal glass containing a syllabub, the rich, creamy dessert she could never resist, for an instant his smile lit his eyes with the memories of a long ago ball, a shared syllabub, and a first kiss.

She felt her cheeks flush again, as if she was still seventeen. Until his expression changed within a moment, gentle humor fading as his gaze focused over her shoulder.

The Countess's butler made a short bow to both of them. "Excuse me, sir, miss. Mr. Jarvis has come from Larkfell House with an urgent message for Miss Braithwaite. I have taken the liberty of showing him to the library, sir."

Adam drew her chair back as Emma rose hastily to her feet, her heart pounding. Jarvis—calm, imperturbable Jarvis—would not come to Rengarth after midnight for any minor matter. News too urgent to wait until morning could only be bad news.

CHAPTER 8

An urgent message from Larkfell. Emma started for the door, but stopped after three paces. Where? She'd never been in the library.

Adam placed her hand on his arm and escorted her through the curious glances of the supper crowd and down the grand staircase. In her haste she had left her gloves behind, the fine wool of his black jacket sleeve smooth and soft under her fingers, her pearl bracelet contrasted against the dark. Too bad if anyone was horrified. A minor impropriety to add to all the other gossip about her this evening.

Through the long corridors of the castle, she tried to steady her breathing, but it kept catching, rough and uneven. Her thoughts raced, anticipating any one of a number of fearful possibilities. Perhaps the weaver had died. Or they had found a body in the stables. Or confirmation of her brother's death had arrived. She couldn't think of anything, short of a death, that would bring Jarvis out after midnight.

Jarvis stood waiting in the library, two candelabras lighting the comfortable room, a small tray of refreshments untouched on a table. She'd known the butler all her life. In that empty house with her brother and sisters gone, Jarvis and Mrs. Barnden were almost as close as family.

Adam showed her to a sofa, and stood behind her.

"Major Caldwell, sir," Jarvis began, "I apologize for my intrusion. To you and to Her Ladyship."

Louisa slipped in to the room, and after one quick surmising glance around them all, she sat beside Emma. Adam remained silent, leaving it to Emma to begin.

Emma clasped her hands in her lap, willing herself to remain composed. "You have some news," she said. "Please tell me, Jarvis."

"Miss Braithwaite, it is distressing news I am afraid. The groom that you sent to Halifax this afternoon, with the letters for Mr. Winslow, Mr. Hargraves, and the insurance agent...he returned a short time ago. He was unable to deliver the letter to Mr. Winslow."

He'd spoken in such a roundabout way, perhaps to lead her gently to what was to come. But still she asked, hoping she'd misunderstood, "Why?"

"The groom found the household in shock. There's been a tragedy, miss, and the Halifax constable is making enquiries. Mr. Winslow's body was found in the garden not long before the groom arrived. And...it does not appear to have been a natural death, miss."

"Mr. Winslow is dead?" The words scraped in her throat. She looked around at Adam, saw the harsh lines of his face, and the tiny hope that she misunderstood Jarvis flickered out, leaving only the terrible reality.

First the fire, and now this. Ralph Winslow, her father's partner for decades. Her partner in the company. Her *friend*. Dead. Not a natural death.

"How-" She had to swallow against the sob gripping her throat. "How did he die?"

Jarvis hesitated, waited for a sign from Adam to proceed before he said, "The groom heard that it was head injuries, miss. But Mr. Winslow was on the lawn, and there was nothing nearby to hit his head on. His watch and his snuff box were stolen. The constable at Halifax thinks it's the work of thieves."

"Thieves? It's a walled garden. We often had tea there." She began to shake, unable to hold back the waves of grief and chilling fear. Louisa pressed a handkerchief into her hand and put her arm around her, but Emma couldn't stop the shaking. Her thoughts raced faster, tangling and tripping over each other.

Without Mr. Winslow, the future of the company was precarious. Without him, everything might be lost. Matthew's inheritance. Larkfell. Everyone who relied on the company could lose their livelihoods. She might go to debtor's prison.

She had to think, *think*, how to deal with this. Not cry. Not cry in front of Adam and Louisa and Jarvis. If she stayed here on the soft sofa she might be tempted to lay her head against the cushions, or Louisa's shoulder, and weep.

She pushed herself to her feet. Hugging her arms around her waist she paced to the window. Carriage lights passed outside. Someone going home now that supper was over.

She must decide what needed to be done before morning. What needed to be done for Mr. Winslow.

She turned to find Adam in front of her, holding a glass out to her.

"He has no family. The funeral... I must-"

"Sip this, Emma. It will help with the shock."

Her hands shook but he made sure she had a firm grip of the stem before he let go of the glass. The first sip of fiery liquid stung her throat. Brandy. Another sip, and the jolt of warmth began to spread. But her thoughts still leapt all over the place, desperately seeking solutions, solace, hope.

The candlelight reflected off the golden liquid in the crystal glass, and more softly off the pearls around her wrists.

Desperation made her decisive. "I can sell my pearls. I kept them because they were my great-grandmother's. But I can't keep them now." The lovely parure—bracelets, necklace, earrings—would be no good to her in prison. They'd pay for Mr. Winslow's funeral, and then some debts. The only jewelry she had left from her mother. With her free hand, she began to work at the catch of the bracelet on the other hand, but the brandy sloshed around in the glass as her vision blurred.

Adam took the glass from her and set it on a side table. She tried again to loosen the bracelet catch but her fingers were clumsy, tears falling on to them. His hands closed over hers and held them.

Muscular hands, tanned against her pale skin. He'd left his gloves in the supper room, too. "Don't, Emma. Let yourself grieve for now."

"I can't..." She needed to stay strong, keep functioning.

Someone put a shawl around her shoulders. Louisa. "Have a good cry. You've had so many shocks today. It's perfectly natural to cry."

Louisa's compassion, like a sister, and the gentleness of Adam's hands undid her defenses. Her heart tightened in her chest and she fought for breath through sobs. Every day of loneliness, every moment of worry, all the months of grief for her father and fear for her brother crashed down on her. Too much. Too much to bear. A wave of giddiness filled her head and she stumbled towards the sofa.

Strong arms caught her and she rested her face, the heaviness of her head, against fine soft wool. Adam's voice murmured, "It's all right, Emma, I've got you. You're not alone. We'll stand by you. I promise you I'll keep you safe."

Safe. His heart beat through the cloth under her cheek and his strength wrapped around her. A sanctuary. She wanted to stay there, safe, cared for, hiding from pain and confusion and fear. But as she regained control over her sobs, coherent thought returned. People relied on her. She had to deal with the situation, not hide from it.

"I have to go home." She lifted her head, and Adam's hold loosened as she stepped away from his warmth and strength. Reluctant to break the contact completely, she let her hand remain on his arm for a moment. Social etiquette provided words when she needed them. "Please give my apologies to your mother. But I must...I have to write some letters." To several creditors. To ask them for patience for a few days while she sorted things out. "And in the morning, after the warehouse, I must go to Halifax." To see what she could do for Mr. Winslow. To find out more about his death. To see her solicitor. The list in her head rapidly grew longer.

"I'll see you safely back to Larkfell," Adam said. "And I'll go with you tomorrow, if you wish. We'll do whatever we can to help until this is solved."

The candlelight behind him cast his face into shadow, but she didn't need to see the details of his expression to know that his solemn words were a promise.

She did not have to face this nightmare alone.

~

Daylight and a servant entering the room woke Adam after less than two hours' sleep. He dragged himself properly awake, pushing back the covers and swinging his legs over the edge of the bed to resist the temptation to return his head to the pillow. Threads of dreams clung like spider webs in his mind and for a few moments it took effort to separate them from realities.

He'd held Emma. Hurting, afraid, and overwhelmed with grief, she probably wouldn't remember those moments in the study when he'd caught her in his arms to keep her from falling. A memory to join the others he'd held on to, year after year. Memories that often replayed themselves in his dreams.

He always welcomed those dreams. A respite of grace and peace from the nightmares of war. Sometimes, when rest would not come, he'd imagined embracing her. Just lying with her in his arms, her head on his chest, her fingers clasped in his, still and trusting and peaceful. Sometimes it was the only way he *could* drift to sleep. But in the cold light of day, time and again he'd reminded himself that it was unreal, that he had no right to hold on to those thoughts and memories in such a manner, that time altered people and she'd be a different person from the girl he remembered. A small piece of honor he'd clung to—until the next time he lay awake, sleepless in the dark.

The servant assigned to valet for him nervously laid out wash cloths and his razor, and Adam splashed his face with water to banish the last fog of sleep. This morning he had no time for dreaming.

Everything about Emma's situation disturbed him. The rumors circulating about her company, and Francis Braithwaite's insinuations were serious on their own. But the threat to her life yesterday, the destruction of the warehouse, and the murder of Winslow multiplied his concerns tenfold.

Adam doubted the Halifax constable's conclusion of theft as the motive for Winslow's murder. Thieves entering a gentleman's garden? Perhaps. But the occurrence of that on the same day that the gentleman's business interests were attacked being merely a coincidence? Unlikely.

If the fire at the warehouse was not accidental—and he couldn't prove that, yet—then who was being targeted? Emma or Winslow? Or the company itself? He knew nothing about Winslow, other than his involvement in Braithwaite and Co. He knew little enough about the company itself, other than some financial constraints due in large part to Josiah's death and Matthew's absence.

He intended to find out. He'd promised last night to meet Emma at the warehouse, and accompany her to Halifax after the insurance assessment. With one partner in the company murdered, the other narrowly escaping with her life from a fire, ensuring Emma's safety must be his first priority.

He shaved and dressed with haste and went downstairs to the morning room, where breakfast was already laid out. His brothers were at the table, Benjamin reading aloud from a newspaper. Benjamin and Jeremy both rose to their feet and bid him good morning. Polite. As if he was a stranger.

But he could spend fifty years separated from Oliver and they'd never be strangers. Of all his family, he'd missed Oliver the most. Barely a year between them in age, much less of a gap when they were young than the two years between Adam and their eldest brother, George. The measles that had taken Oliver's sight when he was eleven had almost taken his life, too. Although his blindness had denied him attendance at school, he accepted no pity and had proved a far more determined scholar, and a far, far better musician, than Adam could ever dream of being.

Oliver nodded in his general direction but his deerhound, Zeus, stood alert beside him, watching Adam's every move. Zeus didn't know him well enough to relax, either. In the small hours of the morning, while Adam updated Oliver on the evening's occurrences, Zeus had stared at him with canine disapproval for a steady hour.

Oliver's hand settled unerringly on the dog's head. "Lie down, Zeus. Adam's no threat."

The dog settled, but didn't seem convinced. Neither did Adam's youngest brothers, sitting stiffly and attending to their meal with downcast eyes.

Adam served himself ham, eggs, and a fresh soft roll before he carried his plate to the table.

"You were reading something about Wellington, I think?" Adam asked Benjamin. "Do go on."

"He's leaving for France on Tuesday, it says." Benjamin pushed aside his plate, found his place in the column of the newspaper again and read, "*'This information he gave to a deputation from the Corporation of Bath, who waited on him on Tuesday at Cheltenham, with an invitation to honour the City with his company to dinner. The Duke regretted his inability to accept it on account of his leaving England on the sixth instant.'*"

Adam spread butter on his still-warm, not-French, roll. The sixth. Four days ago. News took its time to reach the provincial papers.

He had no wish to be back in the embassy in Paris with Wellington. No great desire to be back with his regiment, either. The notion of resigning his commission and of making this period of leave permanent increasingly appealed to him.

He ate while Benjamin continued reading about reductions in the military, executions of conspirators against the King in France, and the supply of clothing in military stores before he paused.

"The next columns are all the cases tried at the assizes. Do you want me to read them?"

"No," Oliver replied. "It's Jeremy's turn. Is there any news from Nepal?"

Jeremy eagerly took the paper from his brother and scanned the pages. "Here it is. "*'The War with Nepal, which has at least given occasion to sinister rumours, if not to untoward events, is at an end. We are enabled to state, on official authority, that, on the 4th of March, the Treaty, so long concluded between the Indian and Nepal Governments, obtained its full ratification.'*"

As his brother read about 'several smart actions' and the enemy resisting 'with great bravery', Adam's appetite faded and he paused in eating.

"I told you our troops would be victorious," Jeremy pronounced when he finished reading. "Five hundred of the enemy dead, and our losses were small."

Adam set down his fork. "Whether victory or defeat, the cost of battle is men's lives, and grief and pain for thousands. I suggest you don't speak lightly of 'victory' in front of our sister."

Jeremy gaped. "But-"

"We will not discuss war at the breakfast table, Jeremy." His firm tone was more fatherly than brotherly. Phoebe might come in at any moment.

Jeremy still had a finger holding his place in the column of print. "Do you want me to read more?" His gaze darted between Adam and Oliver. Adam left it to his brother to decide.

Oliver felt for his cup and unerringly poured tea from the pot. "No, that's enough for this morning. Thank you, both."

Benjamin breathed an audible sigh of relief. "May we be excused?"

"Do you have commitments today?" Adam asked on a whim. "Either of you?"

The boys exchanged glances and looked to Oliver.

"You may be excused your lessons for today, if Adam needs you."

"Then go and get ready to ride to Hartdale and Halifax," Adam told them. At their quick, wide grins, he added firmly, "It will not be an entertaining excursion. We will ride with Miss Braithwaite's carriage and provide protection for her. You will follow my orders at all times. Jeremy, you wish to be a soldier. Should a threat arise, your duty is to protect Miss Braithwaite at all costs."

Jeremy stood straight and at least two inches taller than a moment ago. "Yes, sir."

Adam eyed his youngest brother, still a boy. "Benjamin, if any trouble arises, your duty is to immediately ride for help. Do I make myself clear?"

The lad reached scarcely to Jeremy's shoulder, but he solemnly echoed his brother. "Yes, sir."

Adam's military sternness hardly dented their enthusiasm. Although they left the room sedately, there was a noisy clatter of boots on the stairs.

"Have I just made a mistake, asking them to come?" Adam asked his brother.

"No. They're a little wild, but reliable, and it will do them good to have responsibility. I usually examine them both on what they read each morning," Oliver went on to explain. "Benjamin will be joining Jeremy at school in September. His last tutor was not as strict as the masters will be. We're trying to prepare him. He'll benefit from being with the other boys. He misses Jeremy during term time. Cecilia, too, now that she's gone to school."

Adam took a sip of coffee. Benjamin must be nearing twelve. Old enough to take on some responsibilities. And he had soldiers younger than Jeremy in his battalion.

"It's strange to see them so grown up," he mused. "In my head, they're still small children." But they weren't, and already there was another generation of the family. Phoebe's son, just over a year old. George's daughters, bright happy girls despite the cloud of their father's illness. "You're much better suited to overseeing boys than I am."

"Says the officer highly regarded by his soldiers." As usual, Oliver cloaked his disagreement in a mild, unarguable point of fact.

Adam argued, anyway. "The army is quite different. I can't order a child around."

"Some people do. You won't. You'll adapt. Besides, I won't be here."

A sharp spear of fear hit Adam. "What do you mean, not here?"

Attuned to every nuance of sound, Oliver must have heard the dread in his voice. "Not that. I'm perfectly well. But I'll be staying in London again for some time. Perhaps I'll go to Europe, now that the war is truly over."

For an instant, Adam envied his brother's freedom. An unfair envy, given the blindness forever trapping Oliver in darkness, rendering him unable to travel without a guide. And given his own relative freedom since he'd finished school—a freedom to choose his own career, to follow his own path. That he'd chosen eleven years in the army, bound to the demands of service and war, was still a choice.

On his way to London from Paris, he'd entertained the idea of eventually escaping Europe and all its rivalries and wars and emigrating to the new colony in New South Wales where free land and a new start awaited.

Until he saw how ill George had become. Now his own birth position in the family dictated his duty. Responsibility for Rengarth and its estates might soon become his, either as a guardian for a nephew—Hannah was sure the babe was a boy—or as the earl himself. Unless George recovered, his future lay here, at Rengarth.

"You should travel," he urged his brother. "Hear the famous musicians and orchestras. Meet all the famous composers. You deserve to become a famous one yourself. Louisa could go with you. Or I'll pay for a companion if need be."

Oliver froze with his cup halfway to his lips, his stillness so sudden that Zeus sat up on his haunches, alert. "I do not need to live on your charity, Adam."

Damn. He'd not intended to trample on Oliver's pride. But Louisa arrived in the morning room and he and Oliver rose to greet her, and the moment to apologize passed.

Louisa was dressed to go out, her blue spencer a splash of color over a white dress. She looked unreasonably wide-awake, given that she'd had as little sleep as him, having accompanied Emma back to Larkfell after midnight to see her safely into the care of the housekeeper.

"I know you're planning to ride, but I've ordered the carriage," she informed him airily as she handed her bonnet and gloves to a footman. "We can go via Larkfell and collect Emma."

Adam held out a chair for his sister at the table, and agreed with her plan. Traveling in the coach with the Rengarth crest would emphasize the family's support for Emma. "There's no necessity for you to come, though. It will not be an entertaining time, I'm afraid."

"Of course it's necessary." As decisive and pragmatic as their mother, Louisa added, "She has enough to concern her at the moment without salacious gossip if she's seen traveling alone with a man, with no chaperone. So I will be with you. I told her last night when we took her home that I would accompany her. Besides-" her lighthearted smile was an echo from her girlhood, "I need to go to the stationer's shop in Hartdale. Oliver, I'll get some more of the score paper. We're almost out. And if Emma doesn't need me, I'll visit the bookseller and see what music he has in stock."

Adam poured his sister a cup of tea while she and Oliver discussed paper and music scores. A talented musician herself, Louisa had long been Oliver's primary support in his music, scribing for him and transcribing his compositions.

A caring and capable woman, his sister. And she was right. Escorting Emma unaccompanied risked speculation and gossip. He must find a balance between demonstrating the Caldwell family backing for her, ensuring her safety, and protecting her reputation.

~

Emma dressed in mourning for Mr. Winslow. A plain black worsted dress, with few trimmings, worn over a chemisette with a ruffled falling collar. Respectable. Practical. A dress that she'd had made after her aunt's death three years ago, and worn frequently in the months since her father's death. Out of date now, but it gave due honor to Mr. Winslow and her grief at his passing, and no-one could accuse her of frittering away money on an extensive fashionable wardrobe.

A kind of numbness froze her emotions. Perhaps it was fatigue. She'd hardly slept, staying up in the study until near dawn, working at the accounts, adding assets and amounts owed by debtors, subtracting amounts owed to creditors, searching desperately for the best path through the financial crisis. And when she finally fell asleep, numbers had whirled in her head, and flames, and Francis's face, laughing and laughing.

Mrs. Barnden exclaimed about her paleness and fussed over her when she went downstairs for breakfast.

"Sit down and I'll pour your tea, my dear. Cook's making you a nice plate of eggs, just the way you like them. You should eat a decent, hot meal before going out."

Eat. A meal. Emma stared at the pile of steaming scrambled eggs placed in front of her, with no appetite at all. But with a demanding day ahead and no certainty over where she'd have her next meal, it did make sense to eat a good breakfast. Even though she was so tired and distracted she scarcely noticed the taste.

Hovering like a mother hen, Mrs. Barnden poured more tea for her and offered toast and marmalade the moment she finished her meal. An offer Emma declined, because the Rengarth carriage passed the window and pulled up outside the house.

She pushed herself to her feet. Time to go. Time to go and face the insurance agent. Time to secure the future of Braithwaite and Co., and to honor Mr. Winslow by ensuring that the circumstances of his death were fully investigated, and that he would be laid to rest appropriately.

The knowledge that Louisa and Adam planned to accompany her gave her heart and strengthened her determination. So much hinged on the insurance agent's assessment of the fire and the damage and she could not afford to be ignored. If he was the type of man who disregarded women, the presence of Adam and Louisa—particularly Adam, a man with influence—would not allow that to happen.

"I'll fetch your things," Mrs. Barnden said, as Jarvis announced Adam and Louisa and showed them into the room.

Adam paused inside the door, but Louisa came straight to her and kissed her on the cheek, before holding her at arms' length to search her face. "How are you this morning? Did you manage some sleep?"

"I did, thank you." Without the Caldwell family's support

at the ball, if she'd had to cope alone, she might have fallen into total despair. So much for her usual clear-headed calmness. "I must apologize for my collapse last night," she said. "I'm sorry I was a bother to you. Especially when you had so many other guests."

Louisa waved away her apology. "Pfft. Don't think any more of it. You had an awful shock after a thoroughly unpleasant day. If you'd *not* been distressed I would have been more worried."

"There is nothing to apologize for," Adam added. Once he might have teased her, but now he was quiet, serious. A man she could trust, absolutely.

Mrs. Barnden returned with her pelisse and bonnet, but it was Adam who held open the garment for her and assisted her into it. He stood close to her, and his fingers brushed her cheek as he settled the collar in place. Just one light, accidental touch, and her skin warmed and she almost wished she did not have to step away.

"I will ride beside the carriage," he told her. "And we've brought an extra groom and my younger brothers, so you'll be perfectly safe."

Safe. Adam had ridden beside the carriage last night when he'd escorted her home, and she'd heard him arranging with Jarvis for the grooms and footmen to patrol around the house and grounds. She could not imagine why anyone would try to harm her...but then she couldn't have imagined anyone trying to harm Mr. Winslow, either. She did not worry so much for herself as for Louisa; if there was danger, then Louisa must not be placed at risk.

Adam waited for her response. But with the situation so far outside her experience, she clung to sensible, logical words. "That seems a prudent arrangement, in the circumstances. I trust your judgement, Adam."

The Rengarth coach far surpassed her father's coach in luxury. Fine paneling, velvet upholstery, silk curtains, a generous supply of cushions to ensure their comfort, and the citrus scent of wood polish freshening the air.

The sun made a weak appearance through the clouds, and Louisa opened the carriage curtains to look out over the fields. Although the rain had ceased, the muddy road had been churned up last night by all the carriages travelling to and from the ball, and the coachman drove slowly.

Emma caught sight of Adam through the window every now and then. He rode well, of course, a consummate horseman, relaxed in the saddle, one gloved hand holding the reins. If she could have ridden beside him... No, not today. Not with the ever-threatening rain, and the mud, when she had business to attend to and Louisa for company. And not on a day when rain was not the only threat, and Adam carried a pair of pistols in holsters at the front of his saddle.

Louisa showed more concern for Emma's emotional well-being than fear for their physical safety. Perhaps she, like Emma, trusted in Adam's protection. Or perhaps it was merely that calm, practical Louisa rarely fussed about anything. If she'd noticed the pistols she made no comment, and Emma didn't mention them.

How easily she had slipped back into friendship with the Caldwells, despite the years apart. The constant, underlying sense of loneliness she'd carried for a long time had receded since yesterday. It wasn't that she didn't have other friends. But her two closest friends of her own age had married and moved away, and she increasingly found she had little in common with some of the other ladies. Even Letitia Timms, the vicar's daughter, found cause to gently disapprove of her involvement in business.

There were few families in the district with the friendliness and easy acceptance of the Caldwells. A result, perhaps, of Lady Caroline's unconventional views on education and the roles of women in society. The Countess had educated her children broadly and encouraged them to mix with others in the district. Such as the Braithwaites, despite their lack of aristocratic blood and their status as merchants.

Louisa's determinedly cheerful manner became more contemplative as they passed through the countryside. "I always miss this place, when I'm in London," she mused. "I don't realize how much until I come back. But then, I miss London when I'm here. I'm not sure which is home for me now."

Even in the overcast weather, Emma found the grays and greens of the stone-walled fields beautiful. "This is home, for me. I've only been to London twice. My sisters and I were there the winter before last."

"I was in Paris then, with Oliver. I'm sorry I missed you. I could have introduced you to my friends."

A quieter London season that year than normal, so people had said. With Napoleon exiled to Elba and the French King returned to his throne, many of the French exiles in society returned home, and the English upper classes had taken the opportunity of peace to visit Paris.

Emma's half-formed hope that she might see Adam had been dashed not long after her arrival in the capital, with the news that the family were in France and he had not come home to England. But then she'd been preoccupied with her sisters—one making a good match with a man Emma approved of; her youngest sister a rushed, hasty match that Emma fervently hoped she wouldn't come to regret.

"Both my sisters married while we were there. It was an eventful two months." Not always in a good way. Hectic enough organizing a wedding without the added stress of organizing a second one, at short notice, in less than ideal circumstances. She'd wished, more than once at the time, that the Caldwells had been in London, because she could have done with the advice of friends in the absence of any dependable sense from her aunt. Or her father, for that matter, when he'd come down to town.

"Sophia married Stephen Ridgeway, I do believe?" Louisa asked.

"Yes. She's known Stephen for some years—he's the brother of one of her school friends." Steady, reliable Stephen, the son of a baronet from Leeds, who had courted her sister over several months. Sophia had fallen deeply in love with him and had not hesitated to go with him to India, despite her love of home.

"And Lucy married one of his fellow officers?"

"Yes. Lieutenant Roger Shelbourne." Uncertain how much

Louisa had heard, she added carefully, "It was something of a hurried wedding."

"Oh." Louisa inserted a hundred words of concern and sympathy into the single utterance.

And Emma added a few more to the silent conversation. "Yes."

An unfair implication, perhaps. Roger had been charming, friendly and gentlemanly—at least in Emma's presence. Lucy's flirtations and plans to elope with him may indeed have arisen from her impulsive and adventurous nature rather than his persuasions, and to give the man his due, he had willingly agreed to marry her to protect her name and reputation. Yet Emma had never felt entirely easy about the match.

She certainly understood the appeal of young love and a man in uniform. And maybe it was *because* she understood that she hadn't watched Lucy as closely as she should have. But she had known Adam for months—years, really—before their relatively innocent stolen moments, whereas Lucy had made Lieutenant Shelbourne's acquaintance a bare four weeks before they sailed to India as husband and wife.

"Is Lieutenant Shelbourne a good man?" Louisa asked.

"I hope he is. I did make what enquiries I could. And Father interviewed him." When he'd been hastily summoned from Yorkshire. In just enough time to give his permission for a special license to be issued, two days before the ship sailed.

Emma had not left her family to go with Adam and his regiment at seventeen. She had not been free. But her sisters had been free to go, without responsibilities, and they'd taken their chance and gone with the men they loved. Alone now at Larkfell, Emma could only wait for their irregular letters from across the seas and hope that their marriages made her sisters happy. The thousands of miles, and the months that letters took to travel, rendered her helpless to support the sisters she'd raised through the years of their mother's illness and after her death.

As if she read her thoughts, Louisa said, "I'm glad Phoebe didn't move so far away when she married. And Lilian will mostly be in

London, so I will see her often." She gave a small sigh. "Both of us have younger sisters married. But neither of us have wed." A sparkle brightened her eyes. "Although you, at least, have had a proposal."

Louisa's teasing caught Emma by surprise, and flustered her. Did Louisa know about Adam's proposal...? No. She meant Francis's odd threat, last night.

"Francis doesn't hold any affection for me, so I have no idea why he would want to marry me."

"Because you are beautiful, and intelligent, and passionate?"

"But I'm not. Not beautiful, anyway." Passionate? Perhaps years ago, with Adam... but no man had moved her in the same way since.

Compared to the vivacious Louisa, in her blue silk spencer and fine muslin dress, with fair hair falling in curls from under her bonnet, Emma felt decidedly unremarkable. Not an unfortunate comparison, in the circumstances. Her business with the gentlemen today might proceed more smoothly if they could forget that she was a woman. Quite unfair, given that many women she knew possessed far more intelligence and sense than some men in positions of authority.

Like Louisa. It would be a mistake for any man to only see her beauty and underestimate her astuteness. Or for a woman to underestimate her social acumen. For an Earl's daughter, she had a sound grasp of the realities and complexities of life beyond the castle's walls.

"Oh, Emma, you don't see yourself the way others do. You did not see how the men were gazing at you last night. Your dress suited you perfectly. You have no need for sparkling gems to draw the eye."

More than likely any men gazing were contemplating an object of gossip, not beauty. Straight mouse-brown hair, a plain face and gray eyes did not meet anyone's definition of beauty. Plain and wholesome, perhaps, but not beautiful, especially now that she was no longer a young girl. But she didn't debate that particular point with Louisa. "Francis is wealthy and can choose from many women. Surely he can find someone who has some affection for him?"

"Perhaps you have something that he wants."

A humorless laugh caught in Emma's throat. "It's certainly not wealth. My grandmother left me an annuity, in a trust. It's enough for a modest life only." Not enough to save the company and keep Larkfell running for much longer. There would be another small annuity from her father's estate, too, when it was finalized.

"But you have the Braithwaite company, and its assets. And Larkfell and its land."

"I have only some shares in the company, which will be worthless if I cannot continue trading through this mess. And Larkfell and everything else belongs to Matthew."

"From what you said last night," Louisa said carefully, "Francis believes that Matthew has died. Does he think that you will benefit if that is the case? Do you know how his estate is dispersed?"

"Matthew is alive. We have no evidence of his death. Only a rumor reported by Francis."

Louisa leaned across to clasp her hand. "Believe me, I hope with all my heart that you are right," she said, with fervor. "But since Francis believes otherwise, it may have some impact on his motives."

"Matthew and Papa made sure that their affairs were all in order before Matthew left. They both made provision for me, and for my sisters. If Matthew dies without marrying, then Larkfell passes to me, and some other assets in trust for my sisters."

"But what happens," Louisa asked gently, "If he died before your father?"

A question she'd deliberately avoided asking herself. She'd clung to the thought of Matthew over-wintering at one of the small settlements on the Canadian lakes. Gathered around a fire with the explorers and fur trappers, playing cards and drinking spirits to while away the long winter days and nights.

But with each passing day without word from him—or of him—the terrible possibility had to be contemplated. He might never have made it to safety.

Her heart constricting into a painful knot, she answered Louisa's question. Facts. Just hypothetical facts. "Larkfell would still come to me, should Matthew have no heirs." Larkfell, the beautiful mansion built by her great-grandfather at the height of the Yorkshire worsted trade, sixty years ago. A symbol of the family's wealth and success. The second largest house in the valley, after Rengarth Castle. Admired and envied by many.

A memory fell in to place. A petulant schoolboy, arguing with Matthew.

"I think that's what Francis wants," she said, the memories unfolding into understanding. "Larkfell. He often said his grandfather should have inherited the house. His grandfather was the eldest of the brothers, but our great-grandfather disowned him, and my grandfather inherited Larkfell."

"And Francis believes that Matthew is dead. If he marries you, he gets Larkfell."

"Exactly." All of a woman's possessions became her husband's on marriage. A woman *became* her husband's possession on marriage. Emma didn't try to suppress a shudder. But then the sheer ludicrousness of Francis's idea struck her, and a sudden surge of relief and a reminder of her own strength made her laugh. "There's one significant problem with his plan, though."

"You're not going to marry him."

"Absolutely not. I'd rather go to debtors' prison." She said it with humor but it was no jest. At least, in debtors' prison, she would have a chance of getting out. Not so in a marriage. And a marriage without even the pretense of respect—that would be a life sentence.

As the coach entered the streets of Hartdale, Adam rode past the window, and when they stopped outside the warehouse he had already dismounted and was there to hand her down from the coach.

"It is not quite as bad as I feared it might be," he said quietly.

Although Emma braced herself to see the damaged warehouse, she stopped still when she went around the coach for a clear view across the street. The doorway into the warehouse gaped open, the ruins of the stairwell beyond it black and damp. The shattered windows revealed a layer of soot and ash over the bales of fabric in the lower rooms.

Nor as bad as she'd feared. But to see the building, the heart of the business, so broken and susceptible seemed a reflection of the state of the company itself—in dire need of work to salvage it. Work she would have to manage.

Adam assisted his sister from the carriage and Louisa gave a visible shudder as she surveyed the warehouse beside Emma, unusually somber. "You were in that fire. You could have died. You both could have died."

Determined to keep her thoughts from the nightmare minutes in the loft, Emma emphasized the positive. "Adam arrived in time to help, and we all escaped. That's what matters."

A few men waited in front of the warehouse, in two small groups. Williams the constable, two of his watchmen, and a man she assumed to be the insurance agent in one group. In the other, her employees—Ned and Theo, the clerks, Will, the copy boy and even Tom, the draw boy.

They all watched, measuring her state. She would not give the officials the satisfaction of seeing her uncertain or hesitant, or her employees reason to doubt her conviction or her determination to save the company.

The wind had a cold edge to it and dark clouds threatened rain, and they were all waiting on her. She turned to Louisa. "Go inside where it's warmer and do your shopping. I hope this won't take too long."

Louisa considered the constable and his men with her cool gaze. Even across the street, she made them shift their feet and look away. She turned her attention back to Emma, with a soft hand on her arm that clearly signaled their friendship. "Just call me if you need me. I know you won't let them give you any nonsense."

With a graceful lift of her skirts to keep them off the muddy cobblestones, Louisa headed in to the stationer's shop.

Adam gave his brothers permission to wander for ten minutes, but he remained beside Emma. "I won't say anything unless you ask me too." he said, his voice low. "I'd like to go around the back to look at the stables for a few minutes. But I'll stay with you if you wish."

Confidence. Louisa and Adam had confidence in her. She just had to find it in herself.

She crossed the road, directed a nod at the constable, but she went first to speak with her employees.

They relied on her to be strong. If the company failed, they would be left without livelihoods. Ned, the eldest, barely eighteen, Theo sixteen, Will only twelve, and Tom, nine years old. If she failed them, Ned and Theo might not find another respectable situation, and the younger boys might end up in the factories, working fourteen or more hour days, in dangerous conditions, for minimal wages and with no hope of betterment.

Her father had taken quiet pride in training young sons of widowed mothers to good careers. They all helped to support their families and she must not fail them.

In response to her enquiries, they all assured her they suffered no ill effects from the fire, and Tom informed her that, other than a mild headache, his Uncle Jacob was well and following her instructions to rest.

They'd all showed up for work, but what work could she give them, with the warehouse so damaged?

Ned saw the direction of her gaze. "The constable won't let me in yet, but I reckon we can save some of the stock, miss. Those bales that aren't burnt are sealed up well. The pieces might need airing and drying, but we can manage that."

Assuming the weather cleared long enough. Assuming it cleared soon enough that the pieces weren't ruined. Not a matter she had control over. But any salvageable goods needed to be moved to a safer place. "Ned, when the constable gives leave to go inside, we'll need an accounting of what is burnt or ruined, and what might be recovered. When Mr. Hargraves returns from Halifax with the wagon, help him load up what might be saved and take it to the barn at Larkfell. Tom, you can help Ned and the clerks. There will be a bonus for all of you if you can get that finished today." She couldn't see from here how far the flames had spread on the upper level, and whether the counting room and office were destroyed, but they were certainly inaccessible at present. "Ned, purchase what you will need from the stationer's shop on the account. An account book, quills, ink."

Those easier matters dealt with, she approached the other group of men. Inside, she quaked, but she endeavored to show no sign of it. Confidence. Capability. And a touch of her grandfather's pride. Like a Queen. Like the Dowager Countess, last night. *Take the lead and don't let them see doubt.* "Good morning, gentlemen. Mr. Williams, I am gratified to see that your men have prevented looting overnight. Thank you."

Clearly aware of her arrival with Adam and Louisa in the Rengarth coach, the constable bowed to her and presented the insurance agent, Mr. Penry. A tall man, not much older than Adam, who inclined his head in a cursory greeting.

She did not allow his coolness to daunt her. "Thank you for coming so promptly, Mr. Penry. The men on the fire cart saved the warehouse from much greater destruction, as you see. There is nothing still smoldering, I presume?" She addressed the question to the constable. "Is it safe to inspect inside?"

Williams shook his head, without shifting his gaze from her. "Not yet, miss. A few questions first, if we may."

Wary of the glint of hawkish pleasure in his eyes, she answered, "Of course. What do you want to know?"

Mr. Penry watched her closely but remained silent while the constable asked a series of questions. What time had she come to the warehouse? Who was working there yesterday? When did she notice the fire? Where did it start?

All straight-forward enquiries to answer. She kept a hold on her patience, despite the breeze rising in the street and beginning to chill her. Truly unseasonable weather, for August. Surely he would be finished, soon.

"Was there anything stored in the stable?" Williams continued. "In the loft?"

"Hay. Harnesses. Only the usual sorts of things." Determined to avoid them casting blame on her or her people, she added, "The stable boy sleeps in the warehouse so there would have been no candles in the loft to knock over."

"Then how do you think the fire started?"

She held his gaze, not dropping her own. "I don't know, Mr. Williams. Yesterday people were saying Luddites were likely to blame. I presumed you were making enquiries about them." The Luddite explanation didn't sit entirely comfortably with her, unless they'd targeted her company out of confusion with her cousins' factories. Luddites attacked in mobs at night, made their protest by destroying machinery and then disappeared into the darkness again. It wasn't so much the machinery that concerned them, but the changes in the industry that denied them employment. She wasn't convinced about blaming them, yet she'd had little opportunity to consider alternative possibilities for the cause of the fire.

Williams shrugged. "Don't see why Luddites would attack here, miss, you having no machinery to break. When was the last time you were up there, in the loft?"

The question puzzled her, but she answered it. "Some years ago. We stored some wool up there a few times when the warehouse was full. But I have little necessity now to climb into stable lofts. Why do you ask?"

"A witness saw you at the stables, ma'am. Not long before the fire broke out."

Cold seeped up from the cobblestones under her boots and the wind blew chill air under her bonnet and into her face. "Your witness is mistaken. I was in the courtyard early in the morning to give Mr. Hargraves some instructions before he left for Halifax. I did not go outside again after that. My employees will attest to my presence inside all day."

She could see Ned, at the window of the stationer's shop, but she didn't call him over. He wasn't the only one interested in this scene. Several men stood at the corner, another two not far away, and even the Rengarth groom and coachman watched while they held the horses across the street.

Williams nodded across the street towards Ned. "Well, of course they'd say that, wouldn't they? Trade ain't been going so great, and they want to keep their positions."

She had to avoid dragging Ned and the others into this. "What are you implying, Mr. Williams?"

"Wouldn't be the first time a struggling company set a fire to claim insurance money. Would it, Mr. Penry?"

Penry said nothing, his face devoid of expression so that she could not tell if this ludicrous notion was his idea or the constable's. He simply stood there, observing, his gloved hands resting on the handle of his black cane. The man who had the power to break her business if he believed the constable's nonsense.

Fury rose, burning in her throat, choking her voice. Fury that Williams would accuse her at all, let alone out in the street like a common criminal. Fury that someone had been blackening her name, spreading rumors about the financial state of the company. That circumstances were arraying so many things against her.

And Williams smirked at her, gleeful and confident in his accusations. His two watchmen stepped in closer, on either side of her, both tall and thickset and brutish. If she could find no way to dissuade them of this nonsense, she'd end up in the watch house before long.

CHAPTER 9

From the gaping doorway of the warehouse, Adam saw the men crowding Emma, a pack of wolves around a lamb. She faced them alone, her back straight, her head upright. She didn't see him, clambering over fallen charred timbers from the back of the building to reach her.

Neither did Williams. He grabbed her arm. "You're going to come along with me now, Miss Braithwaite."

She stood her ground and attempted to pull her arm back. "Remove your hand, Mr. Williams."

Adam shoved aside a fallen beam blocking the doorway and stepped out on to the street. "You heard what Miss Braithwaite said, Williams. Remove your hand from her immediately."

Emma exhaled a breath as the constable stepped back a pace. But she continued facing the man, small and vulnerable and astounding in her bravery.

Adam clenched his fists by his side. His glare at the constable's men persuaded them to fall back as well. The insurance agent strolled a few paces away and took an interest in studying the building, as if to disassociate himself from the others.

"What is going on here, Williams?" Adam demanded.

"I'm doing nowt but my job, sir," the man blustered.

Emma spoke, her voice flat. "The constable accused me of starting the fire. For the insurance money." She glanced at the agent.

"Mr. Penry appears to believe him."

"Then Williams is in blatant dereliction of his duties, and Penry is at best a fool." In his anger he didn't care that his words were harsh and blunt. Not as blunt as the fist he'd like to ram into the constable's face.

Williams face reddened as he protested but Penry spoke coolly over him. "I have barely commenced my assessment. Do you have evidence to the contrary, Mr.-?"

The man's calmness and disregard of the constable made Adam revise his initial impression of collusion. There might be more to the agent than he'd first assumed. "Caldwell. Major Adam Caldwell."

"Of the Rengarth Caldwells?"

Adam gave the barest nod of his head. "If the constable had bothered to think, he'd have realized that there is more to this than a simple fire. Because a hay fire doesn't blast through a stone wall."

That caught Penry's interest. "A blast?"

"I'll show you. The constable should also be making enquiries with his counterpart in Halifax about the other attack on Braithwaite and Co. yesterday."

Blank faces showed they'd heard nothing of it. Word had not yet travelled from Halifax this early in the day. Emma's brow creased in a frown, only now connecting the events. He'd said little to her of his suspicions. Last night hadn't been the time to frighten her further, nor this morning. She'd been quiet, still wrapped in grief. Carrying the weight of it with courage and composure.

"You think they're related? Mr. Winslow's-" She hesitated over the word. "Murder? And the fire?"

He could call Louisa to take her to the carriage, or to rest at the inn, but he didn't. She had every right to be informed, and he doubted the knowledge would be too much for her. Some women might collapse in hysterics. Not Emma.

"Yes, I suspect they're connected. I'm concerned that the fire may have been a deliberate attempt to harm you, not just the warehouse. If you come around to the stable, I'll show you why."

He offered her his arm. Partly because the cobblestones were damp and slippery. Partly because he wanted her to know she wasn't alone. Mostly because he had a better chance to protect her, having her right beside him.

Penry and Williams followed them to the end of the building and through the carriage way to the courtyard behind.

Much of the stable had collapsed in on itself, a blackened pile of timber, ash and the twisted metal remains of harnesses. But the front stone wall stood mostly upright, except where it sided against the warehouse building. There, at the loft level, a section was blown out, stones scattered around the courtyard. Through that section, the man-sized hole in the stairwell could be seen.

"Interesting," Penry murmured. "The remainder of the walls have withstood the fire."

"There was a sound," Emma said. "Not long after we smelled the smoke. A very loud sound, like a sharp, deep roll of thunder all around us. The floor shook, and when Jacob opened the door, the burning hay and flames were all around."

Exactly how he'd describe an explosion, if he'd never heard one before. For people who had never been to war, never been involved in mining, thunder was the closest sound they knew. Because no-one fired cannon, in this quiet corner of Yorkshire.

"I strongly suspect someone used a charge of black powder—gun powder—against the wall," he explained, to Emma as much as to Penry, "To deliberately set the warehouse alight."

She stared at him. "But we were inside. They'd have known that, wouldn't they? They'd have known..." Her voice trailed off, her eyes wide and dark with horror as if she relived those terrifying minutes in the loft.

He would relive the horror in his nightmares, those long moments of fear for her life as the fire burned. He could not draw her into his arms and reassure her, remind her of their escape. Not in front of the others. Perhaps never at all.

Williams shifted uneasily on his feet. "But a witness saw her."

Penry's scathing glance visibly withered the constable. "I believe we can discount the veracity of your witness, Williams. Do you have

91

any other evidence, Major?"

Adam's respect for Penry increased. The man seemed to have a good degree of sense. "I spoke with a man yesterday. A soldier. He heard the blast and smelled the black powder."

Penry merely nodded. "I will continue my investigations. Miss Braithwaite, you will be at your residence if I have further questions?"

"I must go to Halifax this afternoon," she said. "I may not be home until late."

Alone at Larkfell she would be only as safe as the few staff could keep her—and at the mercy of the constable if he decided to accost her again there. Adam could hardly protect her there without gossip and scandal. "Miss Braithwaite, my mother has extended an invitation to be her guest at Rengarth Castle until your safety is assured." He spoke honestly; his mother had indeed extended the invitation in their hasty conversation in the small hours of the morning. And it served well now as a reminder to Penry and the Constable that she had the support of the Earl's family.

Emma nodded, a small amount of the tension easing from her face. "Her Ladyship is very kind."

Not exactly an agreement. Perhaps she didn't wish to discuss it in front of the others. But not a disagreement, either, and he was confident that he and Louisa could persuade her to stay at Rengarth for at least the next couple of days. Longer, if they didn't find out who was behind the fire and Winslow's murder. If he had to bring his great-aunt to come and stay after his mother left for London, for propriety's sake, he'd do it. Whatever it took to keep Emma safe.

"A wise plan," Penry agreed. "I'll send word to the Castle if necessary. Miss Braithwaite, it will be helpful if you are able to provide the insurance company with an inventory, or at least an estimate, of the goods in the warehouse."

"I can. The clerks saved most of the ledgers, and I have instructed them to assess the damages. I will have to go home to collect the books. But I can send an inventory to you on Monday."

The wind whistled through the ruins and she shivered, the fine worsted fabric of her pelisse and dress insufficient barrier against the cold. It might as well have been winter, the way the temperature had fallen.

"I believe we are finished here, gentleman," she said, in a manner that invited only agreement. Williams and Penry bowed and murmured their farewells.

Adam escorted her to meet up with Louisa, finalizing her purchases, and the boys, who'd each taken the brief opportunity to buy books. He waited until the coach had departed to Halifax—he'd catch up with it shortly—before he went in search of Garrett.

He found the former soldier waiting for him at a table in a dim corner of the Hartdale Arms, a mug of ale in front of him. Adam tossed a coin to the serving woman and ordered for one himself. The Arms had always been a decent establishment, the tables clean, the floors swept, and the victuals good. Gentlemen and tradesmen patronized it. Some of the guests who'd come for the ball were staying here. Garrett, in his ragged coat, should have looked out of place. But with his upright bearing and combed hair, in the dull light he didn't look like a pauper.

Adam sat down opposite him. The table's position afforded both of them a good view of the room, with a solid wall behind them. "What have you learned?"

Garrett swallowed a mouthful of ale and wiped his mouth with the back of his hand. "There's plenty of talk about the fire. Braithwaites are well thought of in town, especially Miss Braithwaite. She runs a school for the children of their workers. And they pay fair wages and fair piece rates. The rich in town—they're the ones blaming the fire on Luddites. The poorer folk, they aren't." He dropped his voice to a low mutter. "They know. Ain't no-one done any machine-breaking around here for a long time."

Of course the poorer folk had a fair idea about those involved. Luddites were husbands, fathers, brothers, sons. They mounted their attacks at night and then returned in the darkness back to their tight-mouthed communities.

They both remained silent while the serving woman brought Adam's ale. He waited until she left before he commented, "So who attacked the cotton factory near here the other week?" The factory that Francis Braithwaite owned in partnership with another man.

Garrett sipped his ale, his glance darting around for eavesdroppers, as cautious as a soldier in enemy territory. But the few men in the tap room, engrossed in a debate about horses, paid them no attention.

"I went down to the Lion last night," Garrett said. "That's more for the likes of me than this place. Rumor is that the attack were staged. They weren't locals, so they reckon down at the Lion. There's plenty as would like to burn that factory down, the rate the young 'uns there are being hurt or dying, but the place is guarded and they work 'em day and night."

Fifteen hour days for children as young as six. In the conversation at supper last night Adam had learned of the appalling conditions, and that the laws to protect apprentices enacted a decade ago did not apply to non-apprenticed labor, and so factory owners like Francis employed few apprentices and preferred children to whom they owed few obligations. One more reason—not that he needed more—to dislike Francis Braithwaite. One more reason to admire Emma, and her passion for improving the conditions for workers.

But maybe some people didn't admire Emma, for that same reason. Had her activities—her letters to newspapers and parliament, her involvement in local committees, her support of the school for worker's children—had they angered any of the factory owners enough for them to strike at her business? To strike at her?

He took a mouthful of ale to wet his throat. Someone might have aimed at Emma because of her beliefs, but that didn't explain Winslow's murder. Unless he was similarly committed to reform.

"Did anyone see anything?" he asked Garrett. "Know anything? About who was responsible for the fire?"

"Nothing sure, sir. Someone saw a stranger outside the stable a couple of nights ago, but that don't mean nowt. There be plenty of men around, looking for work. Or a warm place to sleep."

Adam's vain hope that the arsonist had been seen faded. Even in a small town like Hartdale, a stranger didn't stand out. Plenty of people traveling along the canal paths, along the river, even the new toll road, stopped in Hartdale. In yesterday's rain, few locals had been out unless they had to be.

"What do you know about the constable? Bert Williams?"

"Ah. A man to steer clear of." He shrugged. "Unless you have coin to spare. He doesn't trouble those who have it and who share it with him."

"He takes bribes." No surprise in that.

Garrett gave a world-weary nod. "Aye. He's no help to those who can't pay. And some folks say that the men who work for him are worse than thieves and ruffians."

The two men who'd almost laid hands on Emma. If he hadn't been there, if they'd dragged her away... He tightened his hands around his tankard as if it was the constable's neck. *Don't think about it.* Thinking about what might have happened only clouded his mind with rage. It hadn't happened. This time. But only because he was there. For all Emma's courage, they'd have dragged her off to the town prison if he hadn't been there to stand up for her. And that had only worked without a fight because of his status and family connections.

He swallowed back his disgust at the unjustness with a slug of ale. Malty and earthy. Wholesome and honest, not pretending to be anything fancy. Like the man in front of him. Who'd lost a leg serving his country.

"Do you need anything?" he asked abruptly. "You receive a pension, don't you?"

"Aye. Nine pence a day, sir."

Nine pence per day. Less than 6 shillings per week. Not enough for a man to live on. "Do you have family? A wife?"

"No, sir." Garrett's straight gaze and the firm set of his jaw belied the words, and he knew it.

There had to be a story there. Garrett didn't strike him as a man who'd desert a needy family. But some men had good reason to remain estranged from their families. Adam might have probed, but footsteps, firm and quick, descended the stairwell behind them and Francis Braithwaite strode through the tap room. Intent on his purpose, he did not see Adam in the dim corner, and he exited to the stable yard.

Adam crossed to the window. With a quick word to the coachman, Braithwaite stepped up into a waiting carriage. Neither the coachman nor the two grooms wore livery of any form, and they'd certainly not been employed for their fine looks.

Garrett came up beside him. "Might be nothing to do with Miss Braithwaite," he murmured. "But that gentleman were talking to the constable this morning. About an hour ago, outside the watch house. And I think—can't be certain though—that some coin changed hands."

Braithwaite bribing the constable? Adam couldn't loathe either man any more than he did already. But bribery for what purpose? If Braithwaite was behind the attempt to take Emma into custody...

He was halfway to the door to confront him when the coachman flicked the reins, the boy holding the horses jumped back, and the carriage clattered out of the stable yard. He spun on his heel to head to the front entrance, to halt the carriage when it turned on to the street, but two men came down the stairs carrying a trunk, blocking the narrow passage way. And behind them, exhorting them to be careful, came Robert Braithwaite.

The narrow passage impassable as the men maneuvered the trunk around the corner, Adam called back to Garrett, "Find out which way that coach went."

He flattened against the wall to allow the trunk-bearers to pass and immediately stepped out to block Robert's path, chest to chest.

He didn't waste breath on social niceties. "What the hell are you and your brother up to?"

"My brother?" The elder Braithwaite seemed genuinely confused, but whether that was the question or the abrupt manner of it Adam couldn't tell. "Other than normal business," he continued, his brow furrowed, "I don't know what you mean. I haven't seen him since last night at Rengarth Castle."

Adam stared him down. "You expect me to believe you when he left here less than two minutes ago?"

"We did not share a chamber, sir. Francis leads his own life. His...
entertainments"— the hesitant nature of the word carried a load of
discomfort— "are often not to my taste."

He might be speaking the truth. Other than some facial similarities
and the fact of their familial relationship, Robert's conservative black
suit, precisely-tied cravat, and punctilious ways couldn't have been
more different to his brother's more egotistic, sardonic manner. If
Robert had marital intentions towards Emma, he would court her in
a chaste and respectful manner. Not make lurid threats in the center
of a ball room.

The thought of either man marrying Emma did not improve his
mood.

*Why is your brother acting to blacken Emma's business
reputation?* He bit back the question, having already said too much
within hearing of those in the tap room.

"A word in private, if you will." His tone belied the polite words.
"The upstairs parlor will suffice."

Robert remained motionless for several moments before agreeing
crisply, "I can spare a few minutes." Cooperation, not capitulation,
from a man with a gentleman's pride.

In the empty upstairs parlor, Adam shut the door firmly. He
indicated the two armchairs by the fireplace and they took their
seats, but neither of them relaxed into comfort. Robert faced him
coolly, his hands clasped on top of his cane. The perfect, well-dressed
gentleman, his conservative attire the best in understated quality.

Adam came straight to the point. "I have reason to believe that
your brother has deliberately been acting against Miss Braithwaite's
interests. What do you know about that?"

Eyebrows rose. "Francis only returned home from Canada last
month. He inherited and lives in our mother's house. I did not see
him until yesterday. What evidence do you have to support your
accusation? And what right," Robert fixed him with a glare, "do
you have to involve yourself in my cousin's affairs?"

As protective as a father or brother. Or as concerned as a suitor.
Or perhaps both, and a fair enough question for her relation to ask.

What right indeed.

"We are neighbors, and our families are friends of long standing." He hoped that would suffice. Not that his parents and Emma's had been particularly close, but they'd always been on friendly terms. "And I am making inquiries on behalf of my brother, to investigate probable criminal activity," he added. Much though he disliked using his brother's position, it *was* part of the Earl's responsibility to oversee the peace of the district, and therefore arguably his, given his brother's illness.

"Criminal activity?" Surprise gave the question a sharp edge. "What has that to do with my brother?"

"The fire at the warehouse was not an accident. Last night your brother was overheard repeating rumors about the company, and then he insulted and threatened Emma. This morning, a witness saw him meeting with the constable—who later attempted to accuse her of setting the fire herself."

"Francis could have any number of reasons for meeting with the constable. Luddites are becoming a threat again."

"Luddites didn't set an explosion in Emma's warehouse when she was inside. Nor did they murder her partner, Mr. Winslow."

The color drained from Braithwaite's face. "Ralph Winslow is dead? How? When?"

Adam didn't soften the news. "Yesterday afternoon. Murdered in his garden."

"But who...?" He shook his head, and it seemed to Adam that his shock was genuine. "Winslow was a good man. I can't believe someone would..."

"They will have to start the inquest today. Emma's already on her way and I will catch up with her."

"Emma is going to the inquest? An inquest is too distressing for a lady."

Adam had a higher opinion of Emma's emotional resilience than her cousin did, but he didn't entirely disagree with the sentiment. Deceased bodies laid out on tables tended to leave haunting, unforgettable images in the mind. "I'll try to dissuade her from going to it, as will my sister, I'm sure. But I intend to be there myself."

"But you didn't know Winslow. You seriously think whoever murdered him is some threat to Emma?"

"I have no hard evidence. But I'm not prepared to take the risk."

Robert drew himself up straight, although the attempt at authority came across more school-masterly than military. "I must ask, what are your intentions towards my cousin?"

None of your business, Adam wanted to say. Except that perhaps it was, given Robert was the closest relative Emma had in the district and evidently felt a responsibility to protect her. And there was an honor in that concern for her that Adam respected.

"I wanted to marry her once," he said, slowly, because it was hard to find adequate words to honestly answer the question. "I find that I still do." And that simple statement summarized yet did not do justice to the unexpected depth of feeling and certainty that had struck him in less than a day. He steered his thoughts back to practicalities he did understand. "But I only returned home yesterday after a long absence, and after years at war I'm..." He couldn't explain himself to himself any more, let alone a stranger. "I am no longer the optimistic young fool I was. So my priority right now is her safety. She will stay at Rengarth as a guest of my mother for now. Perhaps later, once we know she's safe and her business concerns have settled, I might address her. Assuming her affections are not engaged elsewhere and she wishes it."

A declaration of intention he had no idea he'd make before he said it. Yet it seemed right, and he didn't regret the words. Not even when he remembered that Robert's behavior towards Emma might be not only a relative's regard, but that of a suitor.

Robert remained silent for a moment before he nodded. If he held plans to court Emma himself, he swallowed back his pride and capitulated with dignity. "With your military experience you are better placed to be able to protect her," he conceded. "And Lady Rengarth's hospitality is gracious. If there is anything I can do for Emma, please let me know."

"You could find out what your brother is up to," Adam said

bluntly.

"Francis is a proud man, competitive and at times impulsive. I'll speak to him about his inappropriate behavior. But I cannot conceive of him doing anything to place our cousin in danger."

Adam could conceive of it, all too easily. A man who spoke so disrespectfully to a woman as Francis had spoken to Emma last night placed no value on her well-being

But if Robert did not believe Francis capable of harming her, then Adam was wasting time here. He bid him a brisk farewell and left, anxious to get on the road and catch up with the coach.

He met Garrett at the bottom of the stairs.

"The coach went along Market Street, sir," he reported. "I sent a lad after him. He said the carriage turned west and stopped at the old mill past the blacksmith's, and the man went inside with another man."

West, not east. Not the road to Halifax. Whatever Francis's business at the mill, it wasn't anywhere near Emma.

Adam gave Garrett some shillings from his coin bag. "Keep asking around, see if you can find out anything more about the fire, or about that man's doings. Can you find your way to Rengarth Castle this evening? It's three miles from here."

"Aye."

"Good. If I'm not back from Halifax, ask for my brother, Oliver, and tell him I said to see that you get food and lodging."

Garrett muttered his thanks, but Adam was already on his way to the stable yard to retrieve his horse and ride after Emma.

CHAPTER 10

The inn near Mr. Winslow's house in Halifax was raucous with those who'd come to observe the inquest. So many that they filled the upstairs parlor where the coroner and the jury heard witnesses. Those that couldn't fit inside lined the stairs, or crowded into the taproom to share their own news and theories about the death.

In the chamber on the top floor that Adam had insisted on engaging, Emma waited with Louisa. The younger Caldwell brothers had taken up stations on the stairs outside the open door, their curiosity about the proceedings in the parlor warring with their promise to Adam to stay with their sister and Emma. But they remained standing, guarding the door, two young sentinels alert and confident that they were ready for anything.

Louisa, at Emma's insistence, was making use of the bed to rest for a little while, but despite the lack of sleep last night, Emma was too unsettled to lie down. Coming to Halifax had resolved little. Only the news from Mr. Hargraves, her factor, that the entire load of fabric had sold at this morning's market for a good price, made a glimmer of good news in among the bad. Her solicitor was out of town. The manager of her bank had taken ill yesterday and was seeing no-one. Mr. Winslow's solicitor was attending the inquest, and not available to consult.

With little constructive to do, she tidied up the remains of their meal on the table and carried fresh cups of tea to the boys, who accepted with polite smiles of thanks. They were probably more grateful for the little honey cakes she'd added to the saucers than for the tea.

"Adam's talking to them now," Jeremy whispered. "Telling them about the fire."

Adam's voice was barely audible over the murmuring of the many watchers, but she concentrated on those deep, familiar tones and heard most of his summary of the fire and his suspicions.

"Is Miss Braithwaite present?" an authoritative voice asked. The coroner, she supposed. The murmuring grew louder and she missed the exchange that followed, catching only brisk words here and there.

The men gathered on the landing below turned and looked up at her, jostling for a better view as if she was a wild animal at the circus. Not Hartdale people who knew her, but strangers. Here in Halifax she had only a small circle of acquaintances, none of them likely to regard an inquest as entertainment.

Adam shouldered his way through the throng. The inn was old and the stairs to this upper level were steep and uneven but he mounted them two at a time.

Grimness made his face hard, yet when he reached her she saw only the gentle concern in his eyes. "Mr. Palmer, the coroner, wants you to appear, Emma. I wanted to spare you this. It may be difficult. You could plead fatigue to be excused. Or distress."

"No. I will come." Finding the truth about her old friend's murder mattered more than her apprehension. "We can be grateful the coroner is being thorough," she added, in a not-entirely-successful attempt to overrule the thudding of her heart.

"I'll come with you," Louisa said from behind her, hastily patting down her slightly tousled hair. "I don't look too disheveled, do I?"

Emma's nervousness dropped down a notch. With Adam and Louisa standing with her, she could face the whole world. "I wish I could wake up as quickly, and as beautifully, from a deep sleep," she reassured her.

Adam told the boys to remain in—or only just outside—the

chamber, and offered his arm to Emma as they descended the steep stairs. She took it, as much for the connection as for safety on the steps. She'd consider the propriety of that later. Right now she was about to walk into a room full of men and face questions and they'd all be watching her, expecting her to be weak and emotional.

She vowed not to give them the satisfaction of living down to their expectations.

Silence fell in the room when they entered. A dozen jurors, the coroner, and twenty or more other men eyed her critically. The only man she recognized, sitting in the back row of chairs, was Mr. Penry, the insurance agent. He must have left Hartdale not long after they had.

A clerk, after a whispered word with Adam, announced, "Miss Braithwaite. Accompanied by Lady Louisa Caldwell."

Adam brought two chairs over and placed them facing the coroner, and despite her bravado, Emma sat with some gratitude, Louisa beside her.

Mr. Winslow's body lay on a table at the side of the room. They'd covered him with a white cloth. Strangely, the sight did not distress her unduly. She'd helped to lay out her mother's body, and her aunt's, a last service of love she could perform for them, and a chance to say what was in her heart.

The dead did not scare her. Mr. Winslow had always been kind and respectful to all during his life. If his spirit hovered near his earthly remains, it must be as benevolent as during his life.

She bowed her head for a moment, and offered a silent prayer for his soul.

Then she raised her eyes and faced the coroner and the jury of twelve men tasked with determining the circumstances of her friend's death. Well-dressed men, probably merchants or in the professions or gentry.

Mr. Palmer, the coroner, had all the sternness and dryness of a lawyer, and began by asking her a number of straight-forward questions. How long she had known Mr. Winslow. What his role was in Braithwaite and Co. What her role was in Braithwaite and

Co.

There was some muttering as she explained that she held shares and was a senior partner, along with her brother. That with Matthew away she managed the company, day to day.

The coroner raised an eyebrow. "It is unusual, is it not, for a woman to bear the responsibility for such a trade?"

As if women of all levels of society hadn't been capably managing their own and their husbands' trade and financial affairs for generations.

Emma gave her frustration a small amount of freedom. "Not as unusual as many think, sir. You might wish to consult Lady Jersey, for example, as to the prevalence and abilities of women engaged in commerce."

Louisa ducked her head to hide a smile and, behind them, someone choked a laugh into a cough. Several gentlemen grinned while others grimaced. Perhaps the latter had accounts at Child's Bank, where the Countess of Jersey, having inherited the senior partnership from her grandfather, led the bank with a firm hand. And she only a few years older than Emma herself.

"Oh, I would never underestimate a lady's abilities," Mr. Palmer said, dry as dust. "However, Sally Jersey is rather...unique." A few more murmurs seemed to agree with him. "She is also," he added, with a firm stare at Emma, "a Countess."

A pointed reminder that Emma was not a member of the aristocracy. Only a clothier's daughter. A merchant's daughter. *Trade*, as some in the upper classes might say disparagingly.

But a daughter proud of her family's history and successes, and the significant contribution of the worsted trade to the nation's wealth.

She lifted her chin and spoke directly to the coroner. "Mr. Winslow was an astute man but he did not know the worsted trade as my family does. He was a close friend of my father's and invested in the business many years ago. His connections in the West Indies added to our trading partners in Europe, Russia and the colonies. I have of course consulted him since my father's death, but he has never been closely involved and was content to leave the decisions to me."

One of the jurors stood, and with a nod from Mr. Palmer, he asked, "Was Winslow aware of the company's financial problems? That you're near bankruptcy?"

She might have objected but in an inquest the jurors had every right to ask questions. "That is a vicious rumor. The company is not bankrupt, nor even near it."

"But you stand to gain from Winslow's death, don't you?" he pressed.

"Gain?" His question made no sense. "Of course not. He was an old and dear family friend."

"Who has left you his entire estate." The juror turned to the coroner. "Now he's been murdered, just when she needs the money most. And her factor and warehouse men were in Halifax yesterday."

Left you his entire estate... The revelation and the accusation hit her so hard she couldn't draw breath, couldn't *think* clearly through the shock. Louisa grasped her hand and whispered something but she didn't hear the words over the commotion that had broken out in the room.

The juror had resumed his seat, and remained in it, smiling.

The coroner pounded the table and raised his voice above the noise. "Silence!" He had to repeat the order before everyone quieted. "Mr. Rickards, you are Winslow's solicitor. Is it true about his will?"

An elderly gentleman in the front row of seats rose to his feet, leaning heavily on a walking stick. "Assuming that there is no later will than the one I hold for him, " he said, slowly and with legal precision, "And assuming that probate is granted, then broadly, yes. Apart from some bequests to household staff and charities, Miss Braithwaite is the primary beneficiary of the estate."

Among the outbreak of muttering, she heard more than one person say, "Hang her."

His hand lightly touching her shoulder, Adam leaned forward to murmur, "We should leave. It may not be safe to stay."

Emma shook her head, determined not to run away and let the

accusation stand unchallenged.

Her heart beat loudly but she stood up and addressed the coroner directly, in a clear voice that stilled the noise around her. "Sir, I was not aware of Mr. Winslow's will. And, as Mr. Rickards has said, we cannot presume until probate is granted that it is his last will or that it will not be contested." Facts that could not be disputed. "I am curious as to how the gentleman on the jury knew of its contents, but, more importantly, his accusations are entirely baseless and malicious. I shall be consulting my own solicitor regarding his slander." The man wasn't smiling now. Good. She intended to carry through on the threat. "I believe I have answered all of your questions. Should you have any more, you may send them via my solicitor, Mr. Galbraith. Good day to you, sir."

She was shaking as she turned and walked towards the door, but she did not look back. She stared straight ahead so that she didn't meet anyone's eyes, lest they see the anger and fear in hers. Adam and Louisa joined her and the men around the doorway and on the landing parted enough to let them through. Lifting her skirts a little to ascend the stairs, she concentrated on one foot after another on the steep narrow steps so that she would not trip in front of them all.

"Benjamin, order the coach to be readied," Adam instructed his youngest brother as they reached the chamber. "With all haste."

Emma stopped and turned so abruptly inside the door that Adam was only inches from her and still moving forward. She steadied herself—and him—with a hand against his chest. In Adam's face, in the tightness of his jaw, she saw her own fears that the crowd might turn against her, that the coroner might be swayed by lies. "I must speak with Mr. Rickards before we leave." In the many strands of thought jostling in her mind, that one stood clearly. "We need to find out who knew about the will. How that juror knew about it."

Through the cloth of his jacket his heart beat against her hand. As if his family weren't in the room, he closed his fingers over hers and nodded. "I'll go and get Rickards. We will find out."

His certainty gave her heart that her own determination was not ill-placed. Yet when he stepped back, released her hand, she had to fight the temptation to take it back, to lean into his strength. She turned away, fidgeting with her handkerchief, her cheeks hot. She had no right to or reason for such intimacy. She would not refuse his help; she had too much at stake, and as a woman with few connections she was at a disadvantage. But he had been home for barely a day, and she had to remember that the closeness once between them no longer existed, except in her memories.

"Ready yourselves to leave," Adam said to all of them, his voice brusque. "Jeremy, do not let anyone enter this room other than me and Rickards."

Jeremy followed him out to guard the door. Louisa hurriedly began to collect her and the boys' things together, and Emma distractedly began to gather her own belongings. Bonnet. Gloves. Reticule. Pelisse.

The everyday reality of the accessories in her hands did little to help her collect her thoughts.

The velvet ribbon on her bonnet was faded.

Mr. Winslow was dead.

Her black gloves were wearing thin.

A man had accused her of arranging Winslow's murder.

She held her pelisse in her hands, and for a moment everything overwhelmed her so powerfully that she could not think clearly enough to remember why she held it. She shook her head, trying to clear the numbness, and a half-laugh, half sob escaped. "To think that this morning I was only worried about debtor's prison," she said to Louisa. "Now someone wants to see me hung."

As if she understood the paralysis, Louisa gently took the garment from her and helped her into it. "You know Adam won't allow that to happen, Emma. *We* won't allow anything so ridiculous to happen. You're going to get to the bottom of this, and everything will work out fine."

But Emma noticed that despite her friend's assurances, Louisa didn't smile. She didn't sit, either, and nor could Emma. They stood together by the window, watching out over the stable yard, waiting.

Dark clouds swept across the sky and the wind made the horses in the yard skittish.

Perhaps that would make for a faster journey back to Rengarth. Feeling as skittish as the horses, Emma yearned to ride back, free from the confines of the coach, free to ride far and fast.

But it wouldn't help her cause to be seen behaving in so unladylike a manner, and she could not outrun her problems.

Nor would it help her cause to stay and confront the challenges head on. Not when so much remained unknown, including the perpetrator—or perpetrators—and their motives and goals.

Adam had served with the Duke of Wellington, famed for his military intelligence and strategy. She trusted that hastening back to Rengarth was a tactical move, a strategic withdrawal to a stronger position from which to gain intelligence and greater advantage.

And she hated that her peaceful life had become so disrupted that she was likening it to a battlefield.

~

Adam rode beside the coach, as alert and wary as if Napoleon's forces lay ahead. Not that Napoleon's plans had ever been as much of a mystery as the attacks on Emma and Winslow.

He had numerous pieces of information but none of them added together to make a pattern, to point to who was behind it all.

Rickards had dismissed a clerk three days ago, for passing copies of confidential letters to a man in an inn. Not related to Winslow's affairs, in that case, Rickards had assured them. But that same clerk had been with the firm since Christmas, and Winslow had updated his will since then. And a clerk who'd betray a confidence for money might easily have done so more than once.

The elderly lawyer had been distressed—Winslow had been his friend, too—and most apologetic to Emma that she had found out about the inheritance in so public a manner. But other than the fact of the clerk's dismissal, and that he himself was overseeing arrangements for the funeral in line with Winslow's wishes, he'd had little other information to share. Winslow, according to his friend, had not an enemy in the world.

Which still left Adam with a hundred unanswered questions, and he heartily wished he had a man in Halifax he could rely on to make inquiries. No time to find one today. With the inquest now adjourned until Monday morning, the coroner and the Halifax constable, and perhaps even Rickards, had another day to investigate the circumstances of Winslow's death.

And Penry. No surprise to see him at the inquest. But he *had* been surprised to be hailed by the agent as he mounted his horse to accompany the coach from the inn.

"I'll keep making enquiries," Penry had said, without preamble or explanation. "May I call on you tomorrow morning?"

"Yes." On a hunch, Adam had asked from the saddle, "You're investigating more than insurance, aren't you?"

Penry had merely inclined his head, and then stepped back to allow Adam and the horse to go after the coach.

And that raised more questions. Exactly *what* was Penry investigating? And for whom? After an hour of riding without incident, almost at Rengarth, Adam had reached the conclusion that he probably—*probably*—could trust Penry. After witnessing all the intrigues of the European courts, he never trusted easily, or entirely, and with Emma's well-being at risk he'd trust no-one but himself with her safety. Yet Penry had the bearing of an officer, despite the fashionable cane. Military bearing, sharp intelligence in his gaze, a disinclination to tolerate fools. Not exactly the kind of man Adam expected to find working for a provincial insurance company. But there were thousands of returned soldiers and officers adjusting to civilian life now that the wars were over. Including himself.

When they turned into the lane leading to the Castle, Adam sent his brothers on ahead to alert his mother to their arrival, and the Countess and his sisters were on the steps to welcome Emma when they drove up.

He handed Louisa and Emma down from the coach, with no small relief that they were safely at Rengarth. The new castle didn't have the moat and fortifications of the old medieval castle, now in ruins in the woods, but the sheer numbers of household and outdoor staff provided security for all inside.

"You'll be safe here," he assured Emma.

Although fatigue clouded her eyes, she gave him a soft, brave smile. "Thank you, Adam. Thank you for everything you've done today."

"I'll keep investigating until we know who is behind this and why." He still had hold of her hand, when he should have released it. He covered that lapse by assisting her up the stairs, Louisa beside them, to his mother.

The Countess greeted her warmly. "You are very welcome, my dear. We'll send word to Larkfell, and the carriage for your maid. Please don't feel that you have to be sociable, if you wish to rest. It's only the family at home now, and we are very informal. Louisa, will you show Emma upstairs? The blue room is ready for her."

As his sister and Emma went indoors, he drew his mother aside and apologized for bringing a house guest, unannounced. She'd clearly been working in her beloved garden, in an older-style print dress he had vague memories of from years ago. She may have whipped off an apron in order to greet Emma, but a few smudges of earth remained on her skirts, and strands of hair had escaped their neat arrangement.

Some ladies might have been flustered by having to greet a guest in such disarray, or made Emma wait until they'd changed. His mother didn't appear at all perturbed. "You did right to bring her here, Adam. Jeremy said there'd been more trouble. You do have another guest, though. He's with Oliver in the music room. When you've finished there, come and tell me all that has happened."

As Adam approached the music room, the unexpected sound of a violin drifted through the open door. Not Oliver's playing. It wasn't one of his preferred instruments, or his style of music. But a slow, haunting Scottish air, played with a deft touch, the lingering notes resonating with heart ache and longing, sorrow and regrets.

Memories flooded back. Long lines of soldiers, ghostly shadows in the night, hunched in the dark against the misty rain. The hushed voices of men trying to make themselves comfortable, knowing that the horror of battle awaited them in the morning.

Adam watched and listened, silent in the doorway, his emotions strangely jumbled. He'd thought of Emma that night. That he would never see her again if he died. The sense of loss and regret had engulfed him and he'd had to hide his face from his comrades. And he thought of her now, grateful beyond measure for her presence in his life again—whatever might come of it.

Garrett stood, balancing with one crutch under the arm holding the violin. Despite the tattered coat, patched breeches, and well-scuffed boot, he held himself with the same pride as many of the more fortunate musicians who'd played in this elegant room.

The man had his back to the door and didn't hear him, but Oliver, standing by the window with his dog at his feet, turned his head as the last notes of the air faded away.

Adam stepped into the room and had to clear the tightness in his throat before he spoke. "Someone played that air the night before Waterloo. Was that you, Garrett?"

"Aye, sir. Not on an instrument as fine as this, though." He kept his face averted as he laid the violin reverently back in its case, open on a table. "I thank 'ee, Mr Caldwell," he said to Oliver after several moments, his voice gruff, "for the privilege. I never hoped to play on such a beauty as that."

"You have a rare talent," Oliver said. "I'd ask you more about the masters who taught you, but I'm sure Adam wants to hear your news."

Garrett reached for his second crutch and maneuvered backwards several feet, away from the violin. "I'm just a soldier, sir, who used to have a fiddle. It helped to pass the time sometimes."

Oliver gave a disbelieving *hrmph*, but the dog rose to nudge against his leg. "I'll take Zeus out. There's a good claret on the table," he added, as he went out to the terrace with the dog by his side.

A good claret and three glasses. Oliver must have ordered it. Adam poured the wine and gestured to Garrett to take a seat at the table.

"Beggin' your pardon, sir, but I daren't. Not with the muck of the world on me."

Adam cursed himself for his thoughtlessness in putting a good man in an awkward position, and took him out on to the terrace, where the chairs did not have valuable velvet cushions. He'd get someone to find a clean suit of clothes for the man, and a place to sleep.

Once they'd settled, Garrett took a cautious sip of wine, holding the crystal glass with care. "I went up to the old mill," he began. "Mr. Braithwaite's carriage was around the back. The mill ain't run for a long time, but Mr. Braithwaite seems to have some men living there. I looked around when they left. There's a fire and victuals and some bedding."

"How many men?"

Garrett shrugged. "Maybe three or four? Hard to tell. I only saw three."

Adam watched his brother throwing a ball for Zeus out on the lawn, and wondered why Francis Braithwaite needed three or four men working for him, in a unused mill.

"I hid in some bushes beside the mill race. Too far to hear anything, but I could see them. Two of the men reported to Braithwaite. He seemed pleased, and gave 'em money. Then they all went off again. He went t' north, but one o' the men went back to town. I were slower than him, but he were coming out of the Lion when I got there. And the constable, he were inside. He were there in the tap room most of the day. Except when he were…" Garrett hesitated. "Being entertained upstairs."

Adam heard his own teeth grind. So much for the constable investigating the fire. Drinking and whoring instead of finding out who had started it; a gross dereliction of duty. Adam took another mouthful of the fine claret, turning over the possibilities. Either someone—perhaps Francis—was paying the constable *not* to investigate, or he already knew who was responsible, and was complicit in the crime.

But he had nothing to directly connect Francis with the threats to Emma—except a burning distrust of the man and his possible connection with the constable.

He needed more information, but he wasn't about to send Garrett out again. He managed his injury well, but it had to be more tiring getting about on one leg and he'd already walked a few miles today.

"I appreciate your help, Garrett. You're welcome to stay here as our guest. I'll have the housekeeper find you a room." He made a list in his mind of other items for the housekeeper to find for him. Washing water. A clean suit. Razor and comb. A new boot.

He was so caught up in his thoughts he didn't notice the shuttering of Garrett's expression. "Thank 'ee, sir," he said, with a veneer of courtesy masking his distance. "But I don't belong in this grand a place." He carefully placed his wine glass back on the table and reached for his crutches. "I'll be on my way, sir."

Adam cursed himself for his stupidity, for once again putting Garrett in an impossible position. Few ordinary soldiers would feel comfortable in the home of an earl, inexperienced in all the social expectations of a house with ladies and children. Especially one who'd been homeless on the streets just yesterday.

He motioned to Garrett to remain seated, and topped up his wine glass. "No need to go rushing off. Stay for a few days. We'll find room for you in the coach house or one of the gardener's cottages, if that's what you'd prefer."

"I'm not a beggar, sir. I don't want charity."

"You've already done good work for me. Besides, Oliver will appreciate your musical skills. Other than my sisters, there's a dearth of talent at Rengarth. My younger brothers could do with some drill and military training before they go off to school. Preferably to dissuade them from joining the army. And as I'm taking over management of the estate for now, I may well need a man I can rely on. So if there's nowhere else you have to be, I can make use of you here."

Garrett considered the offer, as wary as if Napoleon himself had suggested it. But eventually he asked, "Would I have some time of my own, sir?"

"Of course. If that's what you need." Adam refrained from asking why. Not until they'd built more trust between them. "Stay in the coach house for now, Garrett. You can talk with Oliver, meet the boys, and we'll discuss arrangements again in a few days, once you've got to know the place better."

Adam remained on the terrace after the housekeeper took Garrett down to the coach house. Sip by sip, the wine eased away some of the edginess he'd carried all day. Garrett had proved himself useful and thorough, and Adam hoped that he and his prickly pride would stay at Rengarth. But to untangle the threats against Emma, he needed more than Garrett's intelligence.

He had a long list of unanswered questions. Top of the list: what was Francis Braithwaite up to, and who was involved it with him? Who had murdered Ralph Winslow, and how had the juror in Halifax known about Winslow's will? What exactly was Penry's interest in the case, and what had he found out this afternoon?

If Penry didn't provide the answers to that last question, he'd make enquiries in Halifax himself.

CHAPTER 11

An hour's rest in the beautiful guest chamber went some way to reducing Emma's fatigue. She woke as her maid arrived from Larkfell, followed by a footman carrying a small trunk.

"I've brought several evening gowns, Miss," Kate said, hurriedly unlocking the trunk after a brief, awe-struck stare at the size of the room. "And dresses for church tomorrow. Mrs. Barnden will send more things in the morning."

Her evening gowns. She and her father had not often dressed for dinner and her social life, particularly this year, had been minimal. The dresses she'd worn eighteen months ago in London for her sisters' wedding events had seen few wears since.

Kate laid out four gowns on the bed for Emma to choose from.

She'd worn mourning for Mr. Winslow today, but her black net evening dress seemed too austere for what Louisa had assured her would be an informal family dinner.

Instead of the black, Emma chose a silk dinner dress striped in pale blue and trimmed with blond lace. Kate arranged her hair in a simple knot with a blue ribbon twisted through it, clasped a delicate sapphire necklace around her throat, and produced white satin slippers, gloves, and an embroidered muslin shawl from the trunk.

Last night before the ball, Emma had been too distracted to give the mirror more than a cursory glance. Now, with more concerns overall, but much less trepidation about the evening ahead, she considered the serious woman staring back at her from the glass.

Beautiful, Louisa had called her. So had Adam, a long, long time ago. She did not see it in herself, but then what was beauty, anyway? Only the opportunity to catch an eye. Elusive and ephemeral, it said nothing of the intrinsic nature or qualities of a person. It mattered not at all for family, for friendship, for love.

She was presentable, in accordance with social expectations and with her respect for her hostess and the family. That was sufficient.

"You're always frowning, Em." London, the winter before last, and her youngest sister's chiding. The sudden memory made her take a second glance in the mirror. *"You're much prettier when you smile. I'm sure some handsome man will fall for you, if only you'd smile more."*

Lucy, with so much zest for life and hunger for adventure and few responsibilities to temper her enthusiasm. The woman in the mirror gave a wistful smile. Perhaps it did soften her face, ease away the lines of worry around her eyes.

Would Adam still think her beautiful?

She shook away that thought with a dose of reality. Adam, in this past year in the courts of Europe with Wellington, must have met many aristocratic women, more beautiful, worldly, wealthy, and even more educated than she.

He was an earl's son, and she a clothier's daughter, without significant wealth and with little to bring to a marriage.

Except for Mr. Winslow's estate.

She rose abruptly to her feet, impatient with herself. Even if she did inherit something from her old friend—and there was no certainty of that at this stage—Mr. Winslow had led a modest life, and hadn't even kept a horse. At best, his house in Halifax would be a suitable home for her spinsterhood, once Matthew returned to Larkfell. She could perhaps have a small school there, to educate intelligent poor girls beyond the basics of the village school.

It was pointless to think of Adam in any way other than as a friend and neighbor. Eight years was a long time. They'd both changed, grown older, perhaps become wiser, shaped by their experiences—

Adam's far more arduous and confronting than hers. Their friendship had survived, but they hardly knew each other, now.

Kate, arranging the muslin shawl around her in a fashionably casual drape, stopped abruptly with a gasp. "Oh, miss, I almost forgot. I'm sorry. There are letters for you."

There were three letters, one from her sister, Sophia, and two with handwriting Emma didn't recognize.

She turned Sophia's letter over in her hand, tempted to break the seal, but the voices of the younger Caldwell girls sounded out in the corridor, on their way down to dinner, and she should not be late. She placed the letters on the dressing table. They must wait until later.

The few house guests who'd stayed for the ball, including Adam's sister Lilian and her husband, had left earlier in the day, taking advantage of the dry weather for their travel south. That still left eight of the ten brothers and sisters at home, and in the easy and open way of the family they welcomed her with warmth.

As the senior male present, Adam escorted her—the only guest— in to dinner, and drew out a chair for her to the right of his at the head of the table. The perfect gentleman.

It seemed strange, after all the drama of the past two days, to sit down to an elegant table in friendly company. A relaxed and delicious meal, with little formality other than the liveried footmen serving.

With Oliver to her left, and Louisa and Phoebe opposite, conversation flowed throughout the meal over a wide range of subjects. Emma admired the way in which Lady Rengarth encouraged her younger children to participate, although she did detect some awe of their elder brother, particularly from the youngest girls. Perhaps he was more of a stranger to them than he was to her. They were very young children when he joined the army, and she doubted there'd been much relaxed time together since he arrived home yesterday.

Adam remained relatively quiet, as he had at supper last night. Observing, listening, as if finding his place within his family again. His family may not have noticed, given the multiple conversations.

Aware of him beside her, aware of every movement, every comment, Emma did notice.

But everyone fell silent when Phoebe asked him, "What are your plans, Adam? Will you be returning to your regiment after the summer?"

"No." He paused, his glance flicking from his mother, to Oliver, to Phoebe and to Emma. "No. I'll be resigning my commission. I'll stay here, for as long as I'm needed."

Emma attempted to hide the flood of relief by sipping from her glass of wine, but her hand trembled and she set the glass on the table again. He was staying. She did not have to say goodbye again soon.

Louisa's brief mention earlier in the day about their planned journey to London to see George and the rumors she'd overhead last night about the Earl's health and his lack of an heir fitted together to assume a greater significance. Add to that Adam's solemnity...

George must be gravely ill indeed. Over and beyond the concern for a brother, the implications for Adam might be significant. Even if George's Countess was safely delivered of a boy, for Adam to be heir presumptive to an infant was a quite different situation to being heir presumptive to an older, married brother in what should have been the prime of his life.

"I'm very pleased that you're staying, sir," Jeremy said, with genuine enthusiasm. "You'll be wanting a good horse, I presume. Colonel Hampton was just saying last evening how he must sell two fine horses soon as he can no longer ride. I'd be happy to go and look at them with you."

Amusement softened Adam's face. "And you hope one of them might suit you, too? Have you saved enough from your allowance?"

Jeremy's face fell. "I...er..." He shot a pleading glance at his mother.

"Samson is sufficient for you for now, Jeremy," the Countess said. "We will discuss the situation again after I return from London."

At the mention of London, Susanna pleaded, "Mama, I so wish I could come with you to London."

118

"Our visit will be a quiet one, Susanna, with few entertainments," Lady Rengarth said with gentleness. "You will find it more enjoyable here. I am sure you will be a gracious hostess to Miss Braithwaite. And Adam will be grateful for your support in household matters."

"I will indeed," Adam commented. "You have far more knowledge of overseeing a household this size than I have, Susanna."

Whether it was true or not, Susanna blushed with her brother's compliment, and Louisa gave him an approving nod. He might not know the youngest children well, but he would become friends with them, given time.

Lady Rengarth turned to Emma. "I am sorry that I must depart in a few days, Miss Braithwaite, but you are very welcome to the protection of this house for as long as you wish. If your troubles are not resolved before I leave, I will invite my aunt to visit. She is a kindly soul and very practical. I believe you may know of her? Mrs. Thorncroft?"

A widowed aunt to protect Emma's reputation, since Susanna was barely eighteen and therefore not a chaperone in a household to be temporarily overseen by a single man. Lady Rengarth's thoughtfulness, when George's illness must be foremost on her mind, touched Emma.

"I am acquainted with Mrs. Thorncroft," Emma said with a smile, "And it will be lovely to see her again. We have interests in common." She didn't mention what those interests were. Political discussions, unless introduced by the hostess, did not belong at the dinner table. "However, I do hope not to impose on your hospitality for long, my lady."

"Your interests in common are to do with factory conditions, I understand," Lady Rengarth said. "Aunt Thorncroft has been working for that cause for some years."

"Yes." And since the countess had introduced the topic, Emma added, "We were recently involved in gathering information to submit to the parliamentary enquiry." And how many times, in this past year, had she wanted to ask Mrs. Thorncroft if there was news of Adam—and bitten her tongue. She had no right to enquire and no wish to generate speculation by asking about a single man.

Beside her, Oliver asked, "Do you think Peel's factory reform act will pass, Miss Braithwaite?"

A rare occurrence, to be invited by a male to contribute an opinion. Especially a male from the aristocracy. But then the Caldwells were hardly typical of their class. The fact that Oliver, despite his blindness, was informed about the issue shouldn't surprise her. Already the conversation around the table had shown he had many interests beyond music.

Emma still chose her words carefully. "Parliament has risen for the year, but I hope Sir Robert will reintroduce the bill next year. However, there is still much opposition to the proposed changes." From a long list of members of parliament who were also factory owners.

Louisa's lively face stilled into seriousness. "I don't comprehend how anyone can oppose laws to stop little children from working fifteen or even more hours a day."

"Some of those who are opposed argue that if the poor are not kept busy working, they will fall into idleness, vice and crime," Emma explained. "And that the economy is dependent upon the success of the textile trades."

On the edge of her vision, Adam's fingers gripped the stem of his wine glass. "The same is said of the use of slaves," he said.

The hard edge in his voice left no doubt as to his views. "Indeed," she agreed. "And the arguments often come from the same people."

At the other end of the table, the conversation had drifted to other topics as the dessert course drew to a close, and Louisa was distracted by a question from Susanna.

Emma finished her last mouthful of a delicious flummery. Perhaps she was being too forthright, too absorbed in her own interests. Breaking not one, but two social taboos—by discussing politics at the table, and by discussing politics with men.

But Adam leaned forward and asked her, "Is Francis Braithwaite opposed to the reform bill?"

"He has been away for much of the past year. But before he left he was vocal in his opposition to any ideas of factory reform. He is a partner in a cotton factory near Hartdale that-" Even though it was Adam she spoke to, she continued to choose her words with caution, speaking only facts. "That has a reputation for working its employees very hard."

Another reason she found it difficult to comprehend why Francis wanted to marry her, when they held such opposite views.

"I've heard rumors," Adam said. "Is Robert also involved in the cotton factory?"

"Not as far as I know. The woolen mills he and Francis own are better, but Francis is in partnership with some others in the cotton mills. Robert is far from perfect but he is not," She sought for a word. "Callous." *Economical* was a better word for Robert. He did not flaunt his wealth, or seek more with no regard to the source of it. "Francis is very proud of our great-grandfather's wealth and influence, and the fact that he served in parliament for some years and was knighted." A dreadful thought occurred to her. "I hope he does not attempt to enter parliament himself."

Adam's eyes darkened. "He won't," he said in a low growl, "if I have any influence."

There was no more time to continue the conversation as the countess requested tea to be served in the music room, and began to rise. Adam hastened to his feet and drew out Emma's chair for her.

Emma accompanied the countess and her daughters to the music room, a large salon graced with a beautiful pianoforte, not one but two harps, and a collection of smaller instruments. Comfortable chairs and sofas were arranged informally. A room the family clearly felt at home in.

Emma's fears that she'd overstepped ladylike behavior were alleviated when the countess commented as she poured tea, "You may rest assured, Miss Braithwaite, that my son, Lord Rengarth, is in favor of the factory reforms. As am I," she added with a smile as she passed a delicate tea cup to Emma. "Were I not preoccupied with family matters, I would seek your advice on how to support the cause. Perhaps when I return from London." But there was a slight hitch to her voice and a glimpse of pain in her eyes before she dropped her gaze to the pour the next cup of tea.

One more sign that the Earl's illness was serious. She could not intrude upon Lady Rengarth's hospitality for long. Tomorrow or the next day she would leave.

The countess, however, shook off her moment of melancholy and with a bright smile said to her eldest daughter, "Louisa, that new sonata you were practicing earlier—would you like to play it for us when your brothers rejoin us?"

"I could play the first movement," Louisa agreed. "It's very lovely. But I didn't have enough time before dinner to start on the rest of it."

Adam and Oliver joined them within a short time, the younger boys with them. Although the countess included her younger children as if they were adults, Emma presumed that did not include her young sons drinking quantities of port with their adult brothers.

As the menfolk made themselves comfortable, Louisa went to the piano. Confident, graceful, beautiful in her blue silk dress. Emma envied her poise, and her musical talent.

"This is Herr Beethoven's *Sonata quasi una fantasia*," Louisa said. "Oliver and I heard it in Paris a year or so ago, but I only received the music today."

The sonata, when Louisa played the gently flowing notes with the delicate melody floating around them, was one Emma hadn't heard before and was more than 'lovely'.

The exquisite beauty of the music transformed emotion into pure sound, all the things that mattered—the sorrows and joys she could never find words to express—in such exquisite harmony and cadences that her throat tightened and her breath came unevenly.

Perhaps she wasn't the only one so affected. Phoebe sat very still, her face pale against the black of her widow's dress, a tear sliding down her cheek as she touched the mourning locket pinned to her bodice.

With her emotions so stirred, Emma almost wept with Phoebe. How easily it could have been her, widowed and grieving, if she'd accepted Adam's proposal. If he'd been killed in any one of the battles and skirmishes he'd been involved in. With thousands of muskets firing, sabers slashing, and cannon pounding troops, he must have been mere inches from death a hundred times. If she'd married him and loved him and lost him... She could not bear the thought.

She dared not turn her head to look at him for fear her feelings would show on her face. Instead, she closed her eyes to keep the waves of emotions from overwhelming her. But the music held tenderness too, and hope, and peace. As the last, perfect, lingering notes sounded she found herself holding her breath while they hung in the air, until they faded away and there was only the hushed room and the silence.

No-one spoke for some moments. Louisa remained with her fingertips on the keyboard until her mother said, "Thank you, Louisa. That was very moving. A very special piece of music."

"The second movement is quite different," Louisa said. "Not as contemplative. But I have barely begun to learn it."

"You played that first movement better than Parelli did in Paris," Oliver commented. "He rushed it too much."

Emma sipped the last of her tea while the musical ones discussed the sonata. Her musical talent being sufficient only to recognize her limitations, she merely listened. She far preferred dancing to performing.

Perhaps young Cecilia was the same, or perhaps she simply wanted to avoid being sent off to bed, for she pointed out that there were enough people to make a good set. "Please, Mama, may we dance? I so wanted to dance last night."

Susanna's face lit up. "Oh, yes please, Mama!"

"I won't dance," Phoebe said quickly. "But I'm happy to play for a dance or two."

"If your brothers are willing, you may," the countess told her younger daughters, adding, "Miss Braithwaite, please don't feel obliged to join in if you don't wish to."

Emma had no objection. She wouldn't have danced in public so soon after Mr. Winslow's death, but one or two dances in private were a different matter. And, assuming that Lady Rengarth no longer danced, she was needed to make up a four-couple set.

Adam and his brothers apparently had no objection, either, and while Phoebe sat at the piano and sorted dance music and Lady Rengarth uncovered a harp, the menfolk quickly moved a sofa and a chair to clear sufficient space and rolled up a carpet.

When all was ready, Adam bowed before her. "Miss Braithwaite, we did not have the opportunity to dance together last night. May I have the pleasure of this dance?"

Of course he asked her. It was expected of the host to invite the guest to dance. He'd been perfectly polite all evening, calling her 'Miss Braithwaite', drawing out her chair, attending to her comfort. He would do the same for any woman in her place.

Yet as he led her to the floor near the piano and Phoebe asked what dance they wanted, he said, "Something gentle, I think. Perhaps the Hole in the Wall?" He handed Emma in to place, his gaze fixed on hers as he added with the softest of smiles, "If Miss Braithwaite agrees."

An old, old dance, far from the height of fashion. But slow and graceful and she had no doubt he remembered that they'd danced it together in their youth.

Feeling a blush on her cheeks, unsure what to say, Emma smiled shyly and murmured, "Yes."

The others formed into a set below them, Louisa with Oliver, Susanna with Jeremy, Cecilia with Benjamin. Perhaps because of Oliver, they made a neat set, lines straight and couples evenly spaced. He hadn't danced last night in the crowd, but he didn't hesitate to join in now.

The piano opened the music and Emma returned Adam's gaze as she curtsied. She cast off around Louisa while he did the same around Oliver, before they met in the middle and led up. No-one had worn gloves for the informal dinner and his fingers curled around hers, his smile almost as intimate as his touch as he handed her back to place.

Oliver and Louisa cast up around them, their timing impeccable, both exactly where they needed to be. When Emma advanced to change places with Oliver in the next phrase, it was only the lack of focus in his eyes that gave any indication of his blindness. Louisa and Adam advanced and changed places, Louisa's silk skirt swishing softly as she gracefully turned. Then Adam held his hand out to Emma for the half circle around, the touch of his fingers lingering until the last moment before they separated to cast back to second place.

Perhaps she'd imagined it.

Lady Rengarth's harp took over the melody for the next time through the dance, and Emma and Adam danced with Susanna and Jeremy, both of them graceful in their steps. And once again, each time Adam kept hold of her hand as long as the music and the formation allowed.

She might have been seventeen again, with those stolen moments of touch.

Perhaps that was just the way he danced with every lady. Yet she doubted it. She'd never seen him being flirtatious with anyone, even in his youth. Anyone except her.

They danced the next repeat with Cecilia and Benjamin, and Adam was as gracious to them as he was to his older brothers and sisters. Benjamin didn't quite yet have the polish of Jeremy and Oliver, but Cecilia danced prettily, and they were both so thoroughly enjoying themselves that Emma could not help but feel happy along with them. No matter all the troubles and concerns waiting for her, here tonight she could simply enjoy herself.

When she cast off to the bottom of the set at the end of that time through, she smiled across at Adam in gratitude, and for the first time since his return he smiled easily, without the shadows in his eyes.

For a moment it was almost as though nothing had changed between them.

Yet of course it had. Years had passed and they were both older, each shaped by their experiences, his so different from hers that she could scarcely imagine them.

In truth, she hardly knew him now. And she must remember that she had clouds over her name and responsibilities she could not walk away from, and he was the brother of an earl. And, if she read the unspoken concerns correctly, an earl who was seriously ill, with no son as yet.

Adam was surely merely being polite, and a relationship between them was as impossible as it had always been.

CHAPTER 12

After the ladies and the younger boys retired, Adam remained with Oliver in the music room. He should go to bed himself, but until this second glass of port quieted the racing thoughts in his head, he doubted sleep would come to him. His brother's undemanding company required little in the way of conversation and he relaxed into the armchair, letting his head rest against the back.

Oliver began a new piece on his guitar. A few hesitant notes to begin, then a shift of key before he started again. As he played the first phrases, the melody seemed familiar to Adam, but it took him some moments to place it.

Once again, the air that Garrett had played earlier tugged at his memories and emotions, but not as strongly this time. Maybe because he'd heard it already today. Maybe because of the wine at dinner, the port now. Maybe because the sonata Louisa had played and the dance with Emma had dazed his senses.

"It's different when you play it on the guitar," he mused when Oliver finished. "I assume it's an old folk air you've heard before? Or did you memorize it this afternoon?"

"I'd heard it before." He replayed one of the thematic passages of the air, the gentle notes lingering. "It's a lament by Niel Gow, the Scottish composer." His fingers created another cadence of notes before he paused. "What puzzles me, though, is how a man who purports to be a common soldier knows an air published only a few years ago. And where he learned his technique. It was from a master, not from a village fiddler."

The light from the candles his brother could not see danced against his solemn face. Adam did not doubt him. Oliver knew music, had studied violin, harp and guitar with several masters himself. Unlike Adam, who had minimal musical talent and no patience to practice.

"The regiment was in Belgium for a while before Waterloo. There was a whole society of British officers and wives there. He could have heard it anywhere. Or even bought the music himself."

Oliver inclined his head. "As you say. I'm curious, too, about his accent. It wanders up and down the country. I can't place where he's from."

Adam took another sip of the smooth, rich port. "He's been in the army for many years." Not in his own company, but he had a few recollections of the man, during the Peninsular campaign and later. "There are soldiers from all over. Men who join up as youths tend to lose any distinct speech after a year or two."

"So you trust him."

"Aye." And there was a bit of the Yorkshire lad in *him* sneaking out, despite the good schools and the polish of aristocracy.

"What will you do with him?"

"Find work for him. He can drill the boys, keep them out of mischief. Or teach music in Emma's school. He has good sense and useful skills. He lost his leg fighting in my regiment to defeat the French. We owe him more than an inadequate pension for that."

"You can't find work for every injured soldier. It's a bad year coming. It's been too wet for grain to grow properly. It won't be a good harvest. And plenty enough mouths to feed on the estate."

"I know." He'd been uneasily aware of it, on his journey home through France and much of England. "Europe is even worse off than England. The war disrupted farming, so there were hardly any winter crops. But it will be bad enough here. And," he voiced the unspoken truth, "I have to accept that it will be my responsibility to do what I can for the estate." Dozens of families relied on the estate. The staff of the castle, estate workers, tenant farmers, and pensioners in Rengarth village. "I won't manage it as well as Mother does, I'm sure. But it's my duty, not hers. She's carried so much, raising all of us, caring for Father."

Olive rose to lay his guitar on a table, and settled into a more comfortable armchair opposite Adam, clasping his port. "Do you mind so much?"

Adam shrugged. "I had a vague plan, when I left France, that I might go to New South Wales. They're giving out land grants there. A new colony, a chance to help shape it. It seemed like a rational idea, a few weeks ago."

"But you're not thinking that now."

"No. It's impossible at present, of course." In the quietness of the darkened house, honesty came easily. "I can scarcely comprehend the possibility of outliving George. I was always so glad he was the eldest, that I didn't have to deal with account books and running the estate and all the dreary parliamentary business. And now, at least for the short-term, I'll be running the estate."

"You may yet escape the parliamentary business."

Adam conceded the point. "Hannah is sure the baby is a boy. Apparently there are ways women know. She said something about the way it's lying, and no morning sickness. But if the worst happens, I will have to find tutors and see him educated properly to eventually take up his seat in the House of Lords."

"His mother will see to the early years of his education. The child is not even in his cradle yet. And George is still alive and may surprise all of us. Anyway, when you marry, you will have your own children to raise."

If he married. In truth, he'd given little thought to the prospect until his return home yesterday. Yet he meant what he'd told Robert Braithwaite this morning; that he intended to court Emma, if she permitted it. No other woman interested him. Not a one of the other young ladies at the ball last night had caught his notice. He could not remember a single face or name. Just as none of the women at all the balls and receptions in Europe remained in his memory. Only Emma. Emma with her beauty and her gentleness and her passion for helping others.

"Given your silence," Oliver commented, "I take it that your thoughts are occupied on this issue. As they seemed to be over dinner and the dancing." His face relaxed into a grin. "Of course, should you marry Emma, she may be able to provide advice on keeping the Rengarth account books up to date."

He shouldn't be surprised that Oliver had noticed his distracted state, and correctly interpreted it. But he responded as lightly as his brother's remark, and quoted the marriage service. "'*And thereto I plight thee my troth and my account books?*' I doubt that's the recipe for a good marriage."

"Nor is pity." The flat statement might have held an edge of bitterness.

"Indeed." When they were youths, young ladies had frequently gushed their sympathy to Oliver, keen to 'help' him. Determinedly independent, he'd hated it. And apparently still endured it. "Is there anyone who has captured your affections?" Adam asked.

"No." The answer came just a little too quickly. "There are goals I plan to accomplish. Marriage isn't one of my priorities."

Adam didn't press any more questions on the matter. Oliver would tell him when and if he wanted to.

As if sensing that his master was not entirely happy, Zeus stood, stretched, and nudged his knee. Oliver drained his glass and set it down. "It's getting late. I'll take Zeus out, and then head to bed."

On the spur of the moment, Adam asked, "Would you like to ride in the morning? After an early breakfast?"

The slow smile on Oliver's face made the prospect of rising early totally worthwhile. "Yes. That would be good."

As Oliver and the dog left through the terrace door, two of the candles in the candelabra flickered and died in the sudden draught. The remaining one cast only a small circle of light.

Alone in the room, Adam found himself reluctant to move from the soft comfort of the armchair to relight the candles or retire to his room. Fatigue and the effects of the port weighted his limbs.

Yet, despite all his concerns and unsolved problems, a surprising sense of peace settled in him. Probably not entirely due to the port. Being here at Rengarth—home—seemed a world away from the courts and political intrigues of Europe, and from the war-weary soldiers, merchants and peasants who had suffered so much for so long.

Telling his family of his decision to leave the army made it final. But he couldn't, yet, imagine himself as anything other than an army officer.

Eleven years since he'd left school at eighteen and his father had purchased his first commission for him. In the first few years, seeing little serious action, he'd loved the work, the camaraderie, the physical and intellectual challenges. But after his disastrous proposal to Emma, his regiment had shipped out not to the West Indies as he'd expected, but to Portugal and the hell of the Peninsular campaign.

The things he'd seen, participated in, *done*, in those years of war remained with him, memories as harsh and deep as physical wounds, leaving invisible scars. He still sometimes woke in the night, sweating, thrashing, shouting in the grip of nightmares, and there were moments when loud noises or crowds brought a paralyzing sense of alarm and dread.

Yet here at Rengarth—with his family, with Emma—some of the ugliness he'd carried for so long seemed less intense, the scars less painful.

The life ahead required courage, if a different form than battle courage. Oliver was right about the coming challenges: poor harvests, compounded by unemployment and low factory wages. It might well be a bleak winter for many.

He'd have to start imagining himself as Mr. Adam Caldwell, steward of his brother's estate, and become that man.

And he'd have to find a place for himself as older brother of a tribe of brothers and sisters. He could hardly continue to give orders and maintain discipline and performance in the way he'd done in the army.

He set down his empty glass. He could keep the best parts of Major Caldwell, the skills he'd learned, the knowledge of himself and his strengths. Yet there were other aspects of Major Caldwell that he must learn to let go.

Maybe somewhere, maybe, he might find an echo of the light young man who'd laughed with Emma and loved her and believed in a shining future, in that golden summer, long ago.

But that young man had been a fool, lacking in judgement, and for all that she'd been courteous and friendly since his return, that could well be graciousness on her part, despite his ungentlemanly thoughtlessness when he'd delivered his ill-thought proposal.

CHAPTER 13

Emma undressed and unpinned her hair with Kate's assistance and then sent the yawning girl upstairs to her bed with the other maids. Leaving a candle burning and with a shawl over her robe, she sat in the chair before the fire with the three letters Kate had brought.

The pleasant evening with Adam's family made her miss her own family, so she opened Sophia's first, almost crumbling the seal in her hurry to read it. Dated in mid-February, her sister assured her in the first lines that she and her baby daughter were both well, with the little one thriving and growing out of her gowns. Then news of Lucy, that she was safely delivered of a baby girl the week before.

Emma's vision blurred and she closed her eyes and murmured a prayer of thanks that Lucy and her child were safe. Or at least were, back in February, almost six months ago.

Lucy was recovering well, Sophia wrote, and had asked her to pass on to Emma her promise to write soon. But both their husbands had left Calcutta with the regiment for the north, to enforce the treaty in Nepal. Lieutenant Shelbourne, Lucy's husband, barely had time to see his daughter before departing.

Emma sat for some minutes, reading and re-reading the few paragraphs, hearing Sophia's soft voice. Two sisters, two nieces, so far, far away. Her heart ached with longing, and she brushed her fingertips over the inked words, as if that might somehow eradicate the distance and bring her sisters closer. At least the victory in Nepal had been accomplished with minimal losses, Jeremy had mentioned at dinner. There was every chance that her brothers-in-law were safely back home now with her sisters.

Outside in the night, an owl hooted somewhere nearby, stirring her from her thoughts. She refolded Sophia's letter and reached for the others.

The next letter, from her insurance company and dated yesterday in response to hers of the same day, apologized that they would not be able to send an agent until Monday.

Emma put it aside. Mr. Penry had been able to attend, after all.

The address on the third letter was in an untidy, barely legible hand, and the seal an unfamiliar one.

'My dearest Sister...'

The paper shook so much she could scarcely read the words made blurry by welling tears.

'I know this letter may come as a shock. I am deeply sorry that I could not send word before now, as I fear that rumors of my death have been widely spread.'

Her breath catching raggedly in gasps and sobs, she hastily skimmed the next lines. *'...explain when I can...I am in England... injuries healing...home at Larkfell within days.'*

Injuries healing. Home within days. The brief words said so little. What kind of injuries prevented him from returning? Where and how had he been hurt? Where was he now? Why hadn't he come straight home?

She read on, searching for answers.

'I beg of you, tell no-one that you have heard from me. It may be dangerous. And I must warn you, with utmost urgency, against trusting our cousin Francis Braithwaite, in any circumstance. I have every reason to believe that he means you harm.'

Her heart pounded. No answers, and yet more questions. Francis meant her harm? He was annoying, obnoxious, insulting—yes; but dangerous? She could scarcely conceive it. And yet...there'd been the fire, and Mr. Winslow's murder.

'*I did eventually receive your letters of last December and I was saddened to learn of our father's passing. How lonely you must be there...*'

Tears welled in her eyes, blurring the lines again.

'*I am sure that the business is thriving under your stewardship. I hope to soon be in a position to relieve you of that burden.*'

There were only a few more lines on the page, the untidy script a challenge to read. Perhaps he'd injured his hand, and struggled to hold a quill.

'*You may send word to me C/- Mr. David Penry, at the Fat Goose Inn in Halifax. He is making some enquiries on my behalf, and can be trusted.*

Mr. *Penry* was making enquiries for *Matthew?* No, she hadn't mistaken the words.

She checked the date of the letter. Wednesday. Three days ago. He'd engaged Penry before the fire. Before Mr. Winslow's murder. To enquire about...what? And why?

Darn Matthew for being mysterious. Not like him at all—he'd always found it impossible to be anything but open and honest. Disarmingly open, at times.

Something must have occurred to make him so secretive and distrustful. Something significant.

'*...tell no-one that you have heard from me.*'

But she had to tell Adam. Adam could be trusted implicitly, and perhaps he could make some sense of Matthew's warnings, of Mr. Penry's involvement. And she had to tell Adam because her brother was alive, but in danger, and after months of fearing him dead she needed to share that news—the relief and the alarm—with *someone*.

Distracted, hoping he had not retired for the night, she was halfway down the corridor before she remembered she was in her night clothes, her feet bare. She should not see a gentleman in this state of undress. But as she hesitated she heard footsteps, and there was the glow of light from a candle as Adam came to the top of the stairs, and saw her.

Her own candle flickering with the shakiness of her hand, she hesitated. She should go back to her room. She should have gone in search of Louisa, not Adam. She shouldn't be talking with him, alone, in her nightwear.

She didn't move, waiting until he came closer. He carried his jacket over one arm, his white shirt sleeves catching the light of the candle he carried.

He searched her face as he approached. "Is something wrong, Emma?"

"Yes. No." As if that made sense. She had to explain. "This is a letter from Matthew." She kept her voice low, although the words tumbled out quickly. "He's alive. He's in England. But he says there's danger. That Francis is dangerous. And he's been injured, and Mr. Penry is…" She gulped in a breath and thrust the letter at him. It might make things clearer than she was doing, with her thoughts leaping all over the place. "I can't work out what's happening."

Emotion welled again, the overwhelming, conflicting tangle of happiness and uncertainty and fear that wouldn't let her mind rest for even a moment. She covered her mouth with her hand, determined not to cry, not to fall apart as she had last night. But tears brimmed and she turned her face away, tried to wipe her eyes with the back of her hand. "I'm sorry."

He set his candle down on the hall table, the letter beside it, and tossed his jacket over the adjacent chair before he rescued the candle from her unsteady hand.

"Don't apologize, Emma. Sudden good news after so long not knowing is still a shock." They stood close, so close she heard his slow exhalation before he brushed a tear away from her damp cheek with the softest touch of his thumb.

It almost undid her, that gentle caress. The reminder of everything she'd lost in refusing his proposal. The loneliness of the years since then, being strong for everyone else, hiding her own emotions, burying her own dreams, because both her father and her brother were better at dreaming than *doing*. Long, long years when she'd remembered, ached for, the tender intimacies of heart and soul and body they'd shared, and missed them as if he'd torn away a part of herself when he'd left.

If she didn't distance herself from him, she'd make a fool of herself, throw herself into his arms and weep.

"I'm sorry," she said again, although she found insufficient resolve to move away from him. "I should be stronger than this. I shouldn't be crying."

As if to steady her, he placed his hands gently on her shoulders, his palms warm through the fine lawn of her night robe, and she could not draw her gaze away from the intensity of his dark, deep-set eyes. "You're one of the strongest, bravest women I know, Emma. You always were and you still are. A few tears now doesn't change that."

His words and the memories they evoked made her smile, despite the tumbling emotions. And it seemed important, in this moment, to be honest. To match his honesty and to acknowledge the past between them. "You always encouraged me to believe myself capable of strength. I valued that. I value it now. I'm…" She hesitated, afraid of saying too much, of overstepping. But he'd called her courageous. She lifted her chin and finished softly, "I'm very glad that you're staying at Rengarth."

The flickering lights from the candles became a soft glow, and in the quietness of the corridor, the stillness of the darkened house, a sense of calm enveloped her. Adam's friendship could be counted on. His friendship, his support, his help in this current complex situation.

"So am I." A rare smile touched his eyes. "I didn't have much choice," he admitted, "but now I am grateful for it, too."

Muted noises drifted up the stairs from below; servants readying the house for night, dousing candles and closing doors.

"Come in here," Adam said, gesturing to the open door of a sitting room. "While I read Matthew's letter."

She carried in the letter and his coat while he brought the candles, setting them on a writing desk facing the windows. A sofa, a chaise longue, armchairs and a side table completed the furnishings.

Adam closed the door. "Mother mostly uses this room for her morning correspondence, before she goes downstairs." He took his coat from her hands and then hesitated. "Are you warm enough?"

She nodded, drawing her shawl closer around her robe, more for decency than warmth. It was a large shawl and other than the fact that she wore no stays, her night gown, robe and shawl covered her far more thoroughly than a ball dress did. But with her hair in a braid down her back, and her feet bare, she was all too aware of her state of undress, by social standards.

Too restless to sit on the inviting sofa, she remained standing, wandering the room while attempting to settle her thoughts into order.

Adam stood by the desk to read the letter, angling it to catch the light of the candles. His tanned hands contrasted with the white of his shirt sleeves, and he'd loosened his cravat. Although he kept his hair shorter now, the dark locks still tried to curl, skimming the edge of his collar.

She should not be watching him while he read.

She pretended an interest in the books on a shelf, although barely able to read the spines in the dim light. But in Adam's quiet company, the turbulent emotions of the shock of Matthew's letter began to settle. Not exactly to calmness; her brother was not safe and too many questions remained. But he was alive and she would see him soon and together they would deal with whatever threat Francis posed.

Her emotions regarding Adam were an entirely different matter. The play of light and shadow on his face as he read highlighted the changes in him. If she'd never seen him smile she might say his was a hard face, the firm shape of forehead, cheek and jaw without softness. Lines creased his brow as he deciphered the worst of Matthew's script. He'd aged more than eight years during his time at war, become a mature, solemn man who smiled so rarely he might almost be a different person.

And yet it occurred to her that despite the superficial changes, she did know this grave man. That underneath the fun-loving, light-hearted young man there'd always been a solidity. Kindness, self-discipline, courage, responsibility—he'd shown all those qualities in a myriad of small ways even as he laughed and joked. His unobtrusive watchfulness for Oliver. The way he'd looked out for the younger ones. His friendly courtesy to all, regardless of status. And the way he'd loved her, his passion restrained by gentleness and honesty, always considering her wishes first.

Perhaps his character hadn't changed so much as it had developed, fulfilling the promise of his youth. All of his actions these past two days were in keeping with his character and the circumstances. In the urgency of those circumstances she'd seen his courage, his decisiveness, his leadership and his dedication in action.

The truth could not be denied. Her love for him had not faded with time. Instead, she was falling deeper, more certainly, in love with the mature man he'd become.

A love with no future. She turned away from him and faced a portrait on the wall, closing her eyes to control the threat of tears. She must be sensible and remember that. He was helping her as a gentleman neighbor helped a lady with no menfolk to assist her.

Paper rustled as he refolded the letter. Thoughtful, considering for a moment before he spoke. "I spoke with Penry briefly after the inquest. He is going to call tomorrow. He will be able to give us some more answers."

Relieved to think on more practical matters, she schooled her expression to calmness and turned and asked, "He's not an insurance agent, is he?"

"I doubt it. But there are men who are skilled at investigating all kinds of matters."

He held the letter out to her, and she came close enough to take it, tucking it into the pocket in her robe. "I know. I engaged two men in the colonies, recommended by Lord Castlereagh's office, to make enquiries into Matthew's whereabouts. But their names are Ballantyne and Hays. Not Penry."

"Good thinking. I'd probably have done something similar myself."

His matter-of-fact approval of her actions erased the months of uncertainty about whether she'd wasted her money and the agents' time. She'd had no-one to advise her. But he understood that world of intelligence and investigation. He'd have military and government contacts through his work with Wellington and the embassy in Paris, and wouldn't have needed to write to the foreign secretary's office.

"Mr. Hays believes the expedition may have overwintered in the unsettled areas, " she told him. "And promised to make further enquiries."

"It's been a hard winter there. Mail may have been delayed."

"Yes. Especially from the remote settlements." The mere thought of the cold of winter made her pull the shawl closer around her and clasp her hands in front of the crossed ends. "I wish Matthew had been more specific about the danger," she added, speaking her thoughts aloud. "About why he distrusts Francis. They never liked each other much. Although I confess I always found Francis difficult to like, too, but I never had reason to fear him."

"Until now."

"Until last night," she acknowledged. She suppressed a shudder, remembering Francis's despicable remarks.

Perhaps something of her unease showed in her face for he said with a sudden vehemence, "I wish I'd had the satisfaction of throwing him out."

So did she. But Francis wouldn't have gone quietly. "He'd have only made a scene," she said. "None of us needed that."

"No. You're right." He seemed about to say something else, and stopped. He still stood near the desk, and he thrust his hands in his pockets, stared at the floor, the tension in his shoulders evident under the fine linen of his shirt sleeves.

The distant sound of the tall clock in the hall striking midnight brought a reminder that she was in her night clothes, alone with a man. While sneaking time alone together when they were younger had been exciting, she was wiser now of the consequences and had no wish to cause scandal or to discomfort him. "It's very late. I shouldn't keep you up. I'll go."

He looked up again, his face serious, eyes troubled. "Not just yet." He drew in a deep breath. "Emma, there has been no chance to say this, but I have long owed you an apology. I am ashamed of my behavior that summer. I took liberties that I should not have done. And that last day—I have always regretted my discourteous words. I should have apologized long before now."

Their first time alone since his return. Despite the fact she shouldn't be here, he looked so wretched she hastened to close the space between them to reassure him. "Adam, there is nothing to forgive. Everything we did..." Her face flushed with heat but she could not let him think himself to blame. "We did together. You took nothing that I didn't give freely. I could have called a stop if I had wished to. But I chose not to. And that last day..." She laid her hand lightly on his arm. The linen was soft under her fingers, the muscles beneath it tense and hard. She owed him honesty and courage. She lifted her head so that she could see his face. "I have many regrets, too. That I didn't explain properly why I refused you. That I didn't ask you to wait a year. That I didn't tell you how much I wanted to be your wife."

He exhaled a long, long breath, his gaze locked with hers. Reaching out to her, with one thumb he traced a caress on her cheek so gentle her heart faltered in its rhythm, fluttering as if she was seventeen again.

"You were wiser than I was, Emma," he said softly. "We were so young. *I* was so young. I was a fool to think that you could up and leave your family on my whim. And I was a naïve idiot to think that being a junior officer's wife would be any kind of easy life. After a few months in Portugal I was glad, for your sake, that you'd refused me."

"I was never glad of it," she murmured. "It was one of the hardest decisions I've ever had to make. I am sorry that I hurt you."

It was meant to be fleeting, the kiss she touched to his mouth. Just one. Only one caress, one gift of affection, an assurance that she held only fond memories. But one taste of him brought a thousand memories alight. She couldn't draw away and his mouth found hers again in soft kisses of need and longing that became one deep, long, hungry kiss, saturating her senses. There was only Adam holding her to him, and her hands on the solidity of his shoulders and his mouth on hers and desire flaring like a bonfire between them. She could feel his chest through the thin cotton of her night clothes, the woven texture of his silk waistcoat against her breasts, the imprint of his hands on her back, under her shawl and without the barrier of stays, drawing her closer, closer.

Any moment now, one of them would come to their senses. She would come to her senses. Not yet. Please not yet.

Her heart, her soul, remembered their past intimacies and craved *more*. More touch, more kisses and closeness and the heaven of his caresses under their clothes, the bliss of discovering him and his taste and shape and skin with her fingers and her lips.

All the years of remembering and loneliness and futile longing warred with the small part of her that whispered, *this is not wise*. But all her senses felt alive, alight with passion and vitality, and her heart pounded as fast as Adam's did, under her hand. She imagined undoing his waistcoat, button by button, sliding her hands under his shirt...

This is not wise.

The moment she hesitated, paused in kissing him, he stilled and stopped. "Emma?" he asked against her mouth.

"We shouldn't..." She echoed her conscience, which seemed the only coherent part of her. "This is not wise."

But she did not draw away from him, and he kept his arms around her. A small fact to be grateful for because her bones were as useless as flummery to support her.

"Emma, I'm sorry. If I offended you, or made you uncomfortable."

She spoke over him. "No. Don't you dare apologize. I kissed you. We kissed each other. But there are at least a dozen reasons why we should...why we should be sensible." *She* should be sensible. She had to be, to protect her heart. "Perhaps it's just nostalgia. You've been back only a couple of days. It's been eight years, and maybe we hardly know each other anymore. And besides, there are so many uncertainties just now, for me, anyway."

"You are right. I know I've changed, Emma, and I'm not sure I'm near worthy enough for you. And yet..." He traced her cheek with a gentle finger. "It's still there, isn't it? You and I."

She nodded, without words. It was still there, that bond between them. But it was she who was unworthy, not him.

He swallowed, took a small step backwards, drew her shawl over her shoulders. It did not help to warm the chill in her heart.

CHAPTER 14

Adam did not sleep for a long time. Fatigue from too many nights with too little rest made his body heavy, but his mind played his kiss with Emma over and over again and refused to relax into sleep.

During hot summer days stranded behind enemy lines in Spain he'd discovered that a man weak from thirst thinks only of water. It becomes an obsession. One small taste is blissfully sweet but not enough to quench the thirst, only to heighten it.

He turned over, punched the pillow into submission, determined to fix his thoughts on anything but Emma.

He needed to sleep. If he didn't sleep he'd be exhausted, and exhausted men were slow to react and made mistakes. To keep Emma safe he must be rested enough to be alert.

She was right to call a halt to their kiss. He agreed with many of the very sound reasons she'd given as to why they should refrain from such intimacy. He had only just returned. He had changed and she didn't know him now. Hell, he didn't know himself sometimes.

His heart wasn't listening to reason.

And his mind was failing to tear itself away from thoughts of her. Maybe if he contemplated Matthew's guarded revelations? Francis's motives? No, too connected to Emma, and too inclined to rouse his anger.

Accounts. Finances. That should send him to sleep. When he sold his commission and invested the proceeds, what percent could he earn on it? How much would he have to live on? What would he have to offer Emma?

Emma. Everything kept circling back to her.

He gave the pillow another punch. So much for the discipline of his mind. As unruly as the drunkest new recruit. At least where Emma was concerned.

He surrendered to the inevitable. But he would not imagine kissing her. Caressing her. Giving her pleasure. Making love with her.

No. *No.* Dancing with her. That's what he'd think about. He didn't need a great deal of musical talent to replay the music in his head. Melodic. Slow. And Emma, so lovely in her pale blue dress. So graceful in her dancing. Dancing with him. Smiling at him, her eyes shining in the candlelight.

~

Emma stirred from a restless sleep, wisps of dreams clinging and confusing her for a moment as to where she was.

Rengarth Castle. She'd danced with Adam last night. Kissed him. Relived that kiss and yes, imagined more in her dreams. A mix of imagination and memory, if she was being honest with herself.

And that kiss was the most imprudent thing she'd done recently, acting on impulse and desire instead of reason and sense. Yet, like their youthful explorations, she found it hard to regret. At least she knew something of passion and desire as a result, with memories to carry with her in the likely event of her spinsterhood.

Lady Rengarth had told her to sleep as long as she wished as the household did not rise early, but she was wide awake now. She must not waste time brooding on what could not be. Too many other matters awaited her attention.

She pushed back the bedclothes and sat on the edge of the bed. Time to start the day. Fortunately, with more optimism than yesterday. Matthew was alive, and coming home soon. Mr. Penry was calling later and he'd explain what had happened to Matthew, and why Francis was a threat. And Adam... Adam was a true friend she could rely on.

Kate came in with a large jug of washing water, wished her good morning and offered to lay out the gowns she'd brought. Emma chose the grey silk dress she often wore to church. Today she would attend Saint Mary's in Rengarth village with the Caldwell family, rather than her small parish church near Larkfell where she usually attended.

Kate had barely finished arranging her hair when the housekeeper, Mrs. Simpson, knocked on the bedroom door. A kindly woman, dedicated to the family, and helpful to their guest.

"There's a young lad downstairs, miss, who says he has a message for you. But he insists he can tell only you."

A message only for her? It had to be from Matthew.

Emma hastened downstairs with Mrs. Simpson. The youth, maybe fourteen, fifteen years old, waited in the hall under the very watchful eyes of two footmen. Dressed in a well-worn coat, scuffed boots, and holey stockings, he nervously clutched a battered hat in his hands. Not a lad she recognized.

"I am Emma Braithwaite. You have a message for me?"

"Yes'm." He cast a wary glance at the footmen and the housekeeper, and she led him out through the open door on to the portico. Not exactly out of earshot, and definitely not out of the sight of the footmen.

"You can tell me here."

He shifted on his feet, hardly looking at her. "It's the weaver, miss. Jacob Fryer."

Her heart fell. Jacob, not Matthew. She daren't hope for good news. "What is the message?"

"He were choppin' wood and he just fell down." The words rushed out of the boy's mouth. "Out of his senses. Goody Fryer says you must come at once."

Jacob, who'd woven for Braithwaites since she was a child, who'd trained a generation of weavers. Chopping wood after his head injury yesterday was hardly 'resting', but then who else would keep his kitchen fire going for his young family?

"Of course. I'll come directly." A mile or so to Jacob's cottage. About half-way between Rengarth and Larkfell. "Can you run for the doctor in Hartdale?" she asked the lad. "Assure him I will cover his account."

He nodded, and without hesitating in case of payment, he bolted down the staircase, into the grey but dry morning.

Emma returned to the hall. "Has Major Caldwell come down for breakfast?" she asked the footmen.

"The Major has gone riding with Mr. Caldwell, ma'am."

Riding. With Oliver. Now Adam was home, would they be revisiting their old haunts? If they'd ridden up the pack horse paths over the fells behind Rengarth, they might be hours yet.

She could not delay for hours. Jacob might be dying.

Mrs. Simpson waited, in patient attendance.

"Lady Rengarth? Is it too early to see her?" she asked the housekeeper. Probably. Church wasn't for hours yet. No necessity for a lady to be up and dressed this early.

"Her Ladyship and the young ladies have not risen yet, miss," the housekeeper answered, "but the young gentlemen are in the breakfast room."

She could hardly request a carriage without the Countess's authority. A horse, perhaps, but she wasn't dressed for riding. And it was only a mile—she could walk that, in less time than it would take to change into a habit, or to have a horse saddled.

In normal circumstances, she wouldn't hesitate to set off and walk by herself. She'd walked and ridden all over the district, visiting spinners, weavers, woolcombers and their families. But these past two days were far from normal, and although it was only a mile, out of respect for Adam and the family's concern for her she had to be sensible.

"I will ask Master Jeremy and Master Benjamin if they will accompany me. Mrs. Simpson, would you ask Kate to bring down a bonnet and my reticule? And if I could borrow an umbrella?"

"Certainly. Shall I have a footman go with you as well, Miss Braithwaite? You will be able to send him with any messages necessary."

Please God she wouldn't need to send any messages. Not to the vicar, not to the undertaker. "Thank you. That would be wise. And please inform Major Caldwell of my whereabouts when he returns."

Adam's brothers rose to their feet, courteous young gentlemen, as she entered the breakfast room, and Jeremy leapt to pull out a chair for her. When she explained her mission and its urgency, they instantly agreed that she should go at once without waiting for Adam, and that they would accompany her.

As she tied her bonnet on in the hall, she caught a glimpse in the mirror of Jeremy, drawing his brother aside, and, despite his hushed voice, heard him telling Benjamin to follow his orders without hesitation.

"You're not an officer yet," Benjamin retorted. Hard to snap in a whisper, and he didn't succeed.

Jeremy met her gaze in the mirror, and gave up trying to speak quietly. "Then remember what Adam ordered yesterday," he told his brother sharply. "He *is* an officer."

An officer who'd given her young protectors some clear instructions regarding her safety. She didn't ask what they were. Their journey to Halifax and back yesterday was without incident. A one-mile walk in the vicinity of Rengarth surely held little risk.

Within minutes they left the house, one lad on each side of her, a footman following behind, carrying two umbrellas although the clouds were high and non-threatening. Not far from Rengarth they turned off the road to Hartdale and followed the lane to the east, towards Larkfell. Yesterday's cold winds had succeeded in drying the mud, but there was little breeze today and they were not chilled at all.

They walked briskly, companionably but with little conversation. The lane dipped down a slight hill and narrowed as they entered the Rengarth woods. The trees arched overhead, almost forming a tunnel, and the cool, mossy scent of the damp undergrowth filled the air. Centuries of people and carts traversing the lane had worn it down into a wide furrow through the woods, the banks sometimes two or more feet high.

"That's the path to the old chapel ruins." Jeremy pointed to a place where steps were cut into the low bank and a narrow grassy track disappeared into the trees. "I remember the picnic we had there, Miss Braithwaite. You were too young to come, Benjamin."

"It was a lovely picnic," she said.

She remembered every moment of that sun-filled day among the fallen stones in the flower-filled clearing. With her brother and sisters, and most of Adam's, except George and Benjamin. A day away from constraints and responsibilities and full of laughter and games and fun. And she remembered the next day, too, when it had just been her and Adam, stealing some time alone together. Sunshine and magic and the explorations of first love...

Her face warmed and she lowered her head, as if watching her feet on the ruts in the road. The memories belonged in the past, along with the memories of last night. Jacob lay injured, perhaps dying. Loyal, hard-working, he'd raised his brothers, married late, and still had young children of his own. Head injuries could be fatal, even days after the event. She should have insisted on the doctor seeing him on the day of the fire.

The lane curved around and dipped further down to the old stone bridge across the brook. The water flowed quickly, higher than usual with the recent rains, tumbling over the series of low waterfalls. A pretty, peaceful place that on another day she might stop to admire. Not today.

As they approached the bridge, two doves darted out from the trees beyond, fluttering as if startled.

Something moved in the trees and a horse whinnied, another answering it. Emma slowed. So, too, did Jeremy.

Three figures stepped out on to the lane ahead of them. Two men and a younger lad. All three with kerchiefs concealing most of their faces, and clubs in their hands.

Emma's heart began to race and she took hold of Jeremy's arm, warning him in a low voice, "He's the boy who brought the message. I recognize his coat."

The lad wasn't nervous now. He swaggered as he moved forward with the other two men.

A trap. He'd led her in to a trap.

She turned to flee, but two more men had stepped out behind them.

"*Run!*" Jeremy hissed at his brother, pushing him towards the embankment.

Emma strode some paces forward to keep the bandits' attention on her. "What is the meaning of this?" she demanded. "Move out of my way. Lord Rengarth's brother will be along shortly so you'd best run now before he catches you."

The two men and the lad in front were on the bridge, only yards away. "Oh, we're goin' to run all right," one of them said. "But we're taking you with us, miss."

"No. You will not." Jeremy stepped in front of her, a knife in one hand, an umbrella in the other.

Benjamin scrambled up the embankment. She risked a quick glance behind her. One of the men had a pistol raised, aiming at Benjamin. The footman raced at him, umbrella raised, and she heard herself scream "*No!*" as the pistol fired. Benjamin gave a sharp shout as if in pain and disappeared into the undergrowth, as the footman and the shooter fell to the ground, fighting.

She had no weapon, only her reticule weighted with coins and keys, but she swung it as hard as she could at the second man as he advanced towards her. It hit him on the shoulder but he just laughed and grabbed it. She let it go and began to run but he caught up to her and shoved her forward, hard.

She lost her footing, falling fast. Her knees, hands hit the ground and then her face, her bonnet shoved back by the force.

Pain seared through her as a heavy weight pressed on her back, pinning her to the ground. Panicked, she struggled, but the man knelt on her, holding her down.

Not far from her, the shooter punched the footman's head, then pushed himself to his feet. The footman didn't move.

Bracing against pain, Emma turned her throbbing head, trying to see past the crushed remains of her bonnet brim towards the shouts coming from the other direction.

Jeremy fought the men at the bridge. He wielded the umbrella, jabbed with his knife, but it was three against one. They disarmed him quickly, and as he stood, unarmed, crowded by the three of them, one of the men swung his club.

Emma squeezed her brimming eyes shut. But she heard the soft thud of the blow connecting, and when she opened her eyes again, Jeremy lay in a crumpled heap in the lane.

CHAPTER 15

Despite dark clouds to the west, the rain held off. They'd ridden up onto a ridge along the old pack horse tracks, then looped around to come via another ridge to the hill behind the castle. Adam had naturally resumed the habit of alerting Oliver of any rough ground or rocks, as if he hadn't been away for years. As if his brother's horse wasn't accustomed to following, and steady on its feet. Zeus loped along beside them, never far from his master.

At the top of Rengarth Fell, they made their way in unspoken agreement to a rocky overhang, sheltered from the breeze. Tying the horses to a crooked, wind-swept tree, they sat on a large flat rock, with a view out over the castle, the village, and down the valley to Hartdale. A view that Oliver would never see again. A view that Adam had described to him each time they came, noting the changes, describing the activity below. Now he was here again, and there were so many changes he did not know where to start. This valley that was once the center of his world seemed so much smaller than in his memories. A byway, secluded and isolated from the world of kings and emperors, politics and war.

"Is there much that is different?" Oliver asked, when Adam didn't immediately begin to describe the view.

"Mostly me, I think." Not able to elaborate on the muddled state of his mind, he shook the uneasiness away and focused his eyes on the landscape, in an attempt to catalogue the specifics. "Some of the valley has been enclosed into smaller fields. There are more stone fences, and more sheep in the valley rather than on the fells. It's all gray and green with blobs of white. Hartdale has spread. There are three new factories, and rows of houses around two of them." Straight rows, unlike the center of the old town, with its ancient crooked streets around the market square and the churchyard.

So much change, and yet...and yet his ties to this place remained. Strengthened, in the commitments he'd made to act as guardian for George's heir if necessary.

A few days ago the possibility had unsettled him. Now it did not seem so unwelcome. He didn't need to wonder why.

From here he could just see Emma's home, Larkfell, nestled on the other side of the valley, beyond the woods and the scattering of cottages where the lane met the road that went north-east across the hills towards Haworth and Keighley. Matthew Braithwaite would be home soon, perhaps within days, and along with him an explanation of his warning about Francis.

Movement where the lane entered the woods near Rengarth caught his eye. From this distance he couldn't see clearly but he squinted to get a better look. A figure, progressing slowly, waving his arms. As he watched, three figures ran from the house, one of them in white. Emma? One of his sisters? No good reason for any of them to run like that.

Instinct made his pulse race and Adam reached for his horse's reins. "There's something wrong at Rengarth. Someone's in trouble." If he'd been by himself, he'd be down there in minutes. But with Oliver-

"You go," Oliver said instantly.

"I can't leave you here." Not up on the fell, where the path down was steep, and the weather could change quickly.

"I'll walk the horse down, with Zeus. We'll be fine."

The thought of leaving Oliver alone warred with almost every ounce of honor in him. But his brother was remarkably independent, and that small huddle of people, and two figures now running, one to the woods, the other back towards the house, seemed likely to signify trouble.

"Go," Oliver ordered.

Adam swung himself into the saddle and rode off down the path. Slower than he wished, because of loose rocks and the steep slope, but the mare was steady-footed and as soon as they reached the bottom he urged her to a gallop. The path took him to the rear of the castle, where he found a flurry of activity at the stables, and Louisa in a white morning dress with Garrett, who issued orders briskly. Grooms saddled horses, a farm hand harnessed a horse to a farm cart.

Louisa, her face pale, a smear of blood red on her skirt, rushed across to Adam as he dismounted and clutched his arm, words spilling out breathlessly. "Adam! Thank heavens you're back. It's Emma. She's been taken. And Benjamin's been shot and Jeremy's hurt."

Each word speared a shaft of fear into him. Louisa never panicked, but she was close to it now. A groom mounted and wheeled his horse around. Adam took his sister by the shoulders to pull her out of his way. "How?" he demanded of her. "When? Tell me slowly."

She gulped in a breath. "Emma had a message that the weaver had collapsed. You weren't here, so she went with the boys and a footman. They were set upon in the woods. Not long ago. Benjamin was shot in the leg but he made it back here for help. We've sent a groom for the doctor and to raise the hue and cry." She nodded over to where Garrett helped load a stretcher and blankets on to the back of the cart. "Your friend Mr. Garrett suggested the cart to bring Jeremy and the footman back..." She choked on a sob.

Adam fought the urge to leap back on his horse and ride. The mare had already done miles today. With multiple urgent matters to attend to he must *think*, plan, organize. As if this was a battlefield. "Order the fastest horse to be readied for me," he told her. "I want every man who rides to be on a mount and ready to go. Send a boy up Rengarth Fell to find Oliver. Trust Garrett and tell him to go in the cart. Soldiers know what to do with injuries."

He left Louisa already giving more orders and bolted to the

house. He'd go after Emma, but he'd do it prepared, with whatever intelligence there was to be gathered. "Fetch my pistols at once," he told the butler as he entered the house. "My brother is...?"

"In the stillroom, sir."

His sister Phoebe had Benjamin trouserless, tending to his leg, while his mother hastily gathered jars, bottles and linen cloths, packing them into a leather bag.

Benjamin, his face scratched and marked with tear tracks, saw him first and attempted to rise. "I'm sorry, sir. I couldn't... You said to run for help. Jeremy said I had to. But I couldn't help her."

Adam laid a hand on his shoulder and gently pushed him back down on the chair. A quick glance at the wound on his thigh reassured him. A flesh wound, a graze, despite the blood on his shirt tails and discarded britches. Not shredded muscles or shattered bones. Phoebe's ministrations under their mother's guidance would take care of it.

And yet this was his little brother, not a soldier, and Jeremy and Emma were in an even worse predicament. Adam drew on every strand of discipline. Keep the troops calm. Gather intelligence. Make good decisions. "You did the right thing, Benjamin. Now tell me—how many were there, and which way did they go?"

His brother reported concisely. "Four men, and a boy a bit older than me. Four horses, I'm sure. One of them took Emma on his horse. They went east."

Adam made himself speak with a reassurance he didn't feel. "That's helpful. Was Emma hurt?"

"Not much, I don't think. She fought them." He sniffed, his eyes wide, battling to keep control. "They tied her up. But Jeremy's hurt bad, I think. And the footman. They weren't moving."

Adam clenched his jaw so tight his teeth ground together.

His mother fastened the strap on the leather bag. "I'll see to Jeremy and the footman. You're going after Emma?"

"Yes. I have to find her." But which way? East led to the Hartdale to Haworth road. They might have turned towards Hartdale, and from there to almost anywhere. Or they might take the Haworth road, and from there go north or east. Or they could be on any one of the numerous pack horse tracks that wound down from the fells and along the valleys.

His mother slipped two small bottles wrapped in cloth into a pouch and handed them to him. "Laudanum for pain or distress. The other is for wounds. God be with you, Adam."

The butler met him at the door and handed him his greatcoat, hat, and his pistols, already in a saddle holster. "Loaded, sir. Powder and bullets in your holster. And I brought a knife, in case you need it."

"Good. If a man called Penry comes, send him after me." Adam slid the knife into his boot before taking the rest. Outside, a stable-boy held a spirited gelding, with Louisa beside him, the cart coming up behind with Garrett on it and a farm hand driving it, and six men leading out the remaining horses.

Louisa caught his arm. "Mr. Garrett was talking with the grooms last night. One of them overhead something the night of the ball. He thinks it was one of the Braithwaite men. The man said, '*She mustn't be allowed to marry Adam Caldwell.*' It has to be Francis who's taken her, Adam. He wants Larkfell."

And Winslow's money. Francis Braithwaite's actions now made a terrifying sense. Defaming and undermining the company to isolate Emma, and persuade her into marriage so that he'd get whatever wealth she owned. And now he'd given up persuasion and resorted to force.

Adam secured the holster to the saddle and swung up on to the horse. Braithwaite would get neither Emma nor her inheritance.

~

With a dark hood over her head, a gag in her mouth and her hands tied in front of her, Emma had no choice but to cling to the saddle. The man who'd dragged her up on to the horse held her tightly as they cantered, and merely laughed when she tried to struggle.

"If you fall off, lass, you'll be right under the feet of the other horses." She froze as his hand closed tight over her breast, his breath hot against her neck. "But you wriggle all you like, my sweet."

The vile groping hand and stench of ale and stale sweat turned her stomach, but he was right—even if she somehow escaped his grip to throw herself from the horse, the pounding hooves of the horses following them would trample her to death. Groping could be endured. It did make her apprehensive of what worse might be in store for her, but she refused to let fear paralyze her. She must hold on, endure the discomfort, and remain aware and ready to escape the moment an opportunity arose. Everything depended on her remaining as calm as possible.

The sounds of the hoof beats began to have a different quality to them, and the tiny amount of light penetrating the cloth of the hood seemed brighter. They must have come out of the woods. Which meant they'd meet the road in less than a mile, and be more visible to anyone working the fields or traveling along the road.

Surely someone would notice her being carried off. She must look a sight, riding astride with her skirts and petticoats caught up and her stockings showing.

But it was not long before her captor slowed the horse to a halt, and she felt the relative cool of the small copse of trees around the ancient ruins of a convent.

At least two of the men hauled her down to the ground, none too gently. The horse whinnied as she staggered and fell against it, but one of the men gripped her around the waist and carried her in front of him. She heard other horses, and the creak of carriage harness and shafts.

They shoved her inside the carriage, her ankle catching painfully hard against the step and her bound hands barely breaking her fall to the floor. The door slammed shut.

They were taking her away by coach. No-one would see her inside a coach. Not unless she could sit up, pound on the window, make a commotion.

She struggled to sit up in the small space on the floor, reaching for the seat. Her hands found a cloth-covered leg. A man's leg.

She snatched her hand away as he chuckled.

"Hello, Cousin Emma."

Francis's voice. Her skin went cold.

"I do like to see you in your proper place," he continued, "Kneeling at my feet. Stay there and behave yourself, and I won't have to hurt you."

CHAPTER 16

Adam reached the woods within minutes, the half-dozen grooms, gardeners and farmhands close behind him. Near the bridge, Emma's bonnet lay crushed on the ground, not far from where the footman knelt by Jeremy. Anger threatened to cloud his reason. He mustn't let it.

"Keep going, find out which way they went, and follow," Adam instructed the head groom. "I won't be long."

He dismounted and went to his brother. The footman, not much older than Jeremy and almost as pale, dabbed a dampened neckerchief at the wound on Jeremy's forehead. Blood coated the cloth and glistened in his hair.

"Adam!" Jeremy grimaced in pain as he attempted to roll to his side.

Adam dropped to his knee beside his brother. That he was conscious and aware was no guarantee with a head injury. "Stay still. Lie back and keep as still as you can. That's important. Mother is coming. She'll be here very soon."

"I wasn't able to…"

"Don't blame yourself." Nothing was his brother's fault. Only his own. Adam cursed himself for not being there when Emma needed him. For letting his brothers carry the responsibility that should have been his. If Jeremy's injuries proved fatal or disabling, if Emma was harmed, he would never forgive himself. "You did everything you could. They won't get far. Every man in the district will be after them. Can you tell me anything about them?"

"Four men and the boy. Strangers." He frowned, perhaps in pain, perhaps in thought. "Not fine clothes. But one said..." That grimace *was* pain. "To hurry to get her—Miss Braithwaite—to the 'master'."

Jeremy's eyes drifted half-closed. The conflicting needs tore at Adam. *Jeremy or Emma...Jeremy or Emma.* He had to be practical. Help was coming for Jeremy. Emma had no-one but him to help her. "I must go after her, Jeremy. But Mother will be here in minutes. She'll look after you." He grasped his brother's shoulder. If this was the last time he saw Jeremy alive, he had to make it count. "I'm proud of you, Jeremy. Very proud that you're my brother."

Jeremy's eyelids flickered, and his mouth moved into a smile.

His throat painfully tight, Adam gave his brother's shoulder one last reassuring clasp before he pushed himself to his feet.

He caught his horse and set off at a gallop that did nothing to ease the anger raging in him against Braithwaite. The bastard had sent his thugs for Emma. They hadn't cared who they'd hurt to get her. If Emma was harmed, if Jeremy died, he'd see to it that they all hung for their crimes.

Outside a cottage in a small clearing, a man waited by the lane, with his wife and several small children, all neatly dressed. The weaver, Jacob. Hale and, if not hearty, at least upright and conscious.

Adam reined in his horse. "Did you send for Miss Braithwaite?" he demanded.

"No, sir. We didn't. We were inside, getting ready for church. I heard horsemen go past," Jacob added, "half an hour ago, perhaps. But I only just learned from your people what happened. My oldest boy's gone with them. I pray you find her, sir, and soon."

With little faith left in prayers, urgency drove Adam on. After the woodlands, the countryside opened into fields, most now bordered with grey stone walls. On any other day, people would be out working in the fields, to witness Emma's abduction. But on Sunday folk stayed inside, dressing for church or chapel, and few ventured out for anything other than essential chores until it was time to walk to the service.

Where the lane met the road to the north, he caught up with the men from Rengarth. Two of the three cottages here lay empty, falling in to disrepair. His men quizzed an old man outside the third. There'd been horsemen, and a coach. Not a fancy one. No, he hadn't seen which way they went. His wife had called him in for his porridge. But there'd been a cart past on the road a few minutes ago, taking them Methodists to chapel. And the Parson, going the other way.

Adam paused at the junction. The men from Rengarth milled around, the horses obliterating the direction of any wheel tracks turning from the lane. Trees and hedges bordered the road, so that he could not see far in either direction.

Where would Braithwaite take her? Assuming it *was* Braithwaite. He had no hard evidence, nothing other than suspicion and gut instinct. His and Louisa's.

Scotland. If Francis wanted Larkfell, he must believe he would gain it by marrying Emma. Scotland was the only place he could marry her quickly. Once over the border, they could be married with no banns, no license, no waiting. But only if Emma agreed. Or was coerced.

Which way? South back to Hartdale, and then the turnpike roads to the west and then north to Scotland via Carlisle? Or east, past Larkfell, and on towards the turnpike from Keighley through the Dales to Kendall, and the road to Scotland? The first route longer, but on well-maintained major roads. The second route shorter, but on lesser roads.

Adam's horse skittered restlessly. The men looked to him for a decision, but if he made the wrong one, they might never catch up with Emma.

Which way would Braithwaite choose? *Which way?*

A horseman galloped along the lane. Penry. Adam waited for him. He must have called at Rengarth, and heard the news.

Penry reined in the horse when he reached Adam. "Miss

Braithwaite is in great danger."

"Of being forced to marry?"

"Yes. Or worse. Francis Braithwaite believes Matthew is dead because he paid for him to be murdered. And very nearly succeeded."

Reckless. Francis was reckless, over-confident, arrogant. He believed he'd get away with this—with murder, arson, abduction.

Decision made.

"Take the road to Hartdale," he told Penry, "with three of the men. Alert the constable and the magistrate. If you find he's gone that way, go after him."

"And you?"

"I'm going east. Chances are he'll take her to Scotland through the Dales." He took a risk, wagering Emma's safety on the hunch that Francis might choose the shortest route, disregarding the lack of major roads. But minor roads meant fewer people to witness Emma's abduction. Fewer people to help her.

He set off with the remaining men. He sent one to Larkfell, to inform the household. Another two he sent off on the packhorse routes, over the hills to the west, to alert the authorities at Burnley, in case Braithwaite went that way and Penry didn't catch up with him. Surely a pair of horsemen on the hills had a good chance of beating a carriage traveling via the road.

He rode on alone. He had a good horse and none of the others could have kept up with him. Better that they covered the alternate routes, in case he was wrong.

At the first hamlet he came to, he reined in only long enough to question an old man, sitting on a bench beside the blacksmith's forge.

"Yes, sir. A black coach passed by 'ere. Two 'orses, it 'ad. Can't be sure how long ago, mind 'ee. Mebbe an hour. Mebbe less."

"Did you see the passengers? Was there a lady?"

"Can't say, sir. They went past that quick."

Adam rode on, the hoofbeats hammering the road as hard as the doubts hammering in his mind. A black coach could be anyone. A vicar visiting a distant parish. A gentleman traveling home to his family. A doctor called to attend a patient. In this wet summer, anyone who had a coach used it, rather than an open carriage. Braithwaite might have gone in the other direction.

The horse breathed forcefully by the time they reached the toll gate near Haworth, and stood, flanks heaving, while Adam waited impatiently for the toll keeper to amble across to him.

"Did a coach come through here?" he demanded.

"Aye, sir. A half hour or more ago. That'll be a penny, sir, for this section."

Adam delved in his pocket for a coin. "Open the gate. I must catch up with that coach."

The man shrugged as he fumbled with the gate catch. "Everyone's in a hurry. Gent with the coach was in a fine hurry, too."

"What did he look like?"

"Only saw him through the window. Tall. 'Bout your years, sir, far as I could tell. Brown hair, maybe."

All of that might be Braithwaite, and might not. "Did he have a lady with him?"

"Didn't see no lady. Had two men on the back. No livery, though. And two men riding alongside. Not fancy folk."

That sounded more like Braithwaite. Adam steered the horse around to be ready as soon as the way was open.

But the gate dragged on the ground and the toll keeper had to lift it to open it. "Oh, and he musta 'ad a dog inside," he continued conversationally, as if there was no urgency at all. "Heard it whimpering on the floor and I reckon he kicked it."

Adam urged the horse to speed the moment the gap was large enough. Rage thundered in his head. Not a dog. *Emma.* That bastard Braithwaite had Emma trapped in the coach, and he'd kicked her.

~

Emma squirmed her way up to a sitting position, leaning against the seat frame, as far from Francis as possible in the small space. After one try at the toll gate, she made no more attempts to alert anyone to her presence. Defying him only brought pain. And what was the use, when the ropes, gag and hood made her helpless? It made sense to bide her time, wait for a better opportunity to escape.

The road must have been churned up by the recent rains, and every bump of the coach jarred straight through the wooden floor into her bruised body, her thin skirts offering no cushioned protection. Little chance to rest, to preserve her strength. The linen gag made her mouth dry, and her face heated in the stuffiness of the hood. Ladies did not shout, but all the angry words she wanted to yell at him burned in her throat, and hot tears of frustration welled so that she clenched her eyes closed against them.

Calm. She had to remain calm. Fighting anger and fear, she made herself breathe slowly though her nose, in, out. In, out.

Francis had said nothing more after he kicked her and coolly threatened her with further violence if she did not remain silent. She heard the periodic rustle of a newspaper or magazine. He had her bound and gagged on the floor of the coach, and he passed the time by reading.

Everything she thought she knew about her cousin was wrong. This was not the arrogance and petty rivalry of their youth. The violence with which his men had injured the boys and kidnapped her, and his calculated cruelty towards her horrified her.

'I have every reason to believe that he means you harm.' If only Matthew had given more information. Or Mr. Penry. Then she might understand what had happened in Canada to Matthew, and what Francis wanted with her.

If he wanted her dead, she'd have been murdered in the forest. Was he planning to somehow force her in to marriage in order to acquire Larkfell? What seemed like an idle threat at the ball now seemed most likely. As his wife, everything she owned would become his, and she would be subject to his will in all matters. But he must know that she would never willingly consent to marry him. Even if this abduction ruined her reputation. Or ruined her.

Assuming Francis was responsible for Matthew's injuries, she had to keep him away from Larkfell, in case her brother returned there today. He might not be strong enough yet to deal with any further threat from Francis.

That Matthew was alive was knowledge to hold to herself for the moment. If Francis was taking her to Scotland, she could reveal it before any attempt at a marriage. Surely he would see no purpose in wedding her once he knew that Matthew lived. And in the two days it might take to reach the border, Adam, Mr. Penry, and perhaps even Robert, would be searching for her. If Benjamin had escaped, he'd have raised the alarm already. Adam would be in pursuit as soon as he could. Unless... unless his brothers were badly injured. Or worse.

The terror of that possibility brought a fresh wave of sobs that she struggled to suppress. She could not cry, she must not cry, with the gag limiting her breathing. Her fault that the boys were injured. She should have waited until Adam returned. He might never forgive her for her recklessness. He might even now be tending his brothers, or racing for a doctor.

She could not rely on Adam to be chasing the coach, to rescue her. She could only rely on herself to escape from Francis. And escape while the coach was moving was impossible. From time to time, she heard the hoof beats of other horses, and occasionally the voices of the coachman and others. No point throwing herself blindly from the coach with them all around, even if she could.

With her hands tied in front of her, there was a good chance she'd be able to remove the hood, and perhaps the gag, although she'd have to wait until Francis left her alone.

They must surely stop at a coaching inn soon, to change horses. He might go into the inn for refreshment. That would be her opportunity.

Until then, she'd stay huddled in her corner, and let Francis think her cowed and helpless.

~

Although he'd alternated between a canter and a trot, his horse was near the end of its endurance. He needed a fresh horse. A *good* fresh horse, not whatever old nag an inn might grudgingly hire out to him, when he was more than ten miles from Larkfell now and would be riding on for who knew how many more miles.

The toll road took him into Keighley, where Colonel Hampton lived. Hampton no longer rode, but he'd proudly mentioned the other night at the ball that Mrs. Hampton liked spirited horses and kept several.

Logic warred with Adam's reluctance to detour from the pursuit.

Logic won. A fresh horse was his only hope of catching up with Braithwaite's coach.

He sought directions from the toll keeper, who pointed out a large red-brick house on the outskirts of the town. Adam left the road and leapt over a stone wall to take a shortcut across a fallow field.

Admitted to the Colonel's study, Adam hurriedly explained his chase.

"Of course you must take one of our mounts." The Colonel immediately instructed his butler to see to the matter without a moment's delay. He reached for a quill and paper. "I'll give you a note for my old friend Giles, Lord Fairlie. He's at Gargrave, and has an excellent stable. He will not hesitate to assist."

Adam waited by the window, watching for the groom to bring the fresh horse, while the Colonel's quill scratched lightly across the paper. He kept his body still, his feet from pacing, but his thoughts raced even faster than he'd been riding.

Gargrave. Another twelve, thirteen miles beyond Keighley. If Braithwaite went that way. But what other road would he take? If—*if*—he was heading for Scotland, there was a chance he might turn east and cut across to the Great North Road. But that was a much longer route to Scotland than the turnpike along the edge of the Dales and on to Carlisle.

No, the Dales road had to be the most likely. Also the least populated, with only a scattering of villages. Few witnesses to Emma's abduction. Few people to help her.

Every minute ticking away on the mantle clock took her further away from him. What she must be going through, alone and frightened. He *must* find her, *had* to find her, and soon.

The time seemed to drag, yet in reality the clock hand moved less than ten minutes before the Colonel sealed the letter and gave it to Adam, the wax not yet hard.

"Good luck, lad. If I was younger I'd ride with you. Send word when you've found her."

The chestnut mare stretched out her neck and eagerly sped to a canter once they were on the road. The clouds had darkened while he'd been inside with the Colonel, and the wind whipped at the trees along the road.

A storm was coming, and only a fool would stay on the road when it began. A fool or an arrogant bastard like Braithwaite.

~

When they finally stopped to change horses, Emma tensed for a chance to escape. The coach leant slightly as Francis stood. Good. He was getting out.

"Stay exactly where you are, Emma. We won't be long. And my men will be on guard."

A rush of cold air hit her as he opened the door and stepped down, but then the latch clicked back into place and there was silence inside, except for her breathing. Outside, harnesses jingled, horses whinnied, and Francis gave orders for a fast pair to be fetched immediately. And for two of his men to guard the coach. To guard her. He didn't say as much, but his men were well aware she was there, captive. Given what they'd done to Jeremy, she had every reason to distrust and fear them.

She had maybe ten or fifteen minutes alone. Perhaps more, if the hostler and postilions were slow, or if Francis decided to dine at the inn. Perhaps less, if they were efficient, or if Francis tired of the unseasonable cold.

The rope around her wrists had little give in it, but she was able

167

to reach the cord of the sack around her head and loosen it. The fresh, cool air almost made her giddy, but she only lifted the hood a little, and didn't take it off. If her guards looked in the window she wanted them to see nothing amiss.

She listened, as Oliver must listen, to all the sounds around the coach, identifying them, locating them, working out their significance. The door her shoulder touched faced the stables, across a cobbled area. At least three different men, with thick country accents, spoke tersely with the coachman. On the other side of the coach, a jumble of men's voices and harsh laughter drifted from further away; the inn itself. She heard no woman's voice.

There were few sounds beyond the area, other than birds twittering and the ragged bleating of sheep. A village then, or the outskirts of a town. She'd lost track of time, of how far they might have come.

While she listened, she worked at the knot of linen at the back of her head, her bound hands awkward and clumsy with their restricted movement. But gradually the gag loosened enough for her to slide it down, out of her mouth.

Despite the dryness in her mouth she gulped in breath after shaky breath. When the time was right she'd be able to call out for help. Not yet. Outside, her guards complained in vulgar terms about hard cheese and bad ale, and the coach jolted sharply several times amid a volley of loud cursing and a neighing horse. Not, it seemed, the kind of inn where a gentlewoman might find refuge and help.

She risked a peek from under the hood. The blinds were drawn, the interior dim. Good. The bad light would hide her loosening of the hood. And if she could work on undoing the cord around her wrists, that might not be noticed, either.

Surely Francis planned on stopping for the night, although there must still be some hours until evening. His tastes ran to a much better class of establishment, and she could only hope for a chance to escape and to throw herself on the mercy of a kindly innkeeper's wife. Either that, or wait until they reached Scotland.

She hastily pulled the hood down and resumed her meek position when the guards fell suddenly silent, and Francis's angry voice berated the postilion for his slowness.

In a lower voice, just outside the door, he gave orders to his men. "There's a horseman coming at a pace down the hill. If he comes after us, watch for a good place for an ambush once we're out on the road. Then wait, and deal with him. Make sure there's no-one to follow us."

He slammed the door, banged his cane on the roof, and the coach lurched off. As he settled himself comfortably with soft sounds of cloth against leather, he remarked to her, "No-one's going to rescue you, Emma. If that rider is following us, he won't get much further. They'll find his body in a ditch in a few days."

Cold seeped up from the floor boards, chilling her to the bone. If it was Adam... She had to pray that it wasn't, that it was simply some man who lived in the village who would arrive home safely and not venture past it again today. That there was no-one racing to catch the coach, and riding into a trap.

CHAPTER 17

The rain began to fall in large, heavy drops that splashed on the ground as Adam neared the village at the crossroads. Only a small community, a dozen or so rundown houses, and an old inn facing the market square.

In the distance beyond the houses, he caught a glimpse of a coach before it rounded a bend and out of view. A coach with a pair of black horses. At every toll gate, they'd described chestnut horses. But they'd come more than twenty miles, at a fair pace.

Had Braithwaite changed his horses here? Or did he take another road after the last toll gate, and that was some other coach?

Adam rode into the stable yard of the inn and dismounted, calling out to the groom through the open stable door while he walked the horse to stop her cooling down too fast. "The coach that just left— did it change horses here? Who was in it?"

The groom came to the doorway and studied him. A young man, not that much older than Jeremy, but with hard eyes that had seen far more than his brother ever had. "Who wants to know?"

Adam brought the horse around and faced the man. "Adam Caldwell of Rengarth. I'm pursuing a man who has abducted a lady."

The groom shrugged. "Didn't see no lady. Only a gent and his men." Another assessing stare at Adam, before he decided to trust him. "Oy, you," the groom called back into the stable. "Any lady in that coach you came with?"

In the dimness inside the stable, Adam made out the figure of a man, brushing a chestnut horse. Of course. The postilion who'd led the pair of horses until the changeover. He'd stay with the horses in his charge, see that they returned to their home stable.

He came to the doorway, hesitant, remaining under the shelter from the rain. "There were a lady," he acknowledged. "They bundled her in, back towards Hartdale. A madwoman, they said. Dangerous. Reckoned she'd killed a man."

Adam cursed Braithwaite to hell, so violently that the horse shied. A *madwoman*. Emma. Anger threatened to burn away his reason, his control. If Braithwaite stood in front of him now he'd kill him. But the men watched him as if he might be losing his mind.

Discipline. Control. He could not afford to waste a moment in anger. "They lied," he told them bluntly. "She's perfectly sane, and in grave danger."

The postilion had the decency to flush, shame-faced. "I didn't know, sir. I needed the job to get me back to my family. Some folks you just don't ask questions."

Of course not. Not when the pay meant food on the table.

"They must be stopped." He held out the reins to the postilion and nodded towards the taproom, where voices argued. "I'll go ask them for help. Keep walking her. I won't be long at all."

Leaning against the door post, the groom gave a guttural laugh. "Ain't nobody in there going to help. Waste of time askin' that godless lot. And not a decent 'orse between 'em, anyways."

Adam flicked a coin towards the groom. "Then go find someone who *will* help and send them after me." He swung up on to the horse and wheeled her around. "The man is capable of murder. Don't let her be on your conscience."

He'd wasted enough time and didn't wait to see if they acted. If he had to face Braithwaite and his thugs alone, then so be it.

The road from the village wound along beside a stream, the woods thick on the opposite bank. Thunder rumbled in the distance and the rain fell in earnest now. Good. Muddy roads would slow Braithwaite's coach. His sure-footed mare scarcely altered her stride.

After a mile, the road curved to cross the stream at an old gray stone mill, its wheel turning in the swift flow of water fed by the frequent rain. But the mill was shuttered and silent.

He crossed the arched stone bridge. On this side of the stream the dense trees formed a canopy over the road, a semi-dark tunnel. There were few sounds other than the horse's hooves, muffled by the dampness.

The men leapt out at him as he rounded a bend, wielding long, stout leafy branches directly in front of him. The mare squealed and reared and Adam clutched her mane to stay on. But they beat at her with the branches, and as her feet hit the ground again, straining to bolt, one of the branches caught Adam square in the chest.

He hit the ground, instinctively rolling away from the horse's hooves as she bolted off. His fingers closed around the hilt of the knife in his boot and he leapt to his feet.

One on either side of him, they used the branches like jousting sticks, whacking him while staying out of reach of his knife. They caught him at all angles—face, head, knife arm, body, legs.

But the long branches were unbalanced and awkward and rarely hit hard, his greatcoat cushioning the blows. While he twisted and dodged he measured up his opponents. Not just any thugs. Definitely the men he'd seen on the back of Braithwaite's coach in Hartdale yesterday.

The younger of the two men was tall, thickset and powerful; the older man slighter, slower on his feet, yet wily and more strategic. Both held their branches with two hands, and although they might have knives they weren't obviously to hand. Even if they had pistols, they'd be useless in this damp weather.

The tall man swung his branch hard and Adam ducked under it so that the man, expecting resistance, staggered off balance with the momentum. Adam charged in, slashing at his arm, stabbing into his shoulder, wrenching the knife and twisting it while his opponent roared in rage and pain.

The flicker of a shadow alerted him to the second man behind him, and although he dodged, he wasn't fast enough and the stick

172

jarred against his back, knocking his breath from him. A second blow with a fist caught him on the chin and Adam reeled, stumbling to his knees. The tall man, despite his bloodied arm, kicked him hard in the chest and the world spun around him in a whirl of pain and breathlessness. He had no air, no strength.

Emma. If he lost this fight, he might lose Emma. She needed him to get past these men and find her.

Win.

Breathe.

Win.

He dropped into a roll, away from the kicking legs of his assailants. When the tall man came after him, he grabbed his leg mid-kick, wrenching it outwards with all the strength he could muster. The man fell against his partner, toppling both of them, with a howl of agony as his wounded shoulder hit the road.

Adam pushed himself up and across the few yards to where his knife lay. The injured man was still conscious but writhing on the ground, clutching his arm and breathing heavily between spitted curses. Not much of a threat.

The second man scrambled up, pulling a knife from under his coat. One against one now. He and Adam circled, sizing up each other.

Five breaths against his bruised ribs. Six. The fog of pain was clearing from his head. Appealing to the man's reason might end this without further injury. To either of them. "Whatever Braithwaite is paying you won't be much use when you hang."

The man snorted.

"Where's he taking her to? Gretna Green?"

Another snort, and a feint of a lunge that Adam sidestepped easily.

He kept his gaze steady on the man, his knife ready. "You won't win. I will kill you if I have to. So you can go on your way now, and fetch help for your friend, or they'll carry you from here in a shroud."

Hoof beats gradually grew louder behind him. More than one

horse. Maybe three. He didn't take his eyes from the man to see if it was help coming, or highwaymen. If the latter, he'd be dead within minutes.

But as the riders drew closer, his opponent shifted his attention, looking beyond Adam to see them—and in that moment Adam leapt, tackling him to the ground, kneeling on him to hold him down and putting the knife to his throat.

"Where is Braithwaite taking her?" he demanded.

Silence and an insolent glare answered him.

He pressed the knife a fraction harder against the skin to the left of the man's jugular. Enough to draw a wince and a thin line of blood.

His persuasion worked. Eyes narrowed, the man spat a single word. "Scotland."

Although the admission only confirmed Adam's suspicions, the rush of anger caught him and he stared at that line of blood, the knife gripped in his hand. One slash, one deep cut, and...

No. He was not a cold-blooded killer, no matter how heinous the crime.

But he kept the knife pressed against the skin while he glanced across at the riders dismounting nearby. Penry, with the groom and the postilion from the inn.

Penry directed the servants to restrain and guard the injured man, before heading towards Adam. As he approached, the man's eyes flicked towards him. Recognition.

More questions. Adam cursed silently. Instead of finding his horse and going after Braithwaite, he'd have to decide what to do with Braithwaite's men. And whether he could trust Penry.

Adam sent the groom, not needed to guard the other thug, in search of his horse. He observed Penry closely while he told him, "Braithwaite's only a mile or two ahead. He is taking her to Scotland, as we thought." His voice sounded as rough to his ears as his throat felt.

Penry nodded. "No-one saw him on the other road so I figured quickly enough that he'd come this way. I've not been far behind you."

"You sent the men on to alert the constable?"

He rummaged in a saddle-bag and found a length of cord. "I sent them to alert the magistrate. Because the constable is floating face-down in a pond not far from where I left you."

The constable, dead in a pond. Unlikely to be an accident.

"Did you put him there?"

Penry seemed amused rather than offended. "No. The idea might have tempted me, but I'm no murderer. I'd lay a bet that Dutton here," He nudged the prone man none too gently in the shoulder with his boot, "Had something to do with it, though."

Dutton made an attempt to spit, despite being pinned down by Adam's knife.

"You know them."

"That one," he nodded towards the unconscious man, "Is a local, I believe. But Dutton here—we became *acquainted* in the Canadian colonies." Penry knelt down beside him, cord at the ready.

The man shot him a dagger look and jerked back against Adam's hold. "I should have made sure you were fucking dead, Ballantyne."

Penry pulled back the man's head. "A mistake you've made more than once, Dutton." He didn't wait for a reply before he gagged him with his own neckerchief.

"Ballantyne?" Adam queried sharply.

Penry shrugged. "A name I used over there. Penry's the real one."

Assuming Penry told the truth, he had to be one of the agents recommended to Emma.

"We'll truss him up and then you go on and find Braithwaite," Penry continued. "I'll see that these two get locked up until we can send them to the magistrate, pending trial."

"For the constable's murder?"

"Probably. Certainly with Winslow's murder. And with the attempted murder of Matthew Braithwaite. Although if I have my way Dutton will either be shot for desertion or he'll hang for treason."

Treason. Men who committed treason had no loyalty, no honor, no conscience. Adam kept his knife to Dutton's neck, resisting the urge to slit it while they rolled him over. Penry set to work binding his hands securely behind his back. If he'd been investigating deserters and treason, he was either military intelligence or secret service. Secret service, more likely.

"Is Francis Braithwaite involved in this treason?" Adam asked.

"Dutton and his accomplices were selling military information to the Americans both before and after the treaty that ended our war with them." Penry tightened the cord around the man's wrists with no gentleness. "Braithwaite didn't arrive in Kingston until spring last year but there's evidence that he helped finance a band of deserters who caught revolutionary fever from the Americans. They planned to form a militia and overthrow the colonial government. Some powerful men supported them, and promised them land grants."

Adam swore. "Francis was one of them? Why?"

"Trade concessions. Land grants on both sides of the lakes. Investment in new mills over there. It was all in a letter that was inadvertently delivered to Matthew in Kingston, rather than Francis. I thought at first Matthew was involved, but he was incensed when he realized what his cousin was up to."

As Penry moved to the feet, Dutton attempted to thrash them. Adam dissuaded him from that course of action with a tight twist of his hair and a blood-drawing nick of his knife.

"The expedition that Matthew went on—was that connected?"

Penry sat himself on Dutton's legs and looped the cord around them. "Yes. I had intelligence that the deserters had a camp on the lake system north west of Ottawa. The Governor wanted the lakes mapped and a route found up to James Bay, and gave me twenty soldiers to help. Matthew insisted on coming. Family honor, he said. End result, a pitched battle three months later, ten dead, some of the rebels got away, and our soldiers that were left chased after them. Matthew and I had to overwinter at a trading post."

With Dutton immobilized, Adam rose to his feet. "Was that when he was hurt?"

'No." Penry pulled the final cord around Dutton's legs so tight the man grunted loudly. "That was early this spring. We encountered Dutton and his friends on our way back to Ottawa. Francis had sent them back to finish us off. Especially Matthew. They left Matthew and our guide for dead in a freezing river. After they'd killed the settlers we'd stayed with the night before."

Anger and disgust boiling in him, Adam stopped in the act of putting his knife in his boot, his gazing meeting Dutton's hatred-filled eyes. But a gentleman, an officer, did not kill or injure a prisoner unable to defend himself. Not even a murdering, traitorous bastard like Dutton. Adam made himself walk away. Penry's revelations made him all the more desperate to reach Emma.

The groom returned with his horse, uninjured despite her bolt.

Adam still had questions for Penry, but they must wait. "Follow me when you're rid of these bastards. I've lost too much time."

The rain began to fall again as he urged the mare into a gallop. Within minutes it became heavy, and thunder cracked somewhere close by.

He'd lost his hat somewhere along the way and the rain splashed against his face but he rode on, into the storm, determined to find Emma, praying that Braithwaite was too focused on escaping to have harmed her, yet.

CHAPTER 18

The cold seeped through every inch of Emma's body. Cold and aching pain. Rain drummed on the carriage roof and the roads must be becoming muddy because the wheels slid. Rolls of thunder came closer, louder, and the carriage lurched when it cracked overhead in a tremendous boom.

She was thrown against Francis's leg, and scrabbled to keep away from him while the coach jerked and bounced. The horses must be bolting, or trying to.

Francis swore crudely and shouted to the coachman to control the horses. As if the coachman and postilion wouldn't be doing everything they could anyway. But Francis hated having no control over a situation, and when she tumbled into him again he shoved her away roughly, as though he couldn't bear to have her touching him.

A sliver of a silver lining, given her predicament. If he planned a marriage in name only, she would not have to endure his physical attentions. Although she did not intend to allow a marriage to take place, whether in name only or not.

She braced her feet against the seat frame, her back to the opposite one, as the coach bumped at speed over rough ground. Tomorrow she'd be a mass of bruises.

Their speed gradually slowed as the storm continued. The coachman opened the panel at the top of the box. "The postilion won't go no further than the next inn, sir," he shouted. "About a mile, he reckons."

Francis muttered another curse. "As long as it has decent rooms and victuals," he ordered the coachman. "Otherwise we go on."

Emma slowly stretched her legs as best she could in the cramped space, under her skirts so that Francis might not notice. Only a mile to the inn. She must be ready to escape when they stopped. Ready to run from Francis, call for help, throw herself on the mercy of the first respectable person she saw.

She rested her head on her knees, her bound hands near the edge of the hood, ready to push it up the moment Francis left the carriage. If he left the carriage without her.

But when the coach turned in to the inn and stopped, Francis grabbed her by the arm. He lifted the hood roughly from her head, uncaring that it dragged across her face, and gave a hard laugh. He gripped her face painfully tight. "Taking off the gag will do you no good, Emma. If you utter a single word, or cause me any trouble you'll pay for it. Stay silent and do exactly what you're told."

She blinked in the gray light, and nodded mutely. As if she would obey him. Despite her attempts to stretch her legs, they were still stiff and as he hauled her up and out of the carriage, she stumbled on the steps, crashing in to him and struggling to find her footing on the wet cobblestones.

He pulled her close to him but the tight band of his arm around her was neither gentle nor gentlemanly, her bound hands concealed against his coat. The rain soaked her as he dragged her the short distance inside.

The inn-keeper came out from the tap-room and Francis ordered, "I want your best chamber. Now."

Emma pushed hard against Francis, trying to show her tied hands to the man. "Help me. He's kidnapped me..."

Francis yanked her back against him, his hand clamped over her mouth. "Ignore her," he told the inn-keeper. "She's my wife. Some bastard took her and now she's crazed in the head. I'm taking her to a physician in Scotland."

The man looked uneasily from her to Francis. "Is she dangerous?

I don't want no trouble here, sir."

Emma's hopes of help sank lower than the floor. He believed Francis. She briefly considered trying to bite Francis's hand so that she might try again, but that's what the insane did, wasn't it? Bite and scream. Her cousin's lie condemned her and nothing she said now—if he allowed her to speak—would convince the inn-keeper. She could hear no other voices from the taproom. No other possible help.

"I'll keep her restrained," Francis assured the man, as calmly as if he spoke of a dog. "She won't be any bother. Now, where is your best chamber?"

When she hesitated at the foot of the stairs, Francis squeezed her arm again and murmured near her ear, "I will drag you up there if you don't walk yourself."

She believed him. She lifted her skirts as best she could and climbed the stairs beside him. When the inn-keeper unlocked the door to a large room with a table, bed, and cabinet, Francis pushed her inside and took the key from the man.

"Send a meal up in an hour. See to it that we're not disturbed before then."

As Francis closed the door behind their host and turned the key in the lock, Emma backed away from him. The rain drummed so loudly against the window that she could see nothing of the village outside. It must be a village or even a hamlet; she'd heard no sounds of a town, and if this was the inn's best chamber it did not suggest a well-populated or prosperous area.

A flash of lightning lit the room to brightness as a deafening crack of thunder overhead shook the window panes and the floor beneath her feet.

Her heart galloped in her chest, and she swallowed back a sob. What had Adam said last night? *'You're one of the strongest, bravest women I know...'* She felt neither brave nor strong but the words strengthened her determination and she glanced around, looking for something, anything, she might use as a weapon. The poker beside the unlit fireplace, four feet away. Two wooden chairs at the table. A heavy candlestick on the cabinet.

Seemingly in no hurry, Francis shrugged off his greatcoat and hung it on a hook near the door. Ignoring her, he spent a few moments perusing the newspaper on the table. A deliberate ploy to unsettle her, to belittle her.

In the coach, with limited options, she'd allowed him to think her afraid so that he would leave her be. But now he'd referred to her as his wife. He'd ordered that they not be disturbed. And there was a bed just feet away. She did not need imagination to guess what he intended.

Time to leave him in no doubt that she would not surrender to his will. She faced him across the table and stood tall.

"If your plan is to marry me to gain Larkfell, you will fail, Francis. I will not marry you. And anyway, I will not inherit Larkfell, because Matthew is alive."

He pushed the newspaper aside. "Your brother is dead, Emma. I know that for a fact. And you will obey my orders and you will marry me. Because otherwise I have no use for you and you'll join your brother. A tragic accident. After some poor chit has stood in for you before witnesses."

Anger burned beside chilling fear. He 'd just calmly threatened to murder her, if she didn't comply with his plans. And even if she did comply, she doubted his plans included letting her live. If she told him she knew Matthew was definitely alive and in England—that he'd survived whatever Francis had done to him—he would have no reason to keep her alive, and plenty to silence her forever. "You can't hope to get away with this." Surely he would see reason? "People know I was abducted. They will be searching for me."

"And I've rescued you, dear cuz," he drawled. "For which you will be so grateful you'll accept my proposal. And because you've been pining for me all this time I've been away."

The audacity of his blatant lies astounded her. "All this? Just to gain Larkfell?"

He shrugged. "Not only Larkfell. Your company has properties I can use and land with good coal seams. Your plodding old ways are gone, Emma, and there's money to be made with steam and coal-powered production. And Winslow's fortune will set me up to be the most powerful manufacturer in the north. Cotton and coal, dear cuz. That's the future. I'll be a king of industry."

She let his words pass without contradiction. He had everything planned. Nothing she could say would change that. But the more she understood of his plans and his capabilities, the more chance she might have to best him.

"Did you murder Mr. Winslow?" she asked.

He mocked innocence. "I? No, I was in Hartdale that evening. Preparing for the Rengarth ball."

She held her ground. "But you knew about his will. That I inherit."

"Of course. I saw Winslow not long after I came back. Poor fool thought you were managing the business well."

"I am. Despite arson, murder and malicious rumors."

He grinned and didn't deny any of it. "You don't give up easily, do you, dear cuz? You do have some of the better Braithwaite traits. But you've still lost and all this talking is rather tedious. Enough questions."

He strode around the table to her and advanced so close that she had to step back. But he simply crowded her again, towering over her, his breath against her upturned face. She moved to dodge around him but he cut her off. She retreated step by step as he pressed forward, until she felt the wall at her back.

He trapped her there, with his hands on the wall on either side of her, his body barely an inch from hers. He lowered his face towards hers. "You're mine, Emma. I can do anything I want with you. You can fight if you want," His smile made her skin crawl, "But it won't do you any good."

Her heartbeat raced so hard and fast she scarcely found breath to speak. "Don't."

He laughed softly. "Don't what, Emma? Take my pleasure from you? Make you submit to me?"

Anger surged through the cold fear. Not submission. Never

submission. She would fight him any way she could.

"Have you thrown away all honor, Francis?" The words grated in her throat, but she pushed on. "Our great-grandfather would be horrified."

"Honor is for fools, Emma. The victors take the spoils." His mouth crushed against hers, his body driving her hard against the wall. And his hand closed over her breast, fingers digging in painfully.

His mouth smothered her, his tongue forcing into her so that she gagged and struggled for breath. She pushed her bound hands against him. He shifted slightly but only to get a grip on the edge of her bodice. The soft fabric of her chemisette and dress tore away.

Ruined. The word echoed with multiple meanings. He intended to ruin her. She scarcely cared about society's judgement, but she'd darn well fight against the ruin of her hopes, dreams and the yearnings of her heart. Such intimacies belonged only to a husband or lover.

As he groped under the top of her stays she thrust her hands up between their bodies—and scratched her hand on the pin that had fastened the wrap-front of her bodice closed. His assault on her mouth and on her breast continued, but she gripped the pin between her fingers, slipped it from the fabric and turned it to face upwards. A tiny weapon.

Shock. She had to shock him into stopping.

"Between the legs, Em. That's how you stop a fellow if he gets too familiar."

Bless her brother for educating her in a way her school for young ladies never did. Bless providence for Francis standing with his feet on either side of her leg.

If only she had the audacity and strength... She rammed her knee up as hard and high as she could. Francis jerked with a roar and in the moment when he coiled in to protect himself she jammed the pin upwards, into his face.

It hit soft flesh somewhere near his eye but she didn't wait to see, dodging around him and running for the door. She twisted the key with both hands, yanking it out before she lifted the latch. She dashed through, pulling the door behind her. The latch fell into place, but as she fumbled the key into the hole to lock it Francis's heavy, uneven footsteps sounded on the wood floor. The latch shook just as the lock clicked into place, and Francis swore loudly.

The key held tight in her hand, she ran down the corridor. Not towards the stairs they'd come up. Francis banged the door and shouted for the innkeeper; he might appear any moment. She ran instead towards the rear of the inn. There must be back stairs. Yes. She went down them so fast she almost collided with a chambermaid half-way up with arms full of linen.

The young woman's horrified glance took in her ripped dress, bound hands. "Miss! Are you...?"

"Where is a way out?" Emma gasped.

Francis banged on the door and thundered a volley of curses.

The maid hastily put the linen on a small table on the landing. "This way, miss."

Down the stairs, along a short corridor, and the girl opened a door. The laundry room. Francis's shouts still audible, the maid led Emma between hanging sheets and cloths to a door opening on to a walled courtyard.

"Where is the manor?" Emma asked. There had to be a manor nearby. Villages grew up around manors. A gentlemen would help her.

The maid's eyes grew wide. "Oh, no, miss. Don't go to the manor. Sir Phillip is..." She gulped. "It's not safe there, miss."

A drunkard? A lecher? Worse? Whichever, she'd trust that fear in the maid's eyes. "The vicar?"

The girl shook her head emphatically. "There's a gate over there," she pointed. "If you cross the lane you'll be in the woods. Him up there won't see you go. God be with you, miss."

Rain fell heavily, the cobblestones of the laundry courtyard slippery. The gate stood open, and barely visible through the pouring rain, the dark shadows of a forest.

Her clothes already soaked through, her heart racing, Emma crossed the narrow lane and scrambled over the stone fence, dropping to the ground among the thick, wet undergrowth.

Struggling to hold back her sobs, she stumbled through the trees, uncaring which way she went. Only that it was away from Francis and that the forest provided places to hide from him.

CHAPTER 19

About a mile from the next hamlet—Adam could see it from the hillside he rode down—the horse he'd borrowed from the Colonel's friend stumbled on some loose stones washed down by the rain, and began to limp. Adam swore, and dismounted. Despite his need for haste, no decent man rode an injured horse. Especially not a borrowed one.

He paced beside the horse, the wet reins almost slipping through his hands when it shied as thunder cracked across the sky. He'd have left it securely tied to a tree if the weather was better. Not with lightning and thunder and gusting winds all around. The dark clouds and pouring rain made the late afternoon twilight-dark already.

The hamlet had an inn, a building taller and more substantial than the half-dozen cottages around it. Almost as tall as the ancient church. As he trudged towards the inn, three horsemen road out from the coaching yard. He pulled his horse aside into the church gateway to allow one of the men to gallop past him. The other two headed north.

In the coach yard of the inn, a black coach stood to one side, unharnessed. Adam huffed out a breath. Francis's coach. Here. He'd caught up, at last, and Emma must be in the inn, just yards away.

But no-one came to take his horse, even when he shouted. He led her to the stable himself. Carriage horses occupied several of the stalls, the others empty. He quickly secured his horse in one and hurried across the yard in search of the innkeeper. Or Francis. Might be better if he found the innkeeper first. The man might stop him from killing Braithwaite with his bare hands. And help him get Emma away from the bastard.

He followed the sounds of voices and sobs to the kitchen. The innkeeper looked on while a woman—maybe his wife, maybe a cook—tended to the bruised face of a young woman. The man, dressed in the simple, decent clothes of a tradesman, stepped forward protectively between Adam and the women.

"The man from the coach," Adam asked. "Francis Braithwaite—which room is he in?"

The innkeeper shook his head. "Room one, but he ain't there. Gone searching for his missus. Madwoman, he said. Attacked him and locked 'im in the room and ran off. He's sent everyone out looking for her. Promised ten guineas reward for bringing her back. So they've all rushed off to search for her. Stable boy and all."

Emma. Escaped. Relief did not cool his fury with Francis for his lies and machinations. But she was out there, alone in this rain, and with men eager to find her for the sake of a generous reward.

"He lied," Adam said, unable to keep the harshness out of his voice. "He's not her husband, and she's not insane. She's a respectable lady and he abducted her."

The man studied him, wary, not entirely convinced. "And you would be?"

"Major Adam Caldwell. Of Rengarth. The lady," To protect her reputation, he didn't use Emma's name, "is a neighbor and a friend of my sisters. Braithwaite is a violent man and she is in grave danger from him."

A long moment of consideration while the man weighed up Adam's words against the lies Francis had told him. Finally he nodded. "He beat our girl because she didn't stop the lady from running away. In a right rage he was."

"Two men rode north just as I arrived. Was one of them him?"

"Aye, sir. Off to fetch Sir Phillip's bloodhounds, from the manor."

"Sir Phillip?" He searched his memory for gentry in this part of the county. "Sir Phillip Gresham?"

"Aye, sir."

A man with a reputation for hedonism, if his memory served him correctly. Possibly more likely to ally himself with Francis than with Adam. "How long since the lady escaped? Do you know which way she went?"

"A half hour, thereabouts. Peggy showed her out through the side. Leads out on the lane. We didn't tell him that," he added. "Didn't trust him much after he set on Peggy."

The girl—she wasn't much more than a girl—struggled to stifle a sob.

"You did the right thing," Adam assured her. "Was she hurt?"

"Not much that I saw, sir. But her dress... it was torn, sir. Like he'd..." With fearful eyes, she gulped and mimed a hand yanking at a bodice. "That's why I helped her. She went into the woods, sir. I saw her go."

Braithwaite had attempted to rape Emma. Adam's wrath stretched every element of his control.

"If any of the men bring the lady back, ensure she is treated with every respect and care," he ordered briskly, as if they were soldiers. "I will cover any expenses. And send any men who return back out to search for Braithwaite instead. I'll give a reward for anyone who finds him and locks him up. Best go in teams, though. He's likely to be violent."

Despite the warning, avarice glinted in the innkeeper's eyes. "How much reward?"

The man's moral instincts clearly didn't extend beyond his own family. To ensure Emma's safety, Adam multiplied Francis's offer four-fold. "Forty guineas."

With that kind of reward—far more than a year's wages for folks around here—there'd be plenty of people searching for Francis.

His own priority was to find Emma.

In the lane beside the inn, a small footprint filled with water in the mud by the stone wall. Emma's footprint. He swung over the wall and stood for a moment, looking around him. Several men searched a tumble-down cottage further down the lane. In the opposite direction, two others hunted among the gravestones of the churchyard.

Which way had Emma gone? Along the edge of the forest? No, not likely. Too easily seen. She was a level-headed woman. She hadn't panicked when trapped in the warehouse fire, and he doubted she'd be panicking now. Knowing no-one in the hamlet to trust, and with people searching for her within a short time of her escape, she'd surely aim to get away from Francis, as fast and as far as possible, to a secure hiding place.

Through the woods, then.

The trees dripped with the rain, the undergrowth almost as sodden as the fields he'd passed on the way. In half an hour, at a walking pace through the forest, she might have gone a mile or more. If she was aiming to hide but eventually to get somewhere she might find help, chances were she would walk south, back towards home. Perhaps she'd seek help at the last village, or at a respectable farm. But this area between the dales and the forest was wild, isolated country, with few people beyond the hamlets and villages along the turnpike.

The wind gusted strongly, driving rain sideways and bending trees, and with a glance at the dark sky, he set off into the forest.

She was out there, alone, and another storm front was coming over.

He went far enough into the forest to be invisible from the lane and the road, and from anyone venturing in to the edges to search, before he turned south, away from the hills to the west. But even this part of the forest stretched for miles, so dense that he could walk within a few yards of her and not see her.

In between thunder claps he called her name, although if she thought he was Francis she would remain hidden. And his voice probably didn't carry far above the rain, the creaking of branches in the wind, and all the noises of the storm. He listened for the sounds of bloodhounds, dreaded hearing their baying, but there was only the forest and the storm and his own breathing.

He searched for a needle in a haystack. But he went on, hoping, praying, for a glimpse of her, for a footprint, for some sign he was heading in the right direction.

He almost missed it. Only a gust of wind, making it flutter in the breeze, showed him the strip of grey silk caught on a hawthorn bush.

~

Her soaked dress and petticoats clung to her legs, torn and covered in mud, and her light boots squelched with every step. Sometimes she stumbled, a few times she fell. Her legs ached, her body ached, and her wrists and hands were stiff from their enforced position. She'd been unable to budge the knots in the cord binding them.

Despite the pain and fatigue, she pushed herself to keep going, one foot after another, along the path she'd found. Although narrow and overgrown, people had walked here long enough and often enough to carve the way through the trees. Surely it must lead to a hut or a dwelling or some kind of shelter. Even a ruin might provide some protection from the driving wind and rain.

Some of the girls at school had told wild tales about the dales and the forest. Terrifying creatures, murderous highwaymen, cackling witches, and people lost for days on the fells.

So far she'd only seen wet trees. The animals of the forest seemed to be protecting themselves from the storm as best they could. Yet for all her practicality, fear had lodged, tense and tight, in her spine and shoulders. Fear of Francis, more than any forest horrors.

A roar of wind, leaves and twigs and an explosion of light and thunder boomed around her, so loud the reverberations jarred through her and the earth beneath her feet seemed to buckle.

Yes, she was afraid of this storm, too.

As the thunder began to fade, another sound rose above the wind. Deep baying and barking. Hounds. Hunting hounds, coming closer.

For the first time, real terror gripped her. There was only one thing they'd be hunting, out in a storm. Her.

Tears mingling with the rain flowing down her face, her tattered, wet skirts plastered around her legs, she turned and ran.

She could not possibly outrun hounds, but she ran, anyway, stumbling on the rough path, falling, pushing herself up again despite the pain. Hoping, desperately, that against all odds she'd find some safety.

But the baying came louder, closer. And beyond it, the thunder of hoof beats.

A tree branch dangling over the path whipped her in the face and she stumbled and fell again, pain jarring through her body as she hit the ground. She struggled to rise from the slippery, mossy ground, staggering to her feet as a dozen large dogs rounded the bend in the path and came straight for her.

CHAPTER 20

The pack of bloodhounds and four horseman galloped past, oblivious to where he'd ducked off the path and behind a tree when he heard them.

Francis Braithwaite. Even in the dull light, Adam recognized the set of his jaw, the line of his cheek.

He sprinted after them, his heart thudding in his ears as the hounds' baying suddenly swelled in volume and excitement. Pushing low-hanging branches aside, he dashed around the crook in the path and came upon them. The horsemen, reining in their mounts, and beyond them Emma, surrounded by leaping, baying hounds, desperately trying to fend them off.

"Call them off!" he shouted, dodging past the restless horses on the crowded path. "Call the damned dogs off her!" If they drew blood, they might rip her to pieces.

He slashed out with his knife, his fists, fighting his way through the pack to reach her. Thrusting her behind him, he faced the hounds, the animal in him growling and shouting at them aggressively, as if he was the pack leader.

One of the men dismounted, an older, grizzled man in workman's clothes, and he began commanding the dogs, calling them by name, hauling several of them back.

"Leave them be!" Francis ordered.

The man cast an uncertain glance between Francis and Adam.

Adam didn't take his eyes off him. "Call them off or you'll hang for murder," he threatened.

The man put a whistle to his lips, cheeks working as he blew in it, the pitch so high Adam scarcely discerned it but the dogs heard it. In twos and threes, they fell back, milling around, agitated by the excitement. Still dangerous, for all their training and obedience. Any small thing could set them off again.

Another rider dismounted to help with the dogs. Young, maybe a stable or a kennel hand. Possibly not dangerous in himself.

But Francis was more dangerous than the hounds. And the fourth rider, one of his men, had a hard, scarred face. Just as dangerous. As Braithwaite rode forward, Adam wrapped an arm around Emma protectively and she buried her face against his shoulder, gulping in breaths. He stared up at Francis, defiant and on guard, his knife gripped in his free hand.

At least two men against him. Maybe four. But if the youth and the hound master had come from Sir Phillip's manor, their loyalty might not lie with Francis.

"Let go of her, Caldwell, and step away," Francis ordered. "You're coming with me, Emma."

Emma lifted her head and faced her cousin, defiant despite her torn, muddy clothes and her hair falling down around her face. "No, I am not. I will not come with you and I will not marry you."

Francis laughed. "Deal with Caldwell, Barlow. You two, get the woman."

Barlow dismounted. Sir Phillip's men hesitated. The path was wider here but crowded, the dog pack now ten yards or so behind him, Braithwaite and Barlow and horses in front of him.

Adam let go of Emma and stepped in front of her. "Escape the moment you can," he murmured to her.

Barlow circled, eyeing Adam's knife, drawing two of his own with all the assurance of a skilled fighter.

Adam kept his gaze on the man's face, watching for the flicker that would signal a charge.

"You always get others to murder for you, don't you,

193

Braithwaite?" he said loudly, as much to taunt Francis as to sow doubt in Barlow's loyalty, and that of the men from the manor. "Did you murder Winslow for him, Barlow? And attack Matthew Braithwaite?"

Barlow's only reaction was a narrowing of his eyes, the moment he heard Matthew's name. Behind Adam, the crack of a twig under Emma's boot came from a yard or two away. The other men remained on the edge of his vision, watching her.

The rain still fell, and drips of water trickled down Adam's forehead, into the corner of his eye. He blinked once, and Barlow surged forward, signaling his dominant hand by twisting it to strike first.

Adam dodged to that side at the last moment, bringing his knife over and down point first into Barlow's arm as the man slashed unsuccessfully, catching only his coat.

With a roar, Barlow lunged with his second knife, but he was off-balance, half-twisting to swing around to catch Adam, who took the chance to stab again at Barlow's shoulder, and to haul down on the injured arm with his free hand.

Barlow went flying to the ground, spewing curses.

Francis shouted, "Get the woman!"

Adam spun around and saw Emma grappled by the two men from the manor, but before he could reach her, Francis kicked his horse to speed, straight at him.

He didn't dodge quickly enough and the horse's shoulder caught him hard, followed immediately by Francis's booted kick to the side of his head.

He heard Emma scream as he hit the mud, pain and blackness flooding his senses.

~

Emma struggled against the strong hands gripping her arms, choking back sobs of fear and anger. Adam lay motionless on the ground. Trampled by the horse? She didn't know, hadn't seen properly, only Francis riding into him.

Francis turned his horse, scattering the blood hounds.

"Let me go," she pleaded with her captors. "He'll kill him. He tried to kill my brother. He'll kill me, too."

One man's grip lessened and with a rip of sodden silk she wrenched free, dashing out between Francis's horse and Adam's prone body.

The horse's hot breath reached her cheek and she stepped back as Francis yanked the horse aside just in time to avoid her.

He struck out at her with his crop as he wheeled around. "You stupid *bitch!*"

She ducked and the crop whistled bare inches from her face. Her whole body shook uncontrollably but she had to keep him away from Adam. In case he was still alive. Even if she died protecting him.

Francis's horse skittered nervously towards the dog handlers. His face contorted with rage, Francis swiped at them with his crop as well. "I told you fools to hold her. Get her or you'll pay for it."

The men cast uneasy glances at each other but as Emma let go the breath she'd held, a hand clasped firm around her mouth and yanked her back against a hard body. A wave of panic and the strong scent of blood made her gag. The man Adam had fought. The man he'd stabbed in the arm. He only held her with one arm.

She twisted and rammed her elbow back towards his injured arm. Despite the awkwardness of her bound wrists she hit her target and he jerked sharply, cursing her. But his fingers clawed painfully into her cheek and he held on to her, pushing her forward towards Francis.

Her cousin stared down at her from the saddle, his usually cool, arrogant face such an apoplectic red that she feared he'd lost all reason.

Surely he wouldn't kill her with witnesses present? She'd go with him, if it meant getting him away from Adam.

"You win, Francis. I'll go with you. As long as your man goes, too, and you leave Adam alone."

He gave a guttural laugh. "Caldwell's a dead man." But his glance flicked towards where Adam had fallen, and his smirk faded.

Adam stood a few yards away, a long heavy stick in his hands. "You're the dead man, Braithwaite. Matthew is alive and Ballantyne knows everything. He's reported it all to Lord Castlereagh and he's coming after you. You'll swing for Winslow's murder."

"You're lying. He's lying," Francis shouted to the other men, his confidence cracking. "Don't listen to him. Matthew is dead. You told me he was dead, Barlow."

The man holding her swore, and shoved her roughly aside, edging away, looking around for his horse. She backed further away from Francis, to the edge of the path. The older of the dog handlers came to her side, but did not touch her.

Adam took several measured steps towards Francis and his man. "Always make sure a man's dead before you leave him, Barlow. Your friend Dutton is currently confessing everything to Ballantyne, trying to save his own neck. You just can't rely on hired killers, Braithwaite, for any loyalty. Maybe you can make it to a ship at Liverpool before Ballantyne and Castlereagh's agents find you, but I doubt it. You're a dead man if you're caught in England."

Francis roared and kicked his horse forward, straight at Barlow. The man tried to dodge and failed, uttering a strangled cry as he fell under the horse's hooves.

Francis didn't stop, urging the horse on past Emma without a glance and racing off down the path.

Adam knelt by the broken, bloodied man, the rain already washing his face clean. Emma did not need to go closer to know he was dead. She covered her mouth with her hands, trying to hold back gasping sobs.

She felt a hesitant pat on her shoulder. "You're safe now, miss. He's gone. I'm sorry we...he told us...I'm sorry. We'll follow with the hounds, after I've talked to your man."

She nodded, words impossible through the breathless racing of her pulse. Francis was gone, hoof beats thudding into the distance, but moments ago she'd been terrified for her life, for Adam's life.

And the danger wasn't over—they were deep in the woods with the wind picking up again, and darkness falling.

Adam rose to his feet and she stumbled to him, into his arms.

CHAPTER 21

He held her tight, close to him, shifting so that his back was to the wind, his body protecting her. She buried her face against his chest, shaking all over. Relief flooded him and he could scarcely speak, and he couldn't have sworn that the damp on his cheeks only came from the rain and the wetness of her hair. He'd almost lost her.

"Are you hurt?" he asked.

"Very little," she insisted, although her teeth chattered and her body trembled in his arms. "He didn't harm me."

Incredibly brave, and not entirely truthful about her unhurt state. Trying to reassure herself as much as him, in the same way that soldiers insisted they were fine when their insides shuddered from reaction and distress.

The darkening bruises on the side of her face belied her words. He would make Francis regret every blow that had fallen upon her, and the brutality of Barlow's death in front of her.

She was soaked through, wavering on her feet and heroically trying not to cry. The storm blew around them and she had to be chilled to the bone. The rough cord abraded the skin of her wrists and must be painful. He'd retrieved his knife and, keeping her in his hold and turned away from the sight of Barlow's body, he cut gently through the bonds.

The boy had already left with the hounds, following Francis. The kennel master waited, cap in his hands. Respectful. But still wary.

"She needs shelter and safety," he said to the kennel master. "Where's the nearest place I can take her?"

"There's a cottage not more than a hundred yards down the path. The old goodwife died at Christmas. They've taken some things out but it will be dry for you and the lady for tonight."

"Good." First problem solved. "Follow Braithwaite with the hounds as far as a road. Then raise a hue and cry in the village to apprehend him. There'll be a man called Penry along by morning, I expect. Tell him what happened here, and which direction Braithwaite went. And-" Think. He had to think and plan, despite the pounding in his head. "Catch Barlow's horse if you can. We'll take it` back to the village in the morning." Emma could ride it. Better than walking the miles through the sodden woods again.

"Yes, sir. And you are, sir?"

A fair question, given that he'd just issued a string of orders to a man tossed into the middle of this drama with no knowledge of the players. "I'm Adam Caldwell. Brother to the Earl of Rengarth."

The man bobbed his head deferentially. "And the other gentleman, if I might ask? Sir Phillip did not tell us who he is."

He'd need the name to send searchers out. To inform Penry. "He is Mr. Francis Braithwaite, one of the Braithwaites of Sowerby, near Hartdale." Adam said. "A factory owner."

Emma lifted her face to warn, "Be careful of him. He's lost his reason, I think. He's dangerous."

Desperate men took risks and let nothing stand in their way. And Francis had to be desperate now. His only chance of escaping the hangman's noose was to get to a ship and flee the country. Adam had seen that realization in his face, and in the way he'd ridden over his accomplice, a man who could testify against him, without a trace of mercy.

The wind was rising again, tree branches knocking against each other, and the day's grey light was dimming fast. The hound master slowly approached Barlow's horse, skittish from the smell of blood.

Reluctant to put Emma on an unreliable mount, Adam asked her, "Can you walk to the cottage?"

She stretched her freed hands. "Yes. I can walk. It's not far."

With his arm around her to steady and protect her, they followed the path further on. It led directly to the old dwelling, a low stone house in a small clearing.

The garden was overgrown, and no smoke came from the chimney. Desperate to get Emma inside and safe, he lifted the stiff latch and pushed the door open, alert for any threat. The interior was dark but silent, except for a shutter rattling in the wind. He beckoned Emma inside and shut the door firmly against the storm.

His eyes adjusted to the dimness. Just the one room, with a bed in the corner, a table and two benches, a stool by the fire.

Whoever had last been in the place had left it tidy; the doors and windows closed against the weather and the forest creatures, the floors swept. A humble dwelling, but it was out of the rain, and some kind soul had left a pile of wood beside the fire place as if expecting that strangers might need shelter. Also an iron pot. Not that he had any food to cook in it.

Emma stood in the center of the room, drenched clothes clinging to her and dripping on to the stone floor. Her dress was muddied and torn in numerous places, one sleeve ripped at the shoulder, a testament to the hardships and violence she'd endured. She brushed loose strands of wet hair away from her face, pale except for the dark bruise on her cheek.

Half of him craved to simply take her in his arms again, hold her and never let her go. The moments when he'd come so close to losing her were etched in horror on his mind, as terrifying as any of his war experiences.

But she was wet to the skin, shaking from cold and shock, and she needed dry and warmth more than anything else. He shrugged off his greatcoat and laid it on the bench beside her. The thick wool and the capes had not been enough to prevent some damp soaking right through, but damp wool held warmth better than silk and linen. His jacket was barely damp, and he took that off, too.

"You'll be ill if you stay in those wet clothes. My jacket is almost dry, and my coat will cover you properly."

She met his gaze, understanding what he'd left unspoken, and agreed, although her voice was not quite steady. "That is practical, in the circumstances."

There was only this one room. Nowhere for her to undress, no screens for privacy. "I'll build the fire," he said. He cleared his throat and added, "I'll keep my back to you. I promise."

She nodded without words. Like him, a little embarrassed.

He retrieved the small tinderbox he always carried from one of his greatcoat pockets. A soldier's habit. Always prepared for making a fire for heat, for cooking, for lighting a fuse. Cold, wet, hungry soldiers were not good fighters. Cold, wet, exhausted women were vulnerable. Even Emma, for all her resilience. Her strengths were of the mind; physically she was slight and she'd endured far more than any gentlewoman should today.

He prepared a small pile of kindling in the fireplace. A gentlemen would somehow block his mind from the sounds of a lady undressing in the awkwardness of this situation. He would not hear the rustle of damp silk. He would not imagine...No.

He closed his eyes, seeking reason. He was accustomed to the post-battle urge for physical release and the affirmation of life. He was also accustomed to ignoring it. But combined with Emma's presence and his long-held desire for her, it flamed into an acute hunger, straining every element of mental discipline. He was determined to remain in control of his desire, a gentleman, even if he ground his teeth to dust in frustration.

He struck the flint against the steel over the tinder from the box. Once, twice, three times. A spark caught on the charcloth, began to glow. He blew it into a tiny flame, and put a match to it. As lightning flashed outside again the match caught the flame and amplified it. He lit the kindling—bless whoever had left kindling and wood inside, good and dry—and his pile of dry leaves and twigs began to burn.

He stared at the growing tendrils of flame. He'd kept his thoughts away from Emma, removing her soaked clothes behind him, for at least half a minute. She gave a few short, sharp breaths, as if stretching or straining. No maid to help her with the layers of female undergarments. Should he have offered...? No. She would ask if she needed assistance.

He fed a few small sticks into the growing fire and concentrated his thoughts on what needed to be done to keep her safe. Another wave of storm was brewing outside. With any luck, Francis was far away, and the men he'd first sent out searching for her must have given up by now. They didn't know Emma, and her determination. They'd most likely have underestimated her and assumed she'd stayed close to the village, or the road

Night was not far away. Even if the storm blew itself out soon, there was no sense at all in venturing out in the dark, to stumble two miles or more without light to guide them.

They'd spend the night here. He needed to make the place as secure as possible and find a weapon to supplement his knife in case Francis returned. He cursed himself for leaving his pistols behind at the inn. At the time it had been logical—in the rain, they'd be useless. But they and the powder might have dried out by morning.

He looked up when Emma moved in to the edge of his vision. Emma in her chemise and stays, her legs and feet bare, her arms over her breasts. "I'm sorry to ask, Adam, but I can't..." She swallowed before she finished in a rush, "The cord is wet and I can't undo my stays."

She turned her back to him. The fine, damp linen of her chemise concealed little, above or below her stays.

The back of her neck flushed pink. "If you could just loosen the lacing," she said, "I can manage from there."

He focused his gaze on the knot at the bottom of the rows of eyelets and did not—*not*—let it fall lower.

In that summer long ago it was her stays that had held them back from the closest of intimacies. And now he was undoing them, and there would be no such intimacy. The irony of it didn't escape him.

His fingers fumbled as he picked at the knot in the swollen cotton cord and worked it undone.

The cord laced up in a spiral, from the base of the garment to the top. As he loosened each crossing he kept his eyes steady on the eyelets and the cording and avoided touching the small gap in between, where the fine linen of her chemise was the only covering over her skin.

He had to say something, otherwise his fractured breathing would be noticeable in the silence between them.

"Jeremy and Benjamin," she asked, before he could pull together a coherent sentence. "Are they badly injured?"

Caring Emma, thinking of his brothers despite her own terrifying experiences.

"Benjamin is fine. Only a slight wound. Mother is looking after Jeremy. He'll be spending a few days in bed, although he was quite alert and clearly told me what had happened." Not a lie. Emma needed reassurance for now. But he knew how easily a head injury could become fatal, even days after the event, and he dreaded what news might await him when he returned to Rengarth.

She exhaled a breath. "That is a relief. I was afraid for them both. That it might have been worse."

In fear for her life, yet she'd been worried about his brothers. He clenched his jaw tight against memories of the aftermath of skirmishes and village raids, and the raw knowledge of how much worse it could so easily have been. He worked a twisted part of the cord through a tight eyelet and tried to banish the images from his mind. Emma was safe. There was every chance that both his brothers would fully recover.

She spoke into the silence. "Adam, I am more sorry than you know that I didn't wait for you this morning. It's my fault, for walking in to that trap. My fault that the boys were injured."

He touched her shoulder lightly. "Don't, Emma. It wasn't your fault. I should never have gone riding and left you unprotected."

"But I should have waited. Or taken men with me."

"You couldn't have known Francis would be so brazen. He abused your concern for your workers to trap you. He will answer for his actions, Emma. I will see to it."

She gave a slight shudder. "I hate to think that he's still out there. I hope he's caught very soon."

"We should be safe here tonight," he told her. "I doubt any of the searchers will stay out in the storm."

She shot a look back over her shoulder, eyes wide. 'There are others? Searching for me?"

So much for reassuring her. So much for keeping his attention on his task instead of on the smooth curve of her shoulder. On the rose scent she wore that lingered despite the rain. Lacing. Almost done. "He offered a reward. But I offered a much larger one for arresting him. Large enough that he may already be locked in the cellar of the inn."

"If he is, I will repay you for the reward. It should be my responsibility."

He loosened the last loop of the lacing. With gentle hands on her shoulders, he turned her towards him, careful to look no lower than her eyes.

"I offered it. It is my responsibility and I will pay it. I have sisters to protect too," he added, when she began to object. "I do not want that man at loose in this country, or any other. He must pay for his crimes."

She nodded, although she bit her bottom lip and he wasn't sure whether that was disagreement with his offer or fear of Francis remaining at large. Probably fear. In other circumstances he'd have embraced her to comfort her but right now that would lead to a whole lot of complications. He barely had control over his desire. Touching her, however chastely, would render that obvious.

He gave her privacy by turning his back and returning to the fire, adding larger sticks and a piece of wood. Already it gave off some warmth. But it would take a great deal more to warm the stone walls and floor. And to keep Emma from catching a chill. Whereas he could do with a plunge into a cold, cold lake.

"I'll hang these up to dry," she said behind him.

She'd pulled on his greatcoat and it swamped her, covering her completely and trailing on the floor. She thrust the sleeves back as she reached to hang her clothes on the hooks set into the wall. Dress. Petticoat. Stays. Torn stockings. Ruined boots on the hearth.

No chemise, thank the heavens. Or the devil, who seemed determined to take possession of his thoughts. If she'd hung up her chemise and he'd imagined her naked beneath his coat...No. *No.*

The sound of horses drove insanity from his mind. Two horses at least. Slow hoof beats. They passed around to the back of the cottage.

His knife in his hand, he gestured Emma to hide behind the bed curtains, and cautiously opened the back door of the cottage.

In the dull twilight and drizzling rain he recognized Penry, leading Barlow's horse, and he sheathed his knife.

Although the horse was restless and took part of his attention, Penry asked immediately, "How is Miss Braithwaite?"

"Shaken, but her hurts are not severe. Francis Braithwaite escaped though. We need to get men after him."

He nodded briskly, handing the reins of the horse to Adam. "I came upon Gresham's man, who told me what happened. Unfortunately the hounds lost Braithwaite's scent at a stream. I'll ride to the manor and ask Gresham to arrange searchers, but unless Braithwaite goes back to the village, we won't have much chance of finding him in the dark."

Adam led the horse a short distance away from Penry's. "He'll be a few miles away by now. I doubt he'll have gone to the village. But he may not get far before dark. There won't be much moonlight getting through this cloud. He may hole up somewhere."

"Yes. I'd better get moving, myself. I'll send some men from the village to guard the body out there overnight. And to catch Braithwaite if he's idiot enough to return."

That promise relieved Adam of one major concern. With men guarding Barlow's body—and the path to the cottage—Emma should be safe overnight.

Without wasting precious time in talk, Penry turned his horse and left. Adam coaxed Barlow's gelding to the low byre behind the cottage, murmuring calming nonsense for some minutes before he unsaddled it. There was some good hay in the byre—the old goodwife might have kept a cow—and plenty of water in the overflowing water butts.

With the horse safe for the night, he returned through the rain—heavier now—to the cottage. Emma confronted him with a broom, raised and ready to strike, when he opened the cottage door.

He held up his hands and angled his face to the firelight so she could see him clearly. "It's only me."

"I wasn't sure," she apologized, lowering her weapon. "I heard voices and I thought it was all right, but you were gone for longer than I expected."

She'd unpinned her hair and re-braided it into one long plait down her back. Standing in the middle of the room, with the heavy skirts of his coat falling around her to the floor, she could have almost been some medieval queen. Or a Valkyrie from the old legends, a warrior-woman with the courage and strength to defend herself.

"I'm sorry." He gently took the broom from her hands, propping it against the wall near the door. Just in case they needed it later.

For all his determination to protect her, she'd protected herself better than he'd been able to do. She'd saved him as much—more—than he'd saved her. It wasn't his strength or courage or battle tactics that had rescued her. Only the fact that he'd delivered the news about Matthew being alive and Penry having Dutton; intelligence that had made Francis abandon his plans in his panic to escape.

She'd built up the fire, and it blazed hot, driving the chill from the room.

"You're soaked through," she said.

"Yes." He'd hardly noticed his own discomfort, but his waistcoat was damp, his shirtsleeves wet and clinging to his arms. "I'll dry, soon enough. That was Penry. He caught up with me in time to help with Francis's thugs. It turns out that he's also Ballantyne, a name he used in Canada."

Her brow creased in a frown. "Mr. Penry is Mr. Ballantyne?"

"Yes. He was with Matthew in Canada." He briefly told her what he'd learned from Penry on the road earlier.

She stared at him, wide-eyed. "It's true then? Francis tried to have Matthew murdered? That man—Barlow—attacked him and left him for dead?"

"Barlow and another man named Dutton. Penry and I arrested him on the road here."

"Oh." She raised a hand to her mouth and took several fast breaths, her eyes welling with tears. "Oh." She made an attempt to brush the tears away with her fingers, but more welled. "I'm sorry. I..."

"Cry, Emma, if you need to." He folded his arms around her, and without hesitation she leaned into him, her face buried against his shoulder. "You're safe now. Francis will be riding for a port, to escape England. I won't let him harm you or Matthew again."

"I shouldn't be so weak," she whispered, her breath catching on a sob.

"It's not weakness," he assured her. "You've been amazingly brave through the hardest of days. This reaction to being afraid is not unusual."

He held her while she struggled to regain her composure, and in his own fatigue he laid his cheek against her hair for the comfort of being close to her. He'd so nearly lost her, this woman who meant more to him than any other.

He'd believed himself in love with her as a young man. And he had been, as much as any foolish, impetuous youth could be. Yet only now did he understand, as a mature man, the depth of her unique qualities and strengths, and the power of his love and respect for her. He wanted her by his side, as his wife. If she'd have him.

But she'd refused him once, even though she loved him. And although the attraction between them remained, she might feel no more for him than a nostalgic affection.

CHAPTER 22

She drew on Adam's strength, on his gentle care for her, while the waves of emotion surged through her.

Francis was a murderer and a traitor, fleeing into exile to escape the noose. She was safe from him now. Safe from the man who'd terrified her and threatened her and almost killed the two men she cared most about in the world, Matthew and Adam. And he'd murdered—or ordered the murder of—another, Mr. Winslow.

How had the cousin she'd known since childhood become a murderer and a traitor? How had Robert's brother become a murderer and a traitor? The news would shatter Robert. He was not strong, like Adam. He needed his world ordered, obeying the rules. When he found out all that his brother had done... She was fond of her elder cousin, despite his pedantic ways, and she wept a little for him and for the shock and grief that were to come to him.

Robert was not Adam, though, and every one of Adam's actions these past days had shown her why she'd never loved any other man but him. He'd been a rock, a champion, never doubting her. Time and again he'd come to her aid without hesitation. She hated to think what might have happened in the woods, had he not found her when he did. She'd angered Francis beyond measure; she doubted he'd have continued with his plan to marry her. She had truly been terrified for her life, a sense of defenselessness and powerlessness she hoped never to experience again.

Adam's heart beat under her hand through the slight texture of his black worsted waistcoat. Not only her heart but her body stirred, aware of his heart, his body, and the closeness they shared. Beneath his greatcoat she wore only her thin linen chemise, and the heat suffusing her skin had little to do with the layers of broadcloth enveloping her. Memories crowded her thoughts and imaginings and a proper lady would probably have stepped away but she stayed where she was. Safe. Cared for. Cherished.

The wind had dropped, the rain little more than a gentle patter against the shutters. Only the fire lit the room now, flickers reaching into the shadowed corners. For the first time in days—longer—a sense of peace, of calm suffused her.

She lifted her head to study him, this man who meant so much to her. Did he feel as she did? She could not ask him in words. Yet his eyes told her, in the genuine concern with which he returned her gaze, his embrace still gently around her.

He cupped her face, the touch of his hand light and tender. "You have a bruise there," he said softly. "Mother gave me one of her potions for injuries. It's in the left pocket, there."

In truth her face did hurt, and her whole body ached, but his injuries had to be more severe than hers. No-one had hit her with the force used against him, with intent to kill or seriously injure. She delved in the pockets of his coat for the leather pouch she'd found earlier, intending to offer to tend his bruises. But as she held the pouch out to him, the cuff of his coat fell back on her arm, exposing the red abrasions on her wrist, the scratches on her hands and arms.

For a heartbeat, anger flared in his eyes. But not at her. His fingers were gentle as he took the pouch from her. "Sit down here near the fire. The lotion will ease the pain."

As she sat on the bench, the long skirt of his greatcoat draped on the floor and she tucked her bare feet into the folds of fabric, away from the chill of the stone floor. Adam knelt in front of her, taking her hand and pushing back the heavy sleeve from her forearm, and carefully began to apply the Countess's salve to the abrasions around her wrists. The scents of the lotion assailed her, in a pleasant way.

Arnica, of course, for bruising. The fresh tones of bergamot, or perhaps lime. The sweeter scent of lavender.

She watched while he concentrated on his self-appointed task. His damp shirt clung to his shoulders and arms, shaping muscles and male strength usually hidden by jacket sleeves. She swallowed to wet her dry throat.

As if afraid of hurting her, his touch was feather light as he smoothed the salve over her skin. Feather light and...affecting, Not even the slight sting of the lotion on broken skin reduced the pleasurable sensations. Her pulse fluttered under the delicate skin on the inside of her forearms. And she'd never known that a joint as practical as an elbow could be so deliciously sensitive.

They were both silent, the crackling of the fire and the gentle drumming of the rain the only sounds. She could not think what to say. One arm, then the other. By the time he finished she no longer breathed evenly. Neither did he.

He stood up abruptly, turning away as he reached for the cork stopper for the bottle. In his one quick glance at her face, she saw the unmistakable flare of desire in his eyes. But she also saw the bruise darkening on his jaw.

She rose to her feet, too, and took the bottle from his hands. "I'm not the only one with bruises. Let me tend your wounds now."

He didn't move as she deftly spread the thick lotion on his jaw, and on the reddened area just below his temple. She wasn't sure he breathed.

She lay the lightest of kisses on his temple, heard his small sharp intake of breath. "Thank you for coming to my rescue. I'm sorry you were hurt doing so."

"Bruises fade." His fingertips caressed her cheek, so lightly she might have imagined it except that she couldn't imagine the intensity in his eyes. "I wish I'd reached you sooner."

"You found me, that's what matters. And you risked your life for me. I won't forget that."

"And you for me." His arm tightened around her and she moved in closer, so that there was not the slightest gap between their bodies.

Her fingertips rested on the fabric of his waistcoat, brushing the top button. How easy to unbutton it, to push it aside, find the opening in his shirt and press her mouth to his skin. She remembered the taste of him, as clear as if it were yesterday, and the sensual pleasure of those stolen moments of intimacy. Maybe people thought she was virginal, cold, passionless, but she wasn't. Not with him.

Last night she'd kissed his mouth, and she kissed him again now, a brush of her lips over his, another and another as he answered her kisses with his own. Her fingers threading through his hair, she parted her lips for him and he took her mouth, gentleness giving way to the desire driving them both. She craved his touch, his caresses; yearned to show her feelings in countless, wordless ways and give him pleasure, share pleasure with him.

Heady with passion, she swayed when he paused and stepped back a fraction. His hands gripped her shoulders, the pupils of his eyes dark with wanting, his breathing as ragged as hers. But he gave her space, time to think, to find order and coherence in her thoughts.

Last night she'd allowed sense and duty and responsibility to overcome her desire. But last night was before Francis's attack. Before he'd threatened her. Before he'd come close to killing them both.

Her priorities changed by the fear and violence of the day, she made her decision, simply and without doubt. This might be her only ever chance to lie with Adam, to know and love him intimately. No matter what happened in the future, she did not want to regret missing the chance of this moment.

She only had to find the courage to be bold.

The rain pattered against the shutters, light from the fire danced on the white-washed walls, and both of them still breathed unevenly.

"There is only one bed," she began. Now. *Just say it.* "I want you to share it with me, Adam."

His throat moved as he swallowed but he didn't draw away from her. "Emma, it's natural to want...*that*, after fighting for your life. It's natural to crave it. Connection. Release. Life."

He was too honorable, too much in command of himself.

She didn't doubt what he'd said was true—he'd been in too many battles and must know from experience—yet it was only one truth, not the whole of it.

"It means more than that to us though, doesn't it? I wanted it—*you*—before tonight. When Francis tried...I regretted, so much, that we'd never..." Oh, she was making a mess of this. She had to be clear, direct. Brave. "I want you, Adam. I always have. No-one else, only you."

~

Only you.

Only Emma, for him, ever. She was three-quarters—probably more—of his experience. Even in the darkest days of war, even when his comrades turned to prostitutes and camp women and he, too craved the oblivion of carnal release, the thought of laying with another woman turned desire to nausea. Whether that was a matter of honor—he hated seeing women used—or a hopeless devotion to a lost love, he didn't know for sure. Only that his intimacies with Emma were more fulfilling than a fast and frantic coupling with a stranger could possibly be.

He searched her face for any doubt but other than a small, nervous tug on her lips with delicate teeth, she held his gaze with her clear, silver-gray eyes. No girl, but a woman knowing her own mind, waiting for his response.

He held on to one last shred of control, of honor. "I want you too, Emma. More than you can know. But you have to be sure."

"I am sure."

Her fingers trembling, she undid the buttons on his great coat, pulling the heavy cloth open, letting it fall off her shoulders so that she stood before him in only her chemise, the fine linen skimming the peaks of her breasts.

Heat burned through him, drying his mouth. Gentle. He needed to be gentle with her, this beautiful, giving woman he loved beyond any ability he had to express.

Groaning her name, he gathered her into him, determined for the moment to simply hold her, to allow her to feel the evidence of his desire for her, to give her the chance to change her mind. She pressed against him, her hands sliding under his waistcoat, her touch through his shirt heating his skin. She'd know the significance of the hardness in his trousers. They'd been confident, close enough once to explore each other's bodies and he ached to feel the touch of her fingers gripping him once more. Not yet. Not yet. Her comfort, her pleasure came first. As slow and tender and caring as she deserved.

Caressing the elegant line of her shoulder and neck, he kissed her mouth softly and she opened to him immediately, tongues tasting, teasing, tangling as their kiss deepened again in hungry need.

He eventually left her mouth but only to kiss her face, her neck, the dip at the base of her throat. She made a low sound there, and her fingers threaded through his hair to hold him to her.

He trailed kisses lower, down to where her chemise gathered lightly over her breasts. He licked along the edge of the drawstring as his hands cupped her, and she gasped when he circled the hard peaks with his thumbs.

No stays barred his way now, and he lowered his head, taking one nipple into his mouth, sucking, teasing through the linen. With another gasp she arched against his lips, and although his pulse pounded in his ears he pleasured first one breast, then the other until she swayed on her feet and clung to him, her breathing as ragged as his.

He lifted her and she wrapped her legs around him, her mouth finding his again. None too steady himself, he carried her to the bed. Instead of setting her down on it, he sat on the edge so as not to break the kiss, and she unreservedly straddled his lap as if it was the most natural thing in the world to do. Perhaps it was.

He shed his cravat while her fingers worked feverishly at his waistcoat buttons, her face flushed.

"Tell me what to do," she said, her voice husky.

"Do whatever pleases you."

"But what pleases you?"

"You do." And there was a truth. To see her breathless and unreserved with him, trusting him with intimacy, made his heart light. As though she'd cracked open a suit of armor he'd protected himself with for too long.

The neckline of her chemise dipped as she leaned forward to peel his waistcoat back from his shoulders, and the tantalizing glimpse of her breasts beneath the linen blasted another surge of desire through him.

Slow. He had to take this gradually and tenderly for her sake. Even though his cock strained hard against the fall of his trousers, so close to her. So close.

She unbuttoned his collar and trailed fiery kisses on his chest through the slit of his shirt while he fumbled with the buttons on the cuffs. Once freed, he dragged his shirt over his head and she tugged it from his arms.

Her chemise remained the only barrier between their upper bodies. His mouth, his skin, craved hers, but if he loosened the tie gathering the linen over her breasts, or if he slid his hands under the fabric and lifted it over her, he'd explode into flame.

Slow. *Slow.* She deserved so much more than a hasty coupling. He caught her mouth with his again, gentle in his kiss, while he reached behind with one hand to flip back the covers on the bed. And then he lifted her and turned to set her on the sheet. Not as fine a quality as she deserved, but worn and soft with age.

He remained on the edge of the bed to remove his damp boots. She knelt behind him, exploring the skin of his back, his spine, with her hands and mouth. He almost tore his feet off in his haste to be rid of his boots.

She watched in silence, her lips parted, as he dispatched the rest of his clothes. When he stood naked before her, not hiding his arousal, her eyes widened and a shy but oh so sensual smile curved her mouth and made his heart race.

And then she gripped the hem of her chemise, and wriggling it over her thighs, she lifted it over her head, tossing it aside.

Beautiful. So beautiful he could scarcely breathe.

With my body, I thee worship. He would make those vows to her one day, before God and the vicar and their families.

Slow. He climbed on to the bed, drew her down to lie beside him, and skin to skin, began to show her his love in a hundred lingering kisses, a thousand caresses. As he learned the ways of her body, the touches that pleased her, she explored his body in tantalizing strokes. It took all his control to hold his own desire in check until she was breathless with need, reaching for him, wrapping her legs around him.

Slow. Gentle. Careful. She gave one small gasp, her eyes wide open, but when he paused she gripped his hips to keep him there and whispered hoarsely, "*Please.*"

And then there was only Emma, and the exquisite joy of their bodies together, and her fractured breathing as his slow strokes brought her to the edge of release, and he unleashed his control and together they moved, again and again, until the pleasure built into overwhelming sensation and then the shattering ecstasy of completion.

~

"*No!*"

The guttural word and an arm tightening around her dragged Emma abruptly from sleep. A deep, sated, contented sleep so that for a moment confusion muddled her thoughts about where and who and why.

Memory flooded back as Adam tossed his head from side to side and shouted a hoarse, "*No!*" again, and in the faint light from the dying fire his face was tight with pain.

She rolled to her side and touched his cheek gently. "It's just a dream, Adam," she murmured. "Just a dream."

His eyes flew wide open, staring at her for a heartbeat until he fully woke and realized where he was. He muttered a curse, and blinked his eyes closed and open again, a flush reddening his neck. "You must think me a weakling. I was talking in my sleep, wasn't I?

I'm sorry I woke you."

It hurt to see him feel shamed, and for no reason. "Adam, I'd never think less of anyone merely because of a bad dream. Goodness knows, we've endured enough these past few days to give the strongest souls nightmares."

Sitting up, he dragged a hand through his hair. "It's not that, Emma. I wake often, sometimes shouting, fighting. For years. Usually it's battles. Sometimes..." He breathed unevenly, the anguish of the nightmare lingering in his eyes. "Sometimes I fear I am caught in madness. I'm sorry. I shouldn't have-"

With all they'd shared it seemed natural, despite their nakedness, to wrap her arms around him. "Sshh. It was just a dream. Let it go from your mind. You're not in the slightest mad."

"The war's been over for a year and I still... It keeps coming back. You can't imagine what it was like..." His voice trailed away and he stared ahead, every muscle in his body tense.

No, she couldn't imagine war. Battle after battle, thousands of men and muskets and canon and horses, fighting, shouting, dying. Until this week, she couldn't even have imagined the horror of being trapped in a burning building, or the terror of being hit, captured, and in fear for her life. She'd never forget that fear. Yet he'd endured years of the most brutal fighting.

She'd heard that some returned soldiers and officers suffered from nightmares and nerves, profoundly affected by their experiences and unable to settle. The vicar's son scarcely slept, roaming the countryside and shunning company since his return from Waterloo, to the distress of his father and his sister. Patience, Mr. Timms counselled. Patience and acceptance and understanding.

"I read the battle reports in the papers," she said softly, "and I always thought about you being there, in the middle of it all, in all those campaigns that your regiment was in. And I know I can't possibly imagine the true horror of it but what I can imagine is... hellish. I'd read about them and I'd dread hearing..." She shuddered and broke off, resting her head against his shoulder, her palms against his heart. As if somehow, touching his skin with hers, connecting them, might give him ease and slow his racing heartbeat. "Of course those experiences have affected you. You're a man who cares, Adam. If they had not...if they had not changed you, if they did not haunt you, then you wouldn't be the man I know."

He swallowed but made no reply, so that she feared that her words were meaningless for him. Yet he covered her hand with his, drew her closer, and pulled up the blanket to wrap around her shoulders. She remained still, simply holding him, being with him, hoping that he felt her care for him. He rested his head against hers, and with that sign of trust she determined not to move an inch for as long as he wanted her there.

She was aware of their nakedness and every inch of his skin against hers. And desire was still there, but it hummed in the background, muted for now by a greater need. Her heart ached for the hurt buried within such a strong, proud man, and yet she was touched that he trusted her with it, with his vulnerability. And perhaps that made an even greater intimacy than the beauty of the physical closeness they'd shared. Her heart was full of emotions she could scarcely put a name to. If the word *love* covered them all, then she'd barely touched the surface of it, before today.

Outside it was dark and quiet, with only the dripping of soft rain. A small creature scratched in leaves in the garden, and an owl hooted some distance away.

Some instinctive wisdom held her silent. He needed no more words, inadequate as they were. His skin was warm under her hand, and gradually his breathing evened out, his heart rate slowed and the tension in him began to relax.

"You must be cold," he said eventually, raising the hand he held to kiss her knuckles. "I'll build up the fire."

She had only a few moments to admire his tautly muscled body as he slid out from under the covers before he dragged his shirt over his head. But the loose folds of linen draped around him and there was beauty in that, too, as he crossed the room and crouched by the fireplace.

The air was cool and she nestled down under the covers and

watched him. Hands that had stroked her, caressed her, were strong and sure as he added more kindling to the glowing coals and blew them gently into flame. Even such prosaic and practical movements seemed sensual.

Was this how it was for married people? For lovers? Sharing these everyday moments with all the memories and passions of their lovemaking sharpening their awareness? Heightening desire?

She'd never been aware of watching a man's hands before. Not even weavers or wool combers or dyers at their work. Yet Adam's lean, deft fingers as he broke sticks and added them to the flames stirred her desire, as if she was the kindling in his hands. She dropped her gaze to his feet, bare on the stone hearth, and the lean, sinewy muscle of his leg leading to a thigh exposed by the way his shirt fell... oh, my. She didn't need the fire to heat her body.

Perhaps aware of her observation, he looked over his shoulder at her and a slow smile chased the shadows from his face. A smile of love. Of promise. She hoped it was promise. She ached with wanting him again.

As he returned to the bed the linen folds of his shirt failed to hide his readiness. He shed it before he slid under the covers beside her. And although he murmured, "I should let you sleep," she was in no state for sleeping. And neither, it seemed, was he.

She woke in the morning in his arms, her head cradled against his shoulder, and smiled in contentment. Nothing in her dreams, nothing in her imaginings, and definitely nothing in her limited education had prepared her for the pleasures of being with Adam.

She did not regret her decision for an instant.

Birds twittered in the trees outside, and the faint light of dawn edged around the window shutters and under the door. Soon she would have to rise and face the day. Not yet.

The fire had died down again but sometime in the night Adam had placed his greatcoat over her, on top of the threadbare blanket and coverlet. She spared a sympathetic thought for the old goodwife who'd lived here without the benefit of the extra warmth. But if there was any of her spirit still lingering here in her cottage, it felt like a kindly one.

If she was a little girl who believed in wishes, she'd wish that they could stay here in this cottage, just the two of them, hidden from the world.

Impossible, of course. Others were looking for them and would find them, soon enough. And they both had responsibilities to attend to.

The worries she'd pushed aside last night began to edge their way back. Francis's flight removed immediate danger but—but what would it mean for Braithwaite and Co.? For her? There might never be any proof of his murderous plotting against her and the family company. His exile didn't solve the difficulties facing the company. His exile didn't resolve the distrust of her that had been building among her business connections. And nor did it halt the racing spread of factories that was changing everything.

But Matthew was alive, and coming home, and she didn't have to save the family company alone. And Adam was home. Whatever happened after this morning, she would always be glad to have shared this too-brief time with him.

In sleep his face was relaxed, the torments of concern and command and war eased. A young man again, as if his experiences in battle hadn't aged him beyond his years. And yet, she admired his maturity, too, respected his courage, his dedication to others.

She'd fallen in love with him all over again, deeper than ever.

He stirred, his eyelashes flickering as he gradually woke. His arm tightened around her and he rolled on his side to face her, with a slow, delicious smile that made her heart turn a somersault.

He smoothed a loose strand of hair back from her face. "You're not a dream, are you?"

"If I am, it's very clever of us to dream the same dream."

He nuzzled against her neck, his unshaven jaw lightly prickly against her skin. "You will marry me, won't you?"

She drew in a slow breath, battling the desire to say 'yes', knowing she had to say 'no'. Or something like it. The smile was slipping from his eyes as she hesitated. How could she do this gently? "Adam, I didn't sleep with you to trap you, to bind you to me."

He closed his hand over hers. "I know that. I don't feel trapped in the slightest. I truly want to marry you. Will you?"

"Please don't ask me that, Adam. Not now. There's still so much uncertain and...it's too soon after your return. You might change your mind, once you've settled back here."

He might change his mind if Braithwaite and Co. failed, if scandal enveloped her. He might change his mind if he became the earl. If she said yes now, he'd be bound to her yet might come to regret it, even resent her.

And while all those fears chased around in her thoughts, he held her hand, his thumb circling in a soft, calming caress on the back of it.

"I know I won't-" He broke off as the clip-clop of horses sounded close-by, and rolled off the bed in an instant, grabbing his shirt and trousers. As the horse stopped outside, he tossed her chemise to her.

A brisk knock on the door sounded as Emma pulled her chemise over her head and Adam speedily donned shirt and trousers.

"It's only me, Caldwell." Mr. Penry's voice. "Is all well?"

"Yes," Adam called in reply. "I'll be out in just a moment." As he buttoned up his trousers, Adam crossed to where her clothes hung on the hooks on the other side of the room. He gathered them and brought them to her. "Stay inside," he said as he pulled on his boots. "I'll talk with Penry and get the horse ready. We'll likely have to leave soon."

She nodded mutely. Their brief interlude from the world was over. The day might bring explanations and a journey home to Matthew, but she had also to face all the questions, curiosity and judgement of others—and hide her feelings for Adam from them.

As if he shared her thoughts, he pressed a kiss to her mouth before he went to the door, opening it just enough to slip outside.

CHAPTER 23

Penry propped himself against the stone wall of the garden, idly watching birds on the path and loosely holding the reins of two horses while they grazed.

"The mare is for Miss Braithwaite to ride back," Penry said. He glanced sideways at Adam, amusement quirking his mouth. "You can rely on my discretion, Caldwell. Assuming the lady is not hurt or distressed. In which case, I might feel obliged to act on behalf of her brother."

Adam was in no mood to be teased, but the concern for Emma saved Penry from a bruised jaw. Of course Penry had reached the obvious conclusion, when he'd answered the door. Men purely on guard duty did not wander around in untucked shirts and little else. "The lady is neither hurt nor distressed," he assured him, although his discomfort discussing such private matters made it come out sharp. "Has Francis Braithwaite been captured?"

"Unfortunately, no. Not yet. Gresham sent men searching and has sent messengers to other landholders. Needle in a haystack, though. Assuming Braithwaite wants to escape the country, he could have ridden in almost any direction."

Adam nodded, grim at the thought. Francis might be going east to Hull. West to Liverpool. North to Newcastle or Scotland. He might even go south, to London. Easy enough to hide in London, and ships went all over the world from there.

Penry's coat and hat were quite damp, and he hadn't shaved. Probably hadn't slept, either.

"You've been out searching all night."

Penry acknowledged that with a wry smile. "Not much of the night left, by the time I sent men out on the main roads, and went to see Gresham. He's a magistrate, of course. He sent for the coroner last night. The nearest one is Palmer, in Halifax. Gresham expects we'll both be required to attend and give evidence."

"I'd rather be out searching for Braithwaite."

"So would I, but there are more than twenty men out already. Probably more. News of the reward you offered has spread. And Gresham is overseeing the search. Do you know him?"

Adam shook his head. "More by reputation than direct knowledge." A reputation as a hedonistic libertine. Not encouraging. "I met him briefly a few times, many years ago. Will he truly aid the search? He let Braithwaite borrow his hounds."

"He's no particular friend of his. And somewhat disgruntled that not only were his Bacchanalian entertainments interrupted last night, but that Francis lied about why he needed the hounds. I do know something of him and he takes his manorial and magistrate's responsibilities seriously. He's calling together men for a jury this morning. I expect they'll come out to view the remains within a few hours, as soon as the coroner arrives."

Adam refrained from asking how Penry knew of Gresham, and simply accepted the assurance. "Can we keep Miss Braithwaite's name out of the inquest, do you think?"

"Possibly. If the coroner is willing, we may be able to avoid calling her as a witness for the inquest. Might even be able to avoid mentioning her name at all. Make it you and I pursuing Francis and the others for their crimes. But that becomes more complex," he added, "with references to the Canadian business, and is likely to lengthen proceedings. My reports may not have reached London yet so I can't claim Castlereagh's authority. Or anyone else's."

Long proceedings with the scandal of multiple murders and treasonous plots stirring public interest and talk for months to come were exactly what Adam hoped to avoid. He wanted it over and done with today. Preferably within a few hours, to enable Emma to go home.

"We'll have to stick with the simple facts of the truth, then. The abduction is why we chased Francis. I don't see any other way around it. There are plenty of witnesses to him arriving at the inn with her. And half the village was out searching for his 'mad wife'."

"Yes, I believe you're right. Otherwise there will be whispers and talk, and likely outright questions at the inquest."

"I'll speak with the coroner about protecting her reputation and avoiding her name. But if it becomes necessary, I'd rather her name linked to an abduction than to murder and treason." And that would spare Robert Braithwaite the public censure of being a traitor's brother, on top of everything else. But that thought brought to mind a loose end. "Where did you leave Dutton? And what will you do with him?"

"He's locked up in the church crypt at the last village, with the fear of God in his jailers if he's not there when I return, and a nice fat reward if he is. I'll have to consult about him. A charge of treason requires at least two witness. Matthew and I can give evidence against both Francis and Dutton. Francis is the more important one, and perhaps Dutton might be persuaded to add his evidence to ensure a conviction, in exchange for transportation for life rather than the noose." He grimaced. "But the government may not want word of the American plot to get out. They're tetchy about potential revolutions."

Adam nodded. Dissent among the working classes was already punished with harsh sentences, for often lesser crimes. Too harsh, he sometimes thought. But a well-to-do merchant fomenting open rebellion in the colonies? That might inspire others. And might encourage foreign powers to attempt to destabilize Britain. "There are four witnesses to Barlow's murder. That's enough to send Francis to the gallows. But it doesn't deal with Dutton."

"If I can find a witness putting Dutton at Winslow's murder, that will be simpler. Or I can hand him over to his regiment. They came back to England last year."

Adam considered timings and dates. "Was the war already over when he deserted? Will they go lightly on him?"

"The soldiers killed on the expedition to the north were from his regiment. He won't be treated lightly, believe me."

A polite way of saying that Dutton would either face a firing squad or go to the gallows. Assuming he lived that long. Desertion, sedition, treason, murder—they made a combination of crimes powerful enough to raise a mighty anger in his former comrades, and a commanding officer with no strict commitment to procedure might allow his men to administer their own justice.

Not a laxity in discipline Adam would permit, if Dutton had been in his regiment, but others might. Whatever happened, Dutton had only a short and miserable life-span in front of him, and was no longer a threat to anyone. Except Francis. But Francis would hardly be going anywhere near a prison cell, not when Matthew and Penry remained to bear witness against him. And Emma.

The mist was beginning to rise, the weak sunlight reflecting off water droplets hanging on leaves. Perhaps summer might eventually arrive.

"Tell me what happened to Matthew while I see to the horse," Adam said. "I want to get Emma back to the inn as soon as possible."

Penry, leading the horses, followed him around to the back of the cottage, tying them to the timber fence while Adam put a halter on the horse in the byre and brought it out into the overgrown vegetable garden. He had little to feed it, other than this few minutes of foraging in the neglected vegetable patch. And in the wilderness of herbs he saw nothing suitable to pick for Emma to eat. She must be starving. He was hungry enough, and he'd had breakfast yesterday. All the more reason to get the horse saddled quickly.

"Why didn't Matthew send word earlier that he was alive?" he asked as he carried out the saddle. "Why didn't you?"

Penry held the horse for him. "He was badly injured. There were times I thought he was going to die. We travelled slowly and only reached Montreal in May." He scratched the nose of the horse, who seemed to accept the attention. A surprising gentleness at odds with the impression Adam had formed of an unemotional, no-nonsense man. "We didn't know where Francis and his thugs were and the Gulf was still too icy for ships to travel, " he continued, "so we laid low, and didn't get to Quebec until almost the middle of June, when ships were starting to leave. Turns out that Francis and company apparently went south and shipped home from New York. We did send letters with a ship that left a few days before ours, but it was going to Glasgow. We only landed at Liverpool on Tuesday evening. Matthew planned to consult with a physician there, and then travel to his home. He should be there by now."

The horse became skittish as Adam lifted the saddle on to him. Maybe still unsettled from the fight, maybe simply a difficult horse. He pulled up some green grass to offer the beast as a bribe, in hopes he might keep him quietened enough to ride without distraction. "Why did you stay with Matthew and bring him home instead of going after Francis and the others? Emma can't have been paying you that well."

"Hah. No." He gave the horse another good scratch, emotions chasing across his usually unreadable face. "Because if it wasn't for me," he said eventually, a touch of hoarseness in his voice, "If I hadn't got him involved in trying to catch Francis and Dutton and the deserters, he would have been safely home before his father died. And because I wasn't there when Francis caught up with him and ordered his murder."

His concern for Matthew was all well and good, but the moments when Emma had almost died were stark in Adam's memory. "If you'd told me the other day what you knew about Francis, he would never have got near Emma."

Penry took the rebuke as evenly as he treated the horse. "You were already protecting her. I wasn't sure what Francis was up to and didn't expect him to move so quickly. And I was coming to see you yesterday. You and Miss Braithwaite."

All true, and Adam regretted his sharpness. His tension, his hurry to take Emma back to the inn was no excuse for discourtesy. And to make matters worse, he was transferring his disquiet to the horse, who clearly favored Penry's attentions and distrusted his.

"Whoa, boy. Let's all be easy now." He took the time to stroke the gelding's nose. Whether the beast appreciated it or not, he himself found the few moments oddly soothing. "We're just going to saddle up so you can go back to a nice cozy stable, and be looked after properly."

"I can finish saddling him," Penry offered. "You go in and see if Miss Braithwaite is ready. You can tell her Matthew should be home when she gets there. I sent a messenger to him last night, to tell him she is found and unharmed."

Inside, Emma knelt before the fire, scattering the coals. She'd made the bed, and laid his jacket neatly on the table ready for him. She wore his coat, buttoned up to the neck. She'd somehow managed to coil and pin up her braid, despite the lack of brush, comb, or mirror, but loose tendrils of hair almost covered the dark bruise, stark on the pale skin of her face.

She looked up at him with a tentative smile. If a small part of him hoped that she'd changed her mind and wanted to tell him yes, she'd marry him, that hope was dashed with her first question. "Does Mr. Penry have any news of Matthew?"

Of course her thoughts were with her brother. Of course she was anxiously awaiting Penry's news. "Matthew is likely to be at Larkfell when you get home."

"Oh, that is wonderful." A frown dimmed her smile and she hastily began to rise. "But he'll be out of his mind with worry that I'm not there."

Adam held out a hand to assist her to her feet. "Penry sent him word that you're safe. I hope you'll be there later today, if I can arrange it."

She rose a little awkwardly, hampered by the length of his coat on her. When she released his hand to shake out her skirts he immediately missed the warmth of it.

"Is Francis captured?" Her question jolted him back to harsh reality.

"Not yet. But there are dozens of men searching for him. And word has gone out up and down the main roads that he's a fugitive."

"There will be an inquest for that man today, won't there?" she asked. "Will I have to attend it?"

"Not if we can avoid it. My evidence and that of Gresham's men should be quite enough."

The horses whinnied to each other outside.

"I'm all ready to go." She handed him his cravat, neatly folded. He hadn't noticed it on the table beside his jacket. Of course she'd been concerned about Matthew and the inquest, but the soft smile in her eyes now was solely for him, and his heart skipped a beat. "One of us at least should look reputable," she said, and added, "I can tie it for you, if you like."

The linen cloth was far from snowy white after yesterday but he had the grime from horses and tack on his hands. His shirt lay open at the neck from his hurried dressing, and she stepped closer to do up the fine thread buttons. So close her breath feathered across his skin.

When she reached up to wrap the cloth around his neck, the loose heavy coat brushed against him. Her forehead creased in concentration as she arranged the cravat folds, her breath uneven. If only he could take her in his arms, hold on to her, bury his face in her hair and stay with her here in this quiet sanctuary, just the two of them.

Except it wasn't just the two of them. Penry waited outside, Gresham and the jury waited in the village and Emma needed to get home to her brother. It was his responsibility to see that she arrived there safely.

She finished tying the simple knot and tucked the ends into his waistcoat, his skin lighting with every deft touch of her fingers through his shirt. She was not unaffected either, and when it was done, she left one hand against his thudding heart as she raised her face to his gaze.

"There. Almost respectable," she said. Brushing the back of her fingers against the bristles of his unshaved jaw, she teased lightly,

227

"Except for this. Perfectly piratical."

Her determined cheerfulness despite the tears welling in her eyes struck a bayonet through his heart and twisted it. His throat too choked for words, he clasped her hands in his, kissed her fingers.

"Adam, I..." She paused, swallowed nervously. "I'm glad you're home. I'm glad that you're the one who found me. I wish..." She shook her head with the saddest smile. "I wish everything was simpler."

Oh, how he wished it was simple, too. But she'd refused his proposal of marriage this morning and despite all the perfectly logical and sensible reasons, there was a pang of hurt. An inner voice kept muttering, *'You're not worthy enough for her.'*

Damn that nightmare that had woken him—woken both of them—in the night. He'd lasted weeks without a dream that intense, fooling himself into thinking he was cured of that weakness. And now Emma had seen him crying out in his dreams like a child. No surprise she hadn't accepted him, despite the passion and affection between them.

And there was that inner voice again, taunting him.

He ordered it to quit the insubordination and fall back in line. He was a mature man, not a self-centered youth.

And the truth was that he *had* only been back for three days. The certainty he felt about his love for her...he doubted that would ever change. But these last days—these weeks since he'd left France—had been tumultuous enough that a rational man might acknowledge there was a chance he over-felt his emotions.

Not much of a chance. Not when she looked at him with her heart in her eyes and her incredible strength of character and honor.

He accepted and respected her decision. It made all kinds of sense, in the circumstances. And so his path ahead was simple, step by step.

He kissed her fingers again. "We should get going. But in a few days, when you're home and rested and caught up with Matthew, may I call on you?"

She breathed out a sigh of relief. "Yes. Please."

228

Those two modest words offered a world of possibilities. As long as he matched her courage and sense with his own.

They still had a long way to go, but she was there, by his side, and there was a kind of peace in that, and more than a little hope.

But first he had to make sure that Francis Braithwaite was either on a ship headed far away from Britain, or in chains and committed for trial as a murderer, or a traitor, or both.

CHAPTER 24

They rode at walking pace along the path to begin with, Mr. Penry just ahead of her, Adam close behind. Protecting her. Emma stared at her horse's ears as they passed the trampled body of the man, Barlow, guarded by two burly men. Barlow, the man who'd almost murdered Matthew. Perhaps she should be angry with him, or glad he was dead, or…something. Some emotion, other than this numbness. She need not fear him, anyway.

Nor did she fear an attack by Francis. He surely understood that with Matthew's and Mr. Penry's testimony, and with Adam's and her own, he stood no chance of escaping the death penalty if he was caught in England. A rapid escape from England was his only chance of life.

When the path became wider, they cantered, and before long—a much shorter time than she'd taken last night, stumbling through the woods—the path became a wider track, and a few hundred yards along it joined the road, south of the village. Mr. Penry left them there, going along the road a short way to speak to searchers emerging from the woods.

The closer they came to the inn, the tighter dread coiled in Emma's stomach. She wanted only to hide away from questions and stares and whispers.

They'd planned to approach the inn via the lane that ran behind it, to avoid the scrutiny of the public entrance. But the sight of at least ten men on horseback, milling in the lane, and a cart blocking the gate into the garden made that plan unworkable.

A small carriage arrived just ahead of them at the front of the inn, a groom leaping down to hold the door open as the soberly dressed passenger and his clerk stepped down and went inside. Mr. Palmer, the coroner.

Emma kept her face averted, away from the inn's windows, as they rode into the courtyard. There were people here too, a coach and four waiting, footmen strapping trunks on the back, a postilion holding the horses.

Adam assisted her to dismount, an awkward maneuver for her in his big coat when she was not accustomed to riding astride. He steadied her with hands around her waist as she landed on her feet on the cobblestones, and she longed to lean into the warmth and safety of him, hold on to the intimacies of the night and his unwavering support for a short while longer. But not with a yard full of people and horses.

"Would you like to go in the back way?" Adam asked. "I can find the maid and send her to you."

Emma nodded, desperate to escape the curious glances of onlookers in her disheveled state. The postilion was carefully not looking at her from under his hat.

The footmen had other concerns. Their mistress swept out from the inn, clad in fur-trimmed pelisse and hat, calling out criticisms and instructing them to remove the trunks and turn them around.

Emma caught a glimpse of her face under the fur and immediately wished they'd arrived a few minutes earlier or later. She sidestepped to duck behind Adam but she was too late to avoid Lady Beatrice Farringdon's notice.

With one brief, scathing perusal of her from her untidily pinned hair to the mud-spattered bottom of the greatcoat, Lady Beatrice shot straight to the worst conclusion. "Miss Braithwaite! Good heavens, girl! You have been out all night? With a *man*? Have you no shame at *all*?"

Anger giving her courage, Emma inclined her head merely enough to be polite. "Good morning, Lady Beatrice. Given the unavoidable circumstances, Madam, no, I have no shame." Not even for giving herself to Adam. Others might disagree, but despite all the rules and expectations and propriety, she regretted nothing of the night they'd shared.

"You disgrace the memory of your sweet mother, girl," Lady Beatrice scoffed. "I will see that you are not admitted to polite society again."

Emma almost gaped at her, lost for words. Surely the woman had heard from those in the inn about her predicament? Surely she did not think her bedraggled state the result of a willful romp in the woods?

"Madam, Miss Braithwaite was abducted," Adam said with ice cold precision, "A true lady would enquire after her well-being and render assistance."

"Hrmph. Ran off with a paramour, more likely."

"Good day to you, Madam." Adam's harsh tone made it more warning than courtesy. He offered Emma his arm and she placed her hand on it and walked beside him with as much dignity as she could marshal in tattered boots and his long coat threatening to trip her up. They passed her ladyship with the barest of nods.

Lady Beatrice glared at them, unheeding of the rebuff. "It's bad enough that we were forced to take shelter in this odious inn overnight," she said loudly after them. "It's the kind of sinful place you belong, miss."

Adam's face looked like thunder and Emma feared he might be about to turn and demand an apology. She hated scenes. And Lady Beatrice had humiliated her more than enough. Sick to her stomach, she gripped Adam's arm to stop him turning back, but a call came from one of two riders, just entering the stable yard.

"Adam! Miss Braithwaite!"

The groom barely had time to dismount and hold her horse before Mrs. Hampton slid nimbly down.

She hurried straight past Lady Beatrice as if she didn't see her and embraced Emma lightly. "Thank the lord you are safe, my dear.

I've fretted from the moment I heard." She set her at arms' length to assess her state. "Are you hurt?"

The soft scent of rose water and the genuineness of Mrs. Hampton's concern after Lady Beatrice's contempt almost made Emma cry. But she must not cry and make even more of a spectacle of herself. "Nothing of consequence," she managed to say.

"That is such a relief. But you must be exhausted, my dear. Such a traumatic time for you. You will want to rest and refresh yourself, I am sure."

Beside her carriage, Lady Beatrice snorted and Mrs. Hampton noticed her, and the coach at the ready, for the first time. "Oh, are you going with the Farringdons, my dear? That's very kind of them."

Lady Beatrice heard and her face darkened. She couldn't clamber into the carriage fast enough. The door slammed shut.

"Lady Beatrice has a low opinion of me," Emma murmured. "I do hope she doesn't share it."

Mrs. Hampton's mouth firmed into a straight line of disapproval. "Ah, I see. What a miserable woman. Well I am here now, and a perfectly respectable married woman, so she cannot say that you don't have a chaperone."

But she'd had no chaperone last night, and Lady Beatrice knew it. And she wasn't the kind of woman to keep that information to herself. Panic fluttered in Emma's stomach.

Adam seemed more concerned about other immediate matters. "I will arrange a room, and have them send up a meal," he said. "You must be famished, Emma. And you must have had an early start, Mrs. Hampton."

Famished? She'd stopped feeling hungry sometime yesterday. But her last meal...it must have been dinner, the night before last. Perhaps that explained the increasing light-headedness this past hour or so and her emotional fragility. She wished she could simply hide from everything until the dullness cleared from her mind and she could think clearly again.

Mrs. Hampton gathered the trailing skirts of her riding habit with one hand and slipped her other arm through Emma's to go into the inn. "When the Colonel told me of the situation," she said, "I was determined to follow if you did not return last night. I left before dawn. Our coach is coming and will be here soon. A lady needs a female friend in such circumstances. I'll stay with you as long as you like, my dear, and take you to your home in our coach when you are ready."

Overwhelmed by her thoughtfulness and practicality, Emma stammered her thanks. To go home in comfort and privacy, without putting Adam to the expense of hiring horses and the fuss of traveling unchaperoned; Mrs. Hampton's offer solved so many of the difficulties she had dreaded.

The taproom was full with men too old or infirm to go out searching, and a few women. Emma kept her face down and Adam and Mrs. Hampton moved close to her sides to shield her from their view, but people saw her and Adam, anyway, and as he ushered her up the stairs she heard the threads of talk and rumor spreading. *"There he is, he's brought her back." "Mad, I heard." "Ruined, of course."*

On the landing they met the young maid who had helped her escape yesterday—was it only yesterday?

"Oh, miss, sir! Ma said you'd likely be back this morning. We've got a room ready for you. Come along this way."

She showed them to a room larger than the one Francis had been given, with a parlor separate from the bedchamber. A fire burned in the grate, making the room warm. Too warm.

Hot in her skin but cold inside, angry and despairing, Emma struggled with the buttons on the overcoat, her fingers shaking so much she could scarcely work the thick buttons through the holes. While Mrs. Hampton spoke with the maid, making arrangements, Adam helped her with the coat, his long, sure fingers working quickly on the fastenings.

She resisted the urge to lay her head against his shoulder. "They're all going to talk and speculate, aren't they? Even more when it becomes known that he's fleeing murder and treason charges."

His mouth was a hard line. "Yes, there will be talk," he said quietly. "But I'll speak with the coroner. We should be able to avoid mentioning your name at the inquest. It's not relevant to the cause of death."

"But people will still gossip and all sorts of rumors will spread. Lady Beatrice will make sure everyone knows I was involved."

He moved behind her to remove the coat, his hands resting on her shoulders a few moments longer than needed, a small reassuring caress of his thumb against her cheek. "We'll deal with Lady Beatrice. I suspect she's travelling north, not south, so it will be old news before she returns to Hartdale."

How innocent men were of the ways of vicious women, and the slow, poisonous spread of scandalous innuendo. Lady Beatrice was capable of making her a social pariah, especially with Lady Rengarth and Louisa leaving for London shortly and therefore unable to counter her efforts.

And the uncomfortable truth was that although she was totally innocent in Francis's abduction of her, Lady Beatrice's assumptions were entirely correct when it came to how she'd spent the night. In fact, if not in spirit. Nothing about her time with Adam was tawdry or wicked.

Adam laid the greatcoat over a chair before returning to her. As if he read her thoughts, he murmured, "My offer remains open, Emma."

Mrs. Hampton had gone into the bedroom, busy removing her gloves and riding hat. Purposely giving them some privacy, Emma suspected.

Stepping out of her line of sight and keeping her voice low, Emma said, "No, Adam, please don't think that I expect it of you. Not because of fear of gossip or scandal."

She feared hurting him again, but respect for him and for her own self-respect allowed no other course of action.

But he held her gaze, his expression full of tenderness. "You know that's not the reason I asked. So don't hesitate, Emma, if it helps."

There were footsteps outside and a knock on the door. Mrs.

Hampton hurried to answer it, and in the noise of the maid and her mother bringing in trays of food and two lads carting a bath-tub up the stairs, Emma touched her hand to Adam's.

"Ask me again in a month," she whispered. "If you still wish to."

The light in his eyes eased the ache in her heart.

But then, with a brief promise to be back in a few hours, he left to attend the inquest. She blinked back tears. No point at all in crying. She had Mrs. Hampton for company, and although she did not know her well, she admired her calm confidence and her practicality. And especially her friendly acceptance and lack of judgement, a salve to Emma's soul after Lady Beatrice's condemnation.

While the maid laid out dishes on the table, Mrs. Hampton eyed the torn ruins of Emma's dress with understanding and sympathy. "Oh, you poor girl. You have had a rough time, haven't you? Eat first, I think. The bath can wait until you're not reeling from hunger."

Both food and a bath sounded heavenly. Yet she had earthly concerns. "I have no other clothes with me, so I will have to remain bedraggled."

"No need to worry, Emma. I may call you Emma, mayn't I? And I am Julia. We are much of a size, and I thought it wise in the circumstances to pack some clothes for you. My coach is still not here yet but it should arrive by the time you've eaten. Come and sit down, before you fall down."

Emma's relief and gratitude formed a lump in her throat. *'Wise in the circumstances.'* It touched her that Mrs. Hampton—Julia—a lady she hardly knew, had taken the trouble to come after an abducted woman, prepared for the possibility that she'd been molested or otherwise harmed and ready to offer practical, sympathetic support and assistance. She had proved to be a good friend already.

They fussed around her, Julia and Peggy the maid, and for a while Emma allowed herself to be served food and soothed with warm chocolate and kind words. The creamy porridge followed by scrambled eggs and toast gradually eased the sense of emotional fragility, and revived her energy.

She'd not finished her second cup of chocolate when Adam

returned, his face so grave she set down her cup carefully, bracing for bad news.

He accepted Julia's invitation to join them at the table, but declined her offer of chocolate. He was tense, edgy, and didn't relax into the chair. "Francis's horse has been found, less than half a mile away," he told them. "It's possible that the horse fell, or that Francis has been thrown."

"So he may be injured. Or..." Emma did not voice the word. Dead. People died from falling from horses. Especially at speed. Contradictory emotions tangled in her thoughts. For all his crimes, she did not want to wish Francis dead, and yet ... and yet it would be easier, if it was fate or God or anything other than a man having to take his life.

"Yes, he may be hurt," Adam said. "More importantly, he may not be far from here. I want you to stay inside this room for now, in case of danger. We've already sent out more men to search in the direction the horse was found."

"I'll have my groom guard the back stairs," Julia said. "As a precaution."

Guards. Danger. Precaution. All the warmth she'd gained with breakfast faded and Emma suppressed a shudder. "Surely Francis won't be mad enough to come here to the inn? Unless to surrender himself?"

"Unlikely. But desperate men sometimes do rash things. You bested him, Emma. He won't forgive that." He glanced across at Julia. "Mrs. Hampton, it's best if you and Emma remain here this morning. The coroner wants me to visit the site with the jury, but I hope the inquest will be finished within hours. In which case I will escort you to Larkfell."

She did not ask what would happen if the inquest was not finished quickly. Or if Francis was not found. To be on the road, with Francis still free, without Adam's protection... She had not thought herself a coward, but she'd rather stay at the inn another night if necessary. She must be braver. Taking a deep breath, she asked, "Does the Coroner want me to give evidence at the inquest?"

Adam's hesitation warned her of the answer. "I tried to talk him out of it, Emma, but the coroner has asked for your attendance, after we return. It's Mr. Palmer, who conducted the inquest for Winslow. He said to tell you that he will not reveal your name, and he will clear the room of everyone but the jury and his clerk. Of course Julia may accompany you."

"You can refuse, Emma," Julia said, "if you don't feel strong enough."

Strong? She certainly didn't feel strong or confident in her tattered dress, the bodice just pinned closed enough to hide her stays. But there would be time—at least two hours—before the jury returned. Time to prepare herself. And it was her duty to assist, to make sure that the truth was heard. The sooner the inquest was over, the sooner they could all go home. She clasped her hands tightly together in her lap. "I can do it," she said, before cowardice won.

Adam nodded, his mouth a tight line. He didn't argue or try to talk her out of it, but clearly he disliked the prospect as much as she did. But Francis had murdered a man, and even if that man had almost killed Matthew, the truth must be told about his death, and Francis held accountable.

Adam had barely left when Peggy the maid knocked at the door and poked her head around it. "Beggin' your pardon, ma'am, but your coach has arrived and the man is waitin' for orders."

"Thank you, Peggy. Ask him to bring up my valise, and tell him to have a meal, as it may be a few hours before we leave. And would you arrange hot water for Miss Braithwaite's bath, please?"

The prospect of a bath and clean clothes seemed heavenly to Emma. Even borrowed clothes. To be able to look respectable was a kind of emotional armor that her tattered grey silk and torn petticoats did not provide.

She took another sip of the delicious chocolate. Another kind of emotional armor. "Thank you so much for being here," she said to Julia. "You have been so kind, and thoughtful—I don't know what I'd have done without you."

Julia waved her thanks away. "I knew Adam would look after

your safety, but there are matters only another woman can help with. You would do the same thing for a friend." She smiled with genuine warmth. "I know we met only a few days ago, but Adam has been a dear friend to the Colonel and I for a long time. And you are important to Adam, and I like you, so I hope, as you come to know us, that you will consider us your good friends, too."

You are important to Adam. The world of inference behind the words and the knowing sparkle in her eye worried Emma enough to say hastily, "Adam's family and mine have been neighbors and friends for a long time."

"But I think you and Adam are a little more than friends to each other."

Of course she had overheard them earlier, probably seen their unguarded caress. Yet even before then, she'd travelled for several hours in the early morning to assist a woman she barely knew. That must have been out of friendship for Adam, surely.

"We were close once," she acknowledged, a desperate chance that it might satisfactorily explain everything. "Years ago, before he went abroad with his regiment. But I hope he doesn't feel pressured by speculation or gossip about these circumstances. He must be free to make his own choices, when he has had time to settle at home."

Julia held her gaze calmly. "My dear, you have my word that I will not gossip about either of you."

"I know you wouldn't," she clarified hastily. "But Lady Beatrice might."

Julia acknowledged that with a thoughtful nod. "That is a risk, yes. Beatrice is an unhappy woman who regrets her marriage to a man who is a milksop. She is envious of other women. I rather think she is afraid of you and your confidence in taking on the world."

Emma gave a half-gasp, half-laugh and the chocolate sloshed in the cup. She set it down carefully. "Confidence? If you knew how often I quake inside you wouldn't think me confident at all."

"You act on the things you believe in and step up and accept the responsibilities thrust upon you. In spite of the quaking. I am only new to the district but in the past weeks several ladies have mentioned you to me, in admiring tones. So don't allow the Lady Beatrices of this world—or men envious of your abilities," she added, "to shape your opinion of yourself."

Heartwarming words, coming from a woman whose self-assurance she admired. It was true that she tried to live according to her principles and her conscience. Yet that made little difference to people like Lady Beatrice, and others as quick to judge and who held those outside the aristocracy—especially women—to a far higher standard of propriety than their own peers.

A standard Emma had knowingly, willingly, breached in spending the night with Adam and giving him her virginity. Whatever the consequences, she must face them with dignity, to ensure that Adam did not feel trapped into a relationship he might come to regret. Because that would be hellish for both of them.

The bath water, scented with healing oils, initially stung the scratches on her arms and legs. But the pain faded and the warmth eased the tensions in her body. She wished it could ease the tensions in her thoughts as well, but memories, fears, concerns chased each other around and around and not even the scent of lavender oil wafting from bath water quietened her mind. She had yet to face the ordeal of the inquest, and whenever she thought of it, fear rose to choke her throat.

Julia suggested that she rest after the bath, yet despite the freshness of a clean chemise and the comfort of the bed, she could not settle. The inn had fallen quieter after Mr. Palmer and the jury—and Adam and Mr. Penry—had ridden into the forest. Not silent though. Every voice, every foot step, every hoof beat and jingle of harness that drifted up to the room set her on edge. Although Julia's groom and coachman stood guard at the back and front stairs, and the men of the inn knew to capture Francis on sight, the knowledge of Adam's absence left her feeling vulnerable. Too vulnerable to lie in bed, clad only in a chemise.

She pushed aside the bedcovers and rose. Each layer of dress—stockings, shoes, stays, petticoat, chemisette—added a layer of protection, of mental strength. When she donned the blue camlet carriage dress and fastened the bodice and the sleeve cuffs she felt, if not exactly a warrior queen, at least no longer small and helpless.

Hearing the sound of a single, walking horse, Emma went to the bedchamber's window, overlooking the stable yard. A man in the ordinary clothes of a villager dismounted stiffly, as if he'd been riding for some time.

"Have they caught him?" he called to the stable boy, strolling out to take the horse.

Emma pushed the window open to better hear them.

"Nay," the lad answered. "But 'alf the village still be out searching."

"Aye, well, he ain't gone north. Not by the road, anyways."

"And he ain't come back to collect his coach, neither." The boy nodded towards a black coach, pulled to the side at the end of the stable.

The coach she'd traveled all this distance in. Bundled in to it with the hood over her head, dragged out of it by Francis with scarcely a chance to see it. Only the memories of the cold, hard floor, the incessant jolting, the occasional voices of Francis and his men, the hoof beats of the carriage horses and those of the men, riding alongside.

Men. Plural. There'd been two men on the back of the coach; the ones who had dropped off to ambush Adam. At least two riders on horses. She remembered the voices, one rougher than the other. Barlow hadn't spoken much in the confrontation in the forest last night, but he might well have been the rougher one.

She dragged the window closed and hurried in to the parlor. Julia glanced up from her book.

"There's another man," Emma said. "I must tell Adam. Francis brought another man with him, and we haven't accounted for him yet."

CHAPTER 25

He was scarcely more than a boy. Not much older than Benjamin. Adam stared at the lifeless body dragged in to the forest undergrowth, the skull bloodied and broken by a hard blow. Not even a quarter mile from the village. The men who'd been beating through the woods under Gresham's direction, searching for Francis, thrown from his horse, injured, perhaps or—God willing—dead, had found this instead.

Gresham knelt by the corpse, studying it. "It's Jake, Widow Green's eldest. "He's 'prenticed to the smithy."

The name traveled back in murmurs through the small crowd gathered on the forest path. "He were riding Smithy's horse," someone said. "Left at first light."

Adam stepped aside to let Palmer and some of the jurors forward to see the body, and returned to where Penry waited, holding both their horses.

"A riderless horse this morning, and now a horseless rider," Penry commented in a low voice.

"Who didn't fall by accident and crawl into the thicket."

"Definitely dragged?"

"Yes. Some hours ago. Before that shower of rain." Rain that had left its mark on the lad's blood-stained cheek. "He didn't die immediately, but it can't have taken long."

For all the mangled bodies he'd seen in years of war, this one sickened Adam more. The vicious murder of a lad trying to do the right thing. Even if he'd been motivated by the reward. What poor apprentice wouldn't be? It was the reason he'd offered it, to get as many people out searching for Francis as possible. And now this boy, brave and foolhardy enough to search alone, was dead. And now Francis—in all likelihood the deed was done by Francis—again had a horse to ride.

And Emma was at the inn, with only a few people to protect her, because almost every able-bodied man was out here, either gawking at Jake Green's body, or still searching for Francis.

Adam readied his horse to mount. "I'm going back to the inn."

"Nothing more to do here," Penry said. "I'll come with you."

Palmer and the jurors would doubtless follow in a while. One inquest would become two. But there were no witnesses to the lad's death. Only the man who killed him. The man who'd stolen his horse, hours ago.

A dark, hard anger twisted in Adam's gut. Francis did not deserve to escape punishment.

"There's a map at the inn," Adam said over his shoulder to Penry as they set off down the path, too narrow and overhung with trees to canter along. "I doubt he'll have followed the main road. Maybe west, across the farmland, towards Gisburn."

"We could search all over Yorkshire and Lancashire for days," Penry interrupted. "I'd rather see your Emma gets home safely to her brother."

Adam cursed himself for allowing his rage to cloud his judgment. Other men were already hunting for Francis. His duty—his honor, his loyalty—was to escort Emma safely home.

At the inn, he left Penry to see to the horses and hastened upstairs. Peggy the maid was just ahead of him, balancing a tray against her hip as she opened the parlor door.

Emma, sitting opposite Julia Hampton in the armchairs near the fire, quickly rose to her feet when she saw him. Dressed in a gown the deep blue of the sky at twilight and a chemisette white at her throat, the benefits of a good breakfast and safety showed in her face, no longer as pale as it had been earlier.

She stepped towards him as if to embrace him, but abruptly stopped. He'd have closed the gap between them were it not for Peggy, setting plates of bread and lamb stew on the table, and Julia, standing to greet him.

Emma gaze searched his face. "You do not look like the bearer of good news. Or perhaps you're merely tired and hungry."

"The former, alas." The scent of lamb reminded him how little he'd eaten. "Although maybe the latter, too."

She gestured to the table. "Then come and eat. Peggy insists on feeding us at regular intervals." She made a determined attempt at a smile. "I fear she's fattening us up for Christmas."

He was not going to speak of murder while eating. "Let me tell you what has happened, first."

He declined Peggy's offer of an ale, and as the maid reluctantly left, he carried a chair from the table over and set it to face the two armchairs.

Emma swished the back of her skirt into place as she returned to the chair, in that habitual, elegant way of a gentlewoman.

He didn't want to tell her of the lad, bludgeoned to death. To see her eyes cloud in distress. She'd care, about a boy she'd never met. And yet it must be done. She and Julia both waited in apprehensive silence for him to speak.

"Francis has not been found," he began, his throat drier than Portuguese dust. "But we believe he has stolen a horse and escaped on it."

He omitted mention of the boy's mother being a widow. but still Emma's eyes welled before he finished.

"Do you know for sure if it was Francis?" Julia asked.

"There are no witnesses, no proof. But who else could it have been?"

"There was another man. Another two, in fact," Emma said. "He had four men with him, plus the coachman. He ordered the two on the back to ambush you after the last village." The quiver in her voice made her pause for one breath. "There were two men riding

244

horses. One of them must have been Barlow. But I don't know what happened to the other one. Or to the coachman."

Adam recalled Francis and Barlow riding north to the manor for the dogs as he'd approached the inn yesterday. And one man riding south at speed. To search for Emma? Or to collect the other two who'd been sent to attack him? But leaving horseless men to ambush him didn't seem logical, until he thought like a criminal. Because they would have taken his horse after they'd dealt with him. Probably stolen another one from some hapless traveler, and caught up with Francis before too long.

If the groom and Penry hadn't come along in time to help him thwart that plan... No, indulging in *ifs* was a waste of time, an exercise that led only to madness. There was little reason or logic as to where bullets flew, horses charged, sabers slashed. He'd been lucky, and was grateful for it. But now they had not only Francis to find but another two accomplices, and three men made a significantly greater threat than one.

"I may have seen the man on horseback leave here yesterday," he said. "I'll ask Penry if he knows how many men came with Francis from America." His cohorts from over there were already traitors and murderers. Local men might not be. Yet. "It's safest if you remain in here for now. I'll arrange some additional men to come with us when we leave." He'd have taken them away now, but the jury had not yet returned, and Emma still had to speak to them. "Julia, if we cannot make it to Larkfell before dark, may we impose on yours and the Colonel's hospitality for tonight?"

"Of course. You know there's no need to ask."

He'd asked only for courtesy's sake. Some officer's wives were delicate women who distracted their men with neediness or histrionics. Not Julia. She'd followed battles, nursed wounded soldiers, organized camp followers, handled horror and fear and war, scarcely flinching. She'd have made a fine officer herself. It wouldn't surprise him if she had a small pistol somewhere easily to hand. A perfect companion for Emma, in these circumstances.

Not that Emma was helpless. Far from it. She'd saved the drawboy from the fire, and overpowered Francis and escaped from him. Even with her hands bound tightly together. Not a fragile flower. But these recent experiences were more than her gentle soul should ever have had to endure. The sooner she was safe at home and reunited with her brother, the better.

He left the ladies with an assurance he'd return soon, and went straight out to the stables. He met Penry on the way, and with a tilt of his head signaled him to accompany him.

The ostler came over briskly enough when he saw them. Adam jerked a thumb to the black coach in the corner of the yard. "The coachman who came with Braithwaite yesterday—where is he?"

The ostler gave him back the steady-eyed look of a man who held his own no matter who he faced. "I wouldn't know, sir. He went off looking for the lass. Came back not long after you arrived last night, when everyone started looking for the gent. He took a knapsack from under the seat of the coach, and left on foot. I ain't seen 'im since."

Gone to find Francis? Or deserting him? Possibly the latter, since he'd taken his bag. A forty guinea reward out for his master could persuade a man to rethink his allegiances. Adam took a half-crown from his pocket and turned it between his fingers casually. "There were two riders came with Braithwaite. One died last night. Have you seen the other one?"

"Nay, sir. He took 'is horse and went off after the lady, like the others. 'E ain't been back, neither." He eyed the coin in Adam's hand. "They left their luggage, 'cepting the coachman. Didn't have time to get it upstairs before the lady ran off."

Luggage. Which might have clues as to Francis's plans, and the identities of his associates. Adam handed the coin over. He'd used up much of the money he had on him. "Penry, do you have another one of these for the man if he allows us to look at the luggage?"

Penry obliged, reaching for a coin in his pocket. The ostler led them to a storage room at the back of the stables, where he pulled back a blanket covering a trunk and two smaller bags.

While Penry paid the man and dismissed him, Adam knelt and

opened the trunk. Shirts, a good suit, a banyan, and—he shifted the suit aside—a lady's pelisse, of fine green wool. Underneath that, a cream silk gown, a petticoat and a chemise.

Adam sat back on his heels. "Braithwaite had everything planned. He knew they'd be away for days. He brought wedding clothes for them both."

"He must have been confident that he could persuade her to agree."

Persuade? No, Emma would have stood fast in her refusal. "He would never have persuaded her. He must have had some plan to coerce her." There was a harsh taste in his mouth.

Penry rummaged through one of the other bags. "Threatened harm to her?"

"Or someone else. Someone innocent." Adam imagined it all too easily. Some young woman or child, their life threatened unless Emma complied. She'd only have married Francis to save another.

"He'd do that without a twinge of conscience," Penry said. "Maybe that's why he brought several men with him. To take and hold a hostage."

Another reason the bastard should hang. Adam removed the clothes, and found underneath them a wooden writing slope. Heavy, with a dull rattle. But locked.

Penry, having found nothing of interest in the bag he searched, glanced over and commented, "I happen to have lockpicks, if you'd like to see what's inside."

Adam, hoping for letters, notes, anything to use as evidence against Francis, passed the box to him. "Why am I not surprised you can pick locks?"

Penry merely grinned, and the tools came out of an inner pocket in his coat.

Adam returned his attention to the trunk, tapping the base of it, examining the lining for any indication of a false bottom. Unlike its owner, the trunk appeared unexpectedly honest; the lining smooth, the exterior dimensions matching the interior. No hidden compartments. No secrets to reveal.

Adam opened the other bag. A couple of patched shirts, a pair of trousers, shaving kit, spare stockings and cravat. Much like the other offsider's bag. Nothing incriminating. Nothing identifying. Thousands of men traveled up and down the country every day, with as much and as little as this.

Penry made swift work of opening the writing box, and set it between them so that Adam could investigate the contents. A few sheets of blank paper, ink, quills and sealing wafers. In another compartment coins and bank notes. More than enough to finance a journey to Gretna Green and back. Plus a small padded velvet pouch.

Adam untied the ribbon around the pouch, and shook out into his palm a gold ring. Too small for a man's finger. A wedding ring for Emma.

He clenched his hand so tightly around it the metal pressed into his skin. Damn the man to the fiery depths of hell for his callous plans for her. If he could have thrown the ring into the pits of hell, too, he'd have done it.

Penry flicked through the bank notes before replacing them, exactly as he'd found them. "I guess we should hand this lot to Gresham for safe keeping. So Francis doesn't accuse us of theft."

The practical words edged in through the fog of anger. Yet Francis must never be allowed to put the ring on to any woman's finger. He looked around the store room for something, anything to smash it with. Tools lay on a workbench on the corner, and it was a moment or two's work to pound the ring with a hammer, twist it with pliers.

He dropped the mangled piece of gold back in to the velvet pouch, and tossed it back into the writing box. Penry closed the lid, wisely without comment.

Shame for his anger warred with a fierce satisfaction in the destruction of the ring. Not a noble sentiment.

"The jury will be back soon," Penry said. "We should get something to eat before they arrive. They'll probably all want food, too."

A good suggestion. The inn probably rarely had as many patrons as today. And every experienced soldier on campaign knew to eat whenever opportunity arose, because it might not come again. They had a long day still to come, keeping Emma and Julia safe and escorting them at least as far as the Hampton's home. He planned to go on to Larkfell himself, to warn Matthew of Francis's escape, even if it meant riding in the dark.

He'd have sent Penry to warn him, but Penry was as much—probably more—of a danger to Francis than Matthew, and although the man would never admit it, Penry needed protecting, too.

~

The sounds of dozens of men descending the stairs, some of them grumbling loudly, warned Emma that her time to testify was drawing close. Within a few moments, Mr. Palmer's clerk came to summon her to the inquest.

With Julia beside her, she followed the clerk down the corridor to the chamber where Mr. Palmer and the jury waited. She paused before the door, taking deep breaths to still her nerves, glancing around as hasty bootsteps came up the stairs.

Adam. His smile was gentle, encouraging, as if he knew how fast her heart beat. "I'll be here, just outside," he promised. "Waiting for you."

The clerk held the door open for her and, head high, she went inside.

Unlike the inquest for Mr. Winslow, there was no corpse here. She had a starkly clear memory of Barlow's trampled body immediately after death, and had no wish to view it again, even under a covering.

She sat beside Julia in the chairs set out for them, facing the coroner and the men of the jury. Just as she'd done on Saturday, although today there were no observers other than the twelve solemn jurors, and Mr. Palmer. The men of the jury were mostly middle-aged, or older. Rural men, maybe yeoman farmers or tradesmen, all of them dressed conservatively in dark suits, most some years, if not decades, past fashionable.

Mr. Palmer looked up from the notes he was making. "Thank you for attending, Miss…" He hesitated for only an instant. "Miss Smith. We are here to determine the cause of death of the man, Barlow." He spoke briskly, matter-of-factly, as if she appeared before an inquest every day. "Please tell us what happened yesterday, starting in the morning."

In the morning. They wanted to hear everything. In the past hour, she'd rehearsed parts in her mind, imagining saying the words aloud, and being as calm as if it were simply a story that had happened to someone else, not her.

Her imagination was calmer than she was in reality. She did not look at the jury as she spoke. Nor Mr. Palmer. Instead she set her gaze on the young clerk, his head down as he transcribed her words. It helped to think of what she said being written down, and she related the events slowly and clearly, fact by fact.

The message about the weaver collapsing. The ambush in the woods. Benjamin being shot at. Jeremy being attacked. Her struggles with the men holding her. The gag and hood and being manhandled into the coach with her hands bound.

Mr. Palmer raised a hand. "Let me clarify a point, Miss Smith. Was Francis Braithwaite one of the men who attacked you in the woods?"

"No, sir. He was waiting in the coach at the end of the lane."

"But you were unable to see, with your head covered, you said. How can you know it was Braithwaite?"

She stared at him, uncertain of the purpose behind the question. "I've known him all my life. I know his voice. And of course I saw him when we arrived here, at this inn, and he removed the sack from my head."

"Pardon the intrusive question, Miss Smith, but did Braithwaite force himself on you?"

Emma hesitated, and Julia spoke up. "Is that really necessary, sir?"

Mr. Palmer returned her gaze evenly. "It may be relevant to the cause of death, so yes, it is necessary."

In a strange way, his unemotional bluntness made it easier for Emma to respond. "He attempted to, sir, once we were inside the chamber. But I struck him in the face with a pin."

His eyebrows rose. "A pin?"

"A pin from my bodice. They're quite sharp. After I..." She wasn't quite sure how to describe it. "I kicked him. With my knee. Where...where men are vulnerable. And that's how I escaped."

A brief expression of surprise crossed his face. Or perhaps it was a grimace. But there was a grunt and a mutter from the jury, and she made the mistake of looking across at them.

Disapproval. Disgust. Indignation. There was scarcely any face with a neutral expression, and no sympathetic ones. Were they angry that she'd attacked a man in a delicate place? That she'd defended herself the only ways she could? Did they think she should have simply surrendered and allowed Francis to rape her?

"That was very...forthright of you." The way the coroner pronounced 'forthright' did not suggest approval. "So that was how you escaped? By injuring him?"

Julia took a sharp intake of breath, echoing Emma's consternation. Could she have done nothing right, in the opinion of these men?

She could only tell the truth. "Yes. It was the only way to avoid his attack on me. I don't believe he took any lasting injury. Only enough to distract him so that I could escape the room. I went down the back stairs." One more glance at the jury and she determined not to mention Peggy's assistance. "And out through the laundry room. And then into the woods."

Mr. Palmer nodded and jotted a few notes before asking, "Tell us what happened when your cousin found you in the woods."

He'd have heard the testimony of Adam and Sir Phillip's men, but she presumed he wanted to hear hers to confirm their version of events. She did not want to revisit that scene, even in her thoughts, but it must be done.

Her fingers gripped tightly together in her lap, she recounted the events seared in her memories from the moment the hounds rushed upon her. She swallowed back the remembered terror. She had survived. Adam had survived. Both of them relatively unscathed.

Mr. Palmer and the jury listened without interrupting, even when her voice stalled describing the death of the man, Barlow, and she had to pause before she went on. Julia passed her a pocket handkerchief scented with lavender, and the sweet smell helped to calm her tremors.

One of the jurors raised a hand and Mr. Palmer motioned for him to speak. He rose laboriously to his feet. "Miss, you said that Braithwaite rode his horse directly at the dead man. But you can't be certain of that. With all the fighting, and you screaming and swooning, the horse must have been terrified. I'm correct, aren't I?"

Several of the other jurors nodded in agreement.

They were trying to blame the man's death on the *horse*? Or on *her*, for terrifying it? She must have gaped for she had to close her mouth to breathe deeply before answering.

"Sir, I cannot say on oath that I never screamed. I may have once, when Major Caldwell was knocked down." The terror of that moment still caught in her throat. She kept her voice steady with effort. "However, I was certainly not 'screaming and swooning', as you suggest. Francis deliberately aimed at Mr. Barlow with intent to harm him. His face was red with rage."

The juror nodded, in the absent way one might nod at a child telling fairy stories, and resumed his seat.

Mr. Palmer waited a few moments in case there were more questions from the jury, but when none eventuated, he turned to Emma. "Thank you, Miss Smith, you have been most helpful. You are not required any further. You may leave here to return home whenever you wish."

The clerk leapt to his feet to open the door.

Julia's arm steadied her as she rose. Emma's body trembled, but whether from frustration and anger or apprehension, was impossible to know. Or some emotional reaction to all the horrors in her mind, fresh from the telling.

One of the jurors did not even wait until she'd walked the few steps—six or seven—to the door, before he muttered to his neighbor,

"Out all night with him, she was."

Now it was definitely anger that made her shake. One foot in front of the other, through the door, to Adam. He was there, as he'd promised, but so were several men, waiting at the top of the stairs and gawking at her. With the juror's words echoing in her mind, she could not risk speaking to Adam in front of them all.

She turned away from them, and slipped her arm through Julia's as if she wasn't seething inside, and walked to their room without looking back, trusting that Adam would follow soon.

CHAPTER 26

"They did not believe me." Emma came to the end of the room in her pacing and turned around to begin again. "He suggested that *I* was responsible for frightening the horse."

When she finished relating the gist of her experience before the jury, Adam whole-heartedly wished he could return to the inquest, tell them of Emma's bravery, of the way she'd stepped in front of him, prepared to sacrifice herself for him. No screaming and swooning from her. But the jury was already considering their decision, and no-one permitted to enter until it was done.

He'd dismissed the niggling doubts he'd had this morning, when they were out viewing Barlow's body and he'd overheard two of the jurors talking. Dour, respectable men in dark suits. *'We can't assume he intended to kill him.' 'Could have been an accident.'*

He'd dismissed the doubts because surely, surely they'd see the truth in his testimony, in Emma's, in the witness statements of Gresham's men.

But the jurors hadn't been there. They hadn't witnessed Braithwaite's rage, the hatred in his eyes, the harsh snarl of his voice. They didn't realize the violence he was capable of. Was *still* capable of, if he wasn't captured soon. Although the impending result of the inquest concerned Adam, the fact that Francis remained at large concerned him more.

He might be powerless to affect the jury's decision now, but not to act on matters he had influence over.

"The jury may yet deliver a verdict of murder," he reassured Emma, although he held diminishing hope of it himself. "But I don't think we should wait to hear it. Julia, will you give me leave to order your coach to be readied? Will you both be ready to leave as soon as the coach is?"

Emma ceased her pacing, although her agitation showed in her flushed face and dark eyes. "Of course. Do you think we can make it to Larkfell before dark? Or must we stop at Julia's home tonight?"

He planned to get to Larkfell himself tonight, darkness or not, to warn Matthew about Francis. But it was too risky for Emma and the coach to travel in the dark, with her cousin and his men on the loose. "We'll see how we go. If the storm hasn't damaged the roads much, we may make good time."

She nodded, and didn't press him for any more promise than that. Naturally she must want to see her brother as soon as possible, to be at home, and safe, and in her own place again. But she asked for nothing, understanding the circumstances as well as he did.

In the stable yard he spoke with Julia's coachman and the ostler, ordering the coach to be readied and horses saddled for himself, Penry, and Julia's groom. The horse he'd arrived here with needed more rest on its injured leg. He'd ask Gresham if it could be accommodated in his stables for a few days.

Gresham himself strode out of the inn with Penry as Adam finished making arrangements. The baronet, his face dark with anger, signaled him to join them and they crossed the road in front of the inn and walked thirty yards down to the church yard gate.

Adam had learned little of Gresham this morning other than that despite the fashionable, quality suit, he was a man of energy and action, taking charge of the search, planning and directing men as if he had experience as an officer. Perhaps he did. Whatever his private pursuits and entertainments, he'd shown no lack of respect for others, and a dedication to preserving the peace in his corner of the world.

"The jury's returned its verdict," Gresham said, once they

were out of earshot of the inn. He ground it out through his teeth. "Accidental death."

Despite the warning in Emma's experience, despite the foreknowledge of the other man's tight anger, the words hit Adam like a blow to the gut. "Accidental death? Not even manslaughter? What in Hell happened?"

"Elijah Thomson happened." Bitterness edged Gresham's words. "A stubborn, God-fearing man who regards me as the devil incarnate. People look to Elijah because the vicar is a drunkard, and vicious with it."

"Why put him on the jury then?" Penry asked.

Gresham waved a hand at the village. "Look around. The village is small and getting smaller. The nearest town is miles away. It's hard enough to find twelve men for a jury. We don't have the advantage of choice." He aimed a kick of pure frustration at the fence post. "And the end result is that they didn't believe you, or my men, or Miss Braithwaite. Apparently horses—and women—are highly-strung and emotional creatures and not to be trusted."

Men were emotional creatures, too, and Adam stared out over the church yard, struggling to master his own anger. Moss-covered grave-stones hunched and lurched in overgrown grass beyond the gate. Barlow and the 'prentice would lie there soon enough, but with no headstones to mark their place. And no justice for their murders. Unless they found Braithwaite with the apprentice's horse and blood on him, he'd escape charges for that murder, too.

If Francis managed to leave the country, there was little that could be done about it, at least for now. But there remained a chance that he'd be captured before then.

Adam turned away from contemplating the dead. Their only chance for justice lay in action, not contemplation. "I had no choice but to let Braithwaite ride free last night, but I want him captured and brought before a court on other charges. It can't be for Emma's abduction, because that would be a nightmare of public scandal for her."

"Agreed," Penry said soberly, with no trace of his usual devil-may-care mask. "If he's not well on his way to Liverpool and on a ship before we find him, we'll need to pursue him for Winslow's or the constable's deaths. Or treason."

"You'll need evidence that Braithwaite ordered the murders," Gresham said bluntly. "And a charge of treason will need two witnesses here in England. Do you have proof of the treason? Evidence other than your word?"

Penry took no offence at the questions. "Matthew has a copy of the letter sent to him by mistake. The original is with the Lieutenant-Governor's office in York. The Canadian town of York, I mean. But other than that, I don't have much hard evidence. Not here in England. The regiment can testify to the skirmish and the deaths of their men, but not to who ordered it. We do have Dutton, though, and the other man, who might be useful if he came from Canada with Braithwaite, or if he's heard talk since Braithwaite came home."

Adam's thoughts raced, assessing implications and strategies. The treason charge might have a better chance of succeeding than the murder charges, since Francis did not wield the killing blows himself. And that made Francis as much a threat to Penry as he was to Matthew. If Francis wanted to silence potential witnesses against him, Penry must be on top of the list.

"Dutton's evidence," Adam said, thinking aloud, "Assuming we can persuade him to talk, is key to proving both crimes. He must be taken to somewhere he can be securely held. But I have to take Miss Braithwaite to her home, and warn her brother that he may be in danger. Gresham, do you have any influence with the Halifax militia? Can you persuade them to take Dutton into their custody? And can you spare two good men to guard him until he can be handed over to the militia?"

Gresham gave an unamused laugh. "Most of my good men are still riding all over the county with messages about Braithwaite. Including one to the militia. But I have some house guests who plan to head south this afternoon. They're inside the inn. They can travel with you for the first few miles and stop and guard Dutton overnight if need be." His sudden grin had an edge of the devil in it. "I wouldn't call them good men, but they're handy in a fight."

Their virtue or otherwise didn't concern Adam, as long as they didn't let Dutton escape. "Thank you. I plan to leave as soon as the ladies and the carriage are ready."

The ladies were already waiting, standing by the coach and watching his approach. He steeled himself to tell Emma that Francis would not be charged with Barlow's murder. He'd promised to protect her, and to ensure that Francis paid for his crimes. He'd find a way to make that happen, even if it meant dealing with Francis himself.

~

Accidental death.

The words of the verdict echoed again and again in Emma's thoughts. Francis had purposely ridden over a man in rage and hatred and the jury had called it an accident.

In all the noise and movement of horses and people getting ready to depart the inn, there'd been little chance to talk with Adam. Only his assurance, as he'd handed her up into the coach, of his determination to see Francis tried on other charges, if he was caught in England.

The coach set off, with riders placing themselves in front, beside, and behind it as they left the inn. Through the window she caught glimpses of Adam, on Julia's mare, his pistols in their holster in front of him.

Guarding her? Or prepared in case they caught up with Francis? If he'd had the pistols last night... No, rain-dampened powder would never have fired. At least today was dry, and less cloudy than yesterday. Although she did not want to think of anyone—even Francis—being shot.

Julia passed her a cushion. "Do try and get some rest. You'll feel better for it."

"I fear I'm too unsettled to rest." *Unsettled* didn't truly cover the restless discomfort plaguing her thoughts. *Angry* was more correct. She was angry, and she disliked being angry. Anger was not a rational or helpful emotion.

She'd anticipated a possible verdict of manslaughter, but this... this defied any logic. "How could they? Four of us said he rode at that man with intent to harm him, and they've blamed it on the poor horse." Which surely must have been distressed by the event. She couldn't imagine horses understood others' pain or death, but the scent of blood must have frightened it. "I suppose I should be grateful that they didn't blame me."

"Yes. I confess that there was a moment when I was worried that might occur, although I think Mr. Palmer would have guided them away from that path."

Julia's candid agreement caught Emma by surprise, and she stared at her new friend, unsure if she was jesting. No. Julia was one of the most intelligent, astute women she'd ever met. "I think I expected you to tell me I was overwrought, exaggerating the situation."

"No, my dear. There truly was a moment when I'm certain that the idea of making you responsible for frightening the horse occurred to several of the men, but fortunately that moment passed without any of them acting on it, and some degree of sanity prevailed."

"But they did not find Francis responsible."

"No. I have been pondering why. Those men on the jury were faced with a group of strangers. Perhaps they were hesitant to commit a man to trial for a capital crime when he wasn't there to answer for himself."

Emma leaned her weary head back against the cushion. Julia's suggestion was a perspective she'd not considered, but maybe should have, given her own reservations about the death penalty. Especially her reservations about the death penalty for Francis. According to law, he deserved it, but she could not imagine the cousin she'd known all her life walking to the gallows. He had to be stopped from harming anyone else, punished for his crimes, but death? Like the Quakers, she found it hard to countenance. Transportation to New South Wales or Van Diemen's Land? Would that sit better with her conscience? Allowing the possibility of redemption? Although his crimes were so heinous, was redemption even possible?

She closed her eyes and tried to still the turmoil of fruitless thoughts. If only she could rest, she might find some clarity. The carriage rumbled along, jolting with frequent potholes and ruts caused by yesterday's storms, jarring her bruised and tired body. She doubted she could sleep.

She jerked to wakefulness, unable for a moment to discern whether the voices of men shouting were in her restless dream or in reality. But the carriage slowed and stopped, and Adam rode past the window, urging his horse faster.

Her heart thudded from her dream, her thoughts muddy. "What is it?" she asked Julia in a whisper. Highwaymen? Francis?

Julia peered out the other window, but from this angle all Emma could see was thick smoke, clouding the air. "There's a fire. I think maybe the inn. But that's not where Adam and the men went."

A fire. Not highwaymen or some immediate threat to her. Frustrated at spending so much of the day confined—to the inn room, to the carriage—Emma opened the door and was almost down the steps before the groom leapt into position to assist her to the ground. Julia followed her.

They were in a village that straggled along the road, smaller than the one they'd left. Villagers formed a bucket line, carting water from the well on the green outside the inn through to the stable yard. The smoke swirled in the air, but the inn itself didn't seem to be on fire. Only the stables. In a field across the road, six horses walked restlessly near the far fence., agitated but safe.

"Adam's over there," Julia pointed, "In the church yard with the others."

The ancient church stood beyond the coach, and Adam was there with a group of men, deep in discussion. But as Emma started down the road with Julia, Adam went inside the building, with Mr. Penry and Sir Phillip, leaving the horses with Sir Phillip's friends.

A man in a clerical collar saw Emma and Julia approach, and hurried forward to meet them at the gate, his arms wide to stop them. A young man, a curate perhaps, ashen-faced. "Ladies, please, you mustn't come through."

Julia walked right up to him. "We are not easily shocked, sir. We must know what has happened."

Emma edged to one side. A man lay on the ground in the church yard, unmoving. "The men who were being held prisoner here," Her words came surprisingly steadily, despite the knots twisting in her abdomen. "Have they escaped?"

The curate's eyes darted to hers, then away. "No. No, not... escaped."

"They're dead?"

"Yes. And Jem there, who was watching them. The fire started in the stables, you see. And the other two guards ran to save the horses. But Jem stayed. They hurt him badly and he crawled out there but..." The curate swallowed, unable to continue.

Emma needed no more explanation. Someone had set a fire to distract the guards. Someone? Francis. Francis, who killed—or gave orders to kill—with cold, deliberate ease.

The breeze blowing the smoke from the fire came off the hillside, cool as autumn. It was farmland here, open fields with copses of trees here and there. Was Francis hiding there, waiting for them? Or was he already riding to Larkfell, to Matthew?

"How long ago?" Julia asked. "When did the fire start?"

"An hour. Perhaps more. I told the gentlemen—no-one saw anything. We only found," He gestured towards Jem's body. "A short time ago." His mouth trembled, as if he might cry.

Emma cast another wary glance around the fields. Nothing moved except sheep. Nothing she could see. She touched Julia's arm. "We should wait in the coach." Out of sight of anyone watching. And ready to go the moment Adam and the others were finished here. Matthew was alone at Larkfell, unaware of the danger.

They did not have to wait long before Adam returned. He was tight-lipped with anger, and hesitated to speak, as if seeking polite words.

Emma asked outright, "Are they dead because they lied about murdering Matthew? Or because they're witnesses to Francis's crimes?"

He let out a breath, perhaps relieved he didn't have to tell them of the murders. "Probably both. We'll travel to your home, Julia, as fast as we can. Emma must stay with you tonight, so that Penry and I can ride with all speed to Larkfell."

Stay idly with the Hamptons not knowing if Matthew was safe? "No," she said firmly. "If Julia can spare a horse, I'll ride with you."

"*We* will ride with you," Julia said, and Adam nodded, accepting.

The remainder of the journey to the Hamptons' seemed torturously slow, although in truth they made as good a speed as a coach could. They spent little time there, only long enough for Emma to change into one of Julia's riding habits, for Adam to apprise the Colonel of the situation, for Gresham to write a letter to the Halifax militia, and for horses to be readied with side-saddles.

They set off in a thunder of hoof-beats, the men—Adam, Mr. Penry, Sir Phillip and his friends, and two of Julia's grooms—surrounding her and Julia. To be out on the road, in fresh air, after all the hours of inactivity and fretting should have made her feel better, but all she could think of was Matthew, alone at Larkfell except for the staff, fretting about her safety. She'd believe him home and safe only when she saw him with her own eyes.

She held few fears for her own safety, with Adam beside her and the other men riding with them. No-one, not even Francis, would attack such a large group.

They alternated, cantering and walking, keeping moving as much as was wise for the horses. The day's light faded into twilight as they covered the last miles.

Finally they rode through the ornate iron gates into Larkfell's drive, and she cantered to the house. Adam rapidly dismounted to assist her to the ground.

Jarvis, the butler, was already out on the steps to greet her, Mrs. Barnden behind him, anxiety on their faces easing into relief as they saw her.

"We are thankful to see you, Miss. We received word this morning you were safe."

She recalled Mr. Penry saying he'd sent a message late last night. "I am, and unharmed. Please prepare guest rooms and refreshments for Mrs. Hampton, and for Mr. Penry. My brother?"

"He is in the study, miss."

With a brief word of apology to Julia, she ran into the house, through the hall, up the stairs.

She met Matthew in the gallery, coming towards her. He was pale, painfully thin and leaning heavily on a cane, but he was alive and whole and home.

Tears damp and cool on her face, she embraced her brother, and his arm came around her to hold her close.

CHAPTER 27

He'd seen her safely home. Gresham and friends were riding on to Hartdale, keen to reach town before the light fully faded, but Adam left them where the lane led to Rengarth. His first duty had been to Emma, but now his thoughts turned to his family, especially his brothers.

The deepening dusk made it unsafe to canter along the shadowed lane through the woods, past the place where Emma had been ambushed and the boys injured, so he held the horse to a trot. He doubted Francis posed a threat to him here. Not far to Rengarth now. Not long until he found out how severe Jeremy's injury was.

Where the lane came out of the woods near the castle grounds, two men became visible in the gloom, standing on the path, holding long staffs in their hands.

As Adam cursed and reined the horse in to a halt five yards in front of them, one of them men called, "Identify yourself."

In the faint light their faces were indistinct. Perhaps his was likewise hard to recognize. "Adam Caldwell. What is the meaning of this?"

They lowered their weapons and fell back immediately. "I beg your pardon, sir. Of course you may pass."

"You're guarding Rengarth?"

"Yes sir. Since yesterday, sir. Mr. Garrett recommended guards on the entrances and patrols of the grounds, and Lady Rengarth agreed."

Sensible of his mother and Garrett to protect the family and the castle, when unsure of the source of the threat.

"The danger is not here," he told the men. "But tell Garrett I want at least four men sent to Larkfell tonight. They should ask for Mr. Penry there and follow his instructions to secure the house and grounds."

He cantered the remaining hundred yards to the house. A stable boy–not Benjamin this time–rushed to take his horse. In the hall, he shed his greatcoat into the butler's hands, asking, "My brother Jeremy?"

"Is recovering, sir. Lady Rengarth is keeping him to his bed as a precaution."

Despite the reassurance, Adam took the stairs two at a time, anxious to see his brother for himself.

The sounds of piano and violin came from the music room but he didn't stop, continuing on up to the boys' bedchamber in the family wing.

All the fears he'd carried for his brother jammed in his chest as he strode down the corridor. He stopped in the open doorway, his pulse loud in his ears, whether from exertion or dread he couldn't tell.

Jeremy sat propped against a pile of pillows in his bed, the bandage around his head holding a poultice which apparently did not interfere with his game of chess with Benjamin. A quick glance of the board showed Jeremy was winning the game. No damage to his wits, then.

Both boys greeted him with bright eyes and a barrage of questions, eager for news of Emma. Adam pulled a chair up to the bedside and sank into it. His bruised body ached with two days of hard riding and the injuries Francis and his men had inflicted. But relief flooded him, dulling the hurts.

Emma was home safe. Jeremy and Benjamin were recovering from their injuries. He still had to find Francis and ensure he harmed no-one ever again, but for these few hours tonight he could rest, before he met Gresham and Penry in Hartdale in the morning.

After he'd related the major events of the past two days to the boys, and asked after the injured footman—bruised but back at work, the boys told him—he went to his room to strip off his disheveled, travel-worn clothes and make himself respectable to see the rest of the family.

A nervous young valet waited for him in his room—sent by the butler—and a footman brought a tray loaded with supper. After a long day and a long ride, his stomach rumbled in appreciation, and he downed the venison pie while waiting for warm washing water.

Pulling a loose coat on over a clean shirt and waistcoat—no need to dress properly this late in the evening—he returned downstairs. In the music room, Oliver worked with Louisa and Phoebe on some new composition, but they paused long enough to quiz him about Emma's safety and well-being. Once assured of both, Oliver's fingers found the guitar strings again, and Adam left them to their music.

He found his mother in her sitting room, writing letters by the light of a candelabra at her desk. She quickly set down her quill and rose to kiss him on the cheek, welcoming him back and asking immediately about Emma.

He drew up a chair to her desk and in the quiet of her peaceful room where he'd spoken with—kissed—Emma two evenings ago, he gave his mother a summary of the past two days after the abduction. He left out the more intimate details of how they had spent the night, but the tiny rise of one eyebrow indicated his mother's thinking.

She made no comment until he finished. "You're sure it was Francis Braithwaite who murdered the men in the church? And not his accomplice?"

"Both of them, I'd wager. There were signs that two horses had been tethered behind the church." Two sets of hoof prints in the damp ground, nothing stolen from the church, and two men brutally murdered in the crypt. It could have been no-one else but Francis.

"You'll continue searching for them?"

"Yes. I'll leave tomorrow at first light." He told her of the arrangement to meet Gresham and Penry in Hartdale. "I'm not sure when I'll be back. It depends on whether there is any trace of

Braithwaite, and which direction he's going."

"Send word when you can. I shall call on Emma in the morning. Such a frightening time she's had. She is in truth uninjured? Her cousin did not…?" She delicately left the nightmare words unsaid.

"He did not. She has some bruising and other small hurts. She was remarkably courageous and level-headed throughout the ordeal." That was the easy part to tell. He still had to warn his mother about the gossip sure to come. Emma would need her support. "We had the bad luck to meet Beatrice Farringdon first thing yesterday morning on our way into the inn," he explained, and his mother winced. "She dislikes Emma and immediately leapt to conclusions." Not entirely unwarranted conclusions, yet the manner in which the woman had spoken still angered him, as if Emma was a harlot and their being together was an obscenity.

"Oh, that is unfortunate. She is going to her sister's home in Carlisle, I believe. Both of them are unhappy women who seem determined to make everyone else equally so. They may make life very unpleasant for Emma."

He had some sympathy for women trapped in unhappy marriages and powerless to escape, but not so much that he'd forgive the deliberate spreading of malicious gossip to ruin a respectable gentlewoman.

But the honest truth remained that he'd spent the night with Emma and anticipated the marriage vows that they had not yet committed to. Perhaps he deserved the lady's censure, although such criticism scarcely impacted on men's reputations. He would not suffer the social ostracism that Emma would, should the scandal spread. And she would suffer doubly, from speculation about Francis's abduction as well as for rumor about her night alone with Adam.

Maybe he should have been more of a gentleman, more protective of her reputation, and found a way to return her to the inn that evening. Would that have made a difference? Lady Beatrice had been there—he could have handed Emma into her care, to protect and chaperone her. Or even the innkeeper's wife. If he'd done that…if he'd done that, she'd have had to endure another hour or more in the storm, and they might have been easy prey for Francis.

Pointless to even contemplate those 'ifs'. He'd spent the night alone with Emma and now he had to find ways to ensure she didn't suffer from the consequences of his actions.

His mother watched him, expecting some response. A sage woman, one he esteemed highly, even more so now than in the heady days of his youth. He understood her strengths far better than when he'd been relatively innocent of the world. He barely hesitated before he told her outright, "I proposed marriage to Emma."

She gave a small nod. "I'm not particularly surprised. You do have a sound core of honor, Adam. Did she accept?"

"No." It barely stung to confess it. Emma had good reasons for her decision, and he respected them. "She feels it is too soon since my return, and she refuses to be pressured into marriage by scandal."

"Very wise of her. Honor in the face of scandal is well and good, but marriage is too serious a commitment for a woman to make lightly." She considered him with gentleness. "Did she give you any hope?"

"Yes." Far more than hope. She'd given him her affection and her trust. "She suggested asking her again in a month."

"And will you?"

"I will. I hope you have no objections."

"None at all, though it's not my business, other than my wish to see you happy. She is a woman I respect and like, and if she can endure any social discomfort that arises while you and she come to know each other again to confirm your feelings, then waiting is a sensible plan."

It was. An entirely sensible plan. And yet he missed Emma's presence and longed for the day—if it ever came—when she'd be there, by his side, as friend, companion, lover, wife. As soon as Francis was no longer a threat, he'd begin to court her.

~

Emma rose before daybreak, dressing hurriedly to be downstairs before Matthew left with Mr. Penry to go to Hartdale. She worried about her brother, but after months of inactivity and frustration at feeling helpless and useless, he was determined to see the magistrate and authorities about Francis, and to inspect the warehouse damage. He sent for the gig and drove that, rather than riding.

She only hoped he did not over-exert himself, for he was still weak from his many injuries and the chest infection that had followed his near-drowning. The broken bones in his leg had not healed straight, making walking painful. He had yet to regain strength in his broken arm, and he might never regain full movement in the hand crushed by Francis's men. It was a testimony to his strength and Mr. Penry's care that he'd come home at all, and with all his limbs. She barely dared to contemplate what he'd endured. At least he'd promised that he would not attempt to go to Liverpool or anywhere else in pursuit of Francis.

Julia came down not long after the men had left, keen to get home to her beloved Colonel. She waved away Emma's thanks. "You would have done the same for a friend. You must come and visit us, when Matthew has settled back home and you can be spared. Both my husband and I would love to have you come and stay with us. Please consider us your staunch friends."

Julia had no need to be more specific. Staunch friends offering to provide a haven if gossip or scandal became too unpleasant. Emma's throat clogged and she hugged Julia warmly before she mounted her horse and cantered down the drive.

The clerks and warehouse lads arrived promptly at eight, and Emma spent much of the morning in the Larkfell barn, supervising them in the task of inspecting and assessing the warehouse stock. They had moved everything from the fire-damaged building on Saturday, but there'd not been sufficient time before dark for a good assessment of what was too badly damaged, by fire, smoke and water, and what might be saved. So this morning Emma oversaw the opening of every bale to examine and record the damage to the contents, and the repacking of what dry, undamaged goods they found into new bales.

Even with the lads doing all the lifting, she found opening out and inspecting multiple thirty-yard lengths of worsted fabrics to be tiring work. But they finished assessing the bales before noon, and she left her staff to finish repacking the bales, as task that no longer needed her supervision.

She must change her dusty, sooty clothes and make herself neat and tidy. Lady Rengarth had sent a note earlier, saying she intended to call.

Kate took away her dress and petticoat to be brushed and cleaned, while Emma, wearing only her chemise, washed her face and tidied her hair. As she raised her hands to pin back an errant strand of hair, the mirror reflected the semi-sheer drape of her chemise over her breasts.

Her night with Adam remained fresh in her thoughts, never far away, catching her again and again with unbidden memories of touches and caresses and unforgettable pleasures. She remembered the taste of him, the faint salt of his skin under her mouth, the corded muscles under her hands, rippling as they joined together, tensing before that tumultuous, euphoric release.

In the mirror her eyes were bright, her cheeks flushed with pink. And she was fiercely, defiantly glad that she'd had that one night with him. Even if they never married. Even if...she rested her hand against her abdomen. Even if she was with child, and she had to leave Larkfell and go abroad to raise it alone.

Adam must not be coerced into marriage. That was no path to happiness, for either of them. They needed this month, to know their own hearts, to find out where their futures lay.

Restlessness plagued her when she returned downstairs after dressing in a silk gown appropriate for the afternoon. She might have engaged herself with the account books and writing business letters, but those tasks now required consultation with Matthew, and she must wait his return. She might have walked in the garden, but Mr. Penry had cautioned against being outside alone until Francis was either in custody, or confirmed to have left the country. With Larkfell staff and men from Rengarth watching the house and grounds, there would be no privacy, anyway.

She went in search of Mrs. Barnden, to arrange menus and household matters to cater for Matthew and their guest, Mr. Penry. Her role with Braithwaite and Co. had changed, but responsibility for domestic oversight at Larkfell remained. At least until Matthew married, and his wife became Larkfell's mistress.

For all her joy at Matthew's safe return, an unsettling sense of change and uncertainty contributed to her restlessness. In the years since her mother's death, she'd understood that her own role at Larkfell was only temporary. She loved the house and its light, airy rooms filled with joyful memories. But with Matthew home and his injuries healing, albeit slowly, it might not be long before he considered marrying, and she'd no longer be needed here.

Fortunately, she had sufficient funds to live a modest, independent life and no need to rely on the charity of Matthew and his future wife. *If* she inherited Mr. Winslow's house, that provided an opportunity to use it, and her skills, to good purpose. Or if she married Adam… no, there was too much uncertain to even think on that yet.

Returning to the study after consulting with the housekeeper, she heard male voices in the hall. Adam? The quick flutter of anticipation faded when Jarvis came in and announced, "Mr. Robert Braithwaite, miss, enquiring if you or Mr. Matthew are at home."

She hoped she masked her disappointment. "I am at home," she told the butler. "Please show him in, and ask Mrs. Branden for tea."

From the high of the brief hope, her heart slowed down to an uneven, apprehensive beat. She must grant Robert the interview, even though it might be difficult. He wasn't Francis. She doubted he'd had any knowledge of Francis's intentions.

He came in, his drawn face stark white against the black of his suit. Although as immaculately dressed as always, his manner seemed diminished.

He hesitated inside the door of the study, and bowed deeply. "Cousin Emma."

Seeing him thus, with his pride so reduced and his face so troubled, Emma felt for him and greeted him courteously. "Good day to you, Cousin. Matthew has gone to Hartdale, but please come in, be seated. Would you like some tea?"

He took a few steps into the room but made no move towards the chair. "No, thank you. I came only to…"

He bowed his head momentarily and his shoulders shook with a shuddering breath before he looked her in the eye. Anguished words spilled out. "Cousin, I only heard yesterday afternoon of your… I made haste to Hartdale, where I learned last night from Sir Phillip of all Francis's actions and crimes. I am utterly appalled. I can scarcely comprehend…but I am his only family, and must take responsibility and make restitution. Although his wrongs to you and to Matthew are so great that I hardly know how. I will, of course, pay for the rebuilding of your warehouse and the losses, and provide for suitable premises until it is done. We have an old mill, that you may certainly use if Matthew deems it suitable. Or I will pay for something else. As for the rest, I…"

Abruptly the rush of words stalled, and he paused long enough for her to interrupt.

"Robert, please don't distress yourself. I don't hold you to blame at all. You're not responsible for his actions. And as you can see, I have taken little harm."

She'd arranged her hair today to fall in curls over the bruise on her face, and hoped he was distracted enough not to notice it. In truth it was only a small harm. Unlike Matthew, who might bear the reminders of his beating and near-drowning for the rest of his life. But she'd have to leave Matthew to speak for himself, and to make his own peace with Robert.

She remained on her feet, unable to take her seat while Robert stood. Once more she invited him to sit, but he shook his head.

"You are gracious, Cousin Emma, but you may think differently when you have recovered from the shock. It is customary for the perpetrator or his family to pay damages for assault, arson and…" He could not meet her eyes as he added, "Other wrongs." He drew two letters from his pocket. "I have outlined some suggestions. If they are insufficient, please tell me what you expect. Or my solicitor, if you prefer. I will bid you good day now. I must go and search for him."

He placed the letters on the side table near the door and with another deep bow, he left.

Emma sank back into her chair, emotion thickening her throat. Matthew wasn't the only one irrevocably hurt by Francis.

Robert was undoubtedly a good man. Annoyingly punctilious at times, but she could never have imagined seeing him so devastated. She didn't recall him being particularly close to Francis, but there was only the two of them since their parents died years ago, and Robert always took family duty seriously.

When Mrs. Barnden brought in the tea tray, she poured herself a cup and took up the letters from where Robert had left them on the side table. One for Matthew, one addressed to her.

She broke the seal on hers and opened it out to Robert's neat, perfectly-formed handwriting, expressing his horror at his brother's actions and his gratitude that she was safely returned home.

'*As my brother has acted so heinously towards you, besmirching your reputation and placing you in an invidious position through no fault of your own, I offer myself in marriage to protect your honor. I assure you of my life-long respect, fidelity and tender care as a dutiful husband owes to his wife.*'

She stopped and read the lines again. '*I offer myself in marriage...*' Dear, proper Robert, with his stringent sense of duty. Marrying him was impossible, of course. His sense of propriety might tell him that it was the right course to take, but his heart must quail at the thought. She liked and respected him more, after his visit and this letter, than ever before, but not anywhere near enough to marry him. They'd make each other miserable within a week.

She quickly read the remainder of the letter. A proposed marriage settlement, with funds in trust to ensure her relative financial freedom. An offer to add to her dowry should there be someone else she wished to marry, as recompense for the damage Francis had done to her reputation.

He phrased it delicately, but he clearly thought Francis had succeeded in molesting her, and was trying to make amends so she wouldn't be a shamed spinster for the rest of her days.

She must write to him today to take that burden of guilt from his shoulders. And politely decline his offer to add to her dowry. He had her interests at heart, but he owed her nothing, and she would not be beholden to him. She could stare down any gossip or speculation about Francis's abduction. Any scandal that spread as a result of her night with Adam arose from her own choices and decisions, and Robert had no responsibility at all with regard to that.

For all her determination to face the world without flinching, butterflies danced in her stomach when she heard riders arrive, and looked out the window to see Lady Rengarth and Louisa dismounting. She hurried to the hall to welcome them.

Louisa was inside first, taking the stairs in unladylike haste and rushing past Jarvis to envelope Emma in a hug. "We were so worried! You are truly unhurt?" Her gaze flicked to the bruise on Emma's cheek.

"I am," Emma insisted.

The Countess greeted her with a kiss on the unhurt cheek, enquiring after her health, and assuring her, in response to her own anxious enquiries, that both Jeremy and Benjamin were expected to recover fully, after a few more days of rest.

"Not that either of them understand the notion of 'rest'," Louisa remarked.

"It is a family failing, I must admit," the Countess rejoined with a smile. "Although I am still trying to learn the art of it."

Rather than the formal drawing room, Emma showed them to the family sitting room, moving aside her neglected sewing so that the Countess could have the most comfortable chair.

The Countess waved away her apology. "This is such a lovely, welcoming room. Perfect for sewing or reading. I am sorry that we won't be able to stay for long. Louisa may have mentioned that we must leave for London within a few days, and there is a great deal to organize before we do."

"I was sorry to hear of Lord Rengarth's illness. I pray that he is recovered when you see him."

"Thank you, Emma. He has a new physician, who offers more hope. It is unfortunate, though, that I will be away at this time. Adam told me of your encounter with Beatrice Farringdon, and a little of her rudeness to you. I can imagine the rest. I have written to her this morning. I did not outright warn her not to gossip, of course, but I thanked her for the compassion and concern she showed you, our valued friend." Her Ladyship's graceful brows furrowed. "Which of course she did not, but she's hardly likely to admit to it, and she will understand my disapproval of the behavior she did exhibit."

Emma recalled her father's frequent advice; *Make it easy for a man to redeem himself*. It seemed that Lady Rengarth held a similar attitude, leading by example and persuasion instead of confrontation, and appealing to a person's conscience.

"I hope she's squirming," Louisa said with a cheeky smile. "The way I used to at school, when I received letters like that from you."

Emma recalled an incident when Louisa had snuck out one night to hear a famous musician play at the cathedral, only to be discovered by a teacher attending the concert. She'd faced the consequences without protest. But one needed a conscience to squirm, and Emma feared Lady Beatrice might have too great a sense of moral superiority. "To be fair, she did see me in a compromising situation." She refrained from mentioning Adam, unsure of how much his mother had been told.

Lady Rengarth held her gaze, her expression soft and kind. "In exceptional circumstances, my dear. I would hate to think of any of my daughters being out alone, overnight in that storm, after such a terrifying experience. I am glad that Adam found you, and that you sensibly stayed where you were safe."

The Countess's calm manner and lack of judgement gave Emma no indication whether she assumed that the circumstances of the night alone with Adam were entirely innocent, or whether she knew they weren't, and did not mind.

She stayed with safe words. "I am grateful that he found me, too." The memory of the confrontation with Francis in the forest made her shiver. "I don't think I could have escaped Francis again."

"Has there been any word," Lady Rengarth asked delicately, "of your cousin's whereabouts?"

"Not as yet." She looked down at her hands, clasped in her lap, and made herself loosen them. "I'm hoping that Matthew and Mr. Penry will bring news home later today. They planned to meet with Adam and Sir Phillip Gresham in Hartdale this morning."

"Gresham?" Louise asked sharply. "Is he to be trusted?"

Peggy at the inn hadn't thought so, when she'd warned against going to the manor. Yet Emma had heard nothing else against the man, and his brief comments to her on the journey home had been courteous, although distracted. "Adam trusts him. And Mr. Penry." But they'd both only returned to the country recently. "Is there something they should be aware of?"

"There were some rumors, in London." Louisa cast a hesitant glance at her mother.

The Countess appeared unperturbed. "Rumors are unreliable. I won't judge a man on whispers. Besides, he has the confidence of the Home Secretary. Sidmouth himself told me so. He thinks highly of him."

Emma accepted the Countess's—and the Home Secretary's— assurance. Whatever rumors surrounded Gresham need not concern her. She only hoped that others would equally discount any rumors that arose about her. At least she had the Countess's support, and that of the Rengarth family.

The clock chimed the hour in the hall, and the Countess moved to the edge of her chair, ready to rise. "My dear, as long as Jeremy continues to improve, I aim to leave for London on Thursday. I have invited my aunt, Mrs. Thorncroft, to stay at Rengarth, to assist Adam and Susanna with the younger ones. She will arrive tomorrow. Do you think you and Matthew will be recovered enough from your ordeals to come to dinner tomorrow evening? I can invite several influential people, in order to dispel any gossip before it grows."

Tomorrow evening. Wednesday. She was not ready. She had to be ready. Once the Countess and Louisa went to London there would be no such high-ranking support.

"Your Ladyship is most kind. I am quite recovered, but I cannot speak for Matthew. Perhaps we can send word later today, after I have spoken with him?"

She had to go, whether Matthew accompanied her or not. If she didn't face the world and its curiosity, there'd be even more speculation and gossip. She must hold her head high, and face whatever came.

CHAPTER 28

Wednesday

After two days of chasing leads and possibilities with Gresham and Penry, Adam still had no confirmation of Francis Braithwaite's whereabouts. They knew he'd been to his house, on the other side of the river between Hartdale and Sowerby, but they'd been too late yesterday to catch him there. They'd only found the blacksmith's stolen horse wandering in a field, and the edges of burnt letters in the smoldering fire in the grate of Braithwaite's study.

Braithwaite's servants vehemently denied seeing him, of course. Most with fear in their eyes. Except the tall, broad-shouldered man who served as butler-valet. He lied and didn't care that Adam knew it.

Braithwaite must have gone straight to his home that first night, but after that, no-one had seen him. Or admitted to seeing him. Adam had sent Garrett to lurk at the Lion, the least salubrious of Hartdale's public houses where no-one asked too many questions, but even he'd heard nothing useful.

Late in the afternoon, when Adam was discussing the next day's search strategy with Penry and Gresham in a chamber of the Hartdale Arms, one of Gresham's men returned from Liverpool, muddied and exhausted.

Gresham ordered him to sit down while he delivered his news.

He'd asked around all the docks, and last night had seen a man matching Francis's description hurriedly board a ship bound for Boston. The ship had sailed on the early morning tide.

"Are you sure it was Braithwaite?" Adam asked.

The man nodded. "I did see him for a moment t'other night when he came to get the dogs. The man on the gang plank looked like him, and wore a coat like his. They were loading goods and I couldn't get closer. But one of the dock hands had overhead him give his name as Braithwaite."

Gresham dismissed his man, with orders to get food and rest.

"So that's it, then." Penry stared down at the wine in his glass. "He's out of our reach."

The flatness of the pronouncement echoed the unexpected surge of disappointment coursing through Adam. He'd failed. He'd promised Emma that he'd ensure that Francis paid for his crimes, and now her cousin was free and beyond the reach of justice. The only consolation was that Emma and Matthew were out of reach of Francis, and safe from his enmity.

Gresham downed the remainder of his wine in one gulp. "Nothing else we can do. The bastard's escaped the noose. For now. If he ever sets foot in England again, I'll be after him."

"We'll all be after him. But why does it matter to you so much?"

Gresham stared back at him and said harshly, "I don't like being played for a fool. And I despise traitors."

Not for the first time, Adam was unsure whether that was truth or not. Gresham seemed a man of multiple faces. He played the genial squire when it suited his purpose. The terrifying magistrate at other times. And the salacious womanizer, not only with his friends. Yet when just the three of them were together, he'd been driven, single-minded in his efforts to locate Braithwaite.

But Penry knew something of him and trusted him. They clearly had mutual connections, but neither offered any information and Adam didn't ask. Britain had been at war for years, and men had been called to many kinds of duty. As far as he knew, Gresham was no army man, but he carried the same shadow of darkness that

Adam recognized in himself.

The news of Francis's escape brought their mission to an abrupt ending. Too abrupt. They could go, get on with their lives, yet after days of urgent action not one of the three of them moved.

Gresham divided the remaining contents of the bottle between their three glasses. Lifting his own glass in a toast, he said, "Death to traitors!" and drank.

Adam echoed the toast with less enthusiasm. Not that traitors didn't deserve punishment. But there was no glory, no honor, no satisfaction, in sending a man to his death. Only the cold, hard, hand of duty. And the nightmares that came afterwards.

The wine tasted sour in his mouth.

"Let's hope he falls overboard," Penry said more lightly. "Or dies slowly of frostbite, alone in the New England woods."

The wine didn't improve, and the chamber seemed smaller, stuffier, closing in around Adam. A second bottle of wine waited on the table, but he was in no mood for a masculine drinking session. There'd be wine enough tonight at his mother's dinner party. And Emma.

He finished his glass and rose to take his leave. Penry did the same. The Countess's invitation to the Braithwaites included their guest, of course, and Penry had mentioned his intention to attend.

"Will you be joining us for dinner tonight at Rengarth, Gresham?" Adam asked. He'd conveyed his mother's invitation earlier in the day.

Gresham shook his head. "Thank you, but no. Lady Rengarth is gracious, but I'm not suitable company for your sisters." He flashed such a wolfish smile that Adam might have believed him a profligate rake if he hadn't seen the grim, somber nature of the man beneath the many masks.

He rode out of town with Penry, easier in his company than Gresham's. He trusted and liked Matthew's friend, although he wasn't sure he knew him much better now than three days ago. The man didn't reveal much of himself, in that practiced way that intelligence agents had of being friendly and pleasant yet silent about their personal lives.

Walking their horses about a mile before their roads diverged—Penry to Larkfell, he to Rengarth—Adam broached one of the questions he'd pondered about but not yet asked.

"Which are you with—military intelligence, or secret service?" He'd dealt with agents of both, on Wellington's staff. Respected most of them.

"Neither," Penry said, although after a short pause he conceded, "Now. The wars are over, and I find I am surplus to requirements."

"Like many of us." A generation of active men, who had known only war all their lives. He wasn't the only one finding it hard to imagine himself in a settled, peaceful life. The wars had left their mark on them all. "What will you do?"

"I've nothing to keep me here. So the colonies, perhaps." He gave a short laugh. "But not Canada. It's too damned cold, and with shipping unable to move for half the year, too far and too hard to get to."

It had never appealed to Adam, either. Especially after escorting an envoy from Wellington to Russia one winter. He'd endured more than enough of ice and snow. "There's always India," he suggested. "Or the West Indies."

Penry made an exaggerated grimace. "Have you been to the tropics? Awful heat and humidity."

Adam eyed the clouds overhead. Given a choice between hot and humid or cold and humid, he'd choose the cold. "I've heard New South Wales has a pleasant climate," he said. "And there are generous land grants." Facts that no longer held much attraction to him, but might to Penry.

"I'm not sure I'd make a good farmer. And I doubt the governor needs secret agents out there. But who knows? I'm in no hurry to decide. I have enough money for now, and no-one dependent on me."

They parted where the road to Rengarth left the main road, but Penry's last comment stayed with Adam. He, too, had enough for now, enough to invest in a farm or a business of some type. But he'd proposed to Emma, and the hard truth hammered at him: he had little to offer a woman of her intellect, beauty, and social position.

When he'd been imagining his future on his journey back to England from France, he'd figured his financial circumstances sufficient, with plentiful hard work, to establish himself on a farm in the colonies. Marriage had not crossed his mind then. Only escape from the politics and power struggles of the old world.

Emigration to a new colony was certainly not a life to offer a lady accustomed to the standard of living that Emma enjoyed. Besides, he was committed to staying here, at least for the foreseeable future. He had no doubt that George and Hannah's new baby would be a boy. Hannah was convinced of it, and with three daughters already, they surely must have a son next. So until—God willing—George recovered from his illness, or the boy came of age, he must fulfil is promise to manage the estate.

But he'd proposed to Emma with his heart and soul, not his head, with no thought to the practicalities of supporting a wife. Let alone a family. He had no entitlements to Rengarth and refused to be a drain on the estate. According to his conversation with Oliver on their ride the other day, there was little to spare, anyway.

With the sale of his commission he could purchase a house and some land, but unless he bought a farm he'd have no way of earning a living. He couldn't see Emma as a farmer's wife, and he had no trade or training. No experience in anything but war.

Just one of the plentiful reasons why she might refuse him. She'd witnessed him crying out in the night, and had reason to doubt the strength of his reason. And then there was the fact that the brutalities of the war had hardened him, and she might come to fear a man who'd proven capable of killing others. The gentleness of her nature would abhor the very thought of the things he'd done. He'd been prepared to kill Francis the other day, if he'd had the chance. But in the circumstances, allowing him to escape kept Emma safe from him.

He had a month to find a way to offer her a comfortable life. A month to win her love. A month to prove his worth—to himself as well as to her.

But he also had to prepare himself for the real possibility that she might not consider him good enough to marry.

~

Emma had little time to absorb the news of Francis's flight into exile in the rush to dress for dinner. Relief that he was gone mixed with the unsettling feeling that things were not finished, that nothing was truly settled. From so far away, they could not make him answer for poor Mr. Winslow's and the other mens' deaths, or for Matthew's injuries.

Her disquiet was further heightened when she arrived at Rengarth and dinner turned out to be a more formal affair than she'd expected, without the light-hearted presence of the three youngest Caldwells. The vicar, Mr. Timms, and his daughter Letitia, were friends and undaunting, as was the Countess's aunt, Mrs. Thorncroft, but the other guests the Countess had invited at short notice included Mr. Stratham, a partner in her bank and his wife, and three other prominent gentlemen in the district and their wives. Most of them had been at the ball, and witness to the mortifying scene with Francis and Lady Beatrice during the waltz. And they'd all heard at least some rumor of her abduction. Letitia, bless her gentle, pious heart, had whispered her sincere relief that Emma was unharmed, but the others merely cast her curious glances. Perhaps they expected her to break down in distress.

She needed to remain calm and composed in front of these people, hand-picked by the Countess, presumably so that her demonstration of support for Emma reached into the various Hartdale social circles.

As they all gathered before dinner in the drawing room, small groups here and there around the spacious room, Mrs. Stratham approached Emma where she sat with Matthew and two ladies of the district, the wife of the Hartdale mayor, and a baron's wife, Lady Rothingham.

Nodding to the other ladies, Mrs. Stratham seated herself in a vacant chair without invitation. A woman Emma had met a number of times and never warmed to, she was some years younger than her husband and displayed her wealth subtly in the lavish lace on her dress and the jewels around her neck. But not so subtly that one could fail to notice it. After expressing her pleasure to see Matthew safely returned, she added, "I've heard some ridiculous rumors about your cousin. Such a charming man, it's a shame that people spread untruths." Her little smile had poison in it.

The woman's audacity stunned Emma to silence. Stunned everyone nearby to silence. Emma desperately looked around for the Countess, for Louisa, but they were both engaged with Mr. Timms on the far side of the room. She didn't see Adam in that one quick moment.

While words chased in her head—none of them suitable— the glare Matthew directed at Mrs. Stratham came straight from the Canadian ice. Her once easy, good natured brother growled, "Charming to you, perhaps, Madam. But vicious and violent to me."

Her brother's bluntness, as if he cared nothing for other's opinions, strengthened Emma's confidence. In a burst of boldness, she added coolly, "My cousin certainly intended me harm, Mrs. Stratham, when he abducted me. Fortunately I escaped him before he carried out his threats." There, she'd acknowledged out loud that she'd been abducted, but with the facts. That should banish any presumptions of those within hearing.

Mrs. Stratham's smile faltered, but brightened again as she set her gaze on someone behind Emma. Who clearly counted more, in the lady's opinion, than she did.

In clipped tones Adam said, "Out of respect for our neighbors, I urge you to discretion, ma'am. My family will not look kindly on those who gossip about our friends."

"Oh, I would never do that, Major," Mrs. Stratham assured him with a sweetness so false Emma feared the exact opposite was already true.

Yet neither she nor Adam could do anything, say anything, for Lady Rengarth announced it was time for dinner. Unlike the previous time she'd dined with the family, tonight there were other guests, socially superior to her, and Adam was required to offer his arm to Lady Rothingham. So it was Oliver who escorted her, his steady presence calming to her unsettled nerves.

Fortunately, in the gathering of twenty, they were seated some way down the table from Mrs. Stratham and happily across from Mrs. Thorncroft, who proved delightful company. With Oliver on one side of her and Mr. Timms on the other, Emma felt surrounded by friends. Pleasantly candid in her opinions, Mrs. Thorncroft nevertheless listened and asked others' thoughts and the conversation around their part of the table covered a variety of subjects as the courses of the meal were served.

The tightness in the pit of Emma's stomach after the unpleasantness with Mrs. Stratham eased enough that she was able to enjoy the delicious food. At the head of the table, Adam was engrossed in conversation with Baron Rothingham, while the ladies beside him listened without animated interest. Politics, perhaps. Or maybe not. She heard mention of crops and harvest.

He caught her glance once, and his mouth curved into a smile. The second time, as she quickly looked away, she met Mrs. Stratham's knowing smile. Not a pleasant one.

She must, *must*, be more careful. Ignore the pull of attraction and affection and act as though he was nothing more to her than a kindly neighbor.

When dinner finished and the ladies withdrew to the music room, the constant awareness of Adam and the strain of pretending to be unaffected was replaced with her lack of confidence in being in a smaller group of women. She shouldn't be nervous. Phoebe had excused herself to attend to her son but Lady Rengarth, Louisa and Susanna were all friends, and Letitia, and Mrs. Thorncroft. It was the other four ladies she was unsure of.

Although much of the conversation centered on fashion, Mrs. Stratham managed to slip in comments about worsteds being "rather old-fashioned now", about Mr. Braithwaite's lovely cotton prints— "quite the finest made in England"—and, when the talk shifted to a family from a nearby town whose daughter had recently eloped with a young officer of no fortune, she commented that the young woman was "ruined, of course, and no-one will receive her now."

While the first little barbs could—perhaps—be passed off as unintentional, that last arrow struck Emma with a sharp hurt, for herself and for the young woman concerned. That could easily have been her younger self, as well as herself now.

"I will certainly receive her," the Countess said, as smoothly as if she wasn't contradicting a guest. "I hardly think the exuberance of young love is wrong. Unwise and impatient, perhaps, but it risks no-one's happiness but that of the couple themselves. There are far worse sins. Like adultery, for example," she added, carefully looking at no-one in particular, "which frequently ends up hurting the innocent greatly."

There was a small silence. Mrs. Stratham straightened the lace on her sleeve cuff. The mayor's wife stirred her tea, again.

The arrival of the gentlemen broke the silence. Oliver's deerhound had not been in the dining room, but he padded in beside his master before sniffing around the company. Several ladies nervously pulled their skirts aside. He paused by Mrs. Thorncroft, who scratched his ears affectionately. But when Oliver made a move the dog returned instantly to his side, guiding him through the people towards the piano and other instruments.

With twenty occupants, the room seemed crowded, noisy, more so because, under the Countess's direction, the men set out chairs and rearranged the ones the ladies had been using so that there were three rows forming a semi-circle facing the piano and the harp.

The tension in Emma's shoulders began to relax. Not surprising that there would be more music in this house. A pleasure to listen to, with the added advantage that it meant fewer opportunities for Mrs. Stratham or the mayor's wife to aim conversational daggers at her.

Matthew seemed tired and in pain, and headed for a nearby chair. Emma carried a small footstool over for him, and he smiled gratefully.

Mrs. Stratham had set her conversational sights on Mr. Penry, her penchant for attractive men apparently blinding her to the danger rippling under his socially amiable surface. He needed no rescuing, so Emma retreated towards the back row of seats.

A gentleman hesitated at the door. Not one who'd been at dinner. Not a servant. In a plain dark suit, he stood with crutches, one trouser leg pinned up at the knee.

Adam caught sight of him. "Garrett, come on in. We're almost ready." He escorted the man to Oliver, and his brother and the man conversed in low tones as they tuned a guitar and violin while the ladies and gents settled themselves in their seats.

While Adam moved a table and candelabra closer to the musicians, Louisa slipped into the chair beside Emma. "Mr. Garrett is from Adam's regiment," she murmured. "And he plays the violin like an angel." The words rang with an awe rare for Louisa. But then she glanced at Emma with an apologetic smile. "He was invited for dinner, of course, but he declined. He's only been here a few days."

"This is part of a new suite I have been composing," Oliver announced, and everyone quietened. "Mr. Nathaniel Garrett has kindly agreed to perform it with me."

As Mr. Garrett lifted his bow and Oliver played the first notes of the piece on his guitar, Adam sat in the vacant chair beside her. Her ability to concentrate on the music vanished. The notes from the violin and the guitar chased each other in rising cadences, but she was more aware of Adam's breathing, of his arm almost brushing against hers, and his hand resting on his knee.

She lifted her face back towards the music. Mr. Garrett did indeed play the violin beautifully. Emma didn't need talent to recognize the skill in the gliding, soaring, dancing notes, weaving in and out in harmony with Oliver's guitar. Playful. Uplifting.

After the tension of the ladies' conversation, the music gave Emma a sense of lightness, confidence. Or perhaps that was because Adam sat so close she could have touched him. There was pleasure in that, impossible though it was to act on that desire with so many others present.

As the evening came to a finish, the wind picked up and a few drops of rain spattered against the window. The Countess suggested that those travelling to Hartdale and beyond should depart first, before the closer neighbors. In the hubbub of calling for carriages and the ladies and gentlemen gathering in the hall to don their wraps for the drive home, Louisa touched Emma's arm and led her aside into an alcove.

"Emma, we've hardly had time to talk, but I want to tell you…" She was more serious than usual, more hesitant. "You and Adam… It's not my place to say anything, and I wouldn't yet, but I'm going away and…"

Her heart sinking, Emma braced herself for disapproval, for a friendly warning. Or worse.

Louisa glanced over her shoulder to ensure they weren't overhead and hurried on, "I know that you meant something to each other before he went away, and it seems you still do now. So I want you to know that if you and he were to marry," she smiled softly, "I would be very happy to have you as my sister."

Fear rushed faster than hope. "But we're not…" Pointless to deny her attraction to Adam, since she had clearly failed to hide it. "I'm not a suitable wife for Adam. I have no noble family, no wealth."

Louisa's eyes danced. "We don't have much wealth either, to be honest, and you're far more noble than those gossipmongers," she indicated Mrs. Stratham, "and Lady Beatrice. So please don't think yourself unsuitable. Don't let that be a reason to refuse Adam, if he asks you."

The other guests waited in the hall, the great front door opened, and a carriage drew up outside.

Catching Mrs. Stratham's raised eyebrow when she spotted them, Emma murmured, "Scandal is not sufficient reason to marry."

"It isn't," Louisa agreed quietly. "But love is," she added earnestly, before she pasted a social smile on her face and went to attend to her guests.

Emma waited with Matthew and Mr. Penry while the Countess and Louisa bid goodnight to each set of guests at the door, and Adam escorted them to their carriages. The Strathams had travelled from

Hartdale in the mayor's carriage. When the ladies curtsied to the Countess, their bright smiles faded as the Countess said something in a tone too low for Emma to hear. About her, it seemed. Mrs. Stratham's quick glance in her direction radiated displeasure.

Well, it wasn't as though she'd lost a friend there. They'd only ever been polite acquaintances. Not so polite, now, apparently. But as she'd brought at least part of the scandal on herself, she must bear the consequences.

The Larkfell party was the last to leave. Matthew and Mr. Penry bid goodnight to their hosts, and made their slow progress down the grand staircase to the waiting carriage.

The candlelight flickered on the Countess's face, revealing the strain and fatigue under her social poise. That she'd arranged this dinner at short notice the evening before she traveled with half her household to London for an indefinite stay humbled Emma, and stabbed her with guilt.

Emma curtsied low. "My Lady, I can't thank you enough for all you have done for me."

"I apologize for that woman's unpleasantness, Emma. Unfortunately she is a friend of Beatrice Farringdon, but I trust that she understands now that any further discourtesy will have consequences."

Emma didn't ask what consequences. The threat of a shunning by the Countess might be sufficient to deter socially ambitious women from spreading innuendo. Perhaps.

But perhaps not. The possibility of social shame had not stopped her from giving herself to Adam. Lady Beatrice was witness to the truth, albeit slanted with her particular prejudices. If the Countess found out...

She looked into the candid blue eyes, so like Louisa's. '*I hardly think the exuberance of young love is wrong,*' she'd said earlier. Adam's mother guessed the truth. And she'd arranged all this for Emma's sake.

Heat flooded over her face. "I'm more grateful than I can express, my Lady. I wish you a safe journey, and good news about Lord

Rengarth's health when you reach London."

"Thank you." Unexpectedly, she leaned forward and kissed Emma on the cheek. "You are always welcome here, my dear," she murmured. "As a friend, or...more. Do write to us while we're away."

Stammering her thanks, Emma curtsied again. She embraced Louisa, words stalling in her throat, and turned aside before her composure completely failed. Then Adam was beside her, offering his arm.

"The steps may be slippery," he said, as if that were sufficient excuse to draw her close to his side and cover her hand with his. They were far from alone. Below them, Matthew awkwardly stepped up into the carriage, while Mr. Penry provided a firm shoulder to lean on, and a footman stood by with a lantern. Behind them, the rest of the family watched.

They descended the first half of the stairs in silence, but his hand was warm on hers even through her gloves, and under her pelisse the flesh of her arm and shoulder seemed to remember the sensations of lying skin to skin with him. Her breath came unevenly, as if she'd hurried for some distance instead of sedately descending wide steps.

If she slipped on the damp stone, he'd steady her. Catch her. Hold her.

The idea was more tempting than it should be.

"May I call on you?" he asked, his voice deep and solemn. "Tomorrow?"

"Yes." Matthew planned to go to their temporary warehouse in Hartdale tomorrow to arrange matters ready for business. And Mr. Penry had mentioned his intention to meet with Sir Phillip. He'd not said anything about why.

She would be at home alone tomorrow. With Adam. Her heart skipped a beat in anticipation—until fear flooded over the hope and almost overwhelmed it.

The unpleasantness this evening had disconcerted her. She must be careful. If the ladies did not heed the Countess's warning, or if gossip had already spread, association with Adam's family was too great a risk to his young sisters' reputations.

His hand tightened over hers for a moment before they reached the carriage. The only intimacy possible, in such public view. Mr. Penry waited by the open carriage door, but it was Adam who assisted her in. She thanked him and managed to smile at him, but she felt the strain of it and questions flickered in his eyes. As Mr. Penry swung into the carriage and the door clicked shut, she caught only one last glance of Adam's face before the horses moved off.

In the semi-darkness she closed her eyes and rested her head against the high back of the seat, her thoughts a confusion of contradictions and concerns. Too much had happened in less than a week. She needed time to clear her mind, to think through it all. Time to truly know her own heart, to determine if her feelings, seemingly so strong now, were genuine and lasting or simply a response to the intense emotional strain of the events. Adam needed time to adjust to his new life at Rengarth.

And although it was heartening that Louisa believed her a suitable wife for Adam, Emma was not so innocent as to the potential difficulties.

She could not be certain Adam would ask for her hand again. She could not be certain she'd accept him, if he did. Her heart said yes, but her head—her logic, her reason, her intellect—urged caution.

Time. She needed time.

CHAPTER 29

Thursday

Adam supervised the final loading of the luggage wagon and its departure not long after first light, while the travelers ate a hearty breakfast to fortify themselves for the long day ahead. Then there were hat boxes and valises to load on to the coaches, one vehicle for his family, the second for the servants accompanying them.

The sun had barely risen above the treetops when it was time for the final flurry of activity and farewells. He handed Phoebe up into the carriage, and set his young nephew burbling with laughter when he pretended to toss him in. Louisa next, and he held on to Zeus while Oliver stepped in, before the dog leapt up to take his accustomed place beside the coachman.

His mother embraced her aunt and her younger children, with last minute instructions and affectionate words for each of them.

She took his hand at the carriage step, gathering the skirts of her pelisse. "I'm glad you're here, Adam. I know you'll manage everything well. Write to me with all the news." Despite her brimming eyes, she gave him a playful smile. "More regularly than when you were in France. You don't have the excuse of war now."

He deliberately kept the mood light. "Only the command of this band of scoundrels."

"Do you include me as one of these scoundrels?" his great-aunt enquired. Her raised eyebrow competed with the quirk of her mouth, and lost.

He waited with the door open while his mother settled herself beside Phoebe. "Absolutely, Aunt. I believe you have become the ringleader already."

Although they all chuckled, there were some sobs mixed in.

He closed the door, shooed the watchers back from the carriage, and the horses set off. He clapped restraining hands on his brothers' shoulders to hold them back from chasing it. Cecilia sprinted a dozen paces before she realized her brothers weren't with her, and Adam called her back.

They waited until the carriage turned out through the gates. He wasn't used to being the one left behind. Leaving to join his regiment, he'd known Rengarth would always be there. And the times he'd had leave in London, he'd been the one to ride away from his family after a few days, a week or more.

No-one was going off to war, and yet he had a lump in his throat.

"Come on inside," he said to his charges. "It's our turn for breakfast."

He continued the practice of having the boys read the newspaper over breakfast, and included Cecilia as well since they were all there today. He could read whatever they missed later, but Aunt Thorncroft's eyesight for fine print was fading, and she too was interested in the happenings of the world.

But although the boys and Cecilia read well, taking turns, his thoughts kept straying, flitting over and around all the matters requiring his attention. Estate tasks. Household tasks. Emma. How he'd court her. He needed a new suit. He needed to keep both boys quiet for a few more days. How he'd find a way to support her. Emma.

The paper passed to Jeremy. "An attempted elopement..." His brother stopped abruptly, skimming the words. His face went ashen. "Adam..." He thrust the paper across the table, pointing towards the end of the middle column.

It took Adam a moment to focus his eyes on the words.

'An attempted elopement to Gretna Green almost succeeded recently. A gentlemen of a noble house whisked the lady of his affection north along the Kendal road. Her cousin, a respected manufacturer, pursued them, but after a man was killed in an altercation in the woods, the brave gentleman disappeared and has not been seen since. The lady was seen with her lover in a state of considerable déshabillé early in the morning.'

He read it again, rage replacing disbelief and pushing him to his feet, his chair clattering backwards to the floor. A string of curse words ran through his mind but in the presence of the ladies he refrained—barely—from uttering them.

"Read it to our aunt, Jeremy," he said through gritted teeth. "I must warn Emma. I'll ride to Halifax after that and demand a printed apology from the paper."

He strode out, calling for a horse to be readied, taking the stairs at a run to fetch his coat.

They'd print a retraction and apology if he had to set the type for it himself. And they'd tell him who was responsible.

But the damage was already done. That kind of sensational, salacious account would be discussed in every conversation in the West Riding for days. And whoever was behind this would ensure— it could be done with a word here, a suggestion there—that Emma's name was spread, replacing the speculation with 'fact'.

~

Although Emma didn't sleep late, Matthew and Mr. Penry had already left for Hartdale before she rose. She had barely come downstairs when Adam cantered up the drive. In her morning wrapper over her petticoats, her tousled hair stuffed under a muslin cap, she was not ready for visitors but in the hall he asked for her, and he followed the housekeeper in to the breakfast room.

The hard set of his face forestalled her apology for her state of undress. Fury emanated from him, tightly controlled. Not aimed at her, although his voice was brisk as he said, "I'm sorry, Emma.

There's more trouble to bear, unfortunately."

Trouble serious enough to bring him here at an unsociable hour. Before she could ask, he handed her the newspaper he'd brought and indicated an item in it.

Distracted by his agitated pacing, at first the words did not make sense. They hadn't eloped. As she read on, read the twisted lies, a chasm seemed to open up before her, all the tentative hopes she'd dared to hold crashing down into it.

Her hand shook and she let the paper fall onto the table. That her reputation was blackened was not entirely unexpected, but to cast such suspicions about Adam's character...

"How could it *possibly* be any worse? What they insinuate about you, Adam...to imply you murdered him..." Anger rose red before her eyes. "How *dare* they! Oh, I can't believe they could print this slander!"

"I'm more concerned about the attack on you, Emma. It's vicious and unforgivable. I'm going to Halifax from here and I'll find out who is behind this. I'll see that the paper prints a full retraction and an apology in their next edition."

Saturday. The paper didn't come out again until Saturday. In the meantime, everyone would have plenty to gossip about. And no-one took editorial apologies seriously, if they even read them.

This story would be whispered behind her back for years to come.

Anger was fading to an icy numbness. "It will be too late. It was too late the moment it was printed."

"Yes. I'm afraid so. But it may be that we can lessen the damage."

She nodded, but could not see how. No-one would believe protestations of innocence. And she couldn't, in all conscience, claim innocence. Of eloping, yes. That was a lie. Of the rest...no.

Adam could not sit until she did, but she could only hold herself upright by standing. If she allowed a chair, or Adam, or anything to support her, she might collapse into a flood of tears and helplessness.

Standing rigid, she stared out the window to the gray, overcast day. What had been beautiful and perfect between her and Adam, alone in the cottage, would be twisted by the world into something sordid.

There was a soft knock at the open door. Mrs. Barnden with a tea tray. And an air of concern, taking in the tension of the scene, both of them still standing, Emma by the window, Adam by the bookcase.

She asked the housekeeper to pour as she did not entirely trust herself with fine china with the effects of the shock still gripping her. Mrs. Barnden shot her a questioning glance as she unloaded her tray on the breakfast table and filled two cups.

The household would find out before long. Matthew would undoubtedly hear the news in Hartdale, sometime during the day.

"Thank you, Mrs. Barnden." She astonished herself that she could speak with some degree of composure.

As the housekeeper left, Adam accepted the tea cup Emma offered, the delicate white china small in his large hands.

She picked up her own cup, put it down again. Perhaps in a few minutes, hours…a day, a week, the tightness gripping her would ease and she might be able to drink tea.

Think. She must think her way through this, not curl up into a ball and howl.

"It must be Lady Beatrice who sent that story to the paper," she said. "She saw us, she'd have heard about Barlow's death that night at the inn. But she left before the inquest." And she might not have known about Francis disappearing. "Or it may have been Mrs. Stratham. Lady Beatrice may have written to her."

"If I could summon whoever it was to pistols at dawn, I'd be tempted to."

A measure of his anger that he thought it, although she was fairly certain he'd never call anyone out, even if turned out to be a man responsible for the report and not Lady Beatrice or Mrs. Stratham at all. Although he'd defend those he cared about, she doubted he'd ever flout the law in pointless violence.

"Adam, I'm so sorry that you've been caught up in this, that your honor has been maligned. I can't have this scandal affect your family, your sisters. Perhaps it's best if I go away. I can...I can go and visit my sisters in India. I could begin making arrangements immediately."

Expressing the idea out loud made it seem plausible, although her heart tore in two. Why did India have to be so terribly far away? She'd love to see her sisters and her nieces, but it took more than four months simply to sail to Calcutta; if she went, she'd be away for a year at least. She'd have to leave Matthew alone, when he wasn't fully recovered, and had no-one else but her. And she'd have to leave Adam, and his family.

"No..." Adam broke off his objection, pausing for several heartbeats before he continued, "Only if that's what you truly wish to do. But Emma, don't forget that people here know you and respect you. Many of them won't believe these lies."

"But it's not all lies."

He laid his scarcely-touched teacup on the table and crossed to her, a hand gentle on her shoulder. "Emma, what we did was from our hearts and our care for each other. I can't regret it, but I do regret that I didn't find a way to protect your privacy."

She wished she could press her face against the strength of his chest, allow herself to be held by him, but that was a weakness she could not afford to give in to. She must stay clear-headed. She'd caused too much trouble for him already.

She retreated several steps from him, clasping her hands in front of her so that she couldn't reach for him. "It's my fault. I tempted you."

He stood stock still, his eyes darkening. "Emma, it's a damned myth that a man can't resist temptation. We both chose, and I am responsible for my own actions. But even if I'd slept in the cow byre and never touched you, Lady Beatrice would have drawn exactly the same conclusion."

He was right. An unchaperoned night with a man had ruined many a woman, some far more innocent than her. Many a man, too, forced to marry to salvage a lady's reputation. And too many people living in misery as a result, unsuited to a lifetime together.

She wanted to be sure of shared and lasting respect, affection and love before committing herself to any man. Adam deserved no less. Nostalgic fondness for the young people they'd been eight years ago was not enough when they had both grown and changed. She could not allow his sense of honor to tie him to her, unless he was sure his heart desired it.

Better to endure some weeks of gossip than a lifetime of regret. She lifted her head. "Perhaps if we simply go about our lives as usual, as if this wasn't us, the story might soon be forgotten."

"Perhaps." He sounded as convinced as she felt. Not at all. "Emma, we both know that the impact for me is far less than for you. I'm more likely to be congratulated by my peers than censured. I may be spared the attentions of morally upright matrons with daughters of marriageable age, but," he gave a crooked smile. "I confess that is not a matter that perturbs me at all."

She nodded. That was the way of the world. That women were held to such a high level of morality, and men weren't. The unfairness of it made the load heavier to bear, but raging against it wouldn't help alleviate this problem.

She should sit down, think clearly. He saw her move towards the table and drew out a chair for her. He shifted her teacup closer to her before he sat down himself, turning his chair so that he faced her, not the table.

She managed a sip of tea without clattering the cup against the saucer. Good. The comfort of the tea might help her think rationally about what they faced, and what might be done.

"Lady Beatrice prides herself as a moral authority, and is shocked by a great many more matters than seem to trouble Mr. Timms." This was safer ground, thinking, not feeling. "Mrs. Stratham is..." She remembered the Countess's comment, and a few other things she'd observed. "Rather more flexible in her scruples." An understatement, possibly, although for some reason Mrs. Stratham and Lady Beatrice remained friends. "She is socially ambitious, and cultivates the company of attractive men."

He held her gaze. "I'm only interested in one woman, Emma.

Whatever I can do to ease this situation for you, I will do. But I fear you will need all your courage to face down the unpleasantness."

In this whole disastrous mess his honesty remained constant. He didn't lie and pretend it could be easily fixed.

"It is not the worst thing that has ever happened to a woman. I doubt that all my acquaintances will scorn me." She spoke with more hope than certainty. In truth, she had few close friends in the district now. Few people other than her own and Adam's family she could count on to stand up for her. "I'll go away for a while if it becomes too difficult."

"I hope that won't be necessary." He reached a hand towards her before stopping abruptly, as if understanding her need for distance. "Emma, I won't press you about my proposal. You asked me to wait a month, and I'll do that. But if you wish, before the month is up, you need only say the word and I will see the vicar about calling the banns. If my attentions are unwelcome then say so, and I'll not speak of marriage again."

"No. No, it's not that at all. But it's too significant a decision to rush."

"I understand, Emma. It is important for a woman to be certain. And I must warn you," he took a deep breath, every aspect of his face solemn, "that I am not a wealthy man. I can provide only a modest home and income."

She saw that it hurt his pride to tell her that.

"Do you think that matters to me?" She didn't need maids or silk gowns or fancy balls and dinners. A marriage rich in respect and affection was worth more than thousands of pounds.

"No. But it's a factor for you to consider. You deserve so much more than I can offer."

"I have some funds," she told him, determined to be equally as honest about matters of such importance. "But I am no heiress. There are many young women, more beautiful, accomplished and wealthier than I am."

"But there's only one of you," he said softly. "Don't underestimate your qualities and strengths, Emma." He paused, sought for words.

"You're a rare woman, in everything you are, and everything you do."

His sincerity almost undid her control. She lowered her face and bit her lip, clinging to her composure. If only this could have been a simple, uncomplicated courtship. Renewing their acquaintance in everyday social activities. Coming to know each other again gradually.

But no, their every meeting since his return last Friday had been in the midst of drama, emotion and fear. Only those few hours in the cottage, just the two of them, when she'd no longer been afraid or on edge.

When she didn't respond, he shifted his chair back, ready to stand. "I'd best be on my way to Halifax."

He'd had little rest for days, searching for Francis until yesterday. Eight miles to Halifax, and eight miles back again...he'd be gone most of the day. And for what? Another tidbit in the newspaper for people to gossip about. "Adam, I'm not sure an apology is the best thing. It won't change matters greatly, and it might only serve to increase speculation. Perhaps we should wait a day or so, and see what happens before deciding. When we're calmer."

"If that's what you wish," he said slowly. "You're right in that I certainly don't feel calm. I don't want to stand by when you've been insulted like this. But you have my word that I won't do anything without your permission."

"Thank you." As always, he put her wishes before his own wants. He was an officer, a man of action, yet he'd acquiesced to her request not to ride to the newspaper to defend her honor. "I don't know what's best to do, but I don't want to risk making things worse until we know if anyone will actually connect the report with us." A slim hope, but all she had to hold on to for now. "If the worst happens, I may simply have to find the fortitude to brave it out. Or there's always India. I'm told it's very beautiful."

Her attempt at lightness only succeeded in making him wince.

"Emma..." He leaned forward and enclosed one of her hands gently between his. "I understand if you feel the need to go away for a while. But please don't go without telling me." His eyes pleaded with her. "Without saying goodbye."

She curled her fingers into his. "I won't," she promised. Impossible to consider leaving for any length of time without telling him. Whether to India, to her aunt in London, or simply to Julia Hampton. Impossible to consider leaving him at all without a dagger in her heart at the prospect.

Without words to express her feelings, she placed her other hand on his. The lace cuff of her sleeve was white against the tanned skin of his hands. A reminder that she wore only an informal robe over her petticoat.

She withdrew her hands from his with reluctance. "It's as well Lady Beatrice isn't here. I am in a state of far more déshabillé than I was when she saw us."

"And alone with me. We should be more circumspect, shouldn't we? I'll leave you for now. Would you like me to ask my aunt to visit to keep you company?"

Much though she liked Mrs. Thorncroft, she wanted some time to herself. "I know she planned to keep the younger ones occupied exploring the attics today, to soften the blow of the rest of the family leaving. I will be fine, by myself."

Before he left, he kissed her, brushing his mouth against hers. A brief kiss that sent her heart racing. A reminder of all they'd shared, of how much she could lose.

Once he'd ridden away, she fought off despondency by tidying the tea things back on to the tray. She must keep herself occupied. Even with Matthew back now to look after the company, she had work to do here. The unseasonably wet summer risked failed crops, rising prices, and hunger for the most vulnerable. Combined with reduced work for Braithwaite's spinners and weavers, the winter loomed threateningly.

Her problems were minor in comparison.

She made her decision. She would not run away, unless her continued presence hurt others. Because leaving Larkfell and Hartdale—leaving her home, leaving Adam—would take even more courage than she'd need to withstand the criticisms and the shunning of society.

~

Adam left via the path behind Larkfell's stables, up onto the hills to reduce the chance of anyone seeing him leave Emma's home, and cursed himself almost the entire distance back to Rengarth. An entirely useless activity, for all the 'what ifs' and 'if onlys' changed nothing that had happened and did not even serve to improve his mood. A great cloud of scandal hung over Emma, and his actions had contributed to it.

He respected and accepted her reasons for not going straight to the newspaper to demand an apology. Doing nothing sat ill with him, but what could, in truth, be done? Nothing but ensure he provided no more cause for chatter and speculation. No more galloping over to Larkfell before decent visiting hours to see Emma without a chaperone. He'd learned well the tactical advantages of waiting to choose a battleground, assess the enemy's strength, weapons and resources, and reinforce strategic alliances. This situation was little different to war.

The bridle path he followed took him past the woods and up behind Rengarth. From here the estate spread out below him: the Castle, the farm, the village, the dairy. His responsibility, now that his mother had left for London.

He'd had just enough time yesterday evening, before dressing for dinner, to spend an hour with his mother. She'd shown him the various account and ledger books, and gone over the notes she'd written for him about managing the estate. Her most urgent concern—his concern, now—was the harvest, and whether there'd be enough grain and other crops to see them through winter.

Although half his heart and thoughts were with Emma, he had other duties, too, so he headed down the hill to consult with the farmer about crops, and to find out if Sunday's storms had done much damage.

CHAPTER 30

Face the world. Easier said than done. But better to do it while anger and determination still gave her the fortitude to endure any scorn.

Matthew had already taken the gig and could bring home her purchases, so despite the overcast weather she decided to walk into town. It was not unusual for her to do so, and after days confined to the house, she yearned for the exercise and fresh air.

The brisk walk almost succeeded in raising her spirits. Surely no-one would believe the newspaper story referred to her, if she acted with confidence, as if nothing had happened?

Her first call when she reached Hartdale was to the dressmaker, to replace her ruined gowns. With an unusually cool gaze, the dressmaker told her, "I'm afraid, Miss Braithwaite, that I am fully booked. For some time."

Emma stared at her in disbelief for several moments. No, she had not misheard. She almost challenged the bold lie. Almost reminded the haughty woman that she'd been a regular customer for more than ten years. But there were more effective ways of making her point. "That is a pity," she said. "I wanted three gowns made. And I know that Lady Susanna from Rengarth was planning to call in for some evening dresses. I'll tell her not to bother."

She swept out before the dressmaker changed her mind. And before the surge of anger and disbelief that sustained her gave way to shaking and tears.

She could cope with this. She'd buy fabric and she and Kate could sew her gowns. Or she'd find some young woman with dreams but not the means of setting up as a dressmaker, and employ her.

In the draper's shop, she found that the blue silk taffeta she wished to purchase was, the draper she'd dealt with for years told her nervously, on hold for another customer. Likewise the lilac silk twill.

She looked the draper directly in the eye. "It's reserved for Mrs. Stratham, is it?"

Miserably embarrassed, he nodded.

"The blue taffeta is for the mayor's wife, I suppose? And allow me to guess...this lovely lilac stripe is on hold for Lady Beatrice Farringdon? The entire bolt, I imagine?"

He wrung his hands together and gave another wordless, shame-faced nod.

For her entire life, her family company had enjoyed a good relationship with the draper. He was a decent man and must have been placed under considerable pressure to behave so ill towards her now. Was he afraid that all the wealthy ladies of Hartdale might shun his business if he sold fabric to her? Was that what had been threatened?

She recalled Lady Rengarth's example and her father's words: *Make it easy for a man to redeem himself.*

She did not feel quite so charitable at this moment. "Very well," she said. "Since some of the ladies of the town are clearly providing you with considerable business, I presume that the amount that you are in debt to Braithwaite and Co for the worsteds we have supplied to you this year will be paid forthwith? If I recall correctly, it's about one hundred and fifty-seven pounds." In her mind, she could see the line in the ledger book. "And twelve shillings. I'll tell my brother to expect payment this week."

As she opened the door to exit the shop, she caught the reflection in the window glass of his wide-eyed panic. The possibility of debtor's prison was indeed fearful.

She glanced over her shoulder briefly and acted on her father's advice. "Perhaps you can send word to Larkfell when you have more silks in stock."

The shop bell jangled as she allowed the door to fall shut behind her.

There'd likely be a note or a messenger at Larkfell in the morning with samples of 'new' silks. But she doubted the disapproving dressmaker would suddenly find time in her schedule.

She hesitated on the street. She had more items on her list to purchase, but her courage quailed at the possibility of another confrontation.

Matthew. His sympathy and uncritical presence were not far away. If he didn't already know about the newspaper report, she must tell him. She trusted that he'd support her, no matter what.

He'd accepted Robert's offer of the old mill to use as their temporary warehouse. It lay just beyond the town. Once a water-powered fulling mill, Robert had moved his fulling operations to a steam-powered mill beside the new canal. But these old premises were in good repair and large enough for Braithwaite and Co.'s operations in the short term, at least.

She passed Ned and the office boys on her way along the street, purchasing stationery supplies to replace those burned in the fire. On the edge of town, the warehouse lads drove the wagon towards Larkfell to begin transferring the bales of fabric from the barn.

Beyond the last houses of this part of Hartdale a stream bubbled down from the fells, a low weir forming a small pond. She crossed it on the old stone bridge, the water wheel of the flour mill just downstream creaking and splashing as it turned in the mill race. Upstream a little, the wheel of Robert's mill was still and silent, the mill race closed off so the water passed by it.

The old stone building seemed quiet and empty without the lads present, but the door stood open and she went inside, following the stairway up to the office, the flagstones worn with a century or more of footsteps.

"Get out!" Matthew's voice rang out as she neared the top of the stairs.

She stopped, her hand on the wall, uncertain if he addressed her. He couldn't see her from here.

But a harsh, guttural laugh answered her brother, and a male voice drawled, "Oh, but we haven't finished our discussion."

Francis. Francis, *here*, with Matthew but with no other help but her, and none of their employees nearby. There might be men to help at the flour mill...

"Where are the letters, Matthew?"

"I won't tell you."

Something crashed, and Matthew bellowed in pain. She ran up the remaining few stairs, and pushed through the half-open door into the office.

~

After a couple of hours or so, walking around the farm, discussing plans with the farmer, Adam began the ride home, calculating crop yields and number of mouths to feed in his head. Yields were down and the harvest late, but all going well, no-one would starve. He glanced up at the overcast sky. No guarantees that all would go well.

As he was approaching the castle he overtook a boy, a lad of twelve or so, running hard. He slowed the horse and stopped in front of him. The boy, puffing hard, gulped out, "Message for Major Caldwell at the castle, sir. The man said it were urgent."

On hearing Adam's identity, the boy handed over a folded piece of brown paper. Wrapping paper, not writing paper, torn along the edge, without a seal. The few penciled lines read: *Have seen FB in Brook Lane near church walking south. Will inform gents at Arms and try to follow. Please pay boy. I will repay. N.G.*

Garrett. He'd asked this morning if he might ride on the luggage wagon as far as Hartdale. He was a guest, Adam had assured him, and had more than earned his lodging.

Garrett had seen Francis Braithwaite in Hartdale. He trusted Garrett's sighting over that of a man who'd barely glimpsed

Braithwaite two days before, and thought he saw him from a distance at the Liverpool docks in the moonlight. It was highly possible that Francis had sent a decoy.

Adam paid the boy generously, turned his horse and rode at a gallop to Hartdale. Brook Lane followed the path of the stream through a wooded area to the west of the church and the town. He found Penry and Gresham on horseback, conferring, not much further past the church where the lane forked, one road going into town, the other winding down to a footbridge across the stream.

Penry lifted a hand in greeting but wasted no words. "Garrett said Braithwaite was going south. But which way?"

"We didn't see him in town," Gresham added, "but he had a good twenty minutes on us. He could be anywhere."

Adam looked back to the north, a vague memory stirring. An abominably boring dinner, when he was eighteen, in a large house set back from the road. "The Strathams live further up there, north of the church." Given the coincidence, there was every chance Mrs. Stratham had known exactly where Francis was last night, when she was taunting Emma.

Garrett had said he'd try to follow Braithwaite. Adam swung down from his horse, passing the reins to Penry to hold. He walked a few yards down the west fork of the road. Garrett would have kept to the edge, close into the trees, ready to hide. There were footprints in the bare earth of the wheel tracks. A pair of feet. Not Garrett. Adam knelt to examine the grass alongside. It didn't take him long to find indentations, regularly spaced. Garrett's crutches.

"They went this way," he called to the others.

When they joined him he noticed that Gresham carried a pistol in his greatcoat pocket, and wished he'd brought his own.

Penry saw his glance, and after he handed back Adam's reins he pulled a knife from his boot and passed it to him. "I have another one," he said airily. "Or three."

Adam slid the knife in his boot. He'd use his bare hands on Francis if necessary, but a knife gave him better odds.

They'd almost reached the footbridge when a boy in ragged

clothes stepped out from the trees and hailed them. "The soljer said ye'd be along. He said to tell ye that the man went to the cotton fac'try, but he left there with another man and went towards t' old mill."

"How long ago?" Adam asked. "How long have you been waiting for us?"

The boy screwed up his face, thinking. Of course he had no watch, no way of knowing the time. "Got here just afore the church bell tolled," he said.

Adam had heard it as he approached town. Ten minutes or more ago. Probably for the constable's funeral—someone had mentioned last night he'd finally be buried today.

Francis would have reached the mill within minutes of leaving the factory. The mill that Robert Braithwaite had made available for Matthew to use. And Matthew's warehouse men were probably not there—he'd said last night that they planned to move goods from Larkfell today.

But the footbridge was too narrow for horses. They'd have to either go downstream and cross at the main bridge near the mill—in full view of the mill—or upstream to the ford, and ride to the mill in the cover of the trees.

"Go down towards the bridge," he told the others. "But stay hidden, and don't cross it. Ambush him if he goes that way. I'll try to get in from the other side."

Gresham opened his mouth to argue, but Adam cut him off.

"I'll whistle if I need you."

He turned his horse towards the ford, and urged it on.

~

His chair toppled, Matthew struggled to rise from the floor. Francis stood over him, and raised Matthew's cane to hit him.

"Stop it!" Emma shouted. In her anger, in her horror, she didn't pause to think and grabbed at the cane, desperately trying to stop the blow falling on her brother. She was not strong enough, not at all, and the cane burned along her hands as she struggled to wrest control of it from Francis. He swore and swung it, hitting her on the shoulder, pushing her away so hard she stumbled and fell. Her reticule flew across the room, her bonnet slipped off her head, hanging by its ribbons down her back.

A man—not Francis—pulled her to her feet, gripping her arms painfully tight.

Matthew had dragged himself up to lean against the desk. "Let her go," he ordered. "Tell your friend to release her, Francis."

Francis turned to her. His face was marred by a dark bruise, his eye socket swollen and red. "Creating trouble for me again, Emma. And I was just having a chat with Matthew. But it's advantageous that you're here. It saves me having to go and fetch you."

The cold calmness in his voice scared her as much as his rage had in the woods. But if she quailed before him he'd use her fear against her. "What do you want, Francis?"

"I want some letters of mine that Matthew has stolen. I want the fields to the east of Larkfell. I want the portrait of Sir Francis Braithwaite that hangs in the study at the house." He strolled to Matthew's chair and set it upright. "And I want you as my wife. Do sit down, dear cuz."

The man holding her released her, but she made no move towards the chair. She was closer to the fireplace here, and although she didn't dare look properly, she thought there was a poker propped beside it. Matthew's hand on the desk was only inches from a pen knife and she thought he knew it, was hoping to use it.

She must keep Francis's attention away from him. "You're a wanted man, Francis."

He raised his hand in a great show of mock horror. "Me? Wanted? Pray tell me, for what?"

"For murder."

"Murder? Surely you're not referring to that dreadful accident in the forest, when your screams caused my horse to bolt? There was a report of the inquest in the Leeds paper yesterday."

His sheer audacity astounded her. He'd escaped trial, and he knew it. But Matthew's fingers were only an inch from the pen-knife now. "For the other murders," she said, hastily. "Mr. Winslow and the men in the church. And for treason."

He shook his head, pretending sorrow. "You make such grave accusations, Emma, with no evidence to back them up."

Because he'd murdered the witnesses. She turned away from him, as if in desperation, and edged a few inches closer to the fire poker. The other man was by the door, Francis between her and Matthew. One woman and one injured man against two fit and strong men. They'd be beaten in a moment. Unless some opportunity arose and they were able to take advantage of it.

Matthew spoke up. "The Lieutenant Governor has the letters."

Francis whirled around to face him. "He does?"

Matthew had straightened to a stand, and she couldn't see the pen-knife.

Francis's hands clenched by his side and for a moment she thought he might strike Matthew, but then he merely laughed. "Oh, well, too bad if he does. Too bad for you, that is. They're only addressed to Mr. Braithwaite. I'll write to the authorities and sadly report that my cousin has been plotting treason."

"I'm no traitor," Matthew said flatly, but he didn't mention Mr. Penry. Did Francis know about him? Know that he was Mr. Ballantyne? Emma tried to think whether he'd seen Mr. Penry. Perhaps not.

"Of course you are. I'm sure I can find plenty of witnesses to your treasonous plotting."

Matthew's face darkened. "You conniving *bastard*."

He took a step forward but he was unsteady, without his cane, and not quick enough to avoid the punch Francis threw, hard under the jaw, followed by another forceful punch to the body that sent him crashing to the floor again.

Emma rushed to her brother's side. He was curled up with his back to Francis, winded, his eyes closed and his arms across his body in pain. No. His eyes flickered open and his fingers reached for the knife concealed in his sleeve. She shielded him from their cousin's view. Under cover of grasping her brother's hand, begging him to hold still, to be all right, Matthew passed her the small knife. She tucked it into her pelisse sleeve, sharp end first. His breathing was already coming more easily, and he looked into her face he mouthed the word 'pretend'.

She rose to her feet and faced her cousin. She could not hope to overpower him, even with the advantage of the knife. Even if Matthew was able to help. There were only her wits to rely on, while she waited for any chance to best him. But she must not provoke him into rage.

Francis could have killed Matthew before she'd arrived—he could have done it just now—but he hadn't. He must still have some use for him. To blame for the treason? But he could still do that if Matthew was dead. She had to protect her brother.

'*Arrogance,*' Mrs. Thorncroft had once said when they were discussing how to approach a member of parliament about factory children, '*is an emotional weakness in a man. Use flattery as a weapon.*'

Francis was undoubtedly arrogant, and she needed every possible weapon.

Emma clasped her hands in front of her, aiming to appear feminine and harmless while her fingers touched the handle of the knife. "There was no need to hurt him so badly. He's weak and injured and no threat to you. You're too powerful for us."

"I've always been too powerful for you, Emma." Francis sat himself behind her father's desk, rescued from the old warehouse. "I could have put your father out of business any moment I chose. I can do the same to Matthew whenever I wish."

"You're very clever, aren't you, Francis?" she said, to keep his attention on her. "You have everything planned out. But I don't understand why you still want to marry me."

"Winslow's fortune, my dear. I thought about marrying you before that, of course, although Larkfell mightn't have been worth the bother. But then I found out that old Winslow had rather more fortune than we thought."

"Fortune?" She didn't believe a word of it, having seen her friend's careful economies. But better to play along with it to allay Francis's distrust. "I'll be rich?"

"*We* will be rich. And of course I have everything planned. There are opportunities to pursue in New York. You'll come with me as my wife. And as long as you behave yourself and don't cause any difficulties, I will let Matthew live. If you are anything less than an obedient wife, I will lock you in an asylum and send word to my friends here-" He pointed to the other man. "Who will see to it that Matthew meets his maker. And if Matthew does anything stupid, I will hear of it, and take out my anger on you."

So that was it. Control them and guarantee their compliance, by threatening both of them. He was mad enough and arrogant enough to think that it would work. And perhaps it would, if she could find no other way out. He wanted her inheritance. He seemed convinced it was substantial.

"Will I have my own allowance? To use as I wish?" Pretending to negotiate a marriage with Francis curdled her stomach, but she needed him to believe she was seriously considering it.

"We will be in the highest social circles, so you will be dressed by the finest in New York and, when we return, London and Paris. You may have an allowance for trinkets."

"The banns will need to be called. It will be three weeks before we can marry."

He leaned back in the chair, confident and smiling. "I do believe I have some marriage lines already from our sojourn in Gretna Green. Or I can find some."

Forged marriage lines. "No-one will believe it. There wasn't time."

"Hmm." He was thoughtful for a moment before his smile returned. "But we went there the winter before last, when everyone thought you were in London. A secret marriage, because your father and brother bear such a grudge against my side of the family. It has torn my heart in two, to be separated from you for so long. That's why I rushed to save you when Caldwell abducted you."

He'd do it. He'd tell that lie, repeat it, play the hard-done by lover, use all his charm and people would believe it. Just as they'd believed him at the inn, when he'd said she was his wife, and mad. Which might well be her fate again if she defied him.

Matthew still lay prone on the floor, pretending unconsciousness. At least, she hoped he was pretending. She needed to draw Francis away from him, away from here. Out in the open, she might have a better chance of finding an opportunity or help to escape him.

"You win, Francis. When do we leave for New York? Will we sail from Liverpool?"

"I'm glad you see sense. You and I are going to create a dynasty together, beyond anything Sir Francis could have imagined." He began to rise but something made him pause and grimace. He blinked, touched a hand to the side of his face, near the bruise at his eye. It was barely a second before he straightened and walked around the desk towards her but long enough for her to see that the eye pained him. Was that another weakness?

"We'll leave immediately," he said, and took her arm. Fortunately, not the one with the knife.

"May I collect some belongings from home?" If Matthew knew where she was going, he could send help.

"No. We'll get everything you need in port before we sail." He tipped her face up so that she had to look into the hardness of his eyes. "You will be *my wife*." He enunciated the words with harsh clarity. "There is *nothing* that you need from Larkfell."

His grip was tight around her arm and she had no choice but to go with him. His man stood aside at the doorway.

"Watch my cousin," Francis ordered him. "And make sure he does nothing stupid. Then follow me after ten minutes."

The stairwell was gloomy, without natural light. She almost stumbled on the stairs, and her imbalance pulled at Francis so that he had to steady himself with a hand against the wall. 'Watch where you're walking," he snapped.

There were only a few more stairs left. Not enough to do any damage even if she managed to push Francis down them.

313

She must not make him angry. Now that he'd come up with the idea of them having married over a year ago, he didn't really need her alive. He could—and he was probably perfectly willing to—produce forged marriage lines, bribed witnesses, and a convincing story, and claim a dead wife's inheritance.

Adam wouldn't believe him, or Matthew, but he'd shown no restraint in murdering witnesses.

She shivered as they stepped outside, into the light.

~

Adam caught up with Garrett near the edge of the trees. Hard to spot in the shadows of the foliage, he'd found a good position to watch the mill. "Miss Braithwaite is in there," Garrett said.

"*Emma?*" Fear laced through the cold anger of his hunt for Francis. "Emma Braithwaite is there?"

"The lady sitting with you last night when we played. She arrived, not long back. Can't say for certain that Francis Braithwaite went in—I lost sight of him a bit further back—but I haven't seen anyone come out."

Adam dismounted, moving to the very edge of the trees to get a better view and dropping to his knee for concealment. Francis had come this way, and surely, surely he wouldn't simply have walked past when he must know Matthew was there. And now Emma was inside, with them.

The mill house rose tall from the side of the stream, its great wheel motionless and silent. There were stables beyond a courtyard, and a horse grazing in a small corral.

Garrett came up beside him, as silent as a scout despite his disability. "I could go down," he said. "And pretend I'm looking for work. Find out who's inside."

Adam briefly considered it, while he counted exits. One at the front of the building. One into the large workroom. One out to the courtyard.

The front door flew open, and Emma walked out. With Francis

close behind her. Too close. He held her by the arm, and pushed her forwards. Her bonnet had fallen back from her head, hanging from the ribbon around her neck. Even from a distance, he could see the tension in her, the stiffness in the way she held herself.

Adam held his breath. Which way? Which way would Francis take her? Towards him, or the other direction to the stone bridge? And where were Matthew and the other man?

Emma hesitated when they reached the path but Francis steered her to the north, away from the bridge.

"I'll go and confront him," he told Garrett. "Wait until his attention's on me, then see if you can get in by that back door to find Matthew."

He remounted the horse, drew Penry's knife from his boot and rode from the trees on to the path. Confronting Francis carried risks to Emma. Not confronting him carried more.

Emma saw him moments before Francis lifted his head. As soon as he realized, he yanked Emma around and began to drag her to the bridge. Adam let out a loud whistle and cantered after Francis.

Penry and Gresham burst out from the tree line fifty yards away. Francis was almost at the bridge, but he stopped abruptly, and pulled Emma up against him. Although she struggled he held her with an arm around her body, and the light glinted on the knife he raised to her throat.

"Stay back!" Francis shouted. "Or I slice her throat."

Only ten yards away now, Adam pulled his horse to an abrupt halt.

Dread flooded through every vein and he cursed himself for a damned stupid fool. He should have ambushed them in the trees, taken Francis by surprise instead of rushing in.

Everything in him raged to ride down and tear Emma from his grasp, but if he made one more mistake like that, she'd be dead within moments.

Penry and Gresham halted on the other side of the bridge. Adam wheeled the horse around, retreating a few yards. With the beast side-on to Francis, Adam hastily hid the knife in his boot again before he dismounted. A less advantageous position, on foot, but he'd do whatever it took to keep Emma safe. Even if it came to groveling on the ground and begging. He held up his hands, open and empty, and spoke as calmly as he could. "Let her go, Braithwaite. You won't escape the three of us."

Francis kept his grip on Emma, backing off the path. "Stay back, all of you!" he shouted. "Stay back!" He jerked his head rapidly from side to side, watching both ways, dragging Emma with him. The hand holding the knife shook.

Adam swore silently. Francis was panicking, unstable, and more dangerous in that state than in cold-blooded anger. Adam remained where he was, his hands in the air, his heart thudding. "Penry, back off," he called out. Penry paused but Gresham advanced slowly. "Back *off*," he shouted again, desperate.

The stream flowed strongly into the mill pond, its banks muddy from even higher recent flow. In the mill race it rushed under the great wheel, the splashing and creaking adding to the sounds of the machinery inside, turning and grinding. Beyond those thick walls, the miller would be deaf to their shouts.

Emma no longer struggled against Francis. Her arms were fastened against her sides by his grip around her waist. Her gaze met Adam's and she mouthed words but he was too far away to read them properly. She moved a hand, and the light glinted on metal. A knife? A small one, if so. Not solid enough to do much damage. Even if she could use it before Francis used his on her throat. The blade hovered close, too close to her skin.

"Francis!" Adam voice grated in his raw throat. "Let Emma go. You don't want her death on your conscience."

"No!" Francis roared. "She comes with me." He took several more steps backwards, dragging his captive.

Emma's feet slipped on the mud, and Adam shouted her name as she began to fall.

CHAPTER 31

The knot of her bonnet bow jammed hard into her throat for an instant before Francis lowered his hand to take her weight and steady her against him again.

"Careful," he growled.

Emma gulped in breaths as she found her footing on the treacherous mud. If she hadn't been wearing her bonnet, if the ribbon knot hadn't slowed the knife, she'd have died. The thought of dying scared her. The thought of Adam watching her die terrified her even more.

"Please release me, Francis. It's your only hope. They'll come after you if you kill me."

"They'll come after me the moment I release you." His hold loosened slightly as she took her own weight, but he brought the knife up to her neck once more. He muttered close to her hair, "My only escape is with you."

Relief surged through her. He didn't intend to kill her. He was clever enough, thinking clearly enough, to realize that he'd never escape without her.

Adam had scarcely moved, all his attention on Francis. On her. The other men had edged to the bridge. Mr. Penry had his hand on Sir Phillip's arm, motioning him to hold back. They could do nothing while Francis held her hostage, for fear of hurting her.

It was up to her to break the stalemate. She had the pen-knife but didn't dare use it, in case he jerked his knife in shock, or pain provoked him to rage. "I'll go with you," she said. "I'll tell them I'll go with you. Just please take the knife away."

"No. I won't." His voice sounded strange, heavy. "I…"

He staggered back a step and her heels slid on the mud before she steadied herself.

"Head…arrgh…" His hand with the knife flopped down, the blade falling to the ground. His arm gripped her even tighter as he toppled sideways, down the steep, slippery bank of the stream.

She struggled, trying to grasp tufts of grass, stones, anything, but the weight of his body dragged her down. He went suddenly limp as he hit the water, but she could not stop her momentum and she fell in, the stream rushing, dragging her under. The splashing of the mill wheel sounded loud as she fought to the surface, her skirts tangling around her legs.

~

"Close the sluice!" Adam yelled at Gresham as he dragged off his coat. "Close the damn mill race!"

He caught sight of Penry, shedding his coat on the other side of the bridge.

He barely remembered to inhale deeply before he dived in where Emma had disappeared. She couldn't swim. She'd never learned. Girls didn't swim in woodland pools and streams.

The water was murky, silt stirred up by the heavy flow. The undertow pulled at him. To his left, the water flowed under the bridge and over a low weir. But to his right was the sluice gate that funneled water into the mill race. If Emma was pulled that way…

He swam forward, the water stinging his eyes as he sought any glimpse of her. A brown pelisse in brown water. It must be dragging her down, heavy. *She couldn't swim.*

The muck swirled just ahead and he caught a flash of white. He surged forward, narrowly avoiding her kicking foot, and grabbed hold of her wool pelisse, He hauled her to him and fought the pull of the water, kicking hard. His boots were full of water, his lungs screaming for air.

His head reached air and he gulped it, lifting Emma's face out of the water. They were a yard from the sluice gate, a yard from the stone wall at the side of the mill race. The water eddied against the closed gate, the great mill wheel creaking as it slowed.

His feet scraped the bottom and he found he could stand there, using the wall as support, holding Emma upright with her head above the water.

She clung to him and coughed, clearing her lungs, coughing and crying, and he held her close, his heart pounding with the terror of almost losing her.

Gresham threw a rope down and he and the miller helped Emma up and out first, then him. Matthew was there, and Garrett, and the miller's wife. The miller's wife took charge of Emma, lying her on her side, holding her while she coughed up water.

Adam bent over with his hands on his knees, fighting for decent breath while water poured off him. Matthew said something about he and Garrett knocking out and tying up Francis's offsider but Adam barely took it in. Gresham stood nearby, tense, his gaze directed further down beyond the mill.

"Penry?" Adam managed to ask. "Braithwaite?"

"They went over the weir. I can't see them."

Adam straightened up but Gresham was already off, running down along the bank. Below the mill it was overgrown, shaded by woods.

Emma pushed herself to sit up, breathing with less coughing, insisting she was all right, so he followed Gresham. His boots squelched, his legs heavy from exertion, his relief for Emma's safety replaced with concern for Penry.

They found Penry a hundred yards down, dragging Francis's sagging body into the shallows at a bend in the stream.

Adam waded in with Gresham and they hauled Francis up on to the bank. Unconscious. Limp.

Penry scrambled up after them. "He's not breathing," he gasped.

"He didn't struggle at all."

"We need to get his head lower than his body," Gresham said, and they moved him round so that he faced down, towards the water. Gresham pressed on his back, at the bottom of his rib cage, once, again, again. No water came out of Francis's mouth. No breath went in.

Adam remembered a demonstration he'd seen in the army, years ago. "Turn him over, I'll try breathing into him." As soon as they'd flipped Francis on to his back, Adam pried open his mouth.

Francis's teeth were white. There was no mud, no water, no bits of weed in his mouth. Adam felt for a pulse. Nothing. He pressed on the man's abdomen several times, and huffed breaths into Francis's mouth, but there was no response.

He gave up, and sat back on his heels. The dark, blotchy bruise under Francis's eye—probably the result of Emma's pin—wasn't the only one. With his hair wet and plastered to his head, another bruise on his temple was obvious, several days old, just as blotched but much larger than the one under his eye.

"You said he didn't struggle?" he asked Penry.

"Not at all. He fell to one side, then slid into the water. He was sinking when I got hold of him. He's dead, isn't he?"

"Yes. You didn't throw a knife at him, did you?" Gresham hadn't fired his pistol—he'd have heard that, and there'd be evidence. There was no sign of a knife wound, either, but Braithwaite's sodden clothes might hide it.

"No," Penry said drily. "I was damn tempted, believe me. But he had Emma too close."

Adam saw again in his mind Francis's slow fall; his right hand dropping the knife, his right leg crumpling. The bruises were on the left side of his head. That happened with head injuries, sometimes. The opposite side affected. And sometimes, days later.

"I think he must have been dead or close to it before he went into the water. He certainly didn't breathe it. I'm guessing this bruise is from when he fell from the horse. Maybe he's been bleeding in the brain."

Gresham swore and kicked at a clod of mud. "Too damn quick a death. I wanted to watch him hang."

Bone-weary, cold and wet, Adam couldn't summon up the energy for anger. He'd have killed Francis if necessary to save Emma, but there'd have been no pleasure in it. No pleasure or satisfaction in Braithwaite's lifeless body now, only a dull, flat sense of relief. Francis was dead, and Emma safe from him.

People were coming. The miller and his boys. Garrett. Matthew.

He left Penry and Gresham to explain and to send for the Hartdale magistrate. He went up to the house beside the mill to find Emma.

The miller's wife had Emma wrapped up in blankets, in front of a blazing fire, her wet hair unpinned and falling down her back to dry. The woman fussed around her, urging her to drink a tisane, offering a warm brick for her feet. She clearly had no intention of leaving Emma alone with Adam. He respected the concern for her well-being and reputation, but if she wasn't there, he'd have wrapped Emma in his arms and held her until they both stopped shaking.

Emma clutched the blankets around her, exhausted. He felt ragged and drained himself after less time in the water, and she'd come close to dying. But her color was returning, and she asked what had happened.

He pulled up a stool nearby. "Francis is dead, Emma," he said gently. "We tried but couldn't save him. He can't harm you or anyone again."

She nodded, and a tear trickled down her cheek. "Did he drown? He said something about his head, and groaned, before he fell. I think he was in pain."

"No, he didn't drown. It's possible he was bleeding inside his brain. Sometimes head injuries get worse over a few days, not better."

Her gaze flicked to the miller's wife, busying herself with tidying nearby, and she asked in a low voice, "Was it because of the injury under his eye?"

"No." He hoped that was truth. Surely a pin was incapable of reaching the brain, even near the eye. "He had another head injury, a large bruise on his skull, which must be from when he fell from his horse."

She used a corner of the blanket to wipe away her tears. He'd have offered a pocket handkerchief if his wasn't drenched.

"Perhaps I shouldn't weep for him. But he wasn't always..." A sob escaped her. Adam let her talk. Grief and shock needed expression. "He was my cousin, and I doubt he'd have killed me. He was still rational then and knew he'd die if I did." She tried to swallow back another sob. "Robert must be told. Poor Robert. He doesn't deserve..."

At the open kitchen door, Matthew said, "I'll go to Robert and inform him."

Adam stood and offered Matthew his stool near Emma. Matthew declined it with a shake of his head, but laid a gentle hand on his sister's shoulder. "Em, I'll arrange to get you home as soon as possible. I'm sure Adam will escort you. Perhaps the goodwife will be kind enough to lend you some dry clothes?"

The woman bobbed her head. "Of course, sir. Just as soon as she's warmed up. When you gentlemen are out of my kitchen."

Adam and Matthew took the hint and left Emma to her care. Outside, a small crowd had gathered down near Francis's body, and the office lads Adam recognized from the warehouse fire came running across the bridge. With quiet efficiency, Matthew instructed them to fetch the horse and gig and bring them around.

"You're up to driving it, aren't you, Caldwell?" he asked Adam. "And you'll see Emma safely home?"

"Of course."

When the lads had gone, Matthew leaned on the bridge post and regarded him seriously. "I don't need to call you out, do I, Caldwell? You care about Emma, don't you? Those damn lies in the newspaper—you'll do the right thing by her, if necessary?"

The breeze blew cool on his wet shirt sleeves, prickling his skin. For some reason there seemed more at stake now, with Emma's brother, than all those years ago when, young and cocky with confidence, he'd faced her father and asked for her hand. "Yes. I proposed to her. Days ago. From choice, not pressure. Perhaps I should have spoken with you first." Emma was twenty-five. He had no expectations that any suitors for Louisa's hand need consult either George or him, but some men were more conservative in their views.

Matthew waved the semi-apology away. "Oh, it's her decision. She knows her own mind. I'll defend her honor as a brother if necessary, but I'm glad I don't have to." He gave a bitter laugh. "I'm in no state to defeat you if it came to a fight."

"I can't offer her a great deal," Adam said. "She deserves more. She asked me to give her a month to decide. We can discuss a potential settlement once she's recovered from this, if she wishes it."

"If it comes to that, I'll want to make sure she's protected and provided for properly, but in all honesty, she's better at finances and contracts than I am. Possibly even better than Robert." Although he said it lightly, his face clouded. "I must go and tell him of Francis. I'll hire a carriage in town. I assume there'll be an inquest in the morning. Get my sister home, Caldwell."

"I will. And if…if she takes ill, you'll inform me?"

Matthew assured him, but it didn't alleviate Adam's worry.

She'd almost drowned, swallowed pond water, been wet to the skin. He'd get her home safely and soon, but a bad chill or an infection could easily become more lethal than a knife against her throat.

CHAPTER 32

Despite the warm wrappings of wool petticoats, jacket, cloak and shawl, Emma's shivering did not subside. The chill pervaded to her bones, and no matter how tightly she gathered the layers around her they did not help.

She sat beside Adam in the gig, and although he kept up encouraging comments her thoughts were in too much disarray for conversation. He'd raised the gig's hood, and she huddled with the shawl over her head, hoping to pass through Hartdale unrecognized.

When they'd passed the last houses, he reached his arm around her, tucking her into his side, driving with one hand.

"It's the shock that's making you cold," he said.

She was tempted to believe him, were it not for the slight hesitation in his voice betraying his uncertainty. She rested her head against his shoulder, leaning her body in to his, determined to regain control over her shaking body. It *must* be the shock. The sensible part of her knew that she was safe and that Larkfell was not far away. But her mind played the moments when Francis had held the knife to her throat again and again in her memory. Her hand clenched as if she still clasped Matthew's penknife.

"I was going to stab him in the leg," she confessed, trusting Adam with thoughts she could not imagine sharing with anyone else. "That was my plan, as soon as I had a chance. I could have killed him, if I'd hit an artery. I knew that, and I was still going to do it."

His arm tightened around her. "Your life was threatened, Emma. It was brave thinking in a terrifying situation." For a few moments there was only the clopping of the horse's hooves on the road, and the warmth and comfort of his embrace. Until he spoke again, his voice hoarser. "I would have killed him, Emma, if I'd had the chance. Penry and Gresham, too."

She remembered the three of them watching for the moment to make a move, intent and dangerous. If she'd managed to get away from Francis, they'd have sprung at him. "You wanted to save me. But you didn't kill him, in the end," she said gently, "when you pulled him from the water. You tried to save him."

"I thought he was unconscious. One doesn't..." He left the sentence unfinished.

Kill a defenseless man. Honorable men did not take lives lightly. And Adam was honorable to his core.

Whether it was the work of God, or of providence, fate, or simple chance that had taken Francis at that moment, she'd always be thankful that Adam, and the other gentlemen, did not have her cousin's death on their consciences. Adam's war experiences already caused him too much pain. Although she wasn't sure exactly what Mr. Penry had done during the wars, underneath his teasing cheerfulness she sensed at times a much more complex man. And Sir Phillip... despite his air of self-assurance, she'd glimpsed an emptiness in his eyes.

As the gig rounded a wide bend, two people walking came into view ahead. Emma reluctantly moved away from Adam and sat upright with the shawl over her head. As if she was a village woman that he'd kindly given a ride to.

"It may be best if I am not recognized," she murmured to Adam, and kept her face down as they passed the walkers. She almost didn't tell him of the dressmaker's and draper's refusals to serve her but he deserved warning that the scandal was already spreading.

His jaw clenched tightly as she told him what had happened in town. She almost said 'yesterday' but of course it was only this morning. Near-drowning apparently had some effect on one's sense of time.

"The draper admitted that Mrs. Stratham was involved?" he queried.

"He implied it," she said, careful with the truth.

"Gresham is going to call on Stratham. We suspect Francis may have stayed with them. If so, it's possible he or the Strathams were responsible for that newspaper report."

It did seem possible. Her cousins also had a long association with Stratham's bank, and knew him personally. She'd scarcely spoken with Mr. Stratham at the Rengarth dinner, but his wife's taunting comments held added meaning if she'd had knowledge of Francis's whereabouts. And at the ball last week, Francis had known more about her financial situation than he should have.

"If Sir Phillip finds that Mr. Stratham was involved in Francis's plans, please tell me. I'll have to withdraw my account from the bank if I can no longer rely on his judgement."

"If Gresham finds out Stratham was involved, I'll do everything in my power to have him removed from the partnership. Some of Rengarth's accounts are held there, too." He said it with such harsh determination that Emma would have trembled had it been directed at her.

He turned the gig in through Larkfell's gates, and they had only moments of private time left. Not enough for any of the many things she wanted to say, but had no words to express.

Tomorrow he'd be at the inquest. He'd already told her he doubted Mr. Palmer would insist in calling her to give evidence this time, since there were three witnesses including a magistrate, and she hoped he was right.

Mr. Jarvis and Mrs. Barnden came hurrying out as he assisted her down from the gig, but she paused long enough, with her hand still in his, to look him in the face. "You will visit?" she asked in a low voice, "When you're able to?"

"I will," he promised.

She surrendered herself into Mrs. Barnden's care. The housekeeper bustled her in to the kitchen, the warmest room in the house, and gave orders for the fire to be lit in her chamber, the bed to be warmed, and a tisane to be prepared.

Emma lacked the energy to protest the fuss. She told Mrs. Barnden and the avidly listening kitchen maid the bare details of her near-drowning and assured her that Matthew was unharmed and would be home later in the day.

When her room was heated to the housekeeper's satisfaction and fresh nightclothes laid out, Emma made her still-shaking legs climb the stairs. After shedding the borrowed clothes, she crawled under the covers.

Despite her weariness and the peaceful silence, sleep eluded her. Perhaps because of the silence, she found it difficult to erase from her mind the moments of terror when she'd thought she might die.

To counteract those memories, she closed her eyes and brought Adam's face to the front of her thoughts. When he'd promised to visit, whenever he looked at her, his dark eyes reflected the depth of his concern, his tenderness, respect and love. He saw *her*, with all her strengths and weaknesses.

She had no reason to doubt the genuineness of his feelings for her. She was the one hesitating. Holding back through fear. Fear of bringing trouble to his family. Fear of failing him. Fear of not being enough.

But why was she allowing those fears to rule her? A good man had requested her hand in marriage. A man she respected and loved. A man intelligent and mature enough to make his own judgements. She'd spent more time with him in the past intense week than most couples spent together before marriage, and he'd shown in a thousand ways his constancy and affection.

She allowed herself a few brief moments of imagining herself writing to him, telling him '*yes*'. But of course she should not write to an unmarried man, no matter the circumstances.

She pulled the blankets tighter. She was tired and emotional and in no state to make any life-changing decisions. The problems remained. Her family's social status was far below his, and she had little fortune and a reputation threatened by scandal.

But she needed to rest and sleep and recover, and tomorrow was soon enough to be sensible. For now, she let herself dream.

~

Friday

On the road into Hartdale in the morning Adam met up with Matthew and Penry, who assured him that Emma suffered no illness and had breakfasted with them earlier. The news eased the fears that had haunted him, waking him numerous times during the night.

Once in town, they called on Gresham at the Hartdale Arms. He'd had coffee sent up to his room, made in the French way, and Adam savored the aroma and taste. After his years abroad, it was taking him a while to accustom himself to tea again. This gathering had the comfortable familiarity of the many times he'd sat with fellow officers, men not unlike these new friends, drinking coffee in the morning, wine in the evening, to discuss events and plan strategies.

Gresham told them of his interview with Stratham the previous afternoon. "He indignantly denied knowing anything of Francis's plans. But he overdid the bluster and outrage. I'm fairly confident that Francis stayed there, or that he'd at least seen him. So he had to have had some idea of the plans, although maybe not the lengths Francis was prepared to go to. He visibly paled when I told him Francis was dead."

"There may well have been money involved," Penry remarked. "Stratham is a banker. Francis has been investing in factories and coal. Not to mention financing revolution in the colonies. It's possible that Stratham invested his own funds. Or that not all the transactions are recorded in the bank's ledgers."

A good reason for a banker to pale. Adam planned to make some more enquiries. And to withdraw the bulk of Rengarth's funds, in case unwise or fraudulent investments sent the bank into difficulties.

Matthew used his good hand to steady his injured one as he set down his coffee cup. "Francis told Emma yesterday that Winslow had a fortune. I presume he thought Winslow had inherited his father's estates in the West Indies years ago."

"But he didn't?" Adam queried.

"No. Winslow became an abolitionist while he was at Oxford, and his father disowned him. Left everything to a cousin, so my father told me. Winslow never spoke of his family. Not to me, anyway. He worked for the government in London for some years before he inherited his maternal grandmother's house in Halifax. He lived very quietly. He was a good man. And now he's dead. That in itself should damn Francis to hell." He gulped a mouthful of his coffee as if it was strong spirit.

"Did you get anything from the man Matthew and Garrett restrained yesterday?" Adam asked Gresham.

"Palmer arrived last night and he went with the local magistrate to the watch house to have a chat with the man. Turns out he was the fourth man who traveled with the coach abducting Miss Braithwaite. He was desperate to escape the noose, so he readily confessed everything he knew. He insisted he hadn't committed murder. He blamed Dutton and Barlow for Winslow's death and the constable's. He reckoned he had nothing to do with killing Dutton and his mate at the church. But he knew too much about that and his story kept changing, so Palmer ordered him to be taken to the county jail for trial in Wakefield at the next session."

So that was that. Adam found little satisfaction in the news. All those deaths, and only one man left alive to face justice. He and Penry and Gresham still had to give evidence at the trial, but that was weeks away. At least Matthew and Emma would be spared that duty, and that journey.

They were all silent. Downstairs the tap room was filling with men arriving for the inquest into Francis's death. Another duty to perform before this nightmare was over.

The inquest was mercifully brief and straightforward. Adam told the facts of Francis's death, as did Penry; the doctor confirmed their suspicions that he'd died of the brain injury rather than drowning, and the jury returned a verdict of death by natural causes.

Robert Braithwaite sat through the proceedings, silent and dazed. After the inquest finished and the room emptied, he remained, standing by his brother's sheet-covered body on a table. Matthew spoke some brief words with him before he and Adam followed Gresham and Penry out.

Gresham was setting off back home at once, and Adam and the others bid farewell to him in the courtyard. Matthew and Penry left for the warehouse, and Adam had several errands in town.

When he passed the inn again, Robert rode slowly out, following the undertaker's cart carrying his brother's shrouded body. The route to the church lay through the market square and the main road.

Adam fell in beside him. No good man should be unfriended in such grief.

"I will ask the vicar, " Robert said, when he became aware of Adam's presence, "but I do not think he should be buried in the family vault or the church yard. Not in consecrated ground. Not after all he did."

Adam added 'broke his brother's heart' to his mental list of Francis's misdeeds. "He was not tried and found guilty of any crime," he said, legally truthful against his own knowledge and judgement of the man. But in truth the fate of the corpse did not overly concern him. It would lie and rot, consecrated ground or not. Like soldiers of allies and enemies, like peasants and princes. They all decayed the same, in the end. "Perhaps the vicar will suggest trusting to God to judge him."

Robert nodded dully. A very different man from his brother. Honor meant everything to him, and had meant nothing at all to Francis.

Adam rode with him to the churchyard, and left him to discuss arrangements with the vicar.

The sun made a rare appearance as he took the lane home to Rengarth. There'd been a shower of rain earlier and the droplets of water hanging on leaves and branches caught and reflected the light. Small birds flitted in and out of the bushes lining the lane. His somber mood began to lift and somewhere, in the tangle of emotions and scattered thoughts, he recognized peacefulness in this Yorkshire scene, in the sense of being home after all his years away.

Home and, if not exactly settled, then comfortable with his choice to return and stay. Oh, he still had a hundred challenges ahead but now that the emergencies of the past week were over and Francis was no longer a threat to Emma, his future held appealing possibilities he'd never imagined when he left Paris a month ago.

It wasn't only Emma he'd found again. Although Rengarth Castle would never be quite the same without his father there, he was finding his place in the family again. His respect and admiration for his mother grew deeper the more he understood her strengths; she continued to be the pillar the family and Rengarth needed.

In his youthful fondness for his brothers and sisters he'd perhaps not appreciated them as he ought to. Now he was enjoying coming to know them again, each with their individual characters and interests. The younger ones might give him gray hair before they went back to school—Cecilia as well as her brothers—but his mother had raised them well and he liked them and their lively, generous natures. The boys, allowed downstairs this morning for the first time since their injuries, had made him laugh out loud over breakfast. A rusty laugh that surprised him as much as them, but at least he hadn't entirely forgotten how.

On his arrival home, the butler informed him that his aunt was visiting Emma, the young ladies had walked down to the vicarage, and the young gentlemen were out in the kitchen garden with the sheep dog pups from the farm, and did he understand correctly that they were choosing one to keep?

Adam grimaced at the butler's mildly disapproving question. "They caught me in a weak moment and I gave permission. I've told them it will be an outside dog." He didn't confess that was likely to last less than a day. Who could resist a puppy? And the boys and Cecilia were accustomed to Zeus being inside. Regimental discipline was hardly likely to prove effective in the circumstances.

The butler sniffed eloquently and presented him with the silver platter with the day's post. One letter for him.

Adam turned it over as he walked down to the study and lifted the Earl of Rengarth's seal. A letter from George, although not in his writing, but the neat impersonal hand of one trained to be a clerk or a secretary.

Adam read the few lines, and re-read them to verify their words. *'His Lordship desires me to inform you that Lady Rengarth was safely delivered of a daughter yesterday evening. Her Ladyship and the child are both well.'*

A daughter. Adam placed the letter down on the desk. *A daughter.* George and Hannah had another daughter. Not a son. There'd likely be a letter in the next post with more details of the babe's health and name, but nothing changed the inalterable fact that George still had no heir. Only him.

He strolled to the French doors of the study, hardly knowing why he did so, and stared out. The carriage drive and the neat front lawns and terraces of the castle overlooked the fields and woods of the estate.

'George is breathing more easily and ate dinner at a table last night.' The letter from Hannah a few days ago had given him real hope that the new physician's treatments would heal his brother. A wild hope, perhaps—few people recovered from consumption—but if he lived for two, five, even ten years longer, there was every chance he'd conceive a son and heir. Adam could easily imagine a child version of George, as studious and sensible as his father. Not that his brother would value a son above his daughters; he adored and doted on his little girls. Surely they and his beloved Hannah would give him reason to fight his illness and live for many years yet.

But until George recovered from his illness, all this—the people, the farms, the village—were his responsibility. He set aside the letter to reply to later, when his tasks for the day were accomplished and the house quiet.

He had work to do. Planning for a hard winter with potential food shortages required all the skills of strategy and preparedness he'd learned in the army. He needed reliable men, and Garrett had proved himself again and again.

The former soldier knocked on the study door within minutes of Adam sending for him. Freshly shaved, with a clean shirt and neck-cloth, Garrett could almost pass for a gentleman. Except few gentlemen carried the constant watchfulness of soldiers and the hollow cheek lines of long austerity.

As he accepted the seat across from Adam at the desk, the old guardedness of an experienced sergeant called before an officer closed his face.

Adam's thanks for all his assistance were accepted with a bare nod and the level-eyed stare of a man who'd acted as he had because it was the right thing to do, rather than out of any sense of service.

Adam framed his proposal carefully. "My mother has informed me that our old coachman is living in the village, in an estate cottage that's in need of repair. He's getting frail, but has no family left. If you're willing, you can live there with him. He doesn't need much assistance, except company, help with meals, that kind of thing."

"I'm not able to do major repairs," Garrett said bluntly. "Or pay much rent. And I'm not wanting charity."

"It's not charity. I'm offering you employment. We spoke the other day about some help with the boys, and there's your music, of course. You'd be helping out the old man, and overseeing the repairs. But I also want ears and eyes in the village and surrounds. If there's unrest brewing, if it gets worse in fear of crop failures, I want to know who and where."

Garrett's face became harder. "I'll not spy for you, if you're intending to have hungry men convicted and transported to New South Wales. Sir."

Garrett's objection and the grudging 'sir' might have offended other officers, but Adam respected it. Soldiers didn't survive years of war by being meek, and their views were in agreement. "I'm not asking you to spy," he explained. "I'm asking you to keep me informed of the matters concerning people, and of the men—or women—who might be seen as leaders. They're people who are concerned for others, and I want to work with them to plan how we get through winter without anyone starving."

Garrett held his gaze and took his time before he finally nodded. "Aye, if that's what you're wanting."

Good. Several matters dealt with in one arrangement. "I'll take you over to the cottage in the morning, so you can meet the old man and see the place."

After Garrett left, Adam reached for the long list of tasks his mother had written for him. Managing an estate the size of Rengarth without a competent steward required constant attention. In addition to planning for winter, he must resolve a dispute between tenants, find a new assistant gardener, check the terms of the farm lease, arrange repairs for several cottages in the village, and see to at least a dozen other matters his mother had listed as immediately necessary.

The sun shone out on the terrace and he longed to leave duty behind and ride to Larkfell. But after yesterday Emma should rest, without too many visitors, and his aunt would inform him of her health when she returned. Tomorrow was not far away.

He drew a fresh piece of paper from the drawer, selected a quill, and began a letter to the quarry requesting slate to mend the cottages. He was a Caldwell of Rengarth, and must prove himself worthy of the name. And worthy of Emma.

~

Mrs. Thorncroft's visit made a welcome distraction from the work of unpicking the dress ruined in her escape through the woods, in order to salvage what silk she could. Her dress and pelisse from yesterday were beyond any salvaging.

She had no female relatives nearby to confide in, but she counted Mrs. Thorncroft as a friend, and respected her unpretentious manner and her good sense. Although concerned about Emma's well-being after her ordeal, she did not fuss beyond recommending avoiding chills and resting more than usual for the next few days.

With sunshine streaming in the large windows for the first time in weeks, the sitting room was cozy and a delightfully pleasant place to spend time in the company of a friend.

"I do believe," Mrs. Thorncroft declared when Emma expressed her fears about the scurrilous newspaper report, "That the best way to deal with the threat of scandal is to ignore it, and to carry on as if nothing at all is amiss. Besides, yesterday's events and the inquest today will have revealed your cousin's true nature. There will be little sympathy for him, and should anyone assume you are the lady referred to in the report, they will doubt its veracity."

"I am afraid that those assumptions have already been made. And circulated." Without naming the ladies she suspected of involvement, or the establishments, Emma told her of the two refusals to serve her yesterday morning.

Mrs. Thorncroft tut-tutted. "I can guess the persons who may have pressured them, and I'm sure they will come to regret their actions."

Emma doubted that Mrs. Stratham or Lady Beatrice would ever acknowledge their involvement, but both the dressmaker and draper had since attempted to make amends, possibly for financial reasons if not social ones. The draper's boy had brought a range of silk samples this morning, and the dressmaker had sent an apology for 'overestimating her commitments', an offer to come to Larkfell for a consultation, and several suggested designs for the latest in afternoon fashions, with fabric and trim samples.

"My dear," Mrs. Thorncroft continued, "I'm an elderly lady, and I have seen many a scandal in my lifetime. Believe me, society has a very short memory when those involved are otherwise of good character. Don't underestimate the esteem people have for you. This will all be forgotten soon."

Emma wished she shared her friend's optimism, but took heart from her words. Perhaps the ordeal might not be as great as she'd feared. "I hope you are right. I don't want Lady Rengarth's family, her daughters particularly, to suffer from association with me."

"Nonsense. Caroline would far rather that the girls are friends with you than with the daughters of the women attempting to blacken your name. So do come and visit us at any time. And when you are quite recovered, the girls will call on you."

When Mrs. Thorncroft gathered her reticule and gloves to leave, she said, "I have some books you might enjoy reading while you rest." Her eyes sparkled. "Should I ask Adam to bring them over to you tomorrow?"

Heat flamed in Emma's face and she stammered, "Thank you. Yes. If...if he wishes to, that is."

"Oh, I'm sure he will wish to." Her knowing smile was definitely conspiratorial. "And the day after tomorrow, do come and spend the day with us. I'm sure Adam will be happy to escort you to Rengarth."

Lady Rengarth, Louisa and now Mrs. Thorncroft all expressing their welcome and approval; none of them seemed to mind that she had no aristocratic ancestors. But they hadn't faced the lifetime of slights, both intentional and unintentional, that women of her class were accustomed to.

She had little time to consider the matter, though, because shortly after Mrs. Thorncroft departed, Mr. Rickards, Mr. Winslow's solicitor, arrived. Emma requested the housekeeper to bring tea, and received him in the study. A manservant accompanied him, carrying a large box and placing it beside the desk before retiring discreetly to the hall.

Sitting across from her at the desk, Mr. Rickards took glasses from a leather case and perched them on his nose, opening a folder of papers.

"I apologize for my delay in coming to see you, Miss Braithwaite," he said. "Mr. Winslow also retained legal advisers in London, and it was necessary to correspond with them to verify certain matters, and ensure that there was no later will than the one in my possession. Which, I am pleased to say, there is not. I expect the granting of probate to be unimpeded. You have read the copy of the will that I sent to you on Monday?"

Emma inclined her head. "I have." A document she'd read several times and could recall from memory.

'To Miss Emma Elizabeth Braithwaite, daughter of Josiah Braithwaite I give and bequeath my house and land in Halifax and all the goods and chattels contained therein, and the remainder of

my estate, consisting of all my property, assets and investments, not hitherto bequeathed as detailed above to my loyal servants. This bequest to be placed in trust for Miss Braithwaite's sole and personal use, whether she marry or not...'

Concise and unambiguous, yet she did not entirely believe the intention of it. "The will is dated only two weeks before his death. I know Francis Braithwaite saw him about that time and knew I was a beneficiary. Did he apply pressure to Mr. Winslow to make that so?"

"Oh, no, miss. I can relieve you of that concern. Mr. Winslow revised a few minor bequests to his servants. Otherwise, the will is substantially the same as the one he made some two years ago, with the bulk of his estate bequeathed in a trust for your benefit."

Emma almost sagged in relief. The thought of Francis manipulating, perhaps threatening Mr. Winslow had haunted her. "I don't understand why he chose me, though. Surely he has other family?"

"Unfortunately, no. Both he and his father were only sons, and there are no other relations living. You may be aware—it was widely known—that he was estranged from his father for some years, and on Winslow senior's death, his estate passed to his sister's son. However that gentleman died some years later, without marrying, and he bequeathed the estate back to his cousin, Mr. Winslow."

She'd been aware of the basics of her friend's life. That his family's wealth was built in the West Indies, on plantations worked by slaves; that he'd come to abhor slavery, and wanted nothing to do with it. Disowned by his father, he'd left the West Indies with nothing, and made a living for himself in government service, employment that sat better with his conscience. He refused his entire life to take sugar, because its production relied on slavery. That much she knew.

"I believe that he chose to leave his wealth to you, Miss Braithwaite," Mr. Rickards continued, "because of his affection and respect for you, and because he believed you might continue to support certain benevolent interests of his. Although I hasten to add that this is not a condition of the bequest."

"The charities he supported in Halifax and Leeds?" A society that assisted widows. A dispensary for the poor, and several other worthy causes. "Yes, of course I will support those."

"Those and, ah, others. Miss Braithwaite, the point of the matter is that in addition to his residence and the funds in the bank in Halifax, the London solicitors have provided me with a list of other, ah, assets. These, my dear, amount to a considerable estate." He rummaged among his pile of papers and passed three sheets across the desk to her. "The executor of the estate will, I am sure, correspond with you very shortly. This is the interim list of assets that he sent to me this week."

Emma stared down at the first page, too stunned at first to make sense of the lines of dense writing. "But they're...addresses." At least a dozen addresses, most in the new, fashionable parts of London. Several in Bath. Addresses near the docks in London—perhaps warehouses?

"When Mr. Winslow gained his inheritance, he sailed to the West Indies in order to free the slaves he'd inherited, and sell the plantations. After he returned to England, he used the proceeds to invest in London property, predicting that the city will expand considerably. He has used the income derived from letting these properties for the establishment and support of numerous charitable institutions. I have a list of them here." He passed another set of papers across the desk to her. "Some are run by committees of worthy people, but for several smaller concerns he has employed managers. I have brought his more recent account books and letter books, should you wish to peruse them."

She quickly read the lists. A lying-in hospital for poor women. Schools for children in some of the most poverty-stricken areas of London. Dispensaries for medical aid for the destitute. A night school for former slaves. Another list recorded the names of more than a dozen boys and the payments Mr. Winslow had made each term to good schools for their education. There were several girls' names, too, with payments to Ladies' Academies.

"I have taken the liberty, Miss Braithwaite, of preparing a summary, with indicative figures of assets and liabilities, and income and expenditure. The gentlemen in London will provide more details shortly."

The summary pages held a neat tally of bank funds, investments, property values and quarterly expenses and returns. Pounds, shillings and pence. Thousands of pounds. Tens of thousands of pounds. Her mind reeled with the figures.

Mr. Winslow had been an immensely wealthy man, despite his unassuming life. And he'd left it all to her. She was an heiress, with wealth beyond her capacity to have ever imagined.

But despite Mr. Rickards' assurance that it was not a requirement to continue his charitable works, in her heart it was. More than a year ago, over tea in his garden, she'd discussed with Mr. Winslow her fears for the working people in the new age of machinery, with the long hours, low wages, and lack of freedom, and he'd encouraged her to continue to use her education and her position to work for change. And now he'd given her the opportunity—the responsibility—to do so much more than she'd ever been able to do.

Mr. Rickards was explaining something about the trust, about the specific provisions in the event of her marriage, the selection of trustees to ensure the protection of her interests.

The implications sunk in gradually. She was not naïve. He trusted her to use his wealth for good, but in giving it to her, he'd also given her a significant position and influence. Although Adam's family had made their welcome clear, she'd feared that the inequality in her status compared to theirs might impact on society's acceptance if she married Adam. But society rarely shunned an heiress of this degree. Unless she was mired in scandal.

CHAPTER 33

Saturday

Adam took Garrett down to the village in the morning to meet the old coachman. He left them warily sizing up each other. But the old man had also been an army sergeant, decades ago during the American war, and Adam figured they'd find common interests soon enough. Quite possibly in sharing horror stories about incompetent officers.

He walked back to the Castle, his steps light. A groom waited with his horse already saddled, and Aunt Thorncroft's small bundle of books for Emma in a saddle bag. Bless his great-aunt and her not-so-subtle plot to give him time with Emma.

But he'd only reached the gates when a lone horseman cantered in, pulling to a halt on sight of him. Mud-spattered, almost falling to his feet as he dismounted, the man had ridden long and hard.

Adam recognized him instantly: one of the grooms from Rengarth House in London. His heart lurched and he sensed the news before it came. Before he opened the black-edged letter. Before he read the words, blotched with Hannah's tears.

George, his brother, was dead. The kindest, most decent of men. Dead. He'd succumbed to an infection, Hannah wrote, his weak lungs filling with fluid, his heart failing him.

The reality slammed into Adam's chest as hard as the kick of a horse. Somehow in these past couple of weeks a deep part of his mind had convinced itself that George would not allow himself to die, that he'd find a way to solve the problem of his illness. George always found solutions to problems.

Even after the birth of his daughter—*especially* after the birth of his daughter—surely George had been working on ways to avoid Adam inheriting the earldom. Like staying alive.

Adam cursed himself. There he went, trying to deny reality again.

George was dead. Hannah a widow, their daughters fatherless. His older brother, gone forever. A fresh blast of pain tore through his chest.

"Sir?" The groom hesitated. "I am to give you this, as well, my Lord." He held out a small drawstring bag.

Adam felt the object inside through the velvet. His brother's signet ring, with the Rengarth seal. Of course the groom understood the purpose of the message. The significance of it. The reason for the hard ride from London to deliver it. The seal carried all the authority of the Earl of Rengarth.

"No." Adam ground the word out. "Don't call me that. Not now. Not yet. Not until I..."

Not until he informed the rest of his family.

His brothers were engrossed in a game of chess in the library. His aunt had taken the girls to Hartdale. He dreaded telling them. Despite the large gap in ages and George living in London for much of the past few years, he was their brother, too, and they loved him. And Aunt Thorncroft had always been close to George.

After breaking the news to them, he'd have to assemble the staff, inform them. Some of them had served the family since his father's time. There were others who needed to know, too. The vicar. George's friends in the district.

"Did my mother reach London before...?" A senseless question to ask. She'd only left two days ago.

"No, sir. Another messenger was sent to find and inform her on the journey."

His own grief—this harsh, gut-wrenching pain—must be a

shadow of a mother's anguish for a son. He took small consolation in the fact that she had Louisa and Phoebe and Oliver to support her and share her sorrow.

He had to remain strong for the younger ones and his aunt. He had to assume the role and responsibilities of the earldom. He was unready, unsuitable, unprepared. And yet he must.

He gave a handful of shillings from his pocket to the waiting groom and sent him on to the village to have a meal and a rest at the inn. Better there for now than at the castle, where the other servants or even his brothers might press him for the London tidings.

He watched the man ride away. His own horse skittered restlessly, but uncertainty as to his next direction kept him at the gate. He didn't want to face telling his brothers yet. He'd wait until his aunt and the girls returned. Until he found some sort of composure himself before they turned to him for support.

Courage. He'd faced the hell of gun and canon fire a hundred times but this ripped through him, threatening to crack him apart.

He rode up the fell behind the castle, where no-one would see or hear if he howled. A world without George was as inconceivable as a world without Oliver would be. No more of his kindly, encouraging letters that had sustained him through the years of war. Heaven alone knew how George—as peaceful a man as ever lived—somehow understood what he needed to read when the battle horrors wouldn't fade and the grim realities of war marched on and on. When he didn't care if he lived or died, George's letters blew on the embers of his soul and gave him a fire for life again.

He'd never properly thanked him. Never told him how much he valued him, how much the knowledge that George was there in England, a good man carrying on their father's legacy, gave him reason to fight on. And now he'd never be able to tell him how much he'd mattered.

On top of the fell a gentle breeze rippled in the grass, and despite the hazy sky, the sun bathed the Rengarth estate below him in a gentle light. The castle and all its outbuildings, the farms, the village, the church, and the fields and woods that he'd roamed with George and Oliver as boys. Before he left for school at twelve years old, George knew every one of the tenants and villagers by name. The people respected him, as they respected his father and his grandfather before him.

The Earls of Rengarth had guarded this land for hundreds of years. A sacred trust, his father had said. A solemn duty.

Adam would gladly have stood at the gates of Rengarth, sword in hand, and given his life to defend it. But to be the earl in modern times asked far, far more than that. To do his duty—to fulfil the trust—he'd be months in London, every year, attending Parliament. There'd be all the politics, the delicate balancing of negotiation and influence, and all the horrors of the royal court, with its machinations, manipulations and power struggles. All of it two hundred miles from this place he loved, from the woman he loved. Unless she left Larkfell to come with him.

His quiet, studious brother had loved Rengarth as much as him, and he'd done his duty, with courage and devotion. Like Adam— like all the earls before them—the order of birth determined who became the earl, not choice. Only the choice whether to shirk the role and the responsibility, or to fulfil it to the best of one's abilities.

Looking out over Rengarth, on the soft greens of fields and woods, the gray stones of castle and village and farms that housed its people—*his* people—Adam withdrew the velvet pouch from his pocket, and slid the Earl of Rengarth's signet on to his finger.

In a copse of trees part-way down the slope a woodlark sang, its silver notes soft in the breeze. George's favorite bird. He'd spent hours, day after day, up here on the fell, watching for larks and other birds.

After a moment the lark flew, up into the sky, into the rays of sunlight until Adam could no longer see it.

"Godspeed, George," he murmured. "Godspeed."

~

Dressed in her favorite morning gown of fine embroidered

cambric, Emma endeavored to hold her nerves in check by keeping herself occupied until Adam arrived. She selected silks for three new gowns and sent a letter to town to order them. The clothing Matthew had brought back from Canada was past respectable wear. He'd need to order suits from the tailor, but she spread fine linen on the breakfast table, cut out the pieces for two shirts and began to sew them.

However, the fine straight stitching enabled her thoughts to wander, and she went over and over ways to tell Adam what she needed to say. *'There is no necessity to wait a month.'* *'My circumstances have changed.'* Impossible to say straight out, *'I've never loved anyone but you, and if you ask me again, I'll say yes.'*

The sunshine streamed through the window and, too unsettled to find calm in sewing, she set it aside and went out to the walled kitchen garden to the side of the house. Bees buzzed among the herbs, and she gathered a handful of leaves and blooms, lavender and marigold, bee-balm, hyssop and sweet woodruff. They made a pretty, scented bouquet.

Footsteps on the gravel path made her turn, the bouquet in hand. Jarvis came to the gate. "Major Caldwell, miss, enquiring if you are at home."

"Yes." Her breath caught. "Yes, I will see him."

He was there, behind Jarvis, and although he tried to smile as he came in the gate and saw her, it was fleeting, quickly buried in shadows.

He hesitated inside the gate and she stayed where she was, flowers in hand. He lacked his usual energy, as though it was drained from him, and sorrow darkened his eyes. Alarm coiled in her stomach. "Something has happened?"

He swallowed, nodded, grief carved into his face. "George...an infection developed quickly. He has died."

"Oh, Adam!" She tossed the flowers on a nearby bench and went to him, her arms around him, and he pulled her close, burying his face in her hair. She didn't care if anyone saw them. He'd come to her in his sorrow, and she held him as she wished someone had held her in the anguish after her father's death. She held him close, until the tension in his back eased and his heartbeat under her cheek slowed.

Eventually he breathed in deeply, and exhaled slowly. He raised his head, and cupped her face with his hands, his touch gentle. "The messenger came an hour ago. I haven't told the family yet. Would you...will you come back to Rengarth with me? I don't know how to console them. We thought he was improving. They'll be devastated."

Just as he was devastated, despite the stoicism already settling in place. But the four younger ones had limited experience of grief, and their mother and older sisters were far away. "I will come," Emma promised. She glanced down at her dress. "I'll go and change. I won't be long."

He gave a whisper of a smile. "Don't change. It's a lovely dress. You looked like a bride, holding the flowers."

She wished she didn't blush so easily, but she didn't hide her face from him. Not from Adam. If he saw her heart in her eyes, there'd be no need for words. "It's not a dress for riding, though. I truly won't be long."

They cantered, side by side, along the lane between Larkfell and Rengarth, and although there was little opportunity to talk, she hoped her presence eased a little of the loneliness of grief. Despite all the thousand words unspoken and the uncertainty of the future, today, now, she was by his side when he needed her.

He slowed to a walk near where the path lead to the ancient chapel ruins.

"Do you remember?" he asked.

"Yes." Oh, how she remembered.

"I wish that we could go there again, and stay, just you and I and the birds and the old magic spirits of the place."

"I wish so, too."

"Alas, not today." But he held out his hand to her, and she edged her mare closer to take it. As they rode slowly under the dappled sunlight and shadows of the trees, she noticed for the first time the glint of light on the signet ring on his hand. She'd never seen him wear a signet before.

He'd seen the direction of her gaze. "Hannah's babe is born," he said quietly. "A little girl. We heard yesterday."

Another daughter. And now George was dead. She understood the significance all too well. Other men might think fortune had smiled on them in the circumstance, but not Adam. Her hand still rested in his and she tightened her hold in sympathy. "I'm sorry, Adam. I know it's not what you wanted." Not what she wanted, either; another hurdle between them.

"I was dreaming of a simple life in a pleasant cottage, with honest work."

"You'll do this work honestly, too, and well." She remembered his father, and the respect with which the family had been regarded for generations. Unlike many peers, the Earls of Rengarth did not treat the title lightly. Theirs were not lives of luxury, indulgence, and indifference to their people. And now Adam, who had already given so much of himself in his army service, was called to this duty, too. "You will do it as well as your father and brother did."

"I must and I will do it, Emma, as best I can. But I fear there will be no joy in it unless you are with me, by my side. When the month is up, I will ask you again."

A mix of joy and trepidation made her smile tremble. "There are other things we must do today, but we can discuss that tomorrow, when this sorrow is not so fresh." She had yet to tell him about her inheritance. And although she'd almost discounted the threat of scandal and the social disadvantage of her status, marrying an Earl's younger brother was a different matter to marrying an Earl, and not a decision for either of them to make lightly.

~

Hope and concern chased each other within him and he wasn't entirely sure how to interpret her words, but they were nearing Rengarth and she was correct that he had other priorities to attend to. His first duties as Lord Rengarth: informing his family and the household.

His aunt and sisters had arrived home just ahead of them, still taking off bonnets and gloves in the hall as footmen carried parcels from the barouche.

Emma clasped his hand tightly in silent support as he assisted her down from her horse. He offered her his arm at the base of the steps, and together they walked up the grand stairway. He'd walked, run, leapt up these steps without a thought thousands of times before. Before he'd been the Earl of Rengarth, with a duty of care for the Castle and all within it and around it, and with the woman he wanted as his Countess beside him.

I must do it and I will, he'd said to Emma. The vow echoed in his mind.

In the hubbub of the hall, with the girls chattering about their excursion and greeting Emma and the boys emerging from the library, he quietly directed the butler to gather the household in the servant's hall in half an hour. And then he took his aunt aside and told her that he wished to see the family in the library. She smiled broadly, with an approving glance at Emma.

"It's not that," he said quietly, and she looked into his face and guessed the truth.

She nodded, and requested the housekeeper bring tea in ten minutes before she ushered the younger ones down the corridor to the library.

He'd chosen the library because it was quieter, away from the comings and goings of the servants in the hall. His aunt sat between the girls on one sofa, Emma between the boys on another one.

George Adam Caldwell, his father, watched him from the informal portrait on the wall, his kindly face looking up from the book on his knee, captured for eternity on the canvas as he'd been so often in life. And Emma met and held his gaze, a silent encouragement for what he had to do.

He cleared his throat. "A messenger arrived from London earlier," he began, and he told them as gently as he could of Hannah's letter, of George's death. They wept at the news, his aunt and his sisters, and Benjamin. Jeremy tried manfully to hold his tears back, giving his pocket handkerchief to his little brother crying in Emma's arms, but Adam gave him his own and laid a hand on his shoulder. "It's not weak to cry," he told him. "I did." And he had, on his way up the fell, with the breeze drying the moisture on his cheeks and no-one to see.

As the first wave of grief eased and tears were dried, the housekeeper knocked on the door. He took the tea trays from her and the maid without inviting them in, to protect the family's privacy just a little longer. His aunt rose to her feet, still trembling in her grief, and to his discomfort, curtsied as she asked, "Shall I pour, my Lord?"

Susanna stared and Cecilia gasped, as if the implications had not occurred to them.

With light hands on her shoulders, he kissed his great-aunt's cheek and made her sit again. "You never called George that, and I'm Adam to you, as I always have been. 'Rengarth' if you must, although I'm sure I'll forget that means me, just as George used to."

Emma poured the tea, handing around cups with soothing words and encouragement, gentle with their grief.

When he returned from informing the household staff, the family were all still in the library. While the ladies went upstairs to consult about mourning clothes, so much more complicated for women, he took the boys out into the garden. Their healing injuries ruled out a long ride, so they took the puppies—somehow there were two, not one—and rambled in the woods instead. A mostly silent ramble, and the puppies apparently tired quickly and needed carrying and cuddling. He understood that need.

All through the rest of that long, grave day Emma was a quiet comfort to them all, attending to matters with his aunt, arranging for the front door knocker to be swathed in black cloth, the hatchment— the mourning wreath—to be brought down from the attic and set in place outside, and for mourning stationery and supplies of black crape to be ordered from Hartdale. Aunt Thorncroft pressed her to stay the night, and she agreed.

They gathered early for a light, informal dinner, a subdued meal of comforting food. Afterwards his aunt retired to write letters and Emma took the girls upstairs for hot chocolate while they finished adding crape ribbon to their bonnets to wear to church in the morning. His brothers went to their room as well. Adam gave permission for the puppies to be inside, provided the boys filled up and took a sand box as well.

In the study, with a glass of wine at his side, he set himself to the task of writing the necessary letters. To Hannah first, expressing his sincere condolences and promising to look after her and the children. Then to the vicar. The bishop. George's friends in the district. His mother's friends in the district. The mayor and the magistrate and the justice of the peace. He hesitated every time before he used his brother's seal on the wax. His wine was long gone and the candles burnt down low by the time he finished.

~

The hall clock struck midnight as she draped the black arm bands and cravats on the boys' door handle, and on Adam's. Jeremy had told her that they only had white cravats, and that Adam didn't have a proper valet yet. She needed to keep occupied, too unsettled to sleep, so she'd stitched yards and yards of fine black fabric by candlelight. It would help them all tomorrow, to be properly attired at church. Especially the younger ones; the mourning black not only showed respect for the deceased, it reminded people to be tactful and understanding towards the bereaved.

She was almost back at her room when she heard footsteps on the stairs. She paused, turned to see the flickering of a candle ascending. Adam.

He saw her, and came to her. The candle he carried illuminated the weariness in his face, and yet the wild grief and despair of earlier in the day had faded. He'd shouldered the mantle of his new role this afternoon with dignity and grace, and if he wasn't at peace with it yet, he was coming to terms with it.

"I've left a black cravat at your door for you," she said, keeping her voice low. "And ones for the boys."

"Emma, thank you. For that, and for everything today." He touched a hand to her cheek. "It would have been much harder, without you here."

"I wish I could make the pain go away. But if my being here helps you to bear it, then I'm glad."

"It does. You gave me strength, when I needed it most. Or reminded me that I have it."

Sounds drifted up to them; the bolting of the front door, quiet voices on the stairs. She did not want, yet, to say good night to him. To watch him walk away to his bedchamber, alone, when sorrow might catch him in the darkest hours, at his most vulnerable.

She opened her bedroom door, and gestured him inside.

He laid the candles, hers and his, on the dressing table while she closed the door behind them. He hesitated, glancing around the room. "Your maid?"

"She's unwell. She packed clothes and sent them for me, but I told her to stay at home."

It felt entirely natural, right, to step into his embrace, to hold and be held in the circle of his arms. She rested her head against his shoulder, the soft wool of his coat against her cheek, and they stood there motionless in the still, quiet room. Desire hummed with the awareness of his body so close to hers, but there was a peace, too, in simply being together, an intimacy of the heart. A calm certainty settled within her.

After a while, he tipped her face up and brushed her mouth in the softest of kisses. "Come sit with me, Emma. I need to tell you about Rengarth before I propose to you again."

His hand in hers, he led her to the sofa, and drew her down beside him. She slipped off her shoes and curled her feet under her so she could face him in comfort. The sofa was small and they sat close, closer than in a public setting. The moonlight from the window fell on his face. She wanted to reach out and straighten the high collar of his shirt, where he'd run his finger to loosen it from his neck, but if she touched him now—especially in such an intimate, wifely way—

350

they might easily become too distracted.

"Emma," he said, "I can offer you a comfortable life with everything you need, but I must warn you that our family has always lived more simply than many peers, and Rengarth is not as wealthy as some believe. There are my sisters and George's daughters to educate and provide for, the estate to run, and I'm concerned about the winter, and ensuring people are employed and fed. So, unfortunately there will be little for fripperies or jewels or frequent entertainments." He spoke earnestly, as if afraid what he said might make her change her mind. "But I promise you, whatever you bring to the marriage will be preserved for you. I firmly believe in a woman's right to financial independence, even if the law doesn't."

She had no reason at all to doubt his word. It accorded with everything else she knew of his nature and his beliefs.

"I don't need or want fripperies or jewels or entertainments, Adam. They don't make anyone happy." He'd been honest, and she must be as well, so that everything was clear between them before they made their decisions. She had no concerns about his response, but he should understand the circumstances and have the opportunity to ask questions if he wished. "There hasn't been time to tell you yet," she began, "that Mr. Winslow's solicitor called yesterday afternoon. It turns out that Francis was right; his estate is significant."

He listened while she explained about the legacy, and Mr. Winslow's various charitable institutions. It still didn't seem real that all this talk about wealth actually applied to her. She understood it only in theory, in the neat terms of the lawyer's words and the lists and the numbers. Adam raised his eyebrows when she mentioned the sums involved but he didn't interrupt.

"There are some complicated trust arrangements, although I'm not sure how they will work," she explained to finish. "It is not a requirement of the inheritance, but I'd like to ensure Mr. Winslow's charities are continued, as far as possible. That the majority of his fortune is used to benefit those in need."

"Of course it must. I meant what I said, Emma. I have no moral rights to your money. You will be a wonderful Lady Chair of the

Boards of Directors of those institutions." He raised her hand and kissed her fingers. "You will be a wonderful Countess, too," he added.

His confidence in her did not quite erase her uncertainty. Such a huge step for her, and so much in the public eye. She'd spent her entire life being cautious—*sensible*—and despite the certainty of her heart, the habit wasn't easily shaken. "Are you sure, Adam? My family is not the equal of yours. My great-grandfather started as a weaver. And if the scandal spreads further, people may think I am not suitable to be your wife."

She could almost hear her sister Lucy, teasing her for over-worrying, but Adam didn't dismiss her concern. With his steady, honest regard, he said, "Emma, you love this area, Rengarth and Larkfell and Hartdale, and you care about the people here, as they care about and respect you. You have many skills and an immense knowledge about the industries in this district. You have grace and compassion and you face challenges with courage and a quiet dignity. There is no-one more suitable to be Rengarth's Countess."

His thumb made a gentle circle at the base of her ring finger. Perhaps that finger truly did lead to the heart, for the sensation along with his generous words brought a wave of emotion and a lump to her throat.

"As for scandal," he added, "Francis's death has made his perfidy and your innocence more widely known. If there is any speculation about you, I think the gossip will be short-lived, and confined to people who have little influence beyond their small set. I suspect—hope—that it will be replaced with talk of how the new Lord Rengarth is deeply, tenderly, and completely in love with his wife. Because I am."

Her last uncertainty melted away and her eyes filled with tears of happiness. "And she with him," she murmured.

He smiled, his heart and all his love in his eyes, and took both her hands in his. "Will you marry me, Emma?"

"Yes," she promised, without a single doubt as to the rightness of her decision. "Yes, I will marry you."

He drew her towards him and kissed her, and she answered his gentleness with her own, a wordless assurance of her love for him. Time stilled as they shared a hundred kisses. She bestowed them on his mouth, his temple, on the strong line of his jaw, on his neck, loving the taste of him, rediscovering the shape of him. Somehow she was on his lap, and his lips caressed her mouth, her face, her throat, making her breathless with desire when he traced the line of skin along the edge of her evening dress bodice.

She wanted him to peel away the layers of clothes, his and hers, and lay her hands on his skin, his on hers...

The hall clock gave a single low chime, and one of the candles sputtered and died. The other was already low, close to burning out. There was still moonlight through the window, but it had shifted, the beams at an angle.

"Oh dear," she murmured. "I fear the candle will not last long enough for you to reach your room. Perhaps you should stay here, where it's safer."

Amusement curved his delectable mouth. "I've never seen or heard of a ghost or other dangers in the halls of the castle, but perhaps I should stay here. To protect you, just in case."

After another long, lingering kiss, his cravat fell from his neck, his waistcoat lay open, the bodice of her dress was undone and slipping from her shoulders, and she was totally absorbed in the absolute pleasure and slow, sensual delight of mutual undressing.

Eventually she led him to her bed, let her loosened chemise fall to the floor, lifted the fine linen of his shirt over his head, and drew him down beside her to join with him, love him, share herself and her heart with him. Friend, lover, husband of her soul. He took her into his arms, skin to skin, lips to lips. His hands on her body made desire rise to driving hunger and when he lowered his head and kissed and sucked on her breasts her insides clenched with need and any ability to think evaporated. She gripped his hips, opening to him. Gasping for breath, for control, he entered her gently, but she didn't need gentle, only Adam in her and around her and with her as their passion drove them to the pure, joyous pleasure of release.

At first light he left her with the most tender of kisses, slipping away silently before the household staff woke. She curled up under the blankets, missing his presence the moment the door closed behind him. But in a month they'd be married, and she'd wake every day with him by her side.

Later in the morning, she sat beside Adam in the Rengarth pew of the village church as Mr. Timms led prayers for the soul of the late beloved Earl, and for the comfort of his family.

In the soft sunshine outside after the service, she remained with the family while people paid their respects. Their sorrow genuine, they bowed or curtsied and murmured condolences to the new Lord Rengarth. And Adam, quietly courteous, thanked each one, calling them by name, asking after family members he remembered.

A few people whispered, glancing in her direction, but more people greeted her, asking about Matthew, expressing their pleasure that he'd returned safely from abroad.

And she realized, observing the congregation, that the Rengarth villagers, the staff of the castle, the people of the district—they were her people, too. The housemaid at the castle who helped her dress that morning was the daughter of one of the Braithwaite's weavers. The second footman at breakfast was the son of one of their best spinners. And Ned Langton, the clerk at the warehouse, was the grandson of a Rengarth gardener.

She and Adam did not publicly announce their engagement. Not today, when they mourned George. They'd told the family over breakfast, but Matthew and the family in London must be informed before any announcement, and before the banns were read.

They walked back along the lane towards the castle, but once out of the village Adam suggested the others go ahead, and invited her to walk through the orchard with him. The sun shone in a hazy sky, the green leaves cast dappled shadows, and a flock of hens foraged contentedly in the grass.

"You've been quiet," he said. "I hope you have no regrets?"

"No, not at all." Now that they were out of public view, she linked her arm though his to assure him. "I was thinking that Rengarth and Larkfell—Braithwaites—have been intertwined for almost a hundred years. Everyone at church this morning has connections, in one way or another, to both our families, our history."

"Your family has always been highly respected around here. You've provided livelihoods and skills for hundreds, and paid good wages for quality work. That benefits this whole district, including Rengarth."

His words warmed her and yes, she did feel some pride in her family's history, in the values they held with regard to the business. "Things are changing so fast, though. The traditional ways—I don't think they can last, more than ten, maybe twenty years. I confess, sometime I worry about the future. Not about us," she hastened to add. "That aspect of the future fills me with joy."

He paused in the sunlight and drew her to him for a tender kiss. "I wish we didn't have to wait a month to be married. But the ties between our families will be strengthened. They already are. And whatever the future holds, my love, we'll face it side by side, together."

HISTORICAL NOTES

The worsted industry

The worsted textiles that Emma's family company manufactures were once very common fabrics for clothing and household furnishings. They were made of wool, with the fibers combed before spinning to produce a smooth, even yarn. They ranged from coarse, plain fabrics to exquisitely fine fabrics with complex patterns: calamancos, camblets, lastings, amens, and shalloons were just a few types of worsted fabrics. All the thread was hand-spun, all the fabric hand-woven. It was a huge industry in the 1700s, with fabrics exported all over the world. But by the mid 1800s, these textiles had mostly disappeared.

Unfortunately, very few have survived in museums and textile collections, for two main reasons. Wool clothing is not valued and kept in the same way that formal silk or highly embroidered costumes are, and once it was worn out, might be cut up for other uses. Wool textiles are also vulnerable to the ravages of moths.

However, small samples do survive in a number of clothier's sample or pattern books; small rectangles of fabric pasted in books, often with details of lengths, widths and prices. I studied a number of these when I was researching in the UK for my Honors thesis. As I looked at page after page after page of the lovely colours and beautiful woven patterns, and analyzed their structures, I wondered about the people who had made them, the clothiers that funded and organised the production, and how, why and when these lovely, practical fabrics fell out of production and out of our cultural memory. Although there was some mechanized spinning equipment for worsted yarns by 1816, it's my belief that the best of these fabrics could not be replicated by machine, as the spinning is so fine. And so I've given Emma the challenge of managing a company in a traditional industry, in a time of considerable technological change.

1816 - the year without a summer

The summer of 1816 is well-documented as an unusual one, with cold, wet weather across much of the northern hemisphere. A popular theory is that the bad weather was caused by the volcanic eruption, in April 1815, of Mount Tambora, in what is now Indonesia, resulting in a cloud of volcanic ash that drifted across the northern half of the earth, blocking sunlight and impacting on temperature, rainfall, and air quality. The north of England and Scotland fared a little better than parts of Europe and the Americas, with fewer crop failures, however there was widespread concern and in some parts of the world starvation became reality for some. As Emma discovers while waiting to hear from her brother, the cold weather, with frosts and snow into June in the New England states, and even later in Canada, disrupted shipping, particularly in the Saint Lawrence seaway to Quebec.

Music

The lament that Nathaniel Garrett plays is Scottish composer Niel Gow's 'Lament on the death of his second wife'. It's a beautiful piece of music. There's a video clip on YouTube of Scottish musician Paul Anderson playing this piece, in 2014, and it's how I imagine Garrett plays it: https://youtu.be/fRMTmbU7QEk

It's hard to imagine that in the days before recorded music, few people heard classical music performed, and even the musically-appreciative upper classes might only hear some pieces once in their lifetimes. When Louisa plays the relatively new Beethoven sonata (that we now know as the 'Moonlight' sonata), most of her audience has never heard it before. I've tried to imagine, through Emma's experience, what it must have been like to hear that piece for the very first time.

The famous Baroque harpist and composer of the late 1700s, Blind John Parry, lived in the same small town in Wales as my Parry ancestors. I'm not sure if I'm related to him (Parry being about as common a surname in Wales as Smith is elsewhere!) but it seemed entirely right to make Adam's blind brother, Oliver, a musician and composer.

ACKNOWLEDGEMENTS

This book has been my most challenging writing project so far, and I am deeply grateful to many people for their support, encouragement and practical help along the way.

My many friends who have been unstinting in their enthusiasm (and patience!) right from the very beginning of this journey, especially: Kate T. and Emily; Beattie and Fiona; and Helen, Barbara, Elaine, and Lyn from Sydney.

Having the support of a tribe of authors helps make the writing life less lonely. Valerie Parv, Anna Campbell, Anne Gracie, Fiona Macarthur, Kate Rothwell, Pamela Freeman and many others have believed in me and reminded me many times that self-doubt is just part of the process, and that writer's block can be overcome.

The editing and proof-reading skills of Anna Thomson and Margaret Clarke have strengthened the story with their suggestions and corrections.

Lauren Sadow's graphic design skills and her willingness to dress in Regency costume and be photographed on a chilly spring day have made the cover and the printed book beautiful. Andrew Sadow's photography and Andrea Sadow's cheering and encouragement are greatly appreciated.

This book started life as a creative practice project for a PhD; although, as the Scottish poet Robert Burns wrote, *The best laid schemes o' mice and men gang aft agley*, I'm grateful to my supervisors Jeremy Fisher and Elizabeth Hale for supporting the creative research.

Part of the inspiration for this book lies in the research I undertook for my History Honours thesis, some years ago, on 18th century British worsted textiles, which would not have been possible without David Kent's willingness to supervise an unusual topic. His knowledge of 18th and 19th century British social history is inspiring.

The partners of authors are heroes in their own right. Gordon is mine, and I am more than grateful for his patient support, faith in me, and afternoon teas.

CPSIA information can be obtained
at www.ICGtesting.com
Printed in the USA
LVHW050428050720
659748LV00001B/45